Curveball Year Two: That Which Does Not Dream

This is a work of fiction. Names, characters, places and incidents either are products of the author's imagination or are used fictitiously. Any resemblance to actual events, locales, or persons, living or dead, is entirely coincidental.

ISBN 978-1-939633-29-3

 Edited by **Arpista Editing**. Published by **Eviscerati Communications LLC**.

Curveball archives, news, and series information can be found at:

http://www.curveball.xyz

More of Pascalle Lepas' work can be found at:

http://www.wildelifecomic.com

I0686210

More of Garth Graham's work can be found at:

http://www.gcgstudios.com

Arpista Editing can be found at:

http://www.arpistaediting.com

LICENSING INFORMATION

CONTENTS

DEDICATIONS

To everyone I mentioned in the last book, because none of that has changed, but I'm going to go ahead and mention **Patricia** again, because I want to.

CURVEBALL
13
OCT 2013
CURVEBALL
A Prose Comic
SHADOWS
STORY
CHRISTOPHER WRIGHT
COVER
PASCALLE LEPAS
LOGO
GARTH GRAHAM

PART ONE: FARRADAY CITY BUNKER

By mid-morning the rain in Farraday City has increased in strength and in volume. It's dry in the bunker, but it's humid, and they can hear the rain pounding the ground above them. Everything *feels* wet, even though it isn't.

"Coffee," CB says.

He steps into the living area of the bunker carrying a small metal tray with three mugs. The mugs radiate heat, steam evaporating into the air.

Jenny sits on one end of a beat-up vinyl couch, wrapped tightly in a blanket, legs tucked up under her chin. They all changed the moment they got there, but her hair is still damp and she's shivering from cold. Her hands dart out from under the blanket and wrap around a mug, greedily soaking in its heat.

"I've never seen it rain that hard before," Jenny says.

"It's going to get harder," CB says. "Farraday City gets like this every once in a while. It's a pain in the ass."

He holds the tray out to Red Shift. The man is dressed in some of CB's spare clothes—his uniform hangs over a chair in the kitchen, drying out. The clothes look strange on him. He has the build of a runner—which makes sense, since he is the Platonic Ideal of runners everywhere—and he's a little taller than CB, which makes the clothes look both too small and too baggy.

CB sets the tray down on a small table next to an old, leather easy chair. He sinks into the easy chair, takes the last mug off the tray. For the next few minutes they drink in silence.

"Ugh." Jenny lowers her mug and makes a face. "No cream? No sugar?"

"Sorry," CB says. "I'll go shopping soon."

Jenny wraps her blanket tighter around her body. "I'm cold. This isn't normal, is it? This isn't the right season for cold, even with all that rain." She tries to keep her voice casual, but CB can hear the worry in it.

"It's actually perfectly normal for you," CB says. "You're about to start cocooning."

"I don't know what that means," Jenny says.

Red Shift leans forward, staring at Jenny with interest. "Is she now?"

"What are you talking about?" Jenny demands. "What's cocooning?"

"It's something that happens to a lot of metahumans when they get the first full dose of what they can do," CB says. "Your body is having trouble adjusting because of... reasons..." He waves a hand, gesturing vaguely.

"Because for all your life, up to now, your body has always had a pretty good idea of what your limits are," Red Shift says. "Learning your physical limits is a pretty big part of development, and by the time you're an adult—which you are—you know how fast you can run, how strong you are, how much pain you can take before things got dangerous. All those limits are stamped into you. It's instinctive."

"What he said," CB says. "And a few hours ago you blew past all those limits like they were nothing. Your body is now officially 'very confused.'"

Jenny laughs sharply. "I think my mom gave me this talk once."

"Those changes took place gradually," Red Shift says. "This adjustment is going to take a few hours, a few days tops. Your body really isn't going to like that. So it's going to shut down. You'll slip into a coma for a while, then—"

"I'm going to *what?*" Jenny's eyes widen in alarm.

"It's not dangerous," Red Shift says. "Your body is scaling back in order to ease back into itself, try to rebuild its understanding of what you can do. When you wake up, you'll have an easier time adjusting to your new... uh... I don't actually know what you do."

"Liberty's great-granddaughter," CB says.

"Oh," Red Shift says. "OK. So... stronger, faster. Right. Well, Miss Forrest, after you wake up you're going to still need to test the waters a bit, get used to what you can do, but your body will already be a lot of the way there."

Jenny tries to process this. "Did it happen to you? Either of you?"

"Yes," Red Shift says.

CB frowns. "Not exactly. It's complicated."

"I'm *shocked* by your answer," Jenny says. "So basically I'm going to pass out soon."

"You're cold now," CB says. "That's usually the first symptom. You'll get lethargic pretty soon. Then you'll fall into a deep sleep. After that you'll fall into an ever deeper sleep. We'll probably wind up dragging you off to bed."

"The hell you will," Jenny says. She stands, wobbles a bit, then walks out into the hall. "I'll put myself to bed, thank you very much. See you whenever."

CB grins as she leaves the room.

"So she's a metahuman," Red Shift says. "I had no idea."

"She says she was fighting Richter when you showed up," CB says.

Red Shift shakes his head. "She was about to be *executed* by Richter when I showed up. I didn't see what happened before."

"Fair point," CB says. "So why did you? Show up, I mean. Isn't New York your turf?"

"Isn't it yours?" Red Shift asks.

CB scowls. "That was a long time ago."

"And you wound up *here*?" Red Shift shakes his head. "That doesn't makes sense."

"What doesn't make sense?" CB sounds a bit defensive.

Red Shift stares at him levelly. "Look, I know it's been a while, and I know we weren't exactly on the same page when we were *both* working New York, but I'm pretty sure you didn't turn into a guy who decided to move to the most crime-infested city in America and not try to *do* anything about it."

CB doesn't answer.

"But here it is, ten years later, and apparently you're living in a slum on the beach and you have a secret bunker. So you're doing something. But there are no reports of anyone doing *anything* in this city. There are reports of people *trying* and *disappearing*. This is the Bermuda's Triangle of heroes. Nobody ever saves the day."

"Yeah," CB says. "You ever wonder why that is?"

Red Shift frowns.

"I mean, occasionally there's a very public report of a would-be hero of Farraday City getting killed. Every few years, that makes the news. But there are a lot more examples of would-be heroes who actually start to make progress and then they mysteriously disappear."

"Is that why you're here?" Red Shift asks. "To figure out why?"

"I'm here," CB says, "because this city makes no goddamn sense. No sense at all."

"It's a corrupt city run by crooks," Red Shift says. "It seems pretty straightforward to me."

"Yeah," CB says. "I know. Look, I first came down here because a friend needed help. I got pulled into the disappearing hero thing, and while I was nosing around I tried to piece together the power structure. For ten years I've been pulling together bits and pieces of all the little groups and big groups that are involved in running this city. Each time I learn something new I think it'll be the piece that makes it all make sense. Thing is? It doesn't. This city shouldn't *work*."

"I don't understand," Red Shift says.

"Neither do I!" CB gets out of his chair and starts to pace. "There is no single group in this city that has enough pull to tell any of the other groups what to do. Individual criminal groups run different parts of the city, and they all mostly cooperate to keep the whole thing going. But there aren't any power plays. Not that I can see. In the last ten years there hasn't been a single instance of one crime group trying to move into another group's territory. Does that make any sense to you?"

"No," Red Shift says.

"No," CB repeats. "Right. It makes no sense. And none of these groups are big enough to call the shots, but the way the city hangs together it's obvious *someone* is. Someone has to have the bird's-eye view to make the whole thing work. But I can't find any trace of them. No communication. No tribute. Nothing. There's a big empty space where the top dog should be."

"Come on," Red Shift says. "There has to be something."

"I know that," CB says. "I'm not saying they're not there. I'm saying I can't *find* them. And that's pretty significant. I'm good at that kind of stuff. When I was in the Guardians, when it came to discovering something it was either Gladiator or it was me. Want to break down the atomic structure of a new killer virus? Gladiator. Want to trace a weapons shipment to the metahuman gang that sold it? Me. Want to trace the radioactive emissions of a mutated war beast to the lab that created it? Gladiator. Want to find a crime lord's hideout? Me. The fact that I haven't found the asshole who runs this place after ten years of looking for him *makes no sense*."

CB sighs, then sinks back into his easy chair. "There's no reason I shouldn't be able to figure this out. Farraday City is a nasty piece of work. But at the end of the day, it's not particularly *subtle*. It's a big dumb evil city filled with big dumb evil crooks."

"If the structure is as mysterious as you claim," Red Shift says, "then there has to be more than that."

"Doubt it," CB says. "Scratch the surface and you just find more surface."

"You just have to keep digging, I guess," Red Shift says.

"Nah," CB says. "It's surface all the way down."

PART TWO: THE SWORDFISH

Rain turns into torrential rain, torrential rain turns into a tropical depression, and Jerry is having one of his best nights in a long time. The bar is packed with people willing to pay good money to stay dry. The solid, reliable roof of the Swordfish has, for the duration of the storm, become one of the most popular attractions of the boardwalk. Jerry's been making money all day, and as the storm increases in strength, so does his business.

It ought to make him happy. At least, it ought to make him as close to happy as he's ever likely to get. It doesn't.

The Swordfish is large for the kind of bar it is—it's about the size of your typical sports bar, instead of a neighborhood hole in the wall—and even on the busiest of nights it manages to feel roomy. Tonight it actually feels cramped, and the regulars resent it. Earlier in the evening Jerry had to throw a regular out for trying to knife someone trying to "sit in his booth." On most nights Jerry would let something like that slide, but there are too many people in the bar tonight, and some of the new faces are troubling.

There are players in the bar tonight. Not big-league players—not the kind that actually make life or death decisions that affect Farraday City as a whole. But there are people in the bar who have carved out kingdoms for themselves on the boardwalk—the place the civilized people ignore. In a way, in this part of the city, those people are more important. The people who run the city don't care about the boardwalk—at least, it looks that way—and their decisions rarely change life here in any appreciable way. But the people in here tonight do. They're drug lords, or would-be gangsters, or psychotics with delusions of grandeur. They've all carved out little fiefdoms in the boardwalk, and a lot of them are in the Swordfish tonight.

Jerry rushes around making sure each of the petty lords has enough to keep them occupied and in a good mood. He gives them the liquor that isn't watered down. He makes sure they all have tables. He even offers them food, which he almost never does. So far, a delicate peace has been maintained. None of the would-be kings of the boardwalk accost each other, and everyone else does their best not to step on any toes.

Jerry's at the bar, watching everyone, feeling uneasy. He hopes CB doesn't pick this night to show up—that's the last thing he needs.

"Jerry."

Jerry looks up. One of the regulars, a beefy, thick-necked bruiser named Clarence, crowds up to the bar.

Jerry nods once, reaches under the bar, and pulls out a bottle of beer. He hands Clarence the bottle. He prefers a bottle over a glass, and Jerry likes him enough to humor him.

Clarence takes the bottle, slides some money across the bar, and asks, "You hear about the Hyatt?"

Back when Farraday City was a thriving vacation spot, the boardwalk had been lined with tourist-friendly businesses and hotels. After it collapsed in on itself, the tourist-friendly businesses were converted into businesses that better suited the community that moved in—the Swordfish is a prime example of this. Most of the hotels turned into tenement houses. The Hyatt had probably been a high-scale tourist hotel once, but it's now one of the worst slums in the city.

Jerry sneers. "If we're lucky the storm washed that shithole into the ocean."

Clarence doesn't grin. He just shakes his head in a kind of subdued wonder. "They're all *dead*, man."

Jerry looks at him blankly. "What are you talking about?"

Some of the other people at the bar quiet down a little and turn their attention to Clarence.

Clarence nods. "There's a hole in the wall on the ground floor, like a car crashed into it or something. And every fucking person in there is dead. The police even showed up."

Jerry frowns. The police tend to leave the boardwalk alone. "I didn't hear anything on the news."

Clarence snorts once. "That really surprise you? You think the news is going to come all the way out here in this weather? Hell, when I saw the cops out at the Hyatt I thought I was high."

That provokes a round of laughter from the people around him. But Clarence isn't laughing. He's not what Jerry would consider an empathetic man—he believes in looking out for himself, and doesn't usually put much thought into the struggles of his fellow man—but whatever happened at the Hyatt has put him in an unusually sober and reflective mood.

"How'd it happen?" Jerry asks. "Some kind of hit?" He looks around uneasily, wondering if any of the personalities currently drying off in his bar are involved.

Clarence shakes his head, then leans in, lowering his voice. "It was like some kind of plague. They all died of some kind of *disease*, man."

Jerry looks at him, expression flat. "Quit yanking my—"

"I'm not kidding." Clarence holds up his hands for emphasis. "I saw the police on the scene, man. They blocked off the area, put plastic over the hole in the wall, and they were only letting people who were wearing those yellow plastic body suits go in. Like in those virus movies. All the bodies they pulled out were wrapped in plastic, too. Like they were *sealed*. To keep anything from getting out."

The other people at the bar mutter uneasily. Clarence is generally reliable when it comes to information as long as he isn't talking about himself.

Jerry frowns. He doesn't need this kind of talk in the bar right now. It's too late to stop the rumor from spreading—he can see it rippling through the room, a guy from the bar heading over to a table, whispering excitedly, one of those guys darting off to tell a friend on the other side of the room, and so on—but the last thing he needs is everyone worrying about some kind of weird plague. He can't stop the rumor, but he might be able to change its focus.

"What's going to happen to the building?" Jerry asks, raising his voice just a little to make sure the others can hear. "You know who owns it?"

Clarence shakes his head. "Technically I think Hyatt still owns it. Not that I expect them to come down here."

Jerry waves a hand dismissively. "I don't mean that. I mean who controlled the turf? What's going to happen to the building now? Who's moving in?"

Clarence purses his lips thoughtfully. "Don't know," he says. Then, a second later: "Good question."

And all at once, thanks to the nature of life on the boardwalk, the conversation changes from *I hear a bunch of guys died from a plague in the Hyatt* to *I hear the Hyatt is empty and ripe for the picking*. Panic is bad for business. Speculation is *good* for business. Jerry starts to relax as he watches the new rumor spread through the bar. This might be distracting enough to keep everyone occupied—peacefully occupied—until closing. He starts to wipe down the table, smiling ever so slightly to himself. For the first time tonight he starts to think about all the money he's bringing in.

The front door opens, drawing a howl of protest out of the unfortunates standing near it. Rain whips into the room, along with an unseasonably chilly wind that carries all the way to the back. Jerry looks up, annoyed, about to shout "Get inside and close the goddamned door!" but the words die on his lips.

Two men—one thin, a little on the short side, one much larger and heavyset—walk into the bar. They are both dressed in pin-striped business suits, well tailored but not obviously expensive. They both wear bowler hats. The small, thin man has a lean, birdlike face with bright, gleaming eyes, and a polite, vague smile. The large heavyset man looks around the room once, taking everything in with a dark, flat gaze, then sinks into an expression of bored introspection.

The small man steps further into the room, touching the brim of his hat in general greeting, while the large man closes the door fully shut behind him. Despite their appearance—business suits are not common attire on the boardwalk—they are almost universally ignored by everyone else in the room.

The small man carefully makes his way through the crowd of people, nimbly stepping around groups, darting through sudden breaks in the crowd, heading to the back of the room. The large man stays by the door until the small man reaches the bar, then he walks directly to the back. He doesn't bother to navigate the crowd: people unconsciously step out of his way as he walks. It took the small man minutes to reach the bar; it takes the large man seconds.

They stand at the very end of the bar, a little apart from the rest of the patrons. They don't do anything. They stand there, the large man impassive, the small man with a polite and slightly apologetic expression on his face, and they wait. Jerry nods at the small man once. The small man's smile widens, and he bows, ever so slightly, in his direction. Then the small man turns his gaze out into the crowd, watching the goings-on with interest.

Jerry scans the room. He focuses on a man leaning up against the bar nursing a drink. His clothes are newish but filthy, as if he hasn't changed them in weeks. He has a guarded, cautious look—the look of a man who doesn't like where he is and desperately wants to be left alone. Jerry doesn't recognize him, but he recognizes that look.

He moves over to the man, grabs a glass and sets it down in front of him. The sudden motion surprises the stranger, who looks up in a near panic, relaxing slightly only when he recognizes Jerry as the bartender. He looks at Jerry warily.

"You're new in town," Jerry says. It's a statement, not a question.

The man nods unhappily.

Jerry reaches under the bar. "My sympathies." He pulls out a bottle filled with an amber liquid that almost glows in the dim light. He pours it into the glass, filling it about halfway, and pushes it over to the man. "Been on the boardwalk for... I'm guessing a week?"

The man hesitates, then holds up two fingers.

Jerry raises an eyebrow. "Two. Well, I'd say you've earned that."

The man looks at the glass for a moment, then picks it up. He sniffs at the liquid suspiciously. Then, a moment later, his eyes widen, and he downs the liquid quickly. The effect is almost immediate. The heaviness and suspicion on his face fade away, until at last it relaxes into a happy smile. He looks at the glass in wonder. "What is that?"

"Special," Jerry says. "Consider it a consolation prize for winding up here."

"Almost worth it," the man says, and laughs.

Jerry smiles politely.

"I haven't felt this good in a long time," the man adds. He looks at the glass, then at Jerry uncertainly. "Could—could I—would it be all right if—"

Jerry brings out the bottle and fills the glass without a word. The man drinks slowly this time—savoring it—and as he drinks he starts to talk. About his life. About how a business trip ended with a night of revelry turned bad, and how he woke up in debt to some very bad people with no way to contact anyone who might be able to help him. How he wound up on the boardwalk, with nothing but the clothes on his back and a couple of twenties. How the cash was almost gone, and he figured it'd be better to spend the rest of it here, someplace dry, before the inevitable—whatever that was—happened.

Jerry listens. He's a bartender. People expect it.

"I don't know what I'm going to do," the man says. "I don't know what's going to happen next."

Jerry pulls out the bottle and fills his glass a third time. "Don't think about it tonight. You can't do anything about it, but tonight you're warm and you're dry and you have a drink. Sometimes that's as good as it gets. You might as well enjoy it."

The man smiles gratefully and grabs the glass. By the time it's half-empty he's face down on the bar, snoring softly.

Jerry grabs a rag, picks up the glass, and dumps the contents in a small sink behind the bar. He rinses it out carefully and washes his hands afterward. Everyone ignores the sleeping man except for the small man in the bowler. His gaze is locked on the hunched-over form, his smile widening into one of eager delight. The large man is still lost in his own introspective world.

The hours pass, and the people show no sign of leaving. On one level

Jerry understands—it's still raining like crazy—but when it's finally time to close up he shows no mercy.

"Last call!" He ignores the howls of protest, and for the next half hour he's busy sorting through the deluge of last-minute orders as his customers take as long as they possibly can to order. He gives them ten minutes to drink up, then he ushers them all out into the rain—even the players. Everyone protests, but not too much, and eventually everyone leaves.

Everyone but the big man, the small man, and the drunk passed out at the bar.

The last of the customers stumbles out into the torrential rain, cursing loudly, and Jerry closes and locks the door behind him. He wipes the rain from his eyes and turns to face the small man and the big man, still standing in the same spot at the end of the bar. He jerks his head in the direction of the passed-out drunk.

The big man, still apparently lost in a personal reverie, moves to stand next to the drunk. The small man doffs his bowler and bows low, long yellow hair springing out from beneath the hat like coiled springs.

"Thank you, Gerald." The small man's voice is very crisp, very sharp. "This one is *perfect*."

Jerry shrugs, fighting back his unease. "I gotta clean up."

The small man nods. "Of course. Of course. We won't keep you. You've performed your end admirably. Quite admirably. And on such short notice as well! I thought we had you tonight."

Jerry grunts.

The small man nods. "Exactly my point. Well, we won't keep you." He turns and nods to the big man. The big man grabs the drunk and slings him over his shoulder without any visible sign of effort. The drunk keeps snoring.

"And so we part ways again," the small man says. "Alas."

Jerry walks back over to the door and unlocks it. The small man walks briskly to the door, the big man and his burden following close behind. When they reach the door, Jerry pushes it open. Rain and wind blow into the bar.

The small man tips his hat. "Until next time." Then he steps out into the storm, the big man following suit. Jerry closes the door, locks it, and checks each lock twice.

"Until next time," he mutters.

PART THREE: TRIHEALTH EXECUTIVE SUITE

Ronald Holt sits in his office, stares out his window, and sips his coffee with a contented sigh. The TriHealth building isn't the tallest in Farraday City, not by a long shot, but it's the only building on its block, and the top floor gives him a good view of their part of the Uptown business district. The rain disappeared at dawn, but everything is still quite wet, and the streets glisten in the early morning light. It's quite pretty: the sun shines off the water like a veneer of silver coating the entire city.

A beautiful veneer, he thinks. *Just like the city itself.*

He frowns slightly, his mood momentarily spoiled as his thoughts drift to the day ahead. He's going to have to work hard to mend fences after the other night. He sighs, turns away from his window, and returns to his desk.

Holt's office is large and very upscale. The carpet is thick and white—proper carpeting, not the cheap office fuzz you usually see—and the vaulted ceiling has a skylight that allows for plenty of natural light. The office is a large space, larger than many apartments. The center has his desk, his computer, chairs for visitors, and a small closet by the door. To his right is a full entertainment center, complete with couches, chairs, and a fully stocked wet bar. At the far end of the room is a private bathroom, complete with shower. To his left, at the far end, is a wall-mounted zen waterfall. Next to that is a climbing wall that he never uses. There is absolutely nothing between his desk and the waterfall/climbing wall on the far end. He tells himself it's because he really doesn't need anything else, but the real reason is that he likes people to notice how ridiculously big the office really is.

It is nothing *but* excessive, and it's *his*. He likes that. Other people hate it. He likes that, too.

He stares down at the report on his desk. INCIDENT REPORT: TRIHEALTH SECURITY BREACH, SEVENTH FLOOR, FLAG M. "Flag M" meant metahumans were involved in the breach. Unfortunately they have no footage of the people involved, just descriptions taken from the surviving members of the security team sent to apprehend and neutralize.

He sets his coffee down on his desk and picks up the report, paging through it with increasing agitation. He wants to fire the security team. He can't, apparently—the security chief has refused to do it despite being given a direct order, and apparently she has more political pull than Holt knew. He grits his teeth, fighting back a wave of anger. *Someone* needs to be held accountable for this travesty. How much data was stolen? They don't know.

Where did the metahuman and his accomplice go? They don't know.

Someone knows. Based on the questions he's getting from the Executive Board, he's absolutely sure that at least one of the Vice Presidents who sits on the TriHealth board knows *exactly* who this metahuman was, who his accomplice was, and what they were trying to do. But no one is willing to share that information, which leaves Holt in the unenviable position of trying to fix this mess without being able to accurately assess the threat this metahuman poses. He puts the report back down on his desk, leans back in his chair, and rubs his eyes.

The phone beeps.

Holt opens one eye and stares at the phone. His assistant knows better than to contact him before ten.

The phone beeps again. It's his assistant's number. He growls in frustration and hits the speakerphone.

"What is it?" He keeps his tone short and clipped, so she *knows* he's unhappy.

"I'm sorry Mr. Holt, but a representative from the city is here to see you."

He scowls. "Do they have an appointment?"

"Sir, it's a representative from the *city*." The way she stresses the last word clarifies the situation. Holt sits up straight in his chair and grips the edge of his desk tightly.

"Ah. I see. Thank you, I'll be there in a moment."

His hands are shaking so badly he almost knocks over his coffee as he turns off the speakerphone. He takes a deep breath and forces himself to calm down. The last thing he can afford is to look nervous in front of the mob. He stands, straightens his tie, then walks over to the door. He takes his suit jacket from the closet and puts it on, forcing himself not to hurry. His hand drifts to the door, but he hesitates; he walks back to his desk and stares down at the incident report. He frowns, grabs it, shoves it into a desk drawer, then walks back to the door.

Smooth sleeves. Straighten tie. Open door. Step through with a million dollar smile.

"How do you do? I'm Ron Holt."

The reception area for the top floor is a modern, elegant space: glass tables and chrome furniture with white leather cushions. Pleasant-if-trivial music plays over quality speakers in the ceiling. His personal assistant's desk, a modern-looking glass-and-steel wraparound, is clean and well-organized. His personal assistant, a young, pretty college graduate from a prestigious business school Holt never bothered to remember, is also usually clean and well-organized. At the moment, however, she looks flustered. The most likely reason is the two gentlemen who are also in the room.

Holt can't tell if they look like gangsters or not. They are dressed in pinstripe suits—nothing fancy, but nothing shabby either—and wear bowler hats. The very large man on the left is built like a brick wall. He stands stoically behind his companion, a small, thin man with a cheerful yet unnerving tight-lipped smile. The bowler hats work against them, as far as looking like gangsters goes, but there is a definite quality of *menace* about them that he can't dismiss out of hand. Holt immediately thinks of *A Clockwork Orange* with Malcolm McDowell playing Alex.

The small man tips his hat, his smile widening to show perfectly white, smooth teeth. "Ronald! It's good of you to see us at such an early hour. And us without an appointment, too. I hope you don't think too harshly of your lovely assistant here—she didn't want to call you. I insisted."

His assistant is smiling a tight, pleasant smile that she is obviously expending a great deal of effort to maintain.

Holt nods, hoping it looks amiable, and takes the time to steady his voice. "Not at all. Please do come in."

Holt stands aside, holding the door open for the two men. The small man nods once, tips his hat to Holt's assistant, and steps lightly through the door, almost shouting "An invitation!" in a merry tone as he crosses the threshold of the office. The larger man follows, silent and emotionless.

After they step into the office, Holt turns to his assistant. "Did they say what they wanted?" He keeps his voice low.

His assistant shakes her head. "I asked. He acted like I hadn't."

Holt nods. "Hold my calls for as long as they're here."

His assistant nods.

Holt turns back to the office, steps inside, and shuts the door behind him.

"I say!" The small man gazes at the office. "This is a fine place to work! Stylish. Tasteful. *Big*. I had no idea health care was so lucrative!" The large man says nothing. As far as Holt can tell, he isn't even paying attention.

"It's a growth industry," Holt says, laughing nervously. "Would you like a drink?"

"Oh, very kind, very kind," the small man says.

Holt starts over to the wet bar.

"But I think it's too early in the morning for libations," the small man continues. "Though I thank you for your gracious offer."

Holt stops, then turns. "Well, then, how can I help you gentlemen today?"

"Ah, yes," the small man says. "The meat of the matter. The meat. Good enough, then, let's start. Shall we sit?"

The small man gestures to Holt's desk, and the chairs around it.

"Of course," Holt says. He moves to his desk, but the small man almost pirouettes around it and plops down in Holt's chair. He pushes back from the desk and spins, laughing as the chair makes three full revolutions before it slows to a halt. By chance the chair stops facing Holt directly.

"I've always wanted to do that," the small man says, eyes twinkling. "This is a magnificent chair for spinning. Have you done much of that? Spinning?"

"No," Holt lies. He stands in front of the chair, waiting to see if the small man will get up out of it. He doesn't. Holt fights back another wave of frustration, then walks back around the front of his desk and sits down in one of the other chairs.

The large man doesn't sit.

"So... I'm sorry, I don't want to be rude," Holt says, "but I still don't know why you're here."

"Of course you don't!" The small man almost laughs. His voice is friendly, almost intimately so, as if he were a lifelong friend, or a favorite uncle. "How could you? We haven't told you yet. And I'm sorry this is so abrupt—the thing is, the city has a problem, and I'm afraid your company is involved."

"Well it's not my company," Holt says, then breaks off. He hadn't meant to sound so defensive. He tries again. "I am the executive officer for this branch, so of course management of TriHealth in this area is my responsibility. But we are a publicly owned company, so it would be inaccurate, technically speaking, to call it 'my' company."

"Sure, sure." The small man nods agreeably. "I didn't mean to imply that level of possession. It's probably more accurate to say that *you* belong to *it*."

"I... well." Holt frowns. "You could... I don't know that I..."

The small man laughs again. "There's no shame in that! You are a man who serves a *purpose*. From what I see..." He looks around the office appreciatively. "From what I see, that service has been very good for you. Very good indeed."

Holt doesn't know what to say.

"You are, by all appearances, a successful and well-respected man," the small man continues. "Your success comes from your service to your purpose. Just as mine does from mine, I suppose."

Holt nods, trying to look thoughtful. "I suppose it does."

"Of course, the success of your purpose—of this place—is the result of many factors," the small man says. "Your hard work. The hard work of those who work for you, and with you. Employees. Peers. *Partners.*"

The smile on the small man's face fades, ever so slightly. It's not quite as bright, not quite as friendly, and his voice, while still genial, has the faintest hint of an edge to it. "It's easy to forget your partners. The ones who work *with* you to make you the success you are. And from time to time it may be tempting to ignore the agreements you made with them. From time to time."

Holt doesn't reply.

"We expect a certain amount of this, of course." The small man starts spinning in Holt's chair again, around and around and around and around, pushing off the floor with one leg in a lazy, carefree manner. "The *services* we make available through this city are tailored to a certain *element* with a predisposition toward *unreliability*. Even the respectable organizations—or, perhaps, *especially* them—are given to ignoring the rules, whatever they may be, if they think they can profit and get away with it."

"I still don't—" Holt's voice shakes for a moment, and he coughs, covering it up. "Excuse me. If you could just give me a little—"

"Well it's that business yesterday," the small man says. "Which, of course, was tied to that business the night before. Of course, from your perspective I expect the young man started it. That is a mitigating factor, I admit—or it would be, if it were *ipso facto*, but it isn't. It isn't, you see."

"I don't see," Holt protests. "What business yesterday?"

The small man cocks his head to one side, examining Holt closely. Then he turns to the large man, still standing motionless in his spot.

"He doesn't know," the small man says, then he tips his hat. "You were right all along."

"*What* don't I know?" Holt presses.

"He's a marvel," the small man says, gesturing to the large man. "You'll notice he's not one for talking—not to strangers, at any rate—but while I fancy myself a keen judge of character I have to admit that his judgment surpasses mine with uncanny regularity. He always surprises me. He's a pleasure to work with. Truly a pleasure."

The large man doesn't respond. He doesn't even acknowledge the small man's presence, as far as Holt can tell.

"Look," Holt says, "I still don't understand—"

"Rules!" The chair stops spinning abruptly. The small man's voice is loud and sharp. The smile is gone from his face, replaced with a stern, admonishing expression—a father chastising a son. "This city has *rules*, Ronald. Its success requires that our guests obey those rules. And you—rather, the purpose you serve—has not."

"That's not true!" Holt rises out of his chair in protest. Almost immediately the large man is by his side. A large, meaty hand presses down on his shoulder, and Holt immediately collapses back into his chair. He stares up at the large man, eyes wide. The man isn't looking at him, he's staring out the expansive office windows.

"I am willing to believe that you don't know about it." The smile returns, and the small man's voice slips back into its friendly, conversational tone. "You are not, I think, someone who sees the whole picture. Significant pieces of it, perhaps. More significant than you realize, perhaps. But not the entire thing, no. But your masters, well, they know our rules."

Holt sputters in astonishment. "My *masters*?"

The small man shrugs. "No point in calling a ladle a spoon. Whether you see it or not, you are theirs as sure as if they'd bought you. Which, in many ways, they have..." He spins around in Holt's chair again, just once, his arms spread wide to indicate the office. "And they know our rules. They know what we permit, and what we do not. They know that magic is *absolutely not* permitted here."

Holt tries to rise again, but the large man's hand continues to grip his shoulder, making movement impossible. "*Magic*? You can't be serious."

"Oh, but I am!" The small man nods rapidly. "Very serious. We're very generous in many ways, my dear Ronald. We can share wealth. We can share freedom. We can share—we *love* to share—the simple joys of *excess*. But we are, I'm afraid, very possessive when it comes to *that*."

All at once Holt decides these two men are lunatics. There is absolutely no way they represent Farraday City. The interests who control Farraday

City are mobsters, gangsters—cutthroat, murderous criminals, yes, but they approach their work with a certain level of rationality that these men obviously don't have. He's alone in his office with two men who are lying about who they are, and he has to get out.

He opens his mouth to call for help, and the large man squeezes his shoulder. White-hot pain lances down his shoulder and into his side. His cry transforms into a nearly silent squawk of agony. He gasps, taking sharp breaths, as the small man looks on.

"You don't want to do this," Holt says.

"Perhaps," the small man says, "but what of it? We do what we must in the service of our *purpose*."

Holt shakes his head. "You don't understand. As soon as the people in this building realize I'm in trouble, you'll never make it out."

The small man smiles at him fondly. "Ah, Ronald. *You* don't understand. It doesn't matter. They won't know. They'll *never* know. They never do."

PART FOUR: SOMEWHERE UNDERGROUND

Holt wakes up with a sudden, sharp surge of adrenaline, his mind screaming. *Danger! Danger!* Over and over again it screams, urging him to move, urging him to flee, and he's absolutely convinced it is giving him the best advice he's ever received.

It's advice he can't take. He can't move.

He's lying on his back, staring up into darkness. He can't see anything, but he's lying on something cold. Stone, he thinks—it feels like he's lying on smooth stone, maybe concrete. It's cold enough that he shivers slightly—apparently he can move some—but he can't do much else. He can hear sounds: he hears the sound of someone breathing next to him, the slow, regular pattern of someone sleeping. Above him he hears a dull, distant roar... no, not a roar, but the sound of something rushing over him and around him.

Why is it so cold? Holt tries to raise his head, but he can't. He tries to speak, but he can't. He tries to make any noise at all—a whimper, anything—but he can't. The most he can do is breathe. He tries to take a deep breath, and succeeds. He tries to take a series of short, shallow breaths, and succeeds.

"Good morning!" The sound of the small man comes from somewhere to his right. "Very early morning. Almost two, I think. And yes, it's true, you can't move. It's a thing we do. It makes the next part easier."

Holt takes in a quick, deep breath. He tries to cry for help, but he can't.

"Oh, it won't work, Ronald," the small man says. "We've stolen your voice. Stolen right out from under you. That *also* makes the next part easier. There's quite a bit of concentration involved, and it wouldn't do to have you messing that up. We only get one try to get this right..."

Light flickers from the corner of Holt's vision, and a second later torchlight—he thinks it's torchlight—illuminates the only thing he can see. Far above him is a stone ceiling. It's curved ever so slightly, creating a broad dome. Etched into the ceiling are pictures, or symbols, or... something. He doesn't understand what he's looking at. He can't tell if they're abstract pictures of some kind of animal, or if they're letters in a language he's never seen before.

And then, a moment later, he sees the face of the small man peering over him. He's still dressed in that suit, still wearing the bowler hat. The grin is gone from his face, replaced with an expression of pensive solemnity.

"It's raining again," the small man says.

Holt looks up at him, mute and fearful.

"That's significant, you see." The small man nods once. "It was infinitely difficult to build the sewers under this city—oh yes, we had them built when we restored the city. The soil down here makes digging tunnels difficult. Especially near the beaches. And our requirements were rather exact... it was expensive, and took an intolerably long time. But it was worth it."

Holt tries to move his eyes, but he can't. He tries to blink, but he can't do that either. His body can blink—he feels himself do it from time to time—but he can't make himself blink. It's maddening.

"The secret, you see..." The small man looks lost in his own thoughts. More like the expression on the large man's face than his usual manically friendly demeanor. "The secret is that certain parts of the sewer are graded in very specific ways, so that when water comes into the sewers—specifically, the volume of water that comes in from certain storms—certain passages get more water than others. And all those passages connect, and all flow in the same direction, so that after a while you get a current that flows in the shape of a very distinct, very old pattern."

The small man raises a hand and traces a pattern in the air over Holt's face, so he can see it. Every time the small man's hand passes over his face, Holt feels himself shudder. He tries to picture the symbol in his head. He can't, but each line of it fills him with a pain that goes beyond fear.

"It doesn't mean much to you, I'm sure," the small man says. "Well, that's not true. I suspect it means rather a lot to you. Or it will, very soon. From your point of view the meaning is fixed. It has no context to put it in. You simply know that it exists, and its existence will negate your own. Not a happy meaning, I'll grant. But for us... well. I won't bore you. I'm told I can get rhapsodic when I talk about the metaphysics involved."

The small man ducks out of view, walks swiftly back to the right, where Holt first heard him. "Nevermind. It's time to begin."

Steel scrapes against stone. Holt realizes it's the sound of a knife against a whetstone. His flesh crawls as he hears the *skreet skreet skreet* of the metal against the stone. He wants to whimper. He can't.

"It's unfortunate, I suppose," the small man says. "I mean, you really have little to do with any of this. Not that it matters to the ceremony, but you were chosen in order to send a message to your masters, one I hope they will heed in the future. It would be a more effective message, I think, if you were a willing co-conspirator. If they didn't tell you, your loss may not move them overmuch. But it should have some effect, I think. At the very least, they will know that we know. And in the end it will balance the scales somewhat. You will serve the city your masters damaged, in the end."

Steps grow louder, and the small man comes into view once more, peering down at him. "I do regret you must be *awake* for your part, but only one of you can have the mercy of sleep. And he's certainly more deserving of it than you, for many reasons."

The small man shifts his weight, steps back until he is at the corner of Holt's vision. Holt sees a glint of steel, and then his gaze is fixed on the knife held over him. It's a modern knife, with a carbon steel blade and a plastic, ridged grip.

The blade is very long.

The blade is very sharp.

"There was a time," the small man says, "when every farmer knew the best way to secure a good harvest was to spill the blood of a stranger on his soil. Blood is life, after all. Power. That power and that life would seep into the soil, into the roots, and into the crops themselves. Of course, you need more than that—all the blood in the world won't help you if you're a terrible farmer. You also need to know how to grow the crops, and a long succession of lazy, incompetent farmers led people to believe that these rites were nothing more than dark superstition."

The small man's face comes into clearer view as he leans over. "We know better."

His face recedes to the edges again. "Farraday City is full of strangers, Ronald. Very few people actually put down roots here—they come here believing they can get rich quick, enjoy the high life for a while, and then move on. The people who get trapped here never consider it their home, they consider it a prison. There are very few who actually have any true, deep ties to this place, so we have our pick when it comes to finding blood to spill."

The small man holds the knife above Holt's forehead, tip pointed down. The spot where he imagines the tip might come to rest starts to itch furiously.

"Plenty of stranger's blood," the small man continues. "Blood for our farm. Because that's what Farraday City is, in the end. It's a farm, one we have plowed and planted and tended and protected ever since we first set foot on its ground. It is a farm, and we are farmers. And this morning, Ronald, you and your companion will spill your blood upon our farm, and your blood will sink into the soil, and it will go into the roots of our crop, and your blood and your power will nourish it as we tend it, and it will grow larger and stronger. It will grow, and blossom, and flourish, and you will be the reason why."

The tip comes down, ever so gently, on his forehead.

"*But what is this crop?* I hear you ask. Well, it's a fair question, Ronald, and I'll not begrudge you the answer. In truth, your knowledge is needed to make the ceremony work. Did you ever wonder why, in all those stupid, shallow stories, the villain always reveals his master plan to the hero? It makes no sense, but you see it in movies, books—everything. All the time. Did you ever wonder why? Well I'll tell you."

The tip presses down. Just a little.

"It's because the stories are echoes of a shadow of an older truth: desperate, futile knowledge feeds anguish, and anguish feeds what we do. What we grow."

Holt can feel the tip cutting into his forehead. Blood trickles down the side of his face, pooling in his right ear.

"We grow sin," the small man whispers.

CURVEBALL
14
NOV 2013
CURVEBALL
A Prose Comic
MISSING LINKS
STORY
CHRISTOPHER WRIGHT
COVER
PASCALLE LEPAS
LOGO
GARTH GRAHAM

PART ONE: FARRADAY FREE CLINIC

It's been almost an hour and a half since he first filled out all his paperwork, and he's waiting as patiently as he can, despite the fact that his Saturday is slowly slipping away from him. It's another thirty-five minutes before a young nurse finally calls his name, at which point he stands up and shuffles past all the other people in the room, following the nurse into a small examination room in the clinic where he stands, just as awkwardly, looking at the examination bed with the thin paper sheet spread out on top of it.

"Do I have to get on that?" Arthur's voice is rough and gravelly—he's a smoker, though he's gone without cigarettes for the entire week in anticipation of today's exam. He wants a cigarette so badly his hands are almost shaking with desire. He grips his cap tighter, and his knuckles whiten.

"Not right now." The nurse smiles comfortingly. She's a pretty young thing, though he's not sure how much of the beauty is natural and how much is applied. Her dark red hair is obviously not a natural color, and her dark blue eyes might not be natural either. His niece bought contact lenses that turned her eyes purple. Purple! Young people are always trying new things. "We just have a few more questions, then I'm going to take your blood pressure and a blood sample."

"Do I have to..." Arthur pauses and looks away, coloring slightly. "Do I have to take my clothes off?" He hasn't really been to see a doctor since he was in the army, and he's not comfortable with the idea of undressing in front of someone so young.

The nurse does *not* smile, much to his relief. "No," she says. "Not right now. I'm just going to take your pulse, ask you a few questions, and then take a little blood for our tests. Just take a seat right there and roll up that sleeve."

Arthur nods, relieved. He sits in a plastic chair and rolls up his right sleeve past his elbow.

The nurse looks at the tattoo on his arm. "Thank you for your service, sir."

Arthur colors again. "That was a long time ago."

"Was it the Gulf War?" She places the blood pressure cuff on his arm, makes sure everything is arranged correctly, then begins to squeeze the bulb. The cuff tightens. "I had an uncle in Desert Storm."

"Vietnam," Arthur says. "Like I said, long time ago."

She nods and smiles again. Her hair and eyes may be fake, but the smile is genuine. "You have thick calluses. Still working?"

"I do construction," Arthur says, a trace of pride creeping into his voice. "I can keep up with the younger guys OK. The foreman doesn't know how old I am. You're not going to tell him, are you? I need the job..."

The nurse laughs warmly. "Don't worry. All information remains confidential. I'm going to take some blood now, all right?"

Arthur nods, sighing in relief. He hardly notices as she cleans the spot over the vein and draws the blood.

"You put on your form that you can't remember the last time you saw a doctor," the nurse says.

"Yeah." Arthur watches with distracted interest as the blood is drawn out of his vein and siphoned into a small vial. "Since I left the army. Never got sick enough to bother, and it was expensive. Is this visit really free?"

"Sure is." The nurse smiles again. "That's why we're so busy today. Now I'm going to take this down to the lab. The doctor is still with another patient, so there may be another wait. Just make yourself comfortable. You can lie down on the examination table, if you want. The top raises a little if lying flat on your back makes you uncomfortable."

"All right," Arthur says. "Thanks."

"Hopefully the doctor will be by soon," she says. "Then you can enjoy the rest of your Saturday." She flashes him another beautiful, genuine smile, then takes the vial and exits the room, closing the door behind her.

Arthur looks around the small room and suddenly wishes he had a muted television to watch.

The door opens and an older man in a white coat shuffles into the room. He's a rather plain-looking man, about Arthur's age but softer—he's a man who is used to an entirely different type of labor. His hair is short and almost entirely gray. He wears bifocals set in thick, black plastic rims, the kind that were popular in the late 70s. The man smiles at Arthur, showing yellowed smoker's teeth. "Hello, Mr. Franklin! Sorry for the wait. The place is hopping today, I have to say. Let's get everything moving, there are a few things I want to go over before we send you on your way."

The doctor's voice is jovial, but it's a practiced joviality that Arthur suspects comes from saying the same thing to every patient, day after day. The doctor looks down and reads, his pen rapping the clipboard *tap tap tap tap tap* with rapid impatience as his eyes linger on something.

Arthur sits up, the paper crinkling as he swings his legs off the side of the table. The nurse had been right—it was more comfortable with the back raised. He rubs his eyes and stifles a yawn.

"Your blood results are interesting," the doctor begins, and suddenly Arthur is wide awake. He can't think of a single reason why a doctor would find anything about him interesting unless it was bad. The doctor looks up and raises his eyebrows, apparently surprised by the expression on Arthur's face, then says, "Oh, no, no, Mr. Franklin I'm sorry, I didn't mean it that way. We didn't find anything that would concern us."

Arthur exhales slowly and forces himself to calm down. "I thought you were going to tell me I had cancer." His voice is thick and husky.

"No..." The doctor peers at him critically. "But it's obvious you smoke, Mr. Franklin, and you should probably stop."

"Yeah." Arthur's voice shakes a little. "I know. It's not easy."

The doctor nods. "I can provide you with a list of numbers you can call. Support hotlines, a Nicotine Anonymous group. Do you have any insurance?"

Arthur shakes his head.

"Well, we can discuss your options later. Right now I'd like to talk to you about *why* I said your blood was interesting—interesting in a good way, not a bad way."

"OK," Arthur says.

The doctor smiles again, with the same forced jocularity. "This clinic, and a number of other clinics like it, is funded by a group that does a lot of cutting-edge medical research. Specifically genetic research. Are you familiar with genetics, Mr. Franklin?"

Arthur shrugs. "Just... a part of your body that gives you blue eyes or brown eyes."

The doctor smiles again, this time a bit patronizingly. "That's the general idea. You can tell a little bit about your genes based on some very basic blood tests—tests you agreed to when you signed our forms in the lobby. As it happens, you seem to have a genetic profile that our sponsors are very interested in, and they'd like to make you an offer."

Arthur tries not to scowl, but he can't hide the suspicion in his eyes. "Genetic what? I don't want to sell my organs."

The doctor laughs as if Arthur told the funniest joke he'd ever heard. "Lord! No, I daresay you wouldn't! A 'genetic profile' is just a specific combination of genes. It's like only being interested in people with green eyes and red hair, only the specific things they're looking for are inside the body, not on the outside. They just want you to agree to donate some blood once a month for their studies."

Arthur frowns. "They just want blood?"

"That's right," the doctor says. "And a very small amount—it's not like giving blood at the Red Cross. They want a much, much smaller sample than that."

"And what do I get?" Arthur asks. "I mean, do they pay me?"

"Oh yes," the doctor says. "Quite well, actually. They're a very large company, and this genetic combination is very rare. You'll have to sign a paper promising not to talk to anyone about it, and show up once a month for your bloodwork. In return, you'll be paid quite well each month, and you'll also be signed up for a very comprehensive lifetime health insurance plan."

Arthur's frown deepens. "No offense, but that sounds too good."

The doctor nods. "It's a common reaction, especially in Farraday City. If you like I can put you in touch with some other people in the program. TriHealth—that's the insurance company sponsoring the research and providing the insurance—keeps a list of people who have volunteered to talk to new prospective volunteers."

Arthur tries to look over the top of the clipboard to see what's written on it, but the doctor raises it slightly, obscuring the text. "They want to pay me for looking at my blood?"

The doctor nods. "And health insurance."

"Pay how much?" Arthur asks.

The doctor tells him.

Twenty minutes later Arthur is filling out more forms. There will be more tests later today, and he'll have to return to the clinic next week for his first official donation, but suddenly he doesn't mind that so much of his Saturday has been spent sitting around waiting. He's going to make more money from this research than he ever did working construction. He's about to be able to retire. He's going to have more free time than he ever dreamed possible.

For Arthur Franklin, things are finally looking up.

PART TWO: FARRADAY CITY BUNKER

Red Shift is already up—CB isn't sure he really sleeps—and has apparently already made breakfast. A *lot* of breakfast: eggs, sausage, bacon, toast, ham, and various combinations of each. CB steps over a puddle of batter and adds pancakes to the list.

Red Shift sits at the small table, eating what appears to be a five-egg omelet, six pieces of toast, and a pile of sausage and bacon set on top of seven pancakes. In contrast to the enormous volume of food on his plate, he is daintily sipping a mug of coffee. He's bent over Jenny's laptop, staring at the screen intensely.

"Good morning." Red Shift doesn't look up from the screen. "Help yourself to food. I think my metabolism is finally settling down."

CB grunts and pours himself a cup of coffee. He finds a plate, adds two pancakes and some bacon to it, and sits down opposite Red Shift. Halfway through his coffee he realizes he forgot to get a fork. He shrugs, picks up one of the pancakes with his hands, and shoves it into his mouth.

"I was a little worried for a while," Red Shift says. "I was burning through food like it was the old days, back before I knew how to manage everything. It shouldn't be acting like this now."

"Magic." CB's mouth is stuffed full of pancake, and it sounds more like "mavvik."

Red Shift frowns for a moment, trying to process what he said, then nods when the word registers. "Magic. Right. Hadn't thought of that. We haven't really had a lot of experience with it, to be honest."

CB shakes his head, swallows, and rinses it down with more coffee. "Nobody has," he says finally. "Most people who use it try very hard to stay out of sight, and when they finally come out into the open it's... bad. The Guardians had to deal with it twice. Two times too many. Both times there were side effects for everyone who came into contact with it."

"What kind of side effects?" Red Shift asks.

"Different for everyone," CB says. "It seems to affect technology the same way—Grey Falcon and Gladiator found it drained their power like crazy, and nothing worked as well. Everything was weaker. Regiment couldn't shrug it off like he could every other damn thing in the world—it could actually hurt him. And he had trouble controlling his strength. He would wind up accidentally crushing things one second and then not being able to open a door the next. Everything around me got weird and random. I can't explain it more than that. The only person who seemed to be able to work through it was Liberty. Big surprise there, he could work through pretty much everything. Except, apparently, a bullet through his head."

Red Shift looks thoughtful. "So it affects control. Well, that would explain it. When I first started out I was afraid I was going to starve to death if I pushed too hard. This felt like that."

"I hate magic," CB says. "Bad news. And Doyle... Christ. Doyle plus magic is a bad combination."

"Well I'll try to stay clear of him in the future," Red Shift says. "I'll let Miss Liberty handle it. She seems to be immune."

"... Miss Liberty?" CB stares at him blankly.

Red Shift shrugs. "I can't keep calling her 'Miss Forrest.' She's not a civilian any more. And we don't do first names."

"Yeah," CB says. "You guys were pretty funny about that way back when. So basically you're still the most tight-assed vigilante group in the world."

Red Shift laughs. "And you're still *incredibly* polite."

CB grins. "I'm not sure *Miss Liberty* is going to like you using her laptop."

"I was looking over the medical records you pulled out of TriHealth," Red Shift says. "And I noticed something interesting."

"Oh?" CB scoots his chair around the table to look at the screen. "What?"

"Well..." Red Shift opens one of the files. "You already said you thought there was a link between TriHealth and the 'serial killer' you were investigating just before Liberty was murdered."

CB nods. "Most of the victims had TriHealth listed as their insurer."

"Actually," Red Shift says, "they all did."

"No," CB says. "I remember the police files. Some of them were with other providers."

Red Shift nods. "They still had TriHealth as a secondary provider. I took the list you gave me and did some searching. Every single one of the identified victims is a TriHealth customer."

"So there's a solid link there," CB says.

"Yes," Red Shift says. "And there's more. Every single one of them has a flag on their file that I've never seen before. Here..."

He opens one of the files and zooms in on a box that says "other conditions." In it is a six digit code.

"PROD55?" CB asks. "What's that?"

Red Shift shrugs. "Not familiar with it. But every victim has it. I haven't found anything relating to that code yet, but there are a lot of encrypted files I haven't been able to crack open. Maybe Miss Liberty can do that..."

"Who is Miss Liberty?" Jenny stands in the kitchen door, dressed in a plain blue t-shirt and a pair of gray sweat pants. "Do I smell coffee?" Then, a second later: "Do I smell *food*?"

"Help yourself," Red Shift says. "You've been out for two days."

Jenny grunts and descends on the remaining food. She doesn't even bother to take it to the table. CB and Red Shift look on in astonishment.

"Maybe we should start calling her 'The Locust,'" CB says.

"Funny," Jenny says, as she fills a mug with coffee. "Wait... were you calling *me* Miss Liberty?"

CB recognizes the tone in her voice. It sounds uncomfortably like her mother's. "Uh..."

"It seemed thematically appropriate," Red Shift says.

Jenny narrows her eyes. "*Hell no*. Also unacceptable: 'Lady Liberty' and 'Liberty Lass.' As a general rule of thumb, if any 'code name' you come up with feels compelled to announce to the world that I'm a *girl*, it will be disqualified."

CB's mouth quirks. "How about 'Madam'—"

"Shut *up*," Jenny says. "Shut up *so very much*."

CB grins, then laughs.

Red Shift looks confused. "I don't see what's wrong with 'Miss Liberty.'"

Jenny growls.

Time to change the subject. "How are you feeling?" CB asks.

Jenny gives Red Shift one last dark look, then sits down in the remaining chair. "Funny," she admits. "Like my arms and legs are lighter. I'm made out of rubber. Everything wobbles."

"Just give it a few hours," Red Shift says. "You'll feel normal soon. That's the dangerous part—you'll start breaking things then."

"Lucky me," Jenny says. "What are you doing with my laptop?"

"He found a link," CB says. He quickly fills her in on the PROD55 code.

"I'm trying to get a look at their medical histories," Red Shift adds. "I might be able to put that code into some kind of context. But the remaining files are encrypted..."

"Move over," Jenny says, wiping her hands on her shirt.

Red Shift pushes his chair back, then steps aside. "I guess I'll clean up."

Jenny sits down in front of her laptop and starts typing. "I've been meaning to get around to this anyway."

CB gets another cup of coffee. By the time he sits down again Jenny is grinning from ear to ear.

"Did the bad guys do something stupid?"

"Yeah," she says. "When we were at TriHealth I was copying everything I could find. They stored their encryption keys in the same directory they put their files, so I got those as well. That was sloppy. That's the kind of thing that gets you fired. Anyway, the files are unlocked."

She relinquishes the chair. Red Shift resumes his search.

"CB," Jenny says, "we have to talk."

CB raises an eyebrow. He jerks his head in Red Shift's direction. Jenny shakes her head.

"I'll shout when I find something good," Red Shift says amiably.

CB and Jenny go into the bunker's living area.

"Not a whole lot of privacy in this place, is there?" Jenny says. She sits on the vinyl couch—the same place she was when she first heard about cocooning—and fidgets with her hands as she waits for CB to sit.

"What's on your mind?" CB sits in the old recliner.

"'Miss Liberty.'" Jenny stares at the floor.

"I knew that would piss you off. Look, Red doesn't really put a lot of thought into names. I mean, I actually think his is pretty cool, to be honest, but keep in mind one of his co-workers is a guy named 'Vigilante.' A name he took because he decided to become a vigilante."

Jenny waves a hand dismissively. "I don't really care about the sexist bullshit name. Except that I guess he wants me to actually have a..."

CB nods. "He wants you to have a name, yes."

"Why?"

"Ask him," CB says.

"I'm asking you," Jenny says. "At least, I'm asking you first."

CB sighs. "It's a Crossfire thing."

"What does that mean?" Jenny asks. "And how is it you know them? You've been gone ten years."

"Crossfire got started about the same time the Guardians did," CB says. "So yeah, we have some history. We worked together on a few things, we worked against each other on a few things. They have this thing about code names, hero names, villain names. They *only* use them. As far as I know they do it all the time. Back when he thought of you as a 'civilian' you were 'Miss Forrest.' He doesn't think of you as a civilian any more."

"Do you?"

CB frowns. "I *never* thought of you as a civilian. You're family. That's different."

"That's not what I..." Jenny trails off. "I mean... I'm a metahuman. Like you, and Red Shift, and... and great-grandfather."

"Probably more like him than me," CB says. "Or Red. But yes."

"So..." Jenny looks away. "What does that mean, exactly?"

"You know, Jenny..." CB tries to think of a way to put it diplomatically. "In other circumstances, I would give you the 'it can mean anything you want, or nothing at all' speech. That you could use your powers for the betterment of mankind, or for the betterment of yourself, choose to be one of the good guys, or one of the bad guys, or you could not do anything at all and keep living your life. Some metahumans actually go through their lives not using their abilities at all. But I'm not going to give you that speech."

"Why not?" Jenny asks.

"I'm not going to give you that speech because you're neck deep in this thing. So what it means, as far as I'm concerned, is that we need to get you up to speed so that when things go south you'll be able to handle yourself. You've got a chance to do more than crack algorithms or break encryption or any of that other esoteric stuff you do. I mean, keep doing that—that's useful—but when it comes time to stick it to the people who snuffed Alex, this gives you a seat at the table."

"What if I don't want—"

CB cuts her off. "I don't care. Look, don't take this the wrong way, but I should not have let you come with me. It was stupid and careless and I was tired after that fight and pissed off about Alex and I didn't do what I should have done, which was to steal a car and drive off while you were waiting for me to show up. It was dumb and shortsighted and it put you in more risk than you needed to be in."

Jenny clenches her jaw angrily.

"That said," CB continues, "if it weren't for you we wouldn't have those files from TriHealth. Hell, if it weren't for you Doyle probably would have killed me. You've done good. At the end of the day, we're better off with you here. But we're a lot better off with you here if you decide you're going to commit. It's better if I can work with you instead of always having to keep an eye on you."

Jenny doesn't reply.

CB gets off the recliner. "I know this is a shock, Jenny, but consider that we're hiding in a bunker in the most corrupt city in America because someone murdered your great-grandfather, and—if Crossfire's information is right—your *uncle* might be involved."

"I can't believe he would do that," Jenny says. She stares at her hands. Her voice is very small.

"I can," CB says. "He's an asshole. I'm going to take a shower."

He heads off down the hall. Jenny keeps staring at her hands. Half a minute later she hears the shower turn on.

"He's kind of a jerk."

Jenny looks up. Red Shift is standing in the doorway, holding a mug of coffee.

"I like that about him, actually," Red Shift says. "And I guess you're more used to it than I am. I only had to deal with Curveball when he was on the job. Apparently he hasn't mellowed."

"How much of that did you hear?" Jenny asks.

Red Shift shrugs. "Just the tail end. I agree with him, by the way. Given present circumstances it's better for you to step up than it is to keep playing civilian."

"I know," Jenny says. She sighs. "I just wish I didn't have to."

"Understandable," Red Shift says, "but largely irrelevant. You have gifts that can keep you alive. You need to learn to use them."

"I *know*," Jenny says. "I guess I need to come up with a name."

Red Shift smiles slightly. "It'd make life easier on me."

PART THREE: CROSSFIRE SAFEHOUSE

"Are you absolutely sure?" Vigilante is sitting back in an old metal folding chair, arms crossed. He's in civilian clothes today—a dirty gray t-shirt, jeans, tennis shoes—which David *thinks* means he's starting to get used to the "new team." But he still insists on referring to everyone by their code name... except for David, since he doesn't have one any more. He calls him "Lieutenant" instead.

Red Shift nods through the monitor, his face pixellating slightly from the movement. "The victims were all given Dyson-Ferris Assessments, and were scored accordingly."

"That's the part I don't understand," Vigilante says. "You tell me the victims were *not* metahumans. How do they get scores?"

"I don't understand that part either," Red Shift says. "They're not based on the standard scoring system, and we don't have any documents that explain what they mean. We'll pass it along and you can see for yourself."

"OK," Vigilante says. "What are you working on now?"

It's hard to read Red Shift's expression. "We're still trying to assess the tactical environment."

Vigilante hesitates a moment. "OK," he says.

"Red is being polite." A spiky-haired guy who looks roughly David's age, maybe a little younger, leans in-frame and smirks. "What *actually* happened is that I got my ass kicked and we're trying to figure out who they are and how to deal with them."

Curveball. He really doesn't age. I mean, he looked young at Liberty's funeral but I assumed that was all the TV makeup.

"We may have something on that front," Vigilante says. "It's not a lot—just a name. Curveball, does 'Haruspex Analytics' mean anything to you?"

Curveball shakes his head. "No, it—" His gaze shifts to something past the camera.

David can hear someone else talking, too indistinct for the laptop microphone to pick up. A woman's voice. *That would be Miss Forrest.*

"Oh," Curveball says. "Hold on, Jenny knows these guys." Curveball ducks back out of frame, and Red Shift stands up as Miss Forrest takes his seat and stares into the screen.

David has met her before—when he was Sky Commando, Martin Forrest often took his family to police fundraisers that David was required to attend. She was always polite, well-mannered, and completely uninterested in being there, and after one awkward attempt at making conversation he made a point of smiling, saying hello, then leaving her alone. He's struck by how much she looks like her great-grandfather, even in the poor video quality. She even has a similar jaw—not nearly as square as his, but it has the same determined set.

He looks at the others in the room to see if they see it. If Vigilante and Street Ronin do, they don't show it—they're all business, waiting to hear what she has to say. Scrapper Jack is frowning slightly—he doesn't quite see it, but something is tugging at him. LaFleur, on the other hand... Overmind is sitting forward in his chair, eyes raised, gazing at her with unabashed interest. He glances at David for a moment, nodding slightly—as if to say *yes, Lieutenant, I see it as well*—then returns to studying Miss Forrest.

"I wouldn't say I *know* them," Jenny says. "I've never worked with them. But I've heard of them. They work in my field, at least peripherally."

"What's your field, Miss Forrest?" Vigilante asks.

"Security," she says. "Network security, mostly. Haruspex Analytics provides some very sophisticated tools to the American Intelligence Community. They might do other things, too, but I don't know anything about that. I just know their security tools are... really very good. And *ridiculously expensive*."

"That's a good place to start," Vigilante says. He looks over to LaFleur. "You have any contacts who can look into these guys? We don't really focus on spooks, we're out of luck there."

LaFleur nods.

"Wait." Curveball sticks his head back in-frame. "Vigilante are you talking to LaFleur? Is he there?"

Vigilante looks at LaFleur again. He smiles, amused, and nods slightly.

"Yeah," Vigilante says. "Everyone's here who isn't there."

"OK. LaFleur, there's something else I need you to look into." Curveball frowns. "Uh... more accurately, there's something else that I don't think any of the rest of us have a snowball's chance in hell of looking into."

"Of course," LaFleur says. He raises his voice loud enough to be heard clearly, but he doesn't bother getting in-frame. "How can I help you?"

"Magic," Curveball says. "A guy I used to know named *Plague* is sporting runes of some sort. He's graduated from scary to terrifying as a result. The only thing we have going for us at the moment is that he still has a weakness for blondes..."

Jenny apparently kicks him under the table. Curveball yelps in pain.

“Thing is,” Curveball says, “there aren’t a lot of people who really have access to information about—”

“Indeed,” LaFleur says. “Do you happen to have any specific information about the runes themselves?”

Curveball makes a face. “I tried drawing a few. I’ll email them over. The problem is... well, you know the problem.”

“I do,” LaFleur says. “I agree I should probably make that my priority, but this group still needs to be investigated. Jack?”

“Yeah,” Scrapper Jack says. “Give me a list and I’ll run ’em down.”

“I’ll give you two,” LaFleur says. “Green and Red.”

Scrapper Jack nods.

“Jack too,” Curveball says. “Weirdest reunion ever. OK, so on our end I’ll nose around Farraday City to try and figure out where our very special friends are holed up. And Red Shift has offered to train Jenny, which is probably a good idea.”

Miss Forrest grows very still. “He has?”

“Yeah,” Curveball says. “You need to start learning to cope with your new limits, and I don’t project an impenetrable force field every time I move.”

Miss Forrest stares fixedly at the monitor and doesn’t reply.

“Right,” Curveball says. “I guess we’re signing off so we can fight a little.”

“I’m not trying to—!”

The screen goes dark.

Everyone is silent for a moment, then Street Ronin starts laughing. Scrapper Jack joins in a few seconds later, then David, and finally Vigilante. Even LaFleur looks amused.

“He is still a jerk,” Vigilante says, still chuckling.

“I never worked with him,” David says. “Lots of stories around the precinct, though.”

“I was still on the force when he was pardoned,” Vigilante says. “And the next thing you know, Liberty shows up with Curveball as his sidekick. Nobody expected that to go well.”

“And it didn’t,” Street Ronin says. He and Vigilante laugh again.

“OK,” Vigilante says, “a moment of silence for the rookie and then we need to get to work. We have three separate leads to chase down: TriHealth, Haruspex Analytics, and this business with magic. Jack, you doing your part solo?”

Scrapper Jack nods.

"Right. Well, Street Ronin and I can try to run down this TriHealth thing. Lieutenant, we'll need you here to monitor communications and coordinate between—"

"Actually," LaFleur says, "I could use Mr. Bernard's help."

David stares at LaFleur in astonishment. "You could?"

Scrapper Jack frowns. "I don't think that's a good—"

"No," LaFleur says. "I agree. But I'm afraid it's necessary. Curveball is absolutely right, of course—the presence of magical involvement in this matter makes our situation that much more precarious, and the more we know about it the better. But this course of investigation is dangerous. I'll need another pair of eyes."

Scrapper Jack nods reluctantly. Vigilante and Street Ronin look at David thoughtfully.

"You look a lot better, Lieutenant," Vigilante says. "How do you feel?"

"Pretty good, actually," David says. "But I'm obviously not at a hundred percent."

"It'll take a while before you are," Street Ronin says.

"I figured. I don't know what kind of help you want, Overmind, but if you're looking for someone to fight—"

"I can't promise there won't be fighting," LaFleur says, "but that's not the trouble I anticipate."

"Maybe you could tell us what you *do* anticipate," David says.

"Magic." LaFleur looks around the room. "How much do you know about it?"

"Absolutely nothing," David says. Street Ronin nods in agreement.

"It's not very common," Vigilante says.

"Indeed not." Overmind sighs, then stands, facing the rest of them, as if he were delivering a lecture. "Actual magic is one of the rarest forms of power on the planet. Naturally, given my aims, I've been tempted to explore every avenue of power, to determine its suitability to my... goals."

David tries not to think too hard about that.

"And so there was a time when I tried to learn as much of it as I could. And I quickly learned to stay far away from it. Working with magic is not... healthy."

"What is it?" Street Ronin asks.

"I'm tempted to say 'it's magic, of course,' but that is too glib," LaFleur says. “It’s power. It’s power that has existed for a very long time. It predates any civilization that we are aware of. It is not found in history books—the people who claimed to be magicians were, by and large, charlatans. The knowledge is not shared freely: the practice of magic is as much a religion as it is a discipline, and the power seems to represent a very specific point of view that is absolutely opposed to any other point of view. The belief system it represents is largely alien to our understanding.”

“We’re talking Lovecraftian cults?” Street Ronin asks. “Books written in blood, on pages made of human flesh, that kind of thing?”

LaFleur raises an eyebrow.

Street Ronin smiles slightly. “We *do* read, you know.”

“It’s an apt comparison,” LaFleur says. “There is no city sleeping beneath the ocean, of course—at least, not to my knowledge—but it’s quite possible his stories were influenced by something he encountered once and could not reconcile with his rational mind. It is unpleasant knowledge to have, and is very good at encouraging people to forget it exists. It is also very difficult to use in any capacity. It causes harm to those around it, even those wielding it.”

“What kind of harm?” David asks.

“It harms the soul,” LaFleur says. "The essence of your ‘life force,’ if the term ‘soul’ offends you. Most of us, metahuman or not, are equally vulnerable to it. Jack is almost as invulnerable as Regiment, but he can still be harmed by it.”

Jack nods curtly.

“What does provide some protection,” LaFleur continues, “is strength of will. One who has the will to resist can do so—not completely, but perhaps long enough to survive. I believe I will be safer in this investigation if I am accompanied, and your strength of will, Mr. Bernard, is equal to any in this room.”

David thinks it over. “Why do you want someone with you?”

“Because when I was younger, I tried to study it alone,” LaFleur says. “And I was nearly destroyed in the process.”

Everyone looks at David expectantly.

“It’s your call,” Vigilante says.

“Well.” David stretches in his chair, then gets to his feet. “I didn’t join this outfit just to watch the rest of you work.”

LaFleur nods approvingly. “I did not think you had.”

PART FOUR: NEW YORK CITY, 2 AM

Phillip Henry is dreaming his favorite dream.

He's retired, sitting in his living room, watching television when the doorbell rings. He tries to ignore it, sinking further into his favorite chair and trying to concentrate on the infomercial for denture cream so strong it can also be used to tile your kitchen floor. The doorbell rings again, and again, and again and again until finally he decides whoever it is isn't going away.

He turns off his television, gets out of his chair, and goes to the front door. Standing on his stoop are two men in dark suits, wearing dark sunglasses, waiting stoically for the door to open. Phillip tightens his bathrobe and opens the door.

"Agent Henry, the United States Government requires your help on an urgent matter." No introduction, no preliminary small talk. "It is a matter of National Security, and the President himself has requested your involvement."

The two men stand there expectantly, waiting for him to answer.

Phillip straightens, looks at both men, and nods once.

"No," he says.

He shuts the door, locks it, and goes back to his chair, smiling as he turns on the television and turns up the sound to drown out the urgent ringing of the doorbell.

* * *

He wakes up to the sound of his cell phone. It's his government phone—the one he's not allowed to turn off—and it takes him a few seconds for the sound to register. It's one of the special ringtones that means someone is calling him on an emergency line. He sits up quickly, grabbing for the flashing, vibrating phone sitting on the hotel room nightstand.

"This is Henry." His voice is still thick with fatigue.

"Phillip."

Phillip Henry recognizes the voice, and decides it's time to wake up *now*.

"Travers." Phillip exhales heavily. "I guess we haven't changed any of the emergency access codes yet."

Travers chuckles. "Most were changed. A few were overlooked. It took a few tries."

"And you used one of the unchanged codes to contact me directly." Phillip minimizes the phone display and switches over to text messaging. He composes a quick message—TRACE THIS PHONE NOW—and sends it off to Division M. "I suppose I'm flattered."

"You sound tired." Travers sounds the way he always does—mild, vaguely friendly, unconcerned. As if he were simply calling to catch up with an old friend. "Are you getting enough sleep?"

"You aren't helping that at the moment," Phillip says. He switches back to the phone interface, turns on the speakerphone, and sets the phone down on the table.

"Sorry for waking you," Travers says, "but I thought we should talk."

"I'll be more than happy to listen to anything you have to say." Phillip grabs a pair of pants slung over the back of a chair. "Turn yourself in first."

Travers laughs. "I like that you're giving me that option. It's very by-the-book. Are we on speakerphone?"

"I'm getting dressed," Phillip says, grabbing his shirt. "Why are you calling me, Travers?"

"I told you. I thought we should talk."

"That's not very specific..." Phillip rummages through one of the hotel drawers for a clean pair of socks. "What are we talking about?"

"We made eye contact. Right before I... left the office early."

"We did," Phillip says. He grabs a pair of dark socks and sits on the bed.

"You and I both know what that means. I wasn't lying to you—I *couldn't*. So you know I'm not a traitor."

"No," Phillip says. "I don't know anything. I'd like to remind you that just before you delivered that grand, dramatic speech of yours, you attacked us with a neurotoxin."

"It wasn't lethal," Travers says.

"No it wasn't," Phillip agrees. "But it was a *neuro*toxin. I have no idea how it may have affected my talents. For all I know it was making me believe everything you said was the truth whether it was or not."

Phillip can't tell if Travers is silent, or if he hung up the phone. For a second he's afraid the line has gone dead... then he hears Travers sigh.

"Fair enough," Travers says. "I wasn't taking into account that scenario when I first installed it. I suppose I'll have to rely on your instinct, then."

"My instinct says you deployed a neurotoxin device in a federal building."

"That's not your instinct, that's your rational mind."

"Fine," Phillip says. "My *rational mind* says you deployed a *neurotoxin device* in a *federal building*, and my *instinct* tells me there's no reason a federal employee would set that up in his office, on the 28th floor, unless he was afraid *another federal employee* would be coming after him."

"What was my biggest assignment in the last decade, Phillip?" Travers sounds defensive—that's good. Defensive people tend to focus on their justifications more than what's going on around them. "What was my biggest case?"

"PRODIGY was an outlier," Phillip says.

"An *outlier*? All that money that went into its infrastructure, all those dummy corporations, all the military investment that went into creating drones based off those poor kids—you think that was a one-time, off-the-cuff operation? No, Phillip. The resources necessary to support that operation were significantly larger than the ones we found. The people behind PRODIGY are still out there, and they're still in the government. If they weren't I would have found more."

Phillip grabs his shoes. "Travers, we've had this discussion before, and my answer is the same now that it was then: sometimes, no matter how ridiculous it sounds, the answer to the question includes a magic bullet. You would be more convincing if you could point to anything—anything at all—that would serve as *proof.*"

"I hope to get that for you," Travers says.

"Oh?" Phillip doesn't bother hiding his impatience. "When exactly will that be?"

"It's been three minutes," Travers says. "You should have your trace by now. Keep your eyes open."

The phone goes dead.

"Damn it..." Phillip straps on his shoulder holster, then reaches for his jacket.

His phone rings. It's a Division M number.

"This is Agent Henry."

"We traced the call," the voice on the line says.

"Good." Phillip takes a pair of sunglasses out of his jacket's inside pocket and puts them on. "Send me the location. Deploy my team and send backup. I'll be there soon."

* * *

Travers' call is traced to one of the parts of the city that has been largely ignored by city leaders. It's "old school" New York—graffiti over every exposed surface, broken windows, bars in window frames and across doors, and not a single working street light on the entire block. When Phillip drives to the address he sees Division M has closed in around a small, grimy motel. The parking lot is full of police cars, and police on the scene are shoving a line of handcuffed people into the backs of cars.

There shouldn't be police here.

As soon as he turns into the parking lot his car is blocked by four cops with weapons drawn, shouting commands for him to keep his hands on the steering wheel, stop the car, unroll the window, keep the window rolled up, get out of the car, stay in the car—none of them are giving him a coherent set of instructions, and if he reaches for his badge one of the idiots is probably going to shoot. It's not until a man wearing a dark trenchcoat grabs one of the police by the arm, shouting at the top of his lungs, that they stop.

Phillip gets his badge out, makes sure it's hanging visibly from his jacket's breast pocket, then turns off his car. He steps out into the humid evening, his face set in a snarl of anger.

"Grant, what the *hell* is going on here?"

The man in the trenchcoat, a tall, thin man with dark, slicked-back hair, still has one of the officers held in a firm grip. "Not sure, boss. We're trying to figure that out now. But first I'm trying to keep these idiots from shooting a *highly decorated federal agent*!"

The officer opens his mouth to protest, then closes it again immediately, nodding once, looking chagrined. Grant lets go of his hand. "All right. This man—" Grant points at Phillip. "Is my *boss*. That means *he is in charge of this scene*."

The cop quickly switches from *chagrin* to *outrage*. "Bullshit. Why do the feds care about a vice sting?"

"*It's not a vice sting!*" Grant sounds like he's about to pop. "I told you assholes, we are trying to track down a dangerous fugitive—"

"Grant." Phillip has collected himself and steps up to place a restraining hand on the agent's shoulder. "I'll take it from here."

Grant nods once and steps aside. Phillip looks at the four police who tried to intercept him, smooths out his jacket's left sleeve, and says, "I'm Phllip Henry. DHS is tracking a rogue federal agent with suspected ties to metahuman terrorist groups. He made a telephone call from one of the rooms in that motel."

The police officer's eyes widen in surprise.

"Agent Grant," Phillip continues, "I need you back on the scene, now."

"I'm there," Grant says. "Frank and Hu are bringing in our gear. Second floor, room 221."

Phillip nods and keeps his attention focused on the one who spoke earlier. "I need to speak to the officer in charge, as soon as possible."

The man looks at Grant, then back at Phillip, and nods reluctantly. "Follow me."

Phillip starts to follow. "Grant, keep the scene secure."

"Already on it," Grant calls back. He glowers at the police. "Now if you'll get the hell out of our way, I'm going to park my boss's car..."

Phillip follows the officer to the other side of the motel, where even more flashing police cars are parked in a line at the end of the lot.

"You have a lot of police on the scene for a prostitution raid," Phillip says.

"Yeah." The officer shrugs. "I didn't plan it, Agent Henry. You need to talk to the Lieutenant."

They walk to the center of the line of cars, where a number of men dressed in tactical uniforms—body armor with police logos—are standing in a group talking. The officer stops a short distance away and shifts his weight nervously, not quite willing to get their attention. Phillip steps up next to the officer's side and waits.

Finally the man at the center of the group looks up. He's a middle-aged, weather-beaten man with short, gray hair, pattern baldness accentuating his widow's peak. He looks from the officer to Phillip, then he frowns.

"What?" His voice is brisk and sharp. He's used to being in charge.

The officer gestures toward Phillip. "The Department of Homeland Security showed up..."

"Agent Phillip Henry, Division M." Phillip steps forward and extends his hand. "It looks like we've stepped on each other's toes."

The man narrows his eyes. He shakes Phillip's hand briefly—reluctantly—and says, "Clive Darius. Vice. All due respect, why the fuck do the Feds care about gang prostitution?"

Phillip raises an eyebrow. "We don't. We're chasing a fugitive and possible terrorist."

"I don't know anything about that," Darius says. "I've been planning this sting for weeks. I'm not saying your job ain't important, but that don't give you the right to step all over ours."

Phillip stares at Darius for a long moment, then nods. "Lieutenant Darius, it's not our wish to interfere with your operation. Our suspect checked into Room 221. We'll need a copy of the ledger at the front desk to see what alias he was using when he checked in, as well as how he paid for his room, and we'll need your men to stay away from that part of the motel while we perform our investigation. Once it's complete I promise you we'll be on our way."

"I want to say no," Darius says, "but the Captain will chew my ass out if I do. Fine. Keep your guys away from my guys, and maybe we can both go home happy."

"Thank you, Lieutenant." Phillip turns and walks back to the motel. He pulls out his cell phone and calls Agent Grant.

"Yeah, boss." Grant's voice is a lot calmer now.

"Meet me at the lobby. We need to check the ledger."

"The ledger," Grant says. "Yeah, funny story about that ledger. It's not there any more."

Phillip takes a deep breath. "Tell me at the lobby."

Agent Grant is waiting for him in the lobby. Grant is best described as a "rumpled" man—he wears the "uniform" of Division M (dark slacks, coat and tie, white collared shirt) very reluctantly and takes it out on the Federal Government by looking like a slob. He's in his early thirties and still dresses like a college student. Phillip is hoping he'll grow out of it soon.

"So the ledger," Grant says, pointing at the table. "You'll notice it's not here."

"I do, in fact, notice that," Phillip says. "Where is it, Agent Grant?"

Grant shrugs. "When I saw the cops all over the place, I made a beeline for it while we entered the room. Of course I saw a uniform trying to pick it up and put it in one of their plastic baggies—I told him to cut it out on the grounds that I had a much better-looking badge. So naturally we started shouting at each other."

"Naturally," Phillip says. Phillip doesn't consider himself a very social man—he hasn't developed any skills that make it easier for strangers to like him. Agent Grant, by way of contrast, has spent a lot of time improving his ability to really piss people off.

"At one point in the argument, we both noticed the ledger was gone.

Somebody made off with it while we were preoccupied." Grant smiles slightly. "It's a big mystery."

Some of the weight that had been pushing down on Phillip's head since his conversation with Lieutenant Darius lightens a bit. "OK. Well, we'll have to investigate the scene, then."

"Yeah," Grant says. "I recommend that."

Grant leads them up the outside staircase to the top balcony. 221 is at the far end. When they get there, the door is open. Two uniformed Division M agents are standing at each side, armed with rifles.

"Everyone's inside," Grant says. "I'm gonna go check the trash, I don't think the police have screwed that part up yet."

Phillip nods and steps through the door as Grant heads back to the balcony stairs.

It's a very standard motel room: two double beds set against one wall, a single curtained window next to the door, the radiator/air conditioning unit set under the window. Across from the beds is a desk, a table, and an old, broken television that is chained to the table. The sink and bathroom are at the other end of the room. The carpet smells strongly of mildew.

Two men and a woman are in the room. Agent Brian Frank, a short, wide-shouldered man with a thick, blonde mustache, is running a black light over the sink and surrounding fixtures. Agent Lijuan Hu, a tall Asian woman with a distinctly reddish tint to her skin, is running a much more sophisticated scanning device along one of the walls. Reclining on one of the beds, paging through what appears to be the hotel ledger, is Agent Grant.

"Looks like he checked in a few days ago," Grant says, not bothering to look up. "Under your name, boss."

"You're kidding." Phillip walks over to Grant and picks up the ledger.

"Line 34," Grant says. "It's not hard to miss. Most people check in here as 'Mr. and Mrs. Smith.'"

"I'll bet they do," Agent Hu says, trying not to laugh.

Phillip looks at line 34. Definitely his name, definitely Travers' handwriting.

"Are you absolutely sure nobody saw you take this?" Phillip says, gesturing with the ledger.

"Nobody saw a thing," Grant says. "They were too busy watching me tear into the other guy. We'd just cleared the scene here, so I flipped, grabbed it, then flipped up here. Once we noticed it was missing I accused the poor cop of getting one of his buddies to make off with it while we were fighting."

"Why did he use your name?" Hu asks. "Is he playing a game?"

"Yes," Phillip says. "Just not sure which game. He wanted us to trace his call."

"He hasn't left any prints," Agent Frank says, turning off the black light. "If I break out the more expensive tools I'll probably find DNA, but—"

"No need," Phillip says. "Travers was here. The question is, did he leave before the police arrived, or did they get him?"

Hu, Frank, and Grant look at Phillip in surprise.

"The cops?" Grant asks. "Those jokers? The ones who almost shot you?"

"No," Phillip says. "I doubt they were involved. But their Lieutenant—I want a profile on Lieutenant Clive Darius on my desk by noon."

"He lie to you, Phillip?" Agent Hu asks. Everyone in the group knows that's a bad idea.

"He tried very hard not to," Phillip says. "And he almost pulled it off."

CURVEBALL
15
FEB 2014
CURVEBALL
A Prose Comic
BLURRED LINES
STORY
CHRISTOPHER WRIGHT
COVER
PASCALLE LEPAS
LOGO
GARTH GRAHAM

PART ONE: FARRADAY CITY SLUMS

Water sprays in all directions as CB misses a step, stumbling into an ankle-deep puddle. He fights back the urge to swear and steadies his pace as he races down the alley. He sees a flash of green—BDU pants—as Bruiser disappears around the corner of a building at the far end.

CB ignores the water seeping into his left sock and runs. He's fast, but Bruiser has a head start. He reaches the corner and emerges from the alley into an abandoned street. It looks like it was evacuated during a hurricane, and nobody ever bothered to come back—storefront windows are boarded, doors are barricaded—but the boards are warped and cracked, and some are falling away. The road looks like a shattered window, spidery web-like fractures running through the asphalt, making it look more like a series of shattered windows laid out on the ground.

No sign of Bruiser.

CB slows, then stops, listening intently. He reaches into his trenchcoat pocket, pulls out a pack of cigarettes, and fishes for one of his last three. He stops, ignoring the chase for a moment, and lights up, glad to smell something other than wet, moldy city. For a moment everything is silent.

There. Off in the distance. Splashing footsteps. He thinks a moment, trying to match the direction of the sound with his knowledge of the city. A moment later he realizes what Bruiser did, and where he's probably going to be in the next twenty seconds.

CB runs down the cracked sidewalk, stride lengthening with each step, cigarette hanging out the corner of his mouth. He reaches down to his waist and with a smooth motion unloops a worn leather belt from his jeans. Still running, he wraps one end around his right hand, letting the heavy metal buckle trail behind him.

Two buildings down is an abandoned store with a large sign hanging over the barricaded front door. The wood in the sign is mostly rotted away, but it has a metal frame, and hangs from a thick, rusted metal chain on each end. CB runs, jumps, and with a *snap* the belt arcs over the frame, threads itself through the chain, and CB's left hand closes around the buckle just as his momentum causes the belt to snap tight. The entire sign jerks to one side, the chains rattle, rusted bolts groan but don't give. CB's arms burn from the force, but he keeps his grip and pulls, flipping up and over the sign, into the rotted wood covering a second story window. The boards crumble away as he smashes into them. He releases the buckle as he arcs through the window, belt trailing behind him, and lands into a roll on the soft, sagging wood floor.

It's a small room; it might have been an upstairs office once. The door is open to the hall, and on the other side is a window covered with a single sheet of particle board.

CB gets to his feet and runs. At the last moment he jumps; his feet hit the board first. Nails pop, and it falls outward like a drawbridge opening. The board falls to the ground. So does CB.

He lands harder than he wants—the ground is concrete, covered in a layer of wet, foul-smelling mud. He falls into a roll, managing to shake the worst of it, but it hurts, and now he's filthy. His cigarette, which managed to survive to this point, falls out of his mouth and disappears into the mud. CB growls in frustration and climbs to his feet.

He stands in a service road. Immediately to his left is a narrow alley that winds off in the direction he wants. He sets off, feet sliding over the slick road until he reaches the alley, where the ground is drier. By the time he reaches the privacy fence he's at a full sprint: he jumps, vaults over the top, and hurtles into a busy street. Farraday City is like that, sometimes—one street completely abandoned, the next street over full of people.

Pedestrians scatter out of his way as he lands in a crouch on the sidewalk. Cars swerve at his sudden appearance. Car horns honk frantically as other cars swerve in turn. Today there are no accidents, only near misses. CB takes a moment to orient himself, then sprints down the sidewalk. As soon as he runs off, people go back to their business. It's Farraday City. This kind of thing isn't unusual.

As he nears the end of the block he sees a young, muscular man wearing a white tank top and green BDU on the intersecting sidewalk. It's Bruiser—not running now, not even really paying attention to his surroundings because he thinks he's safe. CB gauges the distance between himself and the corner, between Bruiser and the corner, and focuses on a street light set right at the point where both sidewalks meet.

Bruiser looks up just in time to see CB leap toward the streetlight, leather belt looping around the pole, then snapping taut as CB whips around the pole and smashes feet-first into his chest. Bruiser launches back, a full four feet into the air, before he tumbles onto the concrete walk. After that, all he can do is gasp and writhe in agony.

CB stands over him. "Think you cracked a rib, Bruiser." He leans over and hauls Bruiser to his feet, ignoring his cries of pain. "We need to talk. Asshole."

CB half-carries, half-drags Bruiser back to the service road. He isn't followed: the locals have decided that what's going on is none of their business. He binds Bruiser's arms behind his back with the leather belt and forces him to sit up against the crumbling brick foundation of one of the old stores. Bruiser isn't going anywhere. His shoulders sag in defeat.

CB fishes a cigarette out of his pocket. "For the record, 'Bruiser' is a *really* stupid name."

Bruiser glares at him, but it's all show.

"I mean, if you were over six feet, weighed in at maybe two-fifty, it might work. But you're not. People hear the name 'Bruiser' they expect a linebacker. You're not a linebacker. You look more like a basketball player. Not out of shape, just the *wrong* shape. Your handle needs to fit you, or people are just... going to laugh."

Bruiser struggles not to rise to the bait.

"I bet you get laughed at *all the time*."

The young man's eyes flash. "Fuck you, man."

"Oh, so he *can* talk." CB nods, satisfied, then lights his cigarette. "I wasted a perfectly good cigarette trying to track you down. Right over there." CB gestures to a muddy spot on the other side of the street. "And there's only one left after this. For the record: my patience will probably last as long as it takes me to smoke both cigarettes."

"I got nothing to say," Bruiser looks down at the muddy ground, face sullen.

CB shrugs. "Suits me. 'Course, if you haven't started talking by the time I finish my second cigarette, I'm going to drag your ass down to the boardwalk and leave you there. I'm sure somebody will find a use for you."

Bruiser stares at him in disbelief. "You're full of shit."

CB shrugs again. "Guess we'll find out in..." he scrutinizes the burning cigarette. "One and three quarters of a cigarette from now."

"They'd kill me!"

CB nods. "Probably. It's one of the things they like to do."

Bruiser's eyes narrow. "You're full of *shit*. I know who you are. I know who you run with. You're one of the *heroes*, man, you wouldn't leave me on the Boardwalk like that."

"Know what I was before I became one of the heroes, Bruiser?" CB flicks his cigarette absently. The ash disappears into the muddy street. "I was a bona-fide, Grade A, big-league villain. FBI had a file on me. Hero groups tried to take me down. You know why I stopped being a villain?"

Bruiser struggles against the leather strap binding his arms, but he feels shooting pain in his sides every time he tries to get free.

"One guy," CB says. "One guy talked me down. Seriously, like out of a goddamned movie—he gave a little speech about 'choices' and 'possibilities' and he *turned me away from a life of crime*. That guy was Liberty. If you were wondering."

CB blows out a stream of smoke in Bruiser's direction. It dissipates long before it reaches his face, but he coughs reflexively. Coughing hurts as much as struggling.

"He was my conscience for a long time," CB continues. "Any time I'd find myself in a thorny moral dilemma I'd ask myself 'what would Liberty say?' And then I'd do whatever I decided he'd say. The thing is, I got into thorny moral dilemmas a *lot*. Still do, apparently. I seem to be in one now. Think about it—right now I'm contemplating abandoning a wounded, bound man in the middle of the Farraday City Boardwalk, which would *surely* end in the wounded, bound man dying in some horrible and potentially undignified manner."

"Come on—" Bruiser doesn't get a chance to finish. CB cuts him off.

"So I'm asking myself 'well, what would Liberty say?' It's the question I always ask myself in situations like this. Do you know what the answer is?"

Bruiser tries to scoot a little to one side, edging away from CB, but his legs can't get purchase in the mud.

CB takes a step forward, looming over him. "Hey. Bruiser. I asked you a question. And we're down to one and a half cigarettes."

Bruiser looks up at CB and flinches. "Liberty... he would say... 'don't do it.'"

CB crouches down in front of Bruiser, so that their heads are almost level. His expression is soft. His voice is soft. "That's just it, Bruiser. He wouldn't. He can't. He's dead."

Bruiser shrinks back. He's seen that expression before. He knows exactly what it means.

"You know who killed him, right?" The words come out almost jovial, as if CB were about to tell Bruiser a secret joke. "Johann Richter. I know you know who he is. You're *working* for him."

"I never saw him!" Bruiser protests.

"Of *course* you never saw him," CB snaps. "Richter isn't an idiot. But you're smart enough to have figured it out—though you're not much smarter. Bragging to your girlfriend about it? Dumb."

Bruiser shakes his head in confusion. "How do you know Gabby?"

"Funny nickname," CB says. "Appropriate, too. I don't know your girlfriend, moron. I know *gossip*. I heard from a guy who heard from *his* girlfriend about a girl who goes clubbing with yours, and about how she couldn't stop talking about the new crew you were running with."

"Goddamn it!" Bruiser shouts. "When I find her I'm gonna—"

"If you ever see her again," CB says, "you will be so happy to be *alive* that you'll let it pass."

Bruiser falls silent.

CB stands again, stretches, takes a step back. "You don't work directly for the people I'm looking for, so I don't really care about you, or your girlfriend. Or pretty much anything that has to do with your life. Not today, at any rate. You tell me who your contacts are. You tell me everything you know about their operation. In return I'll loosen that belt a little and be on my way. Not a bad offer compared to what I'm willing to do if you keep standing in my way."

Bruiser looks up at CB and shudders. "If I say anything and they find out..."

CB shrugs. "Not my problem. That said, I don't plan to tell them we talked."

CB looks at his cigarette, now burned down almost to the filter, and throws it out into the street. He reaches into a trenchcoat pocket and pulls out a rumpled pack. He holds it up in front of Bruiser.

"Last cigarette, Bruiser," CB says.

Bruiser starts talking.

PART TWO: FARRADAY CITY BUNKER

"You're cheating."

Jenny tries to wipe sweat off her face with the back of her arm as she glares at Red Shift. He stares back serenely, not even the faintest trace of perspiration on his forehead.

"No I'm not," Red Shift says. "The whole point of having 'super powers' is that they give you advantages. The whole point of *training* with someone who has 'super powers' is to learn how to adapt to their advantages, and to use *your* advantages in a way that allows you to control the fight."

"Fine," Jenny mutters, and lowers herself into a crouch.

Red Shift waits.

Jenny isn't sure why speedsters don't get more press. Red Shift has been kicking her ass all morning, and he's not even winded. *He caught a bullet.* He moves faster than she can track and hits with the force of a guy three times his weight. *He caught a bullet.* And to top off the indignities, he's holding back. *And he caught a bullet!*

"How did you catch that bullet?"

"You're supposed to be fighting me, not chatting me up."

Jenny glares at him. "I'm not *chatting you up*. I'm trying to figure out how you *work*. How did you catch that bullet? I know you run fast—*really* fast—but that's just... nuts."

"I don't usually discuss tactics with my enemies," Red Shift says good-naturedly, "but since you're actually a *student*—sort of—I guess it's relevant to what I'm trying to teach."

Jenny relaxes out of her stance and waits.

They're in the bunker's living area. All the furniture is pushed down to one end, giving the two of them a reasonable space to spar in. The bare floor is covered with a number of gym mats Elliot Grady delivered the day before. Jenny is dressed in an old, third-hand pair of sweat pants and a mismatched sweat shirt. Red Shift is in his Crossfire uniform.

From a psychological perspective, Jenny has already lost the fight.

"Are you familiar with 'bullet time?'" Red Shift asks.

Jenny laughs. "From the video games?"

"Yes. You press a button and for a while in the game everything slows down to a crawl, making it a lot easier for the character to deal with the bad guys."

"Yeah," Jenny says. "Max Payne. Loved that game... when I was in *high school.*"

"Ouch." Red Shift rubs the back of his neck ruefully.

Jenny laughs.

"Anyway," Red Shift says, "it's a really good analogy for how things get when I speed up. The faster I go, the slower everything else looks. And if I focus I can push it even further. When I saw Richter pull the trigger, I pushed. The world slowed down. I saw the bullet."

"So you're not always fast, all the time," Jenny says. "Like, right now, you're just a normal guy who moves at normal speed?"

Red Shift shakes his head. "Not quite, but you get points for trying to work it out. My 'default setting' is a little above human limits."

"So how come you haven't gone crazy?" Jenny asks. "I mean... sorry. It's just that if that was my default state, I'd be so impatient all the time, waiting for people to finish what they were doing..."

"Well, I was a scientist before I became a masked vigilante," Red Shift says. "The kind of research I was doing involved a lot of waiting before I could get on with the next bit. I've had a lot of practice waiting. I'm pretty good at it."

"I'm not," Jenny says.

"You're *great* at stalling." Red Shift flashes a grin. "Come on. Are you going to hit me or not?"

Jenny rolls her eyes. "I think we both know the answer to that question."

"I'll move slow enough for you to hit me," Red Shift says. "If you try."

Jenny growls, then crouches again.

Now that she knows how he sees the world when he's moving, she figures it's pointless to try to attack him head-on. He'd see all her moves in slow motion and have plenty of time to counter them.

But there has to be a way to fight him. He said he'd be moving slow enough for me to hit him if I tried. How do I pull that off?

She lashes out with her right, missing by inches. She follows up with her left, and Red Shift's arm blurs, batting it aside. A low kick, a high kick, a feint on the left followed by a knee—every attempt fails by inches. She's breathing heavily now—and, as far as she can tell, Red Shift is barely paying attention.

Damn him. From his perspective I'm moving so slow I'm telegraphing everything I do. I need to... trick him.

The problem with a feint is that Red Shift will, in theory, have as much time to react to a feint as he will to a straight-out attack. She'll have to be proactive to counter that. Her mind races through all the memories of her great-grandfather teaching her to fight, and in a moment she settles on a move that, at the time, she thought was needlessly clever. She can't remember its proper name—it sounds German, or maybe Dutch—but she remembers calling it "The Plan B." The Plan B is a double-feint—a feint followed up by a second feint, each intended to position the target for a hold-and-throw. If Red Shift isn't expecting her to be that elaborate, it might work.

Jenny feints with her right, and swings hard with her left. As soon as the feint stops, Jenny moves her right arm into position—much too soon under normal circumstances, but she's anticipating the speed of his counter. The gamble pays off: he blocks the attack the way he's supposed to, and just when she feels his arm batting her left aside, her right closes on his wrist. Suddenly she's in control: she twists, his eyes widen in surprise, she pulls, he loses his balance, then her left locks in and she throws him over her shoulder, onto the mat. He hits the floor with a very satisfying *thud.*

Jenny stares down at him and grins. "Got y—"

A moment later she's flat on her back, staring at the ceiling. Red Shift stands over her, frowning slightly.

"You didn't hit me," he says. "I told you to hit me."

"I *threw* you," Jenny says. "That's better."

"It was a good move," Red Shift agrees. "Didn't take me out of the fight, though. You need to take this more seriously."

Jenny stays on her back, staring up at the ceiling.

"Ah," Red Shift says. "Cold feet?"

Jenny shrugs. "I really don't have a choice, do I? CB was right—I'm in the middle of this already, I *have* to commit. But I really, *really* don't want to. I didn't realize how much I didn't want to until just now."

Red Shift nods. "OK. Let's talk about that."

Jenny sits up and stares at a fixed point on the wall. "I grew up surrounded by it. Liberty was my great-grandfather, CB was a family friend, Grey Falcon and Regiment stopped by from time to time—not Gladiator, not as much, but I sort of thought of all of them as uncles. And all I wanted was to be like *them*, so I could go on amazing adventures and save the world..."

Jenny laughs self-consciously.

"I knew what kind of hero I wanted to be, too—I wanted to be just like Mental Marvel. Remember her? When I was in my teens I thought she was perfect—beautiful, powerful, could fly, read people's minds..."

"Never met her," Red Shift says, "but I think her story is more tragic than inspiring."

"Yeah," Jenny says. "That's the point. I got older, I started noticing the other side. Mental Marvel went insane. Grey Falcon died. CB is... *disillusioned*, I guess. And there are people like you—no offense, you seem like a nice guy, but you and your friends spend most of your free time *killing people*."

"We do," Red Shift says. His usually cheerful, friendly voice is strangely flat and matter-of-fact.

Jenny shudders. "God, and you're the *nice* one. This world is screwed up, and I'm part of it now. I guess I'm grieving, a little."

Red Shift is silent a moment.

"OK," he says, finally. "I guess I can see that. I don't know how to help you through it, though. I have a philosophy that I'm pretty sure you won't like, and I'm also pretty sure Curveball would take issue with me trying to win you over on it."

"So what?" Jenny says, anger tinting her voice. "When did he become my lord and master?"

"I didn't mean it like that," Red Shift says.

Jenny stands. "Yeah, but you said it like that anyway. Just like you tried to name me 'Miss Liberty'—I'm sure you didn't mean any offense then, either."

"I didn't," Red Shift says. "It just seemed like an appropriate nod to Liberty, sort of a classic—"

"A classic?" Jenny snorts. "I can just imagine my new career as 'Miss Liberty,' in my brand new costume. I guess that'd be a red, white, and blue *thong*."

Red Shift stares at her blankly. "Thongs aren't really practical in fights."

Jenny rolls her eyes. "Practicality wasn't really part of the equation for Mental Marvel's costumes. I didn't realize that till later, but just before she 'retired' most of her promo posters looked like pin-up spreads. And what about Desire? Have you seen what *she* wears? Also, what's with a major hero going by the name *Desire*?"

"Well," Red Shift says, "it fits. She emits pheromones that—"

"—I know what she can do." Jenny speaks through clenched teeth. "I can read the papers. Of course, the ability she's *famous* for is the one she *hardly ever uses*. Most of the time she makes bad guys *afraid*, or *confused*, or she overloads their... I don't know, neural pathways or something and knocks them out. But the *one time* she decides the easiest way to resolve a hostage situation is to sweet-talk a guy into turning himself in, some hack from the Tribune nicknames her 'Desire' and it sticks."

"Hey, I didn't name her," Red Shift says.

"You wanted to call me *Miss Liberty*," Jenny snarls, then slugs him.

It's a sucker punch. Red Shift's eyes widen in surprise for the second time as he doubles over from the blow. He makes a series of quick, gasping, choking sounds. Jenny panics for a second, thinking she really hurt him, then relaxes when she realizes he's laughing. Or trying to laugh.

"So... hey. What are we talking about?"

Jenny turns to see CB, covered in mud, standing in the hallway. "What the hell happened to you?"

"Working," CB says. He looks at Jenny, then at Red Shift, then at Jenny again. "Everything OK?"

"Everything's fine," Jenny says. "We're talking about how heroes are a pack of sexist assholes."

CB nods. "OK." He looks at Red Shift again. He looks like he's trying not to laugh. "I'm going to take a shower."

CB stomps off down the hall.

Jenny turns back to Red Shift. He's standing up straight now. "Uh... sorry."

"At least I got you to hit me." Red Shift *also* looks like he's trying not to laugh. "I'd like to take credit for that, but I hadn't planned to push buttons today. Still, it's a start. And as far as things go, you're not wrong. The metahuman world is subject to the same prejudices and narrow-mindedness as everywhere else. Myself included. For my part, *mea culpa*."

"I thought heroes were supposed to rise above all that," Jenny says.

"Well, you'd expect that," Red Shift says. "But I might not be the best person to talk to about what heroes are *supposed* to be."

"Right," Jenny says. "Crossfire is not my role model. No offense."

"None taken," Red Shift says. "For what it's worth, I can tell you that we've worked with groups that aren't representative of what you see in the mainstream. The new groups, the unregistered groups, the... well, the *vigilante* groups. They're a lot more inclusive."

"It was bad enough at my job," Jenny says. "Now I have to deal with the same shit, only in spandex and the ratios are even worse."

"Ratios?" Red Shift cocks his head to one side. "What are you talking about?"

"Ratios," Jenny repeats. "You know. Men outnumbering women in the metahuman game. By a lot."

"No they don't," Red Shift says.

"Weren't we just talking about how they did?" Jenny asks, slightly exasperated.

"No," Red Shift says. "We were talking about public perceptions, not actual facts. And the facts are, there are probably as many women who are metahumans in the world as there are men."

"*Probably*?" Jenny shakes her head, confused. "What does that even mean, *probably*?"

"Well no one is really sure about metahuman genesis," Red Shift says. "Or... well, we know in the beginning people like Liberty were *engineered*, but at some point metahumans started showing up on their own. That's the part we haven't figured out. The most popular theory—one I agree with—is that there are a set of genetic traits that all need to be present in order for someone to have latent metahuman abilities. There's nothing to suggest it targets men over women."

"But..." Jenny shakes her head. "That doesn't make any sense."

"I don't know much about sociology, but I assume it has something to do with—"

"Not *that*," Jenny says. "I mean yes, that, but that's not what I'm talking about. The tests. The tests you've been looking at—the ones we got from TriHealth. You said the test subjects were all getting... uh... the metahuman test."

"The Dyson-Ferris Assessment?" Red Shift asks.

"Yeah," Jenny says. "That. *That* doesn't make any sense. It made sense before, when I thought that I could count the number of female metahumans on one hand, but if *half* the metahumans in the world are women, how come the only people in those files are *men*?"

Red Shift blinks. "You're right. That *doesn't* make sense."

"That's weird, right?"

"Yes..." Red Shift frowns. "It's not just weird, it's bad science. Why limit your tests to only half the available genetic pool? Uh... I hate to cut your training short, but do you mind if I use your laptop? I need to get in touch with Street Ronin."

"Sure," Jenny says.

"Thanks," Red Shift says. "Good catch. I'm kicking myself. I should have caught that."

He heads off to the kitchen. Jenny beams.

"Think of a *name*, Miss Forrest," Red Shift says from the hall. "Or I'll start calling you 'Miss Liberty' till you do."

Jenny scowls.

PART THREE: EARLIER

CB leans against the boardwalk rail, looking at the old Hyatt building tenement he used to call home. A few days ago it was. Then someone from his past showed up, and everyone died. That's the word on the street: no survivors.

The cops have the whole building under wraps—*literally* under wraps, covered in some kind of industrial-grade cellophane or saran wrap. Police tape encircles the entire building. The only way in is through an isolation tent set up in front of the hole Red Shift put through the lobby wall.

CB pushes himself off the rail and heads toward the building. There aren't too many people around—it's still mid-morning, and the Boardwalk is mostly nocturnal. The four cops on the scene are huddled off to one side of the airlock tent, sitting on the hood of a police car, drinking coffee and looking bored.

"Oi!" CB calls out to the cops, waving in their direction. They turn toward him, startled, and gape as he ducks under the police tape, walking toward the tent. Two cops hastily set their coffee on the hood of the car and move to intercept, hands resting on their holsters.

"You can't be here." The first cop to reach him is youngish, lean, and clean-shaven with close-cropped dark hair and sharp eyes. "This is closed off for your protection."

CB nods. "Tell Hoydt I'll be in 313."

The cop draws his gun about an inch out of his holster. "I said this place is *closed*." He sounds a little too eager for CB's liking.

CB stops and turns to face him. The cop slows to a halt, watching him warily. The second cop, a heavier man with a thick mustache that would have fit right in if only they were living in the 1970s, stops three paces behind the first. His hand is on his holster, but he hasn't drawn his weapon. The two officers back at the squad car aren't doing much of anything, other than looking on curiously.

CB ignores the second and focuses his gaze on the first. "I hope that gun is actually a cell phone, and you're planning to use it to call Lieutenant Larry Hoydt of the Farraday City Police Department, to let him know that his 10:30 appointment has arrived. Because if you're planning to shoot me, I promise you two things will happen: first, I'll get *really pissed off*. And second, you're going to shoot a guy that Lieutenant Larry Hoydt of the Farraday City Police Department *really wants to talk to right now*. Are *you* a Lieutenant, officer?"

The cop looks CB up and down and his face twists into a half sneer. "What's your business with the Lieutenant? Mud wrestling?"

CB looks down at his clothes. He's still covered in mud from chasing down Bruiser. He looks back at the cop.

"You," he says, "are *hilarious*. I'm going inside. Make sure you tell Hoydt I'm here. If you don't know his number, here's his card."

CB throws a business card at the cop's feet, winks, then turns to face the tent. Something goes *pop*.

"I said stop!" The cop snarls and tries to draw his weapon, then curses as the hammer of his automatic catches on a fold in his uniform, then curses again—with significantly more alarm—when the gun twists out of his hand and falls to the ground. The gun doesn't fire, but the magazine ejects from the bottom with unusual force, scooting a few feet across the pavement.

"Try not to get yourself killed, officer," CB says, unzipping the front flap of the tent and stepping inside.

"Damn it!" The cop is fuming. "Come on! We have to go in after him."

"Put your gun back together, Dean-o," the second cop says. "And calm down. I think he's legit."

"*Him*?" Incredulity *drips* from the first cop's voice. "Did you see him? He looks like he's slept in a sewer all night."

"Look at the card," the second cop says. "It's legit. Read the front."

CB unzips the back of the tent and steps through. As he does, he hears the first cop reading the card aloud.

"It says 'do not ever call me at this number or I will skin you alive.' And he underlined 'ever' three times."

"Yeah," the second cop says. "That's definitely Hoydt's."

"What do we do?" The first cop, deprived of his chance to shoot someone in an official capacity, is beginning to sound petulant.

"You've got his card," the second cop says, laughing. "Guess you better call him."

The power's out, of course. CB fishes the mag-lite out of his trenchcoat pocket, turns it on, and makes his way up to the third floor. The place looks empty, and unusually clean: forensics must have confiscated all the trash. There aren't any chalk outlines, but there are numbered cards placed down in every spot CB remembers seeing a body.

There's no sound. No music, no fighting, no partying, no sounds of addicts getting sick through paper-thin walls. CB hadn't thought well of most of his neighbors, but their absence is...

Undeserved. Their absence is undeserved.

He makes his way to his apartment. The door is open. People have obviously rummaged through his stuff—but he'd already taken the important things with him.

Damn, they took the records. Of course they took the records. Bastards.

The room is brighter than the hall—sunlight still filters in through the film they wrapped around the building, and the windows let in enough light to justify turning off the mag-lite. CB throws himself onto the love seat, fishes out the new pack of cigarettes he bought on the way here, and unwraps the plastic. He tosses the wrappings on the floor—no point in being tidy now—and starts packing.

Tap, tap, tap. The sounds echo in the hall beyond. *Tap, tap, tap*. They sound louder than they should. *Tap, tap, tap*. How many times had he done this in the past and never heard it, because of all the noise coming from everywhere else? There's not even the background noise of fans.

He takes out a cigarette, lights up, and waits for Hoydt. He finishes three before the Lieutenant arrives.

Lieutenant Larry Hoydt announces his arrival by slamming the stairwell door open with considerable force, shouting "GOD DAMN IT CB!" then stomping down the hall with all the strength he can muster. The echo of his footsteps rattles the walls. CB sees the beam of a flashlight swivel across the hall, first right, then left, then right, then left. Finally Hoydt rounds the corner and the flashlight shines directly into CB's face.

CB squints, turns his head, and raises his left hand to block the light. "Jesus, Larry."

Hoydt steps into the room, his small, thin frame seeming to expand with the force of his own will. The Lieutenant isn't physically imposing, but he has a presence that can reduce much larger men to quivering lumps of jelly.

"'Jesus *Larry*?'" Larry's voice is thin and sharp, just like the rest of him. "Since when are we on a first name basis, you pompous little *shit*?"

"*Pompous?*" CB feels his back stiffen.

The Lieutenant pauses for a moment, then turns off his flashlight. "Ah, Jesus." He sinks into the old armchair, shaking his head. "Jesus. *Pompous* is the word that gets you. *Jesus*."

CB snorts. "You alone?"

The Lieutenant shrugs. "Far as I can tell. Hard to say. Especially with the way you decided to grab my attention. Christ. 'Lieutenant, I'm sorry to bother you, but some muddy vagrant just bulled his way past us and gave us your card.' What the *fuck*, CB? What part of 'we don't want my superiors to know we're talking' don't you get? And what the *hell* happened to you? You taking up mud wrestling, or something?"

"What is with the mud wrestling?" CB asks. "Is it a cop thing? I didn't think I could call you direct, and we needed to meet somewhere nobody wanted to be. The plague hotel seemed like a good place."

"Yeah, it's great," Hoydt says. "Because what I *really want* is to catch whatever the fuck killed these poor bastards."

"A metahuman killed these poor bastards," CB says. "And he's not here right now."

"A metahuman?" Hoydt shakes his head dismissively. "No metahumans in Farraday City."

"At the moment there are at least five," CB says. "Including yours truly."

Larry frowns. "That's bad. Who?"

"Pretty bad," CB agrees. "One guy spreads disease everywhere he goes. The other guy killed Liberty."

Larry's eyes widen. The effect is magnified through the thick coke-bottle lenses on his glasses, making him look almost like a cartoon. "That's only two."

"The only two anyone needs to know about right now," CB says. "You already know about me."

"*Officially* you're not a metahuman," the Lieutenant says. "*Officially* you're just a sidekick wannabe who manages to be a royal pain in the ass. Don't thank me, but it kept you alive the last few years."

"Yeah, well, that's not going to hold up much longer."

A look of vague alarm skitters across Hoydt's face. "CB, this ain't the kind of city that plays nice with hero types. Or metahuman types. And when you put both together..."

"Don't care," CB says. "What I do care about is where you stand."

"Where *I* stand?" Hoydt's laugh is short and ugly. "What does that have to do with you?"

"Larry, I like you," CB says. "I do. But sooner or later you have to decide if you're clean, or if you're dirty. I gotta know where you stand."

"Oh," Hoydt says. "You 'gotta know.' I see. Well let me clear it up for you right now..."

Hoydt leans forward, into the light. If CB didn't know better, he'd think the guy was a file clerk. Everything about him looks rumpled and shabby, his arms and legs are spindly, and he looks like he'd be blown over by a moderate breeze—a physique better-suited to pushing paper than anything he actually does. But he carries himself with the conviction and certainty of an Olympic athlete, and the eyes behind his coke-bottle glasses are *anything* but weak.

"I will do anything—whatever it takes—to un-fuck this city, CB. If I gotta be a dirty cop, I'll be a dirty cop. If I gotta be clean, I'll be clean. If the city needs a hero, I'll be a hero, and if it needs a monster then by God I'll be the stuff of nightmares. And don't you for one second think the question is whether you can trust *me*. The question, you stupid, mewling little *shit*, is whether you'll be *smart enough* to be around *long enough* to do any good. I gotta say, right now I have my doubts."

The Lieutenant leans back in the chair, drumming the fingers of his right hand on one arm, *bi-di-dip, bi-di-dip, bi-di-dip, bi-di-dip*.

"OK," CB says. He reaches into a pocket and pulls out a folded-up piece of paper. He holds it out to the Lieutenant.

Hoydt looks at the paper. His fingers stop drumming. "What's this?"

"I was tracking down the people who did all this," CB says, gesturing to the building. "Found one of the locals they were using as suppliers. He didn't work with 'em directly, but he figured out who he was working for. He was able to name a number of the middlemen. They're cops."

Hoydt shrugs. "Corrupt police in this city? What are the odds."

"Yeah." CB gestures with the paper. "I got names."

Hoydt hesitates, then reaches out to take the paper. He opens it, frowns, then turns on his flashlight so he can read the text. "Ah, Christ. Some of these guys are on the task force. Well no wonder we keep losing evidence. OK, this is useful. I can use this."

"Good," CB says. "We on the same page now?"

Hoydt thinks it over, then nods once. "Next time you want to meet, arrange it through Jerry. Your buddy at the Swordfish. That'll make less noise than this fiasco."

“Fine,” CB says. “One last thing. What’s the deal with this city, Larry? What’s really going on?”

Hoydt takes a deep breath and exhales in a big, shuddering sigh. “Can’t tell you.”

“Oh, come on, Larry, this is—”

“No,” Hoydt says. He stands, smooths out his jacket. “Pay attention to what I’m saying. I. *Can’t.* Tell you.”

He waits a minute for that to sink in, then turns. “Don’t get dead, CB.”

With that he turns on his flashlight and stomps back down the hall.

CB finishes his cigarette, and leaves the way he came in. He ignores the cops when he exits the tent; the cops ignore him. He walks down the boardwalk for a bit, trying to organize his thoughts—trying to work out what Larry meant when he said he couldn’t tell him anything. A puzzle for another day, he decides. The important thing is that he can probably trust Larry if it comes down to it. With that, CB finally makes his way back to the bunker...

...where he finds Jenny sucker-punching Red Shift while she yells something about ‘Miss Liberty.’

“So... hey. What are we talking about?” CB isn’t sure he wants to know, but he feels compelled to ask.

Jenny turns, looks CB up and down. “What the hell happened to you?”

PART FOUR: JACOB K. JAVITS FEDERAL BUILDING

The 32nd floor of the Jacob K. Javits Federal Building in New York City is devoted to the Department of Homeland Security's Task Force for Metahuman Activity. That's where Division M set up shop, and when Alishia Webb lands on the roof—the Federal Building is a designated Sky Commando refit and refuel center—she sees one of them waiting for her by the lift.

Alishia waits until the outer shell is secured to the roof, then opens it up and steps out in the tactical suit. She takes off her helmet as the agent—an Asian woman with an oddly reddish tint to her skin—approaches.

"Agent Hu," the woman says, hand extended.

Alishia shakes her hand. "Sky Commando," she says. She still gets a rush from saying that.

"We're waiting for you in the conference room. Do you want to change first? Can you sit in the armor, or...?" Agent Hu's voice trails off.

"I'll be fine," Alishia says. The tactical armor isn't much bulkier than the body armor soldiers wear overseas, and with the power reinforced joints it's actually a lot easier to move around in.

Hu nods and motions for Alishia to follow. They go to the lift—a cargo elevator that was refit for the Sky Commando project—and begin to travel down to the 32nd floor.

The first half of the journey is awkwardly silent. Then Hu says, "I'm glad you're working with us. We weren't all convinced you would."

"Why?" Alishia asks.

Hu shrugs. "Because of the way we've been operating. You know, the whole 'Feds moving in to take over the show' thing."

"Which is your cover, right? Play on all the natural resentment so they'll assume you're grandstanding instead of trying to figure out who's working for the bad guys."

Hu smiles. She has dimples. "Yeah, but you know. When you play a part well, people believe it."

Alishia laughs. "Your boss is really good at rubbing people the wrong way."

Hu laughs in return. "Agent Henry is a great boss. I'd take a bullet for him. But he's not our diplomat..."

"So who's the diplomat?" Alishia asks.

"Grant," Hu says, then laughs again.

"So... Division M." Alishia looks at Agent Hu curiously. "All metahuman?"

Hu nods. "All field agents are."

"So... you?" Alishia asks.

"Yep," Hu says.

"So what do you... do?" Alishia feels a little flustered. "I mean, is it rude to ask? I don't know. I usually get dossiers on the metas I'm going to work with, but we don't have anything on you guys."

"It's not rude," Hu says, "but I've been instructed not to tell you anything yet."

Alishia blinks. "You have? Why? Is it classified?"

The corner of Hu's mouth quirks up. "No. Agent Henry's just yanking your chain a little."

Alishia bursts out laughing. "I'm starting to like you guys more. But if anyone calls me rookie I'll shoot them."

Division M has taken over roughly half of the 32nd floor. It has a surprisingly large staff of analysts, technicians, and support personnel. It reminds Alishia of the Sky Commando program.

"They're all in the conference room," Hu says. "This way."

The conference room is a large, well-equipped meeting room with a long table and comfortable chairs. Agent Henry is there, hunched over a black metal box, frowning. Two men and a woman—a tall, thin man, with slicked-back dark hair and a raggedly unshaven face; a short, wide-shouldered man with a thick blonde mustache; and a light-skinned Hispanic—or maybe Indian—woman with thick, dark curly hair are all standing around him peering down at it as well.

The thin, dark-haired man looks up as they walk in. "Hu! He did it." His voice is excited, like a kid who just managed to figure out what he's getting for Christmas without having to unwrap the present. Then he focuses on Alishia, and nods once. "Uh... that'll make sense in a second."

Agent Henry looks up. "Sky Commando, good. Have a seat, we'll start in a moment."

Hu drifts over to the dark-haired man. "What is it?"

Agent Henry waves her off. "You'll have to wait for the presentation." He looks around and frowns. "Where's Collins? She said she was getting everything."

"Yeah." The dark-haired man laughs. "The computer won't connect to the projector. We're trying to hook up mine."

Alishia frowns as she tries to sort that out. The dark-haired man grins.

"Sorry for the delay, Sky Commando," Agent Henry says. "I'm not trying to be dramatic. I just think context is very important in this situation, especially where your input is concerned."

"My input?" Alishia tries not to be put off by Agent Henry's sunglasses.

Agent Henry nods. "We're wading hip-deep into NYPD politics, and I think it's tied up in the investigation. You'll see why in a minute. But we're definitely going to need your guidance in this."

"OK," Alishia says. "But if you're looking for advice on politics, I'm a really bad choice."

The dark-haired man grins at that. The man with the mustache stifles something that might be more than a cough.

"I've read your file," Agent Henry says, as if that explains everything. It might. Alishia doesn't know. She's never read her file.

The door opens, and a tall blonde woman comes in wheeling a laptop tethered to a projector. "Thanks to Agent Grant, we're finally ready to go."

"Good." Agent Henry turns back to Alishia. "Sky Commando, let me introduce you to the team. Agent Collins is my number two." He indicates the blonde woman wheeling in the projector. "She isn't usually relegated to A/V duty, but she recently lost a bet to Agent Grant." The dark-haired man grins. The rest of the group laughs.

"I believe you've already met Agent Hu," Henry continues, and both Alishia and Agent Hu nod. "That leaves Agents Frank, to my left, and Mallory, to my right."

Agent Frank is the wide-shouldered man with the thick mustache. Mallory is the Hispanic-or-Indian woman with dark, curly hair.

"With that out of the way, let's get started. Collins, take us through last night, right up to finding the package."

Agent Collins nods. The projector dims a moment, then displays the picture of an older man with a vaguely pleasant smile.

"That's Pete Travers," Alishia says.

"Yes," Collins says. "Currently a wanted fugitive. Last night Agent Henry received a call on an emergency DHS Line. Agent Henry identified the caller as Peter Raphael Travers. He authorized a trace on the line, and kept Travers on the line long enough to trace the call to a motel in one of the more dangerous parts of the city."

The image on the wall changes to a picture of a motel.

"Oh," Alishia says. "That one."

"You know it?" Grant asks.

"I worked with Vice for a while before I joined the program," Alishia says. "Everyone over there knows it. Lots of drugs and prostitution."

"And Vice, coincidentally." Agent Henry's voice is dry.

"Yes," Collins says. "When Division M arrived at the scene, an NYPD Vice Task Force was already on the scene. Apparently they had scheduled a sweep that night. There was a... significant misunderstanding that prevented us from making significant progress on the site."

"Ah." Alishia smiles. "You ran into one of Darius' operations? I bet he was pissed."

"Not exactly," Agent Henry says. "He acted like he was, but he was lying the whole time."

Alishia looks sidelong at Agent Henry. He can tell when people lie to him. It's part of what he does.

"Our agents located the room Travers rented," Collins continues. "In that room we found the evidence sitting in front of Agent Henry."

Alishia looks at the small metal box. "What is it?"

"Before I tell you what it is," Agent Henry says, "I want to make clear that from this point on, none of the information we view or discuss is to go beyond this group. Absolutely none of it. Understood?"

The other Agents nod in agreement. Alishia nods as well.

"All right," Agent Henry says. "Collins, thanks for that. I'll take it from here."

Collins nods and sits down.

"There was a television in the room," Agent Henry says. "Not a flat screen, the old kind... essentially a large box chained to the table. Travers had opened it up, hollowed it out, and put this inside it." He gestures to the metal box. "It's a recording device. Sensors attach to the box on a side port, and those sensors were threaded all over the television screen. Essentially it was co-opting the TV screen and using it as a lens."

Agent Henry runs a cable from a port in the metal box to the projector. "I'd like to see what's on it." He flips a switch on the box, and suddenly the projector goes white. A moment later, Alishia sees a grainy black and white image of a seedy hotel room. A large bag sits on one of two twin beds. Peter Travers stands at the foot of the bed, talking on the phone, staring straight into the recording device.

"He's on the phone," Collins points out. "He's establishing the time."

"I agree," Agent Henry says. "This is Travers talking to me. I want you to start timing as soon as it's clear he's off the phone."

The image shows Travers talk for a while, then he hangs up. He shoves the phone in his pocket, then steps outside.

"Oh," Agent Henry says. "I see. I see what he did."

A few minutes later the front door bursts open. Men wearing gray commando uniforms enter the room, armed with automatic rifles.

"I recognize them," Alishia says. "They're the soldiers who attacked that newspaper and tried to blow up the entire city block."

"They also attacked the Forrest residence," Henry adds.

"It didn't take long for them to show up," Grant observes. "I don't like what that implies."

"Hold on," Henry says. "Something else is happening..."

A commotion just off-camera causes one of the soldiers in gray to stop what he's doing and turn to face the door. A second later Lieutenant Clive Darius, head of the NYPD Vice Task Force, steps into the room.

Everyone in the conference room watches in stunned silence as Darius starts giving orders. They can't hear what he's saying, but it's obvious that he's giving the orders, and the soldiers are obeying.

"Well," Agent Henry says, "that puts last night in context."

"Darius is dirty," Alishia says. It's hard to believe.

"Yes he is," Agent Henry says. "And the question of the day becomes: now that we know he's not on our side, whose side is he on?"

"Nevermind that," Agent Grant says. "*We* traced the call. Someone from Division M leaked Travers' location to Darius and his people. It's pretty clear that someone up the chain hasn't been playing straight with us through this investigation. Whose side are we on?"

Agent Henry has no answer to that.

CURVEBALL
16
JUL 2014
CURVEBALL
A Prose Comic
POINT OF NO RETURN
STORY
CHRISTOPHER WRIGHT
COVER
PASCALLE LEPAS
LOGO
GARTH GRAHAM

PART ONE: WASHINGTON DC

Senator Tobias Alexander Morgan sits in his DC office, watching television.

He looks a lot like his grandfather, or the way his grandfather might have looked in his late fifties, if he'd aged like other people. Although his hair is dark—he takes after his mother in that respect—he has the same square jaw, and his eyes radiate the same piercing resolve that Liberty was so famous for. His appearance did a lot for his political career in the beginning. He knows it, and he doesn't resent it. There's no point in resenting an advantage.

Tobias is watching his Schenectady house burn to the ground. The networks still play the footage far more than he likes—not twenty-four hours a day, but it's still one of their main stories. His staff turned it into a drinking game, and one of them ended up in the hospital.

There's a new edge to the coverage that's starting to make him nervous. So far he hasn't given any interviews, or issued any statements, and the media is asking why. Some are wondering if he's hiding something. The word "coverup" is starting to be used. He needs to get out in front of this thing, and he's running out of time.

His phone rings. The digital display shows that it's Marcus, his aide. He picks up the phone.

"Senator, I'm sorry to bother you." Marcus is new, and he still sounds nervous on the phone. "I know you said you weren't taking anyone today, but someone showed up from your VIP list, and—"

"That's fine," Tobias says. "It's all right, Marcus. Who is it?"

"Miss Io—" Marcus stumbles over the name. "I'm sorry. Io... ann..."

"*Ioannou*?" Senator Morgan sits up straight and adjusts his tie.

"Yes sir."

"Please send her in." The senator looks around the room quickly. Nothing appears out of place. "And Marcus: while we're talking, absolutely *no one* is to disturb us. Even if it's someone on the VIP list. Even if it's the President."

Mara Ioannou is a beautiful woman, tall and slender, with coppery skin and dark black hair. Her thick curls are pulled back from her face with silver hairpins, and large dark eyes peer out at the world from under thick, long eyelashes. She's dressed simply but elegantly in a white business suit and a skirt that cuts off just below the knees. The only jewelry she wears is large, double epsilon earrings made of silver.

"Mara." Tobias smiles and stands as she walks into the room. "It's good to see you."

Mara smiles in return, gracious and warm. "I only wish it were under happier circumstances."

The Senator steps around his desk and holds the back of a large overstuffed chair as Mara sits. Then he closes his office door and locks it.

"How have you been?" Tobias keeps his voice casual.

"I'm well," Mara replies. "Thank you so much for asking. It's been a busy year, and I haven't had much time to relax."

Tobias nods as he returns to his desk. "I can only imagine. I haven't had much time to look up..."

He reaches into his desk drawer and pulls out a large black globe that looks a bit like a magic 8-ball. He sets it on his desk and twists the top until it clicks. It begins to vibrate, ever so slightly. A moment later it chimes softly.

"OK," Tobias says. "We should be clear."

Mara's gracious, warm smile doesn't fade, but her posture changes: less ease, more authority. She's not here to talk to a US Senator, she's here to talk to an underling, and they both know it.

"I apologize for the delay," Mara says. "The situation is complex."

"I can imagine. I have a few questions..." Tobias nods toward the television, still showing a picture of his house burning to the ground. "I'm sure you can guess about what."

Mara nods. "We think we know who is involved, and we think we know why. It troubles us greatly."

Tobias waits patiently.

"You know by now that our attempt to contain the leak was mostly unsuccessful. He managed to send the file to an account using a Thorpe domain."

"I knew that much," Tobias says. "It wasn't until after Grandfather's funeral that I was called into the special sessions and had to go dark. But I haven't been able to keep in touch with... well, anyone since. I haven't even been able to go home..." His voice trails off, and he stares at the television screen. "Well, that doesn't matter now. The sessions went well, by the way. I got tentative agreement from a majority, and the minority don't object enough to do anything about it."

"Excellent work," Mara says. "The Chairman will be very pleased to hear that."

"In the last update I had access to, I read you brought in a specialized team to track down the leak," Tobias says.

"We did," Mara says. "They're still investigating. However, at this point we've been using them primarily to try to track the location of the file in order to contain it. They've made some progress on that—based on their work we believe we've identified all the civilians and metahumans who are aware of the file's existence."

"Metahumans?" Tobias asks. "More than Curveball, then. Who?"

"Regiment. His presence at the Forrest brownstone during the attack makes him a potential vector. There was a gap between the attack and the arrival of agents on the scene when they would have had more than enough opportunity to exchange information. We don't know what they discussed."

"Anyone else?"

"Sky Commando—the one who recently retired on disability. We believe Peter Travers passed on some information to him. He disappeared shortly after that. And Crossfire, the recipient of that information..."

Tobias' eyes widen in alarm. "Crossfire."

"I'm afraid so," Mara says. "We're certain it was Red Shift who broke into your house and triggered the failsafe on the computer. And we know he survived: we have satellite footage of him traveling at supersonic speed to Farraday City, where Curveball is currently operating."

"Farraday City?" Tobias shakes his head. "That's an odd place for him to be."

"Odd, yes. Also unexpected. Also very inconvenient: he and your niece broke into the TriHealth building there and stole some rather sensitive files."

"My niece? You mean *Jennifer*? She's involved in this?"

"Yes," Mara says. "She's traveling with him."

Tobias closes his eyes. He appears to deflate slightly.

"I'm sorry," Mara says.

"Julie and I were never particularly close," he says. "I hated that she was so involved in that part of my grandfather's life. I thought she was a hero groupie, to be honest. In retrospect that was... that was unkind. We've never really managed to be more than civil to each other, lately. And now this."

"There is very little we can do at this point," Mara says.

"I know." Tobias shakes his head regretfully. "Sacrifices must be made."

PART TWO: FARRADAY CITY BUNKER

"Well that settles it, *Miss Liberty*. I'll tell Vigilante and Street Ronin your new handle, and they'll make sure to leak it to the press."

"The hell you will!" Jenny knows Red Shift is joking, but the constant needling is starting to get to her. It doesn't help that she's going stir crazy: the bunker wasn't designed to hold three metahumans, especially when two of them have spent the last two weeks training. The entire place smells like a gym, and the rest of the bunker feels cramped since the main living space was converted into a sparring room. "I'm not refusing to take a name, I just can't think of one."

They're all sitting around the little table in the kitchen drinking coffee: Red Shift and Jenny sit across from each other—something they've been doing more and more, as their teacher/student relationship grows steadily more adversarial—and CB sits a bit back from the table, an amused spectator, watching them exchange barbs.

"It's not that I'm unsympathetic to your situation, *Miss Liberty*, but we're running out of time. Eventually you're going to go into the field, and when that happens you don't want me calling you 'Miss Forrest' while we're fighting the bad guys."

"I get it," Jenny says, "really. I get it. And it's not like I haven't been *trying*, but I can't think of anything that doesn't sound *stupid*, or *wrong*, or *both*."

"It can be a pretty big step," Red Shift agrees. "Sometimes it's a matter of trying something for a while, just to see if it works. The danger is that if you don't establish a name before the press picks one for you... well, usually the one they pick sticks. Remember our previous conversation about 'Desire.'"

"Yeah," Jenny grumbles.

"And if the press comes up with a name for you," CB adds, "you're screwed."

"Why me, specifically?" Jenny asks. "I thought they were universally bad at this."

"Not really," Red Shift says. "They're the ones who named me. I suppose I got lucky—they zeroed in on the red glow that my force field creates when it's discharging energy as I run, conflated it with some half-remembered facts about the Doppler Effect, and the result was a name that I didn't hate."

"But he's a guy," CB points out. "*You* will get screwed. You are an attractive young woman with metahuman abilities, and I promise you one of two things will happen: if they know who you are, and that Liberty was your great-grandfather, they will call you *Miss* Liberty and that will be that. If they don't know who you are, they will come up with a name that objectifies you so hard that any time the papers write anything about you, half the column will be devoted to what you were wearing at the time and whether it 'worked.'"

"I hate that," Jenny says.

"Well I don't blame you," CB says. "So I'm going to agree with Red on this one: come up with a name."

Jenny stares down at the table.

CB narrows his eyes. He leans forward, elbows resting on the edge of the table, and watches her carefully. "Jenny."

Jenny looks up guardedly.

"Do you want to be the next Liberty?"

Red Shift raises an eyebrow.

Jenny stares at CB, expression blank. "What?"

"Do you want to be the next Liberty? Honest answer."

Jenny looks back down at the table.

"You need to decide that before you decide anything else," CB says. "Look, I don't really think we're going to be able to build a 'secret identity' for you—too many people know you're traveling with me, too many people know you're related to Alex, and your abilities are a little too on the nose for people *not* to make the connection."

"Yeah." Jenny keeps staring at the table. Her voice is tight and unhappy.

"The Press is going to go with Miss Liberty because it's just too obvious not to use. They'll go with 'Miss' Liberty because one, they're still mostly a pack of sexist assholes, and two, it's a little too soon to be passing on the name for most people. But you could decide to pick up the torch on your own, if you wanted. You could *claim* the name—just 'Liberty,' no 'Miss'—and you could probably make it stick. If you wanted."

Jenny doesn't answer.

Red Shift looks from CB to Jenny, and nods thoughtfully. "Could work. It would be polarizing."

"It would be *very* polarizing," CB agrees. "Some people will love the idea of his great-granddaughter picking up the name, others will hate it. But Jenny—look, I don't have any experience with legacies, OK? But you've got one, and it's a hell of a thing. You have to figure out how you want to approach that, and the first step is to decide whether you want to *take up his cause*. Because if you take his name, Jenny, you damn well better take up his cause."

"I don't..." Jenny shakes her head. "No. I don't want to do that. I don't want to be Liberty."

"OK," CB says. "So who do you want to be?"

Jenny shrugs.

"Don't think about this from an adult's perspective," CB says. "Think back to when the Guardians were still doing their thing—you were, what? Eleven? Twelve? You ever think about what your life would be like if *you* were in the group?"

Jenny blushes slightly.

"Well what did you think of? Who did you see yourself as?"

"Doesn't work," Jenny says. "I always wanted to be like Gladiator. Powered suit. High-tech gadgets. I came up with names like 'Aegis' and 'Silicon Justice' and 'Möbius.' None of those really—"

CB bursts out laughing. Jenny's blush deepens.

"Sorry," CB says. "But there's already an 'Aegis' and 'Silicon Justice' sounds like a Crossfire reject."

"And 'Möbius' is a villain's name," Red Shift says. He's deliberately *not* smiling, which Jenny finds somehow more uncomfortable than CB's undisguised mirth.

"He was a German mathematician!" Jenny protests.

"That just makes it more villainous," Red Shift says. "German name plus metahuman plus post World War II equals villain. Unless you're actually *from* Germany. Then it's all right."

"That's completely unfair," Jenny says.

"Yep," CB says. "Still a villain's name, though. On the other hand, it's definitely a boss villain. You'd be the one in charge... at least, you would until we showed up to kick your ass and put you in jail."

"I still don't see how Möbius is a—"

CB presses on, ignoring Jenny's protest completely. "Look, thinking up a hero or villain name is a lot like thinking up a name for a band. It doesn't always matter what the words *really* mean—you're essentially labeling your sound, and that label will be affected by how people *perceive* that label.

When I turned hero I was able to keep using 'Curveball' because my 'sound' didn't really change. I just switched record labels."

Jenny rolls her eyes. "You *would* figure out a way to make this about music..."

"Hey, it works. A band tries to create a sound and an image that people respond to and the wrong name can hurt that. I mean, if the Beatles called themselves 'We Can't Play' it wouldn't have worked in the 60s." CB breaks into a grin. "Might have worked in the 90s, though."

"Well that's settled," Jenny says. "I'll just hop onto the web and look for one of those random band name generators. Problem solved."

Red Shift and CB laugh.

"They have superhero name generators too, you know." Red Shift nods gravely. "Street Ronin stumbled across one once, and we wasted three days clicking the refresh button over and over again. My favorite was *Commander Rapid Catman*."

CB chokes on his coffee.

"There were also a lot of names with variants of 'fist' in it. Stone Fist—which is actually being used, I think. The Crimson Fist..."

"Villain name," CB says.

"Villain *organization*," Red Shift says.

"Yeah, OK, I can see that."

"*Final Fist* almost worked, but we decided it sounded more like a video game title. *Master Fist* and *Fist Master* sounded like cartoon villains..."

"*This isn't helping*," Jenny says. "Once I start laughing there's no going back."

"OK, OK," Red Shift says. "I'll be good."

"You don't want to be Liberty," CB says. "You're not comfortable with taking up his mantle, and that's fine. So maybe we don't choose a name linked with an ideology. We'll focus on your abilities. What do you do?"

"What Liberty did," Red Shift says. "She's pretty much right where he was in terms of strength and reflexes."

"OK," CB says. "So Jenny, you basically put world-class athletes to shame. And you put athletes who use performance-enhancing drugs to shame."

"Apex," Red Shift suggests.

"No way," CB says. "That name is—"

"Cursed?" Red Shift shakes his head. "Didn't think you were that superstitious."

"Five guys with that name," CB says. "All dead within a year. It's the Scottish Play of hero names."

Jenny wrinkles her nose in disdain. "I think it's a bit over the top. I mean I'd basically be calling myself 'the highest point.' How much more arrogant can you get?"

"Of course it's arrogant," Red Shift says. "That's the point. There's no such thing as a modest hero name."

"He's right," CB says. "You never hear about 'Polite Man' and '*No, After You*' teaming up to rid the streets of crime."

"So arrogant is good," Jenny says.

"*Regiment*," CB says. "Guy named himself after an entire freaking army."

"What about 'Athena?' Greek goddess of war, wisdom, and justice. I could get behind that."

"Athena is an excellent name," Red Shift says. "If you're OK with being sued."

Jenny narrows her eyes. "Why would I get sued?"

"Yeah..." CB shifts uncomfortably in his seat. "Well, as it turns out, there are two entertainment companies who create..."

"...entertainment..." Red Shift supplies.

"Right," CB says. "Entertainment. About godlike beings in capes and spandex who go around saving the day."

"They're very protective of their properties," Red Shift says. "And if you're interested in operating in even a semi-legitimate capacity, you do not want them targeting you."

Jenny shakes her head. "You guys get sued by *comic books*?"

"*Very protective of their property*," Red Shift repeats.

"And one of those properties is a woman of Greek origin. She's not Athena, but comparisons will be made—and they'll sue you in a heartbeat."

"They'd lose," Jenny says.

"You'd run out of money first."

"Why would they even care? They don't do anything with that character."

"No they don't," CB says. "And they spend a lot of time making sure *absolutely nobody else will, either*."

"Fine!" Jenny throws up her hands. "I give up. No Athena. So I need to choose a grandiose name that will *resonate* with people that *isn't* cursed and that *won't* get me sued."

CB thinks it over. "Yeah," he says. "That pretty much sums it up."

They lapse into silence again. Jenny stares into her now-empty cup of coffee and restlessly drums her fingers on the table. Red Shift watches her, looking almost serenely patient. CB gets up and claims the last of the coffee.

"The problem is I don't *have* a 'sound,'" Jenny says.

CB tilts his head to one side. "Who's making this about music now?"

"I am," Jenny says. "Don't change the subject. My name is Jennifer Adele Forrest. It has been all of my life. When I think of who I am, and what I represent, that's the name I come up with, time after time. A woman who's spent a lot of time trying to become really good at her job. A job she loves. A career she just *torpedoed* because some asshole murdered her—"

She breaks off then, ducking down as her voice catches.

"My *sound* is who I was *before* this happened. I'm a blank slate. Five, ten years from now I might be like my great-grandfather was. Or I might be an unpredictable pain in the ass like you, CB. Or I might be a surprisingly likable but ultimately *really terrifying monster* like you, Red Shift. No offense."

"None taken," Red Shift says.

"The point is, there is nothing *about* me to base a name on. I don't have a cause, I don't have a theme, I don't have a *context*, and I'm not going to use my great-grandfather's just because we're related. He deserves better than that."

She stands up, chair scraping loudly against the floor as she sets her coffee cup on the table with a loud *clack*. "Call me 'Zero,'" she says. "Got that? *Zero*. That works as well as anything else."

She storms out of the room. A moment later, they hear the door to her room slam shut.

Red Shift and CB sit in silence. CB sips at his coffee.

Red Shift pushes his coffee cup away and turns to CB. "I thought she was too young for Schoolhouse Rock."

"She is," CB says.

They lapse into silence again.

PART THREE: TRIHEALTH, NEW YORK CITY

Vigilante and Street Ronin stand on the roof of the Mercer Actuarial Building and stare down at the street below. Traffic is moderately heavy, and they frequently hear the sound of car horns blaring angrily as vehicles fight for the right of way.

"Audience tonight," Street Ronin says. His voice is calm and steady, but Vigilante can detect an edge to it.

"Yeah," Vigilante says. "That's OK. Fun won't start until we get in."

They gaze at the TriHealth on the other side of the street. Mercer Actuarial is slightly taller than the TriHealth complex, so they're looking down at its roof. The roof is a plain, flat surface with a cluster of exhaust vent pipes and a maintenance hatch.

"No security on the roof," Street Ronin says. "Sure you don't want to go in that way? A lot simpler."

"Simpler," Vigilante agrees. "Also quieter. We want to knock first."

"OK," Street Ronin says. "Help me get set up."

They kneel, hunching over a rectangular metal box as they quickly pop a series of latches across the two long edges. The top slides off, revealing a gray slab of metal and eight spheres, each roughly half the size of a man's fist. Street Ronin picks up the gray slab, turns it over once in his hands, and flicks it away from him with a single, sharp motion. A tripod pops out of the bottom, extending fully. He sets the tripod and slab securely on the ground. Vigilante removes each sphere from the box and sets them down in front of the tripod.

"I was hoping to test these a bit more before we used them in the field," Street Ronin says. He removes a USB cable from a pocket in his combat harness, attaches one end to his visor, and attaches the other to the gray slab. Immediately the sides of the gray slab begin to blink as it boots up. "OK, stand back. I'm going to turn these on."

Vigilante stands back. Street Ronin places his hand on the gray slab, traces a pattern near the upper left corner, and with a low hum the eight spheres rise into the air.

The gray slab is essentially a giant touchpad: individual controls are marked out on an overlay that displays on Street Ronin's visor whenever he looks at it. He sets the spheres to follow mode, designates a leader, and they fly down toward the TriHealth building below.

"How are you going to find the server room?" Vigilante asks.

"Heat," Street Ronin says. "All those computers are going to radiate heat, and the resources put into cooling will be significant. So I'm going to fly the spheres around the building until I find..."

His voice trails off and he hunches forward, making careful, precise gestures on the control surface of the slab.

"Thirteenth floor." Street Ronin grins, his voice rueful. "Damn it. I'll pay you later."

Vigilante chuckles. "They just can't help themselves, sometimes."

"OK, well... I found a vent. That's going to be my way in. As soon as I'm in position I'll start tracking."

Vigilante stretches out on the roof, lying on his back, looking up at the sky. "Let me know when it's my turn. Until then I'll just look at the... smog, I guess."

Street Ronin grins, then gets back to work. He instructs one of the spheres to immolate itself and burn through the vent, then guides the other seven up into the building. Sure enough, the vent is directly under the server room. It's relatively simple to find data connections from there. Ten minutes later he's ready.

"Thomas."

Vigilante stirs slightly—he's fallen asleep.

"*Vigilante.*"

"Yeah." Vigilante sits up.

"I'm ready. Your turn."

"Right..." Vigilante stands, rolls his left shoulder, then his right. Finally he lowers his visor into its locked position. "How's my feed?"

"Visual is fine," Street Ronin says. "Might get spotty inside. I don't know what kind of tech they use, but I expect the server room will make transmitting video a challenge."

"I'm flattered you think I'm going to get that far," Vigilante says. "OK. Start pinging me."

Vigilante hears a soft *ping* in his earpiece, repeating at two-second intervals. It's an audio feed Street Ronin is transmitting directly to him—if it gets cut off, he'll know someone is jamming the line.

"Time to make a mess."

Vigilante steps over the edge of the building and disappears from view.

It takes Vigilante a few seconds before he finally hits the sidewalk. The force of the landing echoes down the street, splitting the concrete as Vigilante immediately leaps across the street, arcing high to avoid the oncoming traffic, and lands neatly in front of the revolving doors that lead into the TriHealth lobby.

Vigilante straightens, grabs the edge of one of the doors, and pushes. The door buckles in its frame, glass shatters, and with a groan the revolving door grinds to a halt. Vigilante turns sideways and slips past the twisted frame, then with a swift kick he shatters the glass in the door blocking his way into the lobby. He steps through.

The lobby is large and spacious—it looks more like the lobby of a modern bank than a health insurance company. There are booths lined up along the walls, and velvet rope lines set up to separate each line. The lobby is empty except for the security desk where a single guard is shouting into a headphone.

"Guard isn't trying to stop me." Vigilante keeps his voice low and conversational—too low for the guard to hear over his own yelling.

"Smart." Street Ronin's voice comes in sharp and clear over the visor's earpiece. "I'm going to send a sphere down to the street, just to keep an eye on things."

"OK." Vigilante waves casually at the security guard and follows the sign that points to the elevators. "I figure they'll do gas or something first."

"Worried about it?" Street Ronin asks.

"Nope." Vigilante ducks around a corner and sees four elevators, all closed. "Found the stairs."

The stairs, as expected, are by the elevators. The door, as expected, is locked. It's a fire door, made of reinforced steel.

"Steel door."

He kicks at the door. It buckles under the force of the blow, but it doesn't fly off its hinges. Vigilante stares at the twisted mass, still sitting in the frame, still attached to its hinges, and still locked.

"Okay... *not* a steel door."

Two more kicks do the job. The door breaks free and falls into the stairwell beyond. Vigilante kicks it out of the way, then starts climbing.

"You were right about the gas," Street Ronin says. "Look at your HUD."

Vigilante looks up into the corner of his visor. There he sees the feed Street Ronin is pumping in—a view of the lobby from across the street. The top-to-bottom glass windows are now shuttered, and the now-broken revolving door is blocked by what looks like a solid steel wall.

"Looks like they're sealing it up," Street Ronin says. "Guess they don't want something leaking out into the street."

"How *thoughtful* of them," Vigilante says.

By the fourth floor the air has a distinctly sharp taste.

"They're deploying the gas, whatever it is." Vigilante feels a vague flash of euphoria as his body adjusts to the attack. "I thought it was a neurotoxin at first, but I'm not sure."

"I'm not going to ask how you know that," Street Ronin says.

"It's too lemony."

He tenses each time he approaches the stairwell landing for a new floor—each landing is basically an enclosed room. There are heavy not-steel doors on every floor, not just leading into the main part of the building, but also separating the stairs from the landing itself. These doors aren't locked, but each time he steps onto a landing he expects an ambush. Each time, the ambush doesn't come. The only sounds he hears are the echo of his footsteps as he climbs and the soft ping of Street Ronin's ambush feed.

Halfway between the seventh and eighth floors, the ambush feed goes dead. They make their move on the eighth floor landing. It's a hell of a move.

Once he steps onto the landing he hears the loud buzz of a klaxon alarm as blast doors descend from the ceiling with a thunk, completely covering each exit. Vigilante clenches his fists and steps into a crouch, but before he can do anything else sections of the landing floor explode in a blaze of white-hot phosphor. Vigilante remembers thinking that an unusual choice—the explosions burn hot, but they aren't very large—and then a moment later the phosphor sparks with the gas in the room.

For a moment the room is full of fire. Then the light dims, the air feels heavy, and the gas condenses, still burning, into a thick, jello-like substance that clings to everything it sticks to. He is, effectively, swimming in napalm.

He starts to scream as the burning gel envelops him, and forces himself to stop before any of it gets into his mouth. As painful as it is—and it is *excruciatingly* painful—his uniform and the organic armor that makes up the outer layer of his epidermis make sure that pain is only skin deep. The last thing he wants is that stuff inside him, burning its way through. That would probably kill him outright, at least for a while. He closes his mouth, closes his eyes, and forces himself to stop breathing.

Vigilante isn't a scientist. He has no explanation for why his body can do what it does, and the scientists he knows can't do any better—he is, in their eyes, a medical and scientific impossibility. But despite his ignorance about *why* and *how*, over time he's learned exactly *what* his body can do and how much punishment it can withstand. He knows how long it takes for his body to neutralize toxins. He knows how long it takes for his body to mend broken bones. He knows how long it takes for his body to completely regrow an arm. Despite the pain of *literally being coated in fire*, he knows he's not even *close* to dying.

The pain makes it hard to focus on anything complicated, so he forces himself to check his gear. His visor is intact—surprising that it withstood both the explosion and the searing heat, but it means he can open his eyes. The rest of his uniform isn't as durable, and most of it has burned away. His skin is blistering.

*Oh, God, it **hurts**.*

The walls are different. They looked like concrete or cinderblock before, but that veneer has crumbled away to reveal glossy white walls. Whatever it is, it isn't affected by the heat. The surface is smooth and unmarred, no visible scorching or warping, though it appears it might be glowing, just a little. The floor has crumbled away to show similar material. It's slippery, though that might just be the gel. The doors look like airlocks from a science fiction movie. Everywhere around him is the dull roar of flame... though it's not quite as loud as it was a few seconds ago. And it's not quite as bright, or as hot. The fire is *dimming*.

Airtight seal. The fire's going out because the room is running out of air.

He imagines a strike team standing patiently just outside the main door, waiting for the fire to consume all the oxygen and put itself out before coming in to clean up. Not a terrible plan, but Vigilante has something else in mind.

Moving is difficult. He wants to curl up into a ball and wait for the pain to stop—that desire occupies most of his conscious thought, and the only way to get past it is to allow himself to get angry. It's dangerous territory, but he needs a motivator that's stronger than pain. His rage will do. He focuses on the anger, and what he wants to do to the people who did this to him. To do that, he needs to get out of this box. To do that, he needs to move. He moves.

He focuses on the door that leads out to the rest of the floor. He backs away from it, until he reaches the far wall, then hurls himself at it with all his strength. The floor is slippery—both from the strange material it's made out of, and from the gel coating it, but pushing off from the wall allows him to build up enough speed for him to make a sizable dent in the door when he hits it. It hurts—everything he does hurts, now—but he just piles that on top of all the other things that are pissing him off. He backs up again, launches again, and the door groans as it buckles almost in half. One more time: he goes back to the wall, charges at the door with everything, and this time the door rips out of the wall, spinning into the wide, short corridor beyond and smashing into the corridor wall.

Vigilante runs into the corridor, bursting into flame all over again as the gel on his body reignites from exposure to fresh air. A roaring wave of heat nearly knocks him down as the gel in the stairwell does the same. Almost immediately sprinklers in the ceiling activate, dousing the corridor in a steady stream of water. It has no effect at all on the burning gel.

He hears a panicked shout, and through the film-encrusted visor he sees armored figures at the end of the hall. He recognizes the armor: the NYPD uses something similar, designed to be worn by specialized SWAT units in situations where metahumans are actively menacing the public. It's not Sky Commando-level tech, but each armored suit is fully enclosed, heavily armored, and heavily armed. These aren't NYPD-issue, however. They don't have the right markings... they don't have any markings at all. Three of the armored suits face him—behind them, the corridor opens into a cube farm, and Vigilante can hear someone frantically barking orders just out of view.

Vigilante takes his first breath in minutes. He can smell the fire behind him, and the charred smell of his own singed hair and burnt flesh. He bellows, his voice cracking with raw, seething rage, and charges directly at the armored figures.

One of them takes a step back, startled by the approach of the yelling, burning, naked man leaving a trail of fiery footprints in the carpet behind him. The other two level their right arms at him. Panels slide over the joints, locking the arm into a rigid, extended position, and a large-caliber gun emerges from the top. A moment later both fire: one hits him squarely in the chest, the other in the face. His visor shatters, and he falls back, skidding a few feet along the ground until he comes to a stop.

He sits up. His face is a bloody, misshapen mess, but he can already feel it starting to knit back together. The armored figure in the middle takes another hesitant step back. The other two don't flinch.

"Deploy stuckey!" The command from the unit on the right is issued in the open air, not over radio, and that's the only reason Vigilante doesn't find himself trapped in goo.

He rolls back, toward the remains of the door he'd cast aside when he first burst out of the stairwell. The stuckeys explode between him and his assailants, completely filling the hallway—a tactical error on the part of the armored units, because it buys him more time—and he grabs the still-burning door with both hands. He notices the fire in the stairwell is rapidly spreading into the hall, despite the sprinklers, and it won't be long before it's completely out of control.

He grits his teeth as he grasps the door, ignoring the searing heat from the alloy, and smashes it into the wall. It's not a load-bearing wall, and it only takes a second swipe with the door to create a hole large enough for him to step through. He's in a long office, a manager's private office from the look of it, and the door at the end looks like it might open into the cube farm.

Vigilante runs down the length of the office and holds the metal door in front of him as he crashes into the much less impressive office door, which splinters into hundreds of bits of particle board upon impact.

He is now in the cube farm, much to the surprise of everyone already there.

A quick scramble as the non-armored personnel duck into various cubicles, attempting to use them as cover. Vigilante is able to count at least five figures in tactical gear before everyone disappears, not counting the three armored units at the very edge of the hall, who are turning to face him.

Eight, at least. But deal with the armor first.

He throws the burning metal door into the hall. It catches the rightmost unit in mid-turn. Vigilante hears a single, sharp scream as the door shears off its right arm. The door continues through the far wall into another office, crashing into a desk which immediately bursts into flame.

The center unit turns to face its crippled comrade, takes a step away—toward the burning hallway, where the wad of stuckey has melted from the raging heat. It stops, seemingly transfixed by the inferno at the end of the hall. Whoever is in that armor is obviously having trouble keeping it together. To Vigilante that makes it the most useful thing in the room.

It takes him five steps to cross the room. The far right unit has now toppled over, its severed arm lying a few feet from the rest of it. The unit on the left shouts "FOCUS!" and levels its heavy gun at him. Vigilante feels his shoulder go numb, but he's too focused on his target to care. The center unit turns just in time to see Vigilante bearing down on it. It raises its arms in a half-hearted attempt to block.

Too little, too late.

Vigilante grabs the armored unit by its chestplate and pushes it as hard as he can into the other. They smash into each other with a *crunch*, and both fall over, the first on top of the second. The operator of the first unit panics, flailing arms and legs in an attempt to get upright.

The second armored unit manages to push the first off, but too late—

Vigilante drives his smoldering fist through the chestplate, burying his arm up to his elbow. When he pulls it back out, his forearm is stained crimson.

He turns to the last armored unit.

The operator panics, deploying every weapon it can. Unfortunately it's still lying prone: the large caliber gun fires wildly through the wall, a small caliber submachine gun sprays bullets uselessly into the ceiling. A series of short, sharp *pops* announces the launch of every high-explosive grenade and stuckey it has.

Vigilante leaps into the cube farm, trying to get as far away as he can. He's about halfway in when all the ordnance goes off at the same time.

A third of the cubicles are blown apart by the force of the blast. Vigilante lands on a desk, smashing it in half and getting briefly tangled in the plugs and cables. When he gets to his feet, the room is silent. Even the fire from the stairwell is muted—the stuckeys have once again fused into a solid block at the mouth of the corridor. There is no sign of the hapless armored unit. He hears groaning from somewhere in the cube farm—at least one of the five non-armored personnel survived—but no one is trying to shoot him at the moment, so he doesn't follow up.

A low rumble fills the air, and the walls shake as Vigilante hears a series of explosions from far above him. It's the "Plan B" signal—if they lose communication, Street Ronin will destroy the spheres as soon as they meet their objective. Time to go...

The last of the gel on his skin has finally burned out, and he can feel his skin starting to regrow. The outer layer is still charred, and it crackles like cellophane when he moves. He looks around the surviving cubes and finds a bright green plastic rain poncho hanging from a hook on one of the cube walls. It's better than nothing, so he puts it on quickly, then runs over to a large panoramic window set into the far wall. It's riddled with bullet holes, so it's easy enough to break—it's a little harder to break without raining bits of glass onto the street below, but he manages to fracture it without shattering, then force his hands through to tear strips off the glass until there's enough space for him to jump through. Then he jumps, angling it so he lands on a ledge of the building across the street. The air is cool on his blackened skin—ironic, since it's summer, but not surprising given where he's been for the last fifteen minutes—and he allows himself to enjoy the relief as he jumps back to the TriHealth building in order to give himself the momentum he needs to make it to a roof in his next jump. From there he makes his way, building by building, to the rendezvous point.

Street Ronin is already there, waiting. He cocks his head to one side when Vigilante lands beside him, taking in the poncho and wrinkling his nose at the scent of charred flesh.

"Trouble," Street Ronin says. It's not a question.

"That was part of the plan," Vigilante says. "But I really didn't expect them to set me on fire." His voice is ragged and angry. It's under control at this point, but he's still in a lot of pain. "Did we get it?"

Street Ronin nods. "We got it. The spheres noticed the traffic about the same time I lost the link with you. I couldn't communicate with them directly, but they emailed me the details."

Vigilante sits down on the rooftop, allowing himself to curl up and just sit there for a moment, waiting for his body to heal, waiting for the pain to subside. Street Ronin sits next to him waiting patiently. When Vigilante speaks again, his voice is steady.

"What did we learn?"

"Pretty much what we expected. Someone pushed a panic button and they immediately began transferring a specific set of files to an alternate location. We couldn't get the files without alerting them, but we did find the alternate location..."

Vigilante nods, satisfied. "Where did it go?"

"Farraday City," Street Ronin says. "Didn't expect that. I don't know where specifically, but I think the newbie might be able to figure it out."

"OK," Vigilante says. "Looks like we're going to Farraday City."

"Overmind and the Lieutenant haven't come back yet," Street Ronin says. "And Scrapper Jack still has business up here."

"Yeah," Vigilante says. "Can't be helped at this point. I can get in touch with Jack, tell him to meet up with us when he can. I assume he knows how to get in touch with Overmind."

"So," Street Ronin says, "mission success. Was it worth it?"

Vigilante gets to his feet. He's sore all over, but his charred skin has turned into blistered skin, and some of those blisters are already fading. His scalp itches as new hair growth starts to appear in patches over his head, and there's little sign he'd been shot in the face with a .50 caliber rifle ten minutes ago.

"I'll tell you tomorrow," he says.

PART FOUR: UNKNOWN LOCATION, TROPICAL CLIMATE

David Bernard struggles to open his eyes as he is suddenly inundated with the cold sting of ocean water rolling over his face.

He chokes, gagging as he tries to simultaneously expel the water he just inhaled and draw fresh air into his lungs. He panics for a moment as his body can't seem to organize itself to do first one, then the other, but then he coughs, retches, and streams of ocean water come out of his mouth and nose. A moment later he breathes in—the air is sharp, and burns, but it's a relief.

He looks down at his hands. They're covered in white sand. He hears the roar of surf, and as he looks around he sees he's on a beach.

A wave of dizziness overtakes him, and he falls to one shoulder just as another wave breaks, covering his face. He just manages to avoid inhaling, and scrambles to his feet before the next wave rolls in.

He's dressed in BDUs. He's armed: an automatic pistol is locked in a shoulder holster, and a combat knife is sheathed on his left hip. He's also wearing a life jacket and a parachute harness.

No parachute. Harness, but no parachute. The secondary chute is still packed.

Must have landed in water.

Another wave of dizziness overtakes him. He staggers, automatically bringing his hand up to his forehead, and draws it back when he feels something wet and sticky. There's blood—he has a cut on his forehead.

He waits a minute, steadying himself, then looks up and down the beach. He's not exactly dressed like he was in his military days, but it's hard not to compare this to an airborne deployment. Since that's the only thing that makes any sense right now, that's what he goes with. If he parachuted in... did he do it alone? It seems unlikely. Who did he come in with?

He tries to remember. He panics as he realizes he can't remember much of anything at all. The last memory he has is in the Suit, responding to a call downtown. Something about a metahuman going crazy, tearing up real estate...

The bus smashes into him harder than anything he's ever felt in his life, he barely notices when he goes through the cinderblock wall—

The dizziness returns, and he has to sink to his hands and knees to get it under control. He's hurt, probably suffering from a concussion, though the thought *that's not possible, they fixed that before we left* comes unbidden into his mind. There's no context for it, but apparently he feels *very indignant* that it didn't turn out to be true.

He gets back to his feet and tries to collect his thoughts. He's on a beach. He stops for a moment and takes it in: it's hot and humid, the water is a very distinctive shade of blue, the sand is very white—he's somewhere in the tropics. He'll have to find a map to learn more.

He frowns, and starts checking his pockets. Does he *have* a map?

He should have a map. If he were going to agree to parachute in to an unknown destination, for whatever reason, he would *demand* a map. And a lot of other things.

Supplies.

His pockets aren't empty, but they aren't exactly informative: he has a rolled-up Boonie hat, six extra magazines in his tactical vest, a silencer of dubious quality, and a small first aid kit. The right inside vest pocket holds a few food bars, a waterproof compass, and a small LED flashlight. A small metal canteen hangs off his belt. The left inside vest pocket is a Rite-in-the-Rain water-resistant notepad and a Fisher Space Pen.

He travels further up the beach, putting himself out of the reach of the waves, as he glances at the notepad. His hands are shaking so badly it's difficult to read—he doubts he's going to want to use his gun any time soon—but he recognizes his own handwriting. It's a fresh pad, and only the first page has anything written on it.

The date at the top makes him pause. Assuming the date is correct, he can't remember the last two months.

The rest of what he wrote is suitably cryptic:

Pt Libertad

No avail map

Compass useless???

Not here (OMs fault?)

He frowns at the notepad. It looks like he was about to write something else, but it's just an interrupted scrawl.

No avail map. That explains why he doesn't have a map, but "Pt Libertad..." *Libertad* meant "liberty" in... Latin? Spanish? He can't remember. Spanish would be likely if he were in the Bahamas, but without a map (*no avail map*) it's impossible to tell. He takes out his compass. The needle wobbles for a moment, then slowly begins to *rotate*, first clockwise, then counter-clockwise, then clockwise again. It keeps switching direction after each rotation. He stares at it for a full minute, waiting for it to settle. It doesn't.

"Compass useless," indeed...

He puts the compass back in its pocket and stares at the last line of the notepad. He has no idea who or what OM is. He doesn't know anyone with those initials. A country, maybe? A political party? A corporation?

He looks up and down the length of the beach. He doesn't see anyone, but he suddenly feels exposed. He supposes if he actually parachuted in here on some sort of mission—which doesn't really make any sense, but nothing else does, either—that it's probably a good idea to stay out of sight. There's a forest beyond the beach. He puts the notepad back in its pocket and heads in that direction, walking briskly, trying to remain level to avoid making himself dizzy again.

David brushes his hand across his forehead. He's still bleeding—he needs to take care of that soon. That's his plan so far: stop bleeding, stay out of sight.

It's not a great plan, but it's the only plan he has.

The mid-morning sun beats down on his neck as he trudges toward the forest, asking himself the same questions over and over again:

Where is he?

Why is he here?

CURVEBALL
17
AUG 2014
CURVEBALL
A Prose Comic
ENEMIES WITHIN
STORY
CHRISTOPHER WRIGHT
COVER
PASCALLE LEPAS
LOGO
GARTH GRAHAM

PART ONE: SKY COMMANDO

Alishia Masters remembers her first week in the Sky Commando program as if it were yesterday. One of the first things she remembers noticing is the press. They were everywhere: any time David would go on day patrol there would always be a few media helicopters trailing him. Any time he set down, there would be a van or two somewhere nearby. They never approached, they never asked for interviews, they just... lurked.

At the end of the first week she remembers asking David why. His response was both direct and unsettling.

"They're waiting for us to fuck up."

Alishia was never sure exactly how serious he was when he said it. David had been a tough mentor, and in the early days he spent a lot of time trying to push her buttons, just to figure out what they were. It was six months before he let her get anywhere near the suit, and the first time she botched a landing, taking out the side of a grocery store in the process, it was another month and a half before he let her try again.

He was pretty possessive about the suit. She knows the feeling.

She's never been particularly comfortable around the press, at least in part because of that conversation, and any time they're on hand she feels less like a hero and more like a public relations disaster waiting to happen. That's why she prefers night patrols—most of the press are at home.

Also, night flying is a hell of a lot more fun.

She's flying over the Verrazano-Narrows Bridge from Brooklyn to Staten Island, taking in the Manhattan skyline. It shines brightly, skyscrapers washing out the night sky. *No stars necessary,* the skyline says. *We make our own light here.*

The skyline blurs slightly as a priority message pops up in the suit's HUD. Alishia sees the phrase *Code Ultraviolet* and immediately sets all thought of fun aside. Code Ultraviolet is reserved for the really important stuff. Usually it means very dangerous metahumans are involved.

"Play message," Alishia orders.

"Code Ultraviolet: TriHealth Building, Manhattan. Metahuman seen entering building approximately twenty minutes ago. Fire on the upper levels. Initial reports on identity of intruder are sketchy, but some civilian footage suggests Crossfire may be involved."

Oh, Christ.

"Response mode." Alishia's voice is tight, her words are clipped. "Dispatch, this is Sky Commando and I am en route. I am requesting MTHD backup, with available units to set up a perimeter and secure the scene. How soon until fire arrives?"

There is a short pause as the dispatcher checks. When the voice returns, the dispatcher—male, older—sounds mystified. "Fire and Rescue is already there, Sky Commando, but they're... they report being denied access to the building."

"They report *what*?"

"MTHD units are already on the scene, and blocking access to the building."

Alishia narrows her eyes. "My ETA is ten minutes. Sky Commando out."

The phrase *Sky Commando out* automatically kills the feed. "Contact MTHD, Ultraviolet band."

The Sky Commando program isn't the only part of the NYPD organized to respond to metahuman threats: NYPD SWAT has the Metahuman Division. MTHD and Sky Commando were, in the very beginning, competitors for attention and funding. Over time it became clear they were a lot more effective when they worked together. That hasn't changed since Alishia took the seat. At least, she hasn't thought so.

She's surprised to see the tired, worn face of Captain Banks on the screen. Paul Banks is the head of the MTHD. He and David got along pretty well. Alishia never had much contact with him directly.

"Sergeant." Captain Banks looks a little surprised to be talking to her, which is fair. While Sky Commando has a direct, private line to the MTHD, it's considered proper to coordinate via dispatch so the entire force can coordinate appropriately. "MTHD is responding per your request. Our closest team is fifteen minutes out, though. I think you're going to get there first."

"Closest team?" She can't hide the surprise in her voice. "Captain... I was calling to follow up on a report we're getting from Fire and Rescue on the scene. They say MTHD units are preventing them from entering the building."

Captain Banks raises an eyebrow. "We don't have any units on the scene."

The Captain has a reputation for honesty. Alishia is inclined to believe him. That said, she never would have pegged Clive Darius as dirty, either. Right now there are only a few people she's certain she can trust, and none of them work for the NYPD.

Alishia nods. "OK. Someone on the scene is obviously confused. I was just calling in case your people had better intel. Sorry."

"I only know what we just heard," Banks says.

"All right. Sorry again, Captain. Sky Commando out."

The Captain's face winks out.

A minute later her comm beeps again. When she answers it, she's surprised to see the scowling face of Lieutenant Clive Darius.

"Lieutenant?"

"Sky Commando." Darius has a low, gravelly voice. "I am already on the scene, and my people have it locked down."

"What is Vice doing on the scene?" Alishia uses every bit of self-control she has to keep the suspicion out of her voice. *And how the hell did you get access to this line?*

"We just finished up a raid four blocks east of here," Darius says. "We were closest, so we were first on the scene."

He's lying. Alishia is positive he's lying.

"OK," Alishia says. "I'll be there in seven minutes."

"There's no need. We've got everything under control here."

God damn it. "Yeah?"

"Yeah," Darius says. "The suspects have already fled the scene. There are wounded, and the building is still on fire, and we need forensics to go over everything, but there's nothing for you to engage here."

He's trying to get her to stay away from the scene, the rat bastard.

She takes a deep breath. "I don't have a choice, Lieutenant. Sky Commando has to respond to every Ultraviolet while on duty. And I can't end an Ultraviolet until I arrive at the scene."

Darius nods stiffly. "Understood. But once you're briefed on the scene *you will call it off.*"

Technically Darius has no authority to give her an order of any kind. Technically Sky Commando calls the shots in these situations—metahuman response is what the program is *for*. Technically, Sky Commando can, during an Ultraviolet, give anyone other than the Mayor or the Chief of Police a direct order and expect it to be followed without hesitation or argument.

"You want to tell me why?" Alishia asks.

Darius just stares at the screen, eyes flat. "Nope."

Practically, she's a Sergeant, he's a Lieutenant, and he's a bona-fide crime-fighting superstar with a hell of a lot of political pull. Technicalities be damned: Darius is giving her a direct order because he knows he can get away with it, at least for the short term. Alishia knows it, too.

"Yes sir," she says.

"Good." Darius nods, apparently satisfied, then kills the line without so much as a goodbye.

"Asshole..." Alishia grits her teeth and quickly calls Agent Phillip Henry's private phone. He picks up on the second ring.

"Agent Henry." He's tired, but he doesn't sound groggy.

"This is Sky Commando, and I don't have a lot of time. How fast can you get your team out to the TriHealth building in Manhattan?" She doesn't waste time on pleasantries, and he picks up on that immediately.

"Fast," Henry says. "Not all of them, but some. Why?"

"Code Ultraviolet," Alishia says. "Crossfire is a possible suspect, and Clive Darius is already on the scene."

"Darius?" Henry is definitely paying attention now. "What's he doing there?"

"Pulling rank," Alishia says. "He just ordered me to call off the Ultraviolet as soon as I arrive."

"Can he do that?" Henry asks. His voice is tight with excitement. It sounds like he's pacing the room.

"It's complicated," Alishia says. "Short version is 'yes, but it'll cost him.'"

"What do you think he's trying to do?" Henry asks.

"Coverup," Alishia says. "Something went wrong tonight and he's trying to make sure nobody finds out what. Pulling rank like this is... well, he can get away with it, because he's connected. But it's *stupid*. Long term, it's stupid, and he doesn't have a reputation for that."

"So whatever he's trying to protect is worth the risk," Agent Henry says.

"I don't know. I think so. Just a hunch."

"OK," Agent Henry says. "How do you want to play this?"

"How fast can you get your people there?"

"I can have Agent Grant on the scene in two minutes. Everyone else will take a bit longer. What do you need?"

Alishia considers her options before replying.

"I need you to live up to your reputation," she says.

* * *

Lieutenant Darius' claim that the scene is locked down and under control turns out to be grossly exaggerated. The press are already there, and Darius' men are struggling to keep back the teams on the ground. They're completely ignoring the two helicopters hovering next to the seventh floor of the TriHealth building, where smoke and flame pour out of a broken panoramic window. Too much fire, too much press, too many bystanders...

...and damned if Fire and Rescue personnel aren't squaring off against armored MTHD personnel.

Alishia frowns as she zooms in on that image. They *aren't* MTHD—the design is slightly different, and there are no official markings of any kind. She zooms in on the armor, saves a few images for later study, then lands by the main entrance to the building.

The revolving door to the TriHealth building is hopelessly twisted out of place; broken glass litters the entrance and scatters into the sidewalk as heavy-booted people move to and fro. The lobby beyond is completely obscured by a solid, metallic curtain. Two of the mysterious, unmarked armored personnel stand on either side of the revolving door.

Lieutenant Darius emerges from a small cluster of uniformed officers off to the right and walks quickly over to Sky Commando. "OK," he says. "I need you to—"

"Hold on a minute, Lieutenant." Alishia smiles as she watches annoyance and frustration play over his face. "I need to check out that fire."

Darius steps back as Sky Commando launches back into the sky, rising up to the seventh floor in order to peek through the broken window into the room beyond. The interior is engulfed in flame: floor, walls, ceiling, all are burning. But other than the flame coming through the window, the fire doesn't appear to be doing any damage to the outer walls. According to her HUD, the surface temperature of the building wall is no greater than that of any other building on the street.

Alishia flies back down to the sidewalk.

Darius scowls, his arms folded across his chest. "Cancel the Ultraviolet."

"The fire on the seventh floor is *not* contained," Alishia says.

"The fire isn't a metahuman, either. Sky Commando, you aren't needed here. Cancel the Ultraviolet and leave the scene."

Alishia wonders how long she can string this out. "Fine. I'll call it in..."

"Don't bother, Sky Commando. This is a federal investigation now."

Lieutenant Darius' expression falls into a carefully maintained mask of neutrality as he stares past Alishia, into the street. Alishia's HUD shows Department of Homeland Security Agent Alan Grant step around one of the fire engines, holding his badge up over his head as if he were using it to ward off evil spirits as he closes the gap between them, the tail of his rumpled trenchcoat flapping behind him as he moves.

A spark of recognition flashes in Darius' eyes.

Grant keeps his badge held over his head as if it were a beacon of truth and righteousness. "Any metahuman incident that occurs within a mile of a federal building is a federal matter, Lieutenant. Half a mile from here is a Veteran's Administration office, so you are out of luck."

Darius glares at Grant. "This is *bullshit*."

"I'm cryin' for ya," Agent Grant says. "Really. I mean we all made such good friends the last time, didn't we? There was *so much cooperation* then."

Darius scowls.

"You got a problem with me being here, feel free to call someone. Call your Captain... oh, but I don't answer to him. I guess you could call the Mayor, but I don't answer to *him*, either. Oh, wait! I know. You can call the *Governor*. That'd be another guy I don't answer to..." Grant finally loops his badge around his neck, then sticks his hands in his trenchcoat pockets as he takes a look around. "*Jesus*. This crime scene really is a *clusterfuck*."

"If you think you can do better—" Darius begins, but Grant cuts him off.

"Of *course* I think I can do better, Lieutenant. This is *amateur hour*. Sky Commando, I'm gonna need you to get those helicopters farther back."

"She doesn't work for you!" Darius is shouting now, spittle spraying out of his mouth.

"Actually she *does*." Grant turns back to Darius and raises his voice. "The Sky Commando Program gets some of its funding from the Department of Homeland Security. That means we can call her in if we deem it appropriate to do so. And hey, guess what? *I deem it appropriate to do so*."

Darius is livid. "You are making a big mistake, 'agent.' You assholes have been throwing your weight around ever since you got here, and it's pissing off all the wrong people."

Agent Grant plants himself directly in front of Darius. Grant is taller, so he leans in until he's only inches away from the Lieutenant's face.

"You know what I'm gonna do about that? Do you?" Grant cocks his head to one side, waiting for a reply.

Darius doesn't answer.

"Well I'll tell you what I'm gonna do," Grant says. "I'm gonna go home, and then I'm gonna cry. I'm gonna cry about how *mean* all the police officers are being to me, and I'm gonna cry about how you hurt my poor, tender feelings. I'm gonna cry, and cry, and cry, and cry, and cry. But then I'm gonna *journal* it, so *I think I'll be OK*."

Alishia is thankful the Sky Commando helmet is completely opaque as she grins from ear to ear. Whatever Agent Grant's metahuman ability may be, it's clear his real super power is being an asshole.

PART TWO: HARUSPEX ANALYTICS

Jason Kline shifts uncomfortably in his chair as he looks at the impassive faces staring back at him. His team has been using the situation room as their primary workspace, and they're used to having it all to themselves. Seeing so many members of the board sitting at the long table is unnerving.

"This sucks." Michelle Lawrence is a small woman who always dresses in sweats—her preferred uniform is gray sweat pants and a blue hoodie. Usually she has the hoodie up, with the drawstring pulled out so far that the hood covers everything but her eyes, nose and mouth. She claims it helps her think, and as far as Jason can tell it works. Today, however, the hood is down, and she's staring at the impassive faces like someone about to face a firing squad.

"You'll be fine," Jason says. "You did all the work, you should get the recognition."

Michelle snorts through her nose, and Jason manages not to smile. The only recognition Michelle is interested in is from people she considers peers. The people who pay the bills are *not* peers.

"Recognition is your job," Michelle says. "You're the team leader, you get the recognition. That was part of the fucking *deal*, dammit."

"OK, yes," Jason says. "I get it. But we don't have enough time to brief me before I brief them. So you have to brief all of us."

Michelle narrows her eyes, but she nods reluctantly.

"We just need a few more minutes to get everything set up," Jason says, turning back to the board members lined up along the far end of the table. As always, they simply stare impassively, betraying no emotion whatsoever.

He turns back to his team. Michelle is staring at her laptop, typing furiously, trying to ignore everything else. To her left Billy and Phyllis are muttering and comparing notes, ever the strange, mismatched, and uncannily effective pair. Billy Davison, a blonde-haired, blue-eyed surfer from California, is pointing at something on his screen, looking at Phyllis questioningly. Phyllis Tanner, a middle-aged black woman with swirls of gray in her hair, shakes her head disapprovingly. Billy shrugs, nods, then turns back to the screen. To *their* left, Simon Yin is hunched over the computer that controls one of the many paneled screens set into all the walls in the room. His long, slender fingers fly over the keyboard, dark eyes glaring at the screen as he frowns slightly.

"Got it." Simon looks up, nodding toward Jason. "He's hooked in."

"All right," Jason says, then stands. "Thank you for your patience. We're still trying to get more intel on what's going on."

"What *is* going on?" asks one of the board members. He's an older, white-haired man with craggy eyebrows and a slightly reddish nose. His expression is just as impassive as the rest of the board members', but his voice betrays impatience.

"Michelle Lawrence was here when it started," Jason says, gesturing to his right. "She'll walk all of us through it as soon as the Chairman arrives."

The members of the board straighten a little. The white-haired man frowns slightly. "He doesn't usually attend meetings."

"Connecting now," Simon says. The paneled screen immediately behind him blinks once, and then the image shifts to display a shadowy silhouette in a darkened room.

"Ah." The Chairman's unmistakable voice comes through the panel speakers crisp and clear. "I can see you all now. Good morning."

"Mr. Chairman," the white-haired board member says respectfully.

"Hello Andrew. I felt circumstances were serious enough for me to sit in on this briefing. Members of the board, I'm afraid we're about to travel through some very unpleasant waters. I'm going to let Jason's team give you the whole story, but the short version is we've just suffered a very serious lapse in security, and it's going to affect how we go forward with Operation Recall."

The impassive mask slips for a moment, and the members of the board look briefly startled.

"Go on, Jason," the Chairman says.

Jason sits, then nods to Michelle. Michelle sighs, then stands.

"I was in the situation room working on something else when one of our triggers went off."

"Triggers?" The white-haired board member, Andrew, leans forward, frowning.

"*Triggers.*" Michelle's eyes blaze. She *hates* being interrupted, especially when it's about something everyone in the audience should know.

"We sent the board a briefing on the changes we made to the security protocols after the assault on the Forrest brownstone," Jason says, trying to give Michelle a little time to calm down. "It was obvious they needed to be updated. One of the changes we made was to put triggers in place to inform us when specific events occurred."

"Please save the rest of your questions until the end," the Chairman adds, and Andrew immediately leans back in his chair, expression neutral.

Jason nods to Michelle.

Michelle takes a quick breath, looks down at her laptop monitor, and continues.

"A little after 1 AM this morning the TriHealth facility in Manhattan was attacked by the metahuman Vigilante of the rogue group Crossfire. The trigger we received was a notice that TriHealth was transferring its sensitive data to its designated remote facility as a result of that breach."

At the mention of *Vigilante* and *Crossfire* Jason can see the board members shifting uncomfortably in their seats. He doesn't blame them. When Michelle first told him, his reaction had bordered on panic. To their credit, they don't interrupt.

"Given the circumstances surrounding the trigger I decided to monitor the situation personally," Michelle says. "It went about as well as could be expected. Security assumed Vigilante was trying to get to the server room, and personnel engaged him on the eighth floor, trying to delay his progress until the data was copied and the servers could be wiped. A security team and three high threat units were on hand as the stairwell underwent rapid sanitization. It is regrettable but not entirely surprising that Vigilante survived. The high threat units and most of the security team did not."

The fidgeting in the audience continues.

"About twelve minutes into the encounter a series of explosions originated from the server room. At that point Vigilante fled the scene. The origin of the explosions has not yet been determined, though it's possible the sanitization agent, which had leaked out of containment and into the 8th floor, was a contributing factor. We'll need time to do a thorough investigation before we can say for certain. We might not get that time."

Jason can see Andrew actively struggling against the desire to interrupt.

Michelle sighs. "A number of protocols are in place to prevent incidents like these from getting even more out of hand. One of the most important is to ensure that our contacts in the NYPD and other response agencies are first responders. Those protocols were in place and, by all appearances, worked well. A highly-placed asset in the NYPD was on the scene and was starting to lock it down when a Code Ultraviolet was issued, and everything started to fall apart."

Andrew apparently can't contain himself any longer. "I apologize

Chairman, and I apologize, Miss Lawrence. But once our assets are on the scene it should be *impossible* for a Code Ultraviolet to be issued."

"I agree," Michelle says. She doesn't sound angry this time. Jason supposes Andrew's apology helped. "As far as we can tell, the Code Ultraviolet did not go through the normal chain of command. I haven't been able to trace its origin yet. Unfortunately, Sky Commando was working the night shift and responded immediately."

Michelle sighs again, this time more heavily. "Our assets attempted to get her to leave—to the extent that they may have compromised themselves, unfortunately—but they were prevented when federal agents intervened. Division M showed up shortly after Sky Commando did and invoked a proximity clause to take control of the scene. Apparently the TriHealth building is close enough to a federal building that the claim had teeth."

"It is." The Chairman has been quiet through the entire briefing, nothing more than a silhouette on his panel. Now all eyes turn toward him. "We have used that proximity to our own benefit on a number of occasions—it's one of the reasons we chose the location. Unfortunately, tonight that worked against us. Miss Lawrence, if you don't mind I'd like to take it from here."

Michelle nods once and sits down, looking relieved.

"Ladies, gentlemen, we have a problem." The Chairman doesn't sound angry, but the tension in the room rises just the same. "If all our protocols were in place and functioning as expected, as Miss Lawrence claims—and I have no reason to doubt it—then there are only two scenarios that adequately explain the Code Ultraviolet being sent out in such an unorthodox fashion."

Jason raises an eyebrow. His team hadn't had any time to speculate on this part of their findings, and in his brief call to the Chairman prior to the meeting they hadn't discussed it.

"First," the Chairman says, "it's possible that Crossfire managed to send it. We have intelligence that links David Bernard, the former Sky Commando, with Crossfire as recently as last week. Bernard was able to seriously complicate our move against the Weekly 832 by calling Sky Commando to the scene, and he may have access to back channels that we're unaware of. Crossfire may have their own access as well—we've long suspected they have their own assets in the NYPD..."

Jason sees some of the board members nodding thoughtfully.

"The other possibility," the Chairman says, "is that the Ultraviolet was triggered by the mole within our organization."

The tension in the room ratchets up even higher.

"You will notice that the entire board was *not* invited to this meeting," the Chairman says. "Those of you who are here have already been vetted and cleared by Kline's team—in other words, the people sitting in this meeting right now are the only people on the Board you can trust. The only exception to that is Mara—she's currently out on assignment, but she has also been cleared and will be briefed accordingly when she returns."

The tension eases a bit.

"Now listen very carefully," the Chairman says. "This incident is going to cost us a great deal. A similar event in our Farraday City location has me convinced that the metahuman Curveball is coordinating with Crossfire, and based on their actions we have to assume that they've made a connection between TriHealth and the death of Liberty. The incident at TriHealth is now a federal matter, and I fully expect that before we can put our own assets on the ground there, the current investigation will uncover a number of very inconvenient things. In other words, there's no doubt we've been compromised and it's going to affect the Project Recall timetable."

The silhouette leans forward so that his features are almost, but not quite, visible. Jason finds himself straining to try to see, but to no avail.

"We're going to have to pivot," the Chairman says, "and put more assets in play. But I don't want to do that until we've found our mole. The damage our traitor did to us this morning will be trivial compared to what he or she might do in the future. That's why I'm directing all of you to make finding this mole your top priority. Project Recall is on *hold* until the traitor is found and dealt with."

Jason looks at his team. Michelle is nodding in agreement. Billy and Phyllis are still hunched over Billy's laptop, murmuring to each other quietly as they argue over some piece of intel they aren't ready to share yet. Simon stares off into space, head tilted to one side... Jason knows that look. Something the Chairman said just gave Yin an idea.

"Everyone in this room now has the same job," the Chairman says. "Find the traitor. Solve the problem. *Make it go away.*"

PART THREE: SCRAPPER JACK

The Tides is an upscale restaurant and nightclub with a downscale gimmick: it only *looks* seedy. The food, drink, and entertainment are top-notch, the service is exceptional, security is always on point. It's the perfect place for rich people to go when they want to feel like they're slumming without actually having to slum. It's also open all night, making it a convenient spot for rich, all-night revelers.

It's 3 AM now, and it looks like business is good.

Jack Barrow stands outside the cinderblock building and stares up at the entrance. There's no one lining up to get in at the moment, but a few seconds ago a rowdy group of well-dressed drunk socialites stumbled through the heavy metal door with more enthusiasm than grace. Standing by the door, leaning against the wall, is a heavily-muscled man in an oil-stained tank top and heavy canvas pants. His massive arms cross in front of his chest, his face wears an expression of disinterested menace. He looks like a thug—a typical street-smart bouncer—but the high-tech earpiece gives it away.

Jack smiles slightly and climbs the steps.

The bouncer eyes him warily. Jack is dressed in his "uniform:" heavy black leather jacket, thick motorcycle boots, white t-shirt, faded denim jeans. It's not the right weather for the jacket, Jack isn't sweating, and the bouncer picks up on that. He doesn't stop leaning against the wall, but Jack can see him tense.

"Not tonight, buddy," the bouncer says.

Jack doesn't stop until he's at the top of the steps, then looks at the bouncer.

"Go on," the bouncer says. "Let's not make this a thing, OK?"

"Then let me in," Jack says.

The bouncer pushes himself off the wall. He doesn't move to Jack, and he doesn't uncross his arms. He's a little taller than Jack is, and he looks bigger. "Management reserves the right to refuse service."

"You're not management," Jack says. "But if Mike Boyle wants to keep me out, that's his business. All he has to do is say so."

The bouncer narrows his eyes. "You know Mike?"

"Knew him," Jack says. "Look, I don't want any trouble. Just tell him that Jack Barrow is here. If he doesn't want to be seen, I'll be on my way."

The bouncer frowns and considers his options. Then he touches his earpiece. "Guy named Jack Barrow wants to see Mike. Claims he knows him."

A brief silence follows as they wait.

The bouncer's hand rises to his earpiece again. "Step over here. They want to see you on camera." He points to a spot immediately in front of the door.

Jack shrugs and stands on the spot, looking around for the camera. He doesn't see anything.

The bouncer holds his hand up to his earpiece, frowning slightly as he listens. Finally he nods. "OK. Sorry for the trouble. Mike's waiting for you at the bar."

"Thanks," Jack says, and steps inside.

The nightclub is to the left, the restaurant is to the right. The first thing Jack notices is that both the nightclub and the restaurant have a bar—for that matter, the nightclub also has tables, and he sees people sitting at the tables eating food as they listen to a guy playing pretty good Spanish guitar on the small stage at the far end of the room.

Jack crosses into the restaurant, which appears to have been designed to look like a saloon from an old western. The floors are scuffed hardwood, the tables are all round with simple straight-backed chairs set around them, and a long bar stretches the length of one wall. Most of the crowd is at the front, near the door. It thins out considerably the farther in you go, and at the very far end, sitting on the very last stool at the bar, is Michael Boyle.

Back in the day he was rail thin and wiry, a little on the short side, with thick, curly red hair. Back then he was always a little unnerving to be around because he was always watching everything, all the time. He'd size you up in a second—you and everyone else in the room—and you could see the wheels turning in his head. It was exhausting to watch him sit and think.

He's not like that now. He looks tired. Haggard. He slumps over the bar, head drooping, one hand idly playing with a half-empty tumbler of yellow-tinted glass. He has more wrinkles than most men at his age, making him look ten or fifteen years older than he should. He doesn't look like Undermind any more. He looks like a tired old guy sitting at a bar.

Boyle doesn't look at him directly, he just glances at Jack's image in the long mirror behind the bar, and raises his glass a few inches off the bar by way of salute. "Jack." Even his voice sounds old and cracked, like a wall just on the verge of crumbling away. "Drink?"

Jack shrugs, then nods. Boyle gestures with his glass to one of the bartenders, and in short order an identical yellow-tinted glass tumbler is set in front of Jack.

They toast in silence, then drink. It's scotch, good scotch. Jack takes a moment to appreciate it.

"You look good," Boyle says.

"Thanks," Jack says. "Sorry for dropping by. If you're anything like me, you don't appreciate reunions."

Boyle smiles slightly. "You, I don't mind. Business or pleasure?"

"Business," Jack says. "Still don't mind?"

Boyle shrugs. "I don't mind, but I don't have much to offer. I'm retired." He gestures vaguely. "Retired, and just tired. I don't really have my head in it any more."

"No shame in that," Jack says. "I like the place."

Boyle's smile grows a little, softening the lines on his face. "Yeah. I did good here. Nobody thought this location would work, but I did my homework. And the staff... it's all about your employees. Mine are only slightly corrupt." He chuckles at that.

"I get that you're out of the game," Jack says. "And I'm the last guy who'd try to pull you back in."

"What about you?" Boyle turns to face Jack now, and there's a hint of his old self in his eyes. "You're the last person I thought would be back in the game."

"I'm not," Jack says. "Not exactly. This is... unique."

The curtain draws back, and suddenly the old Boyle is there: absolutely still on the outside, working like crazy everywhere else. He finishes his drink and sets the empty glass down on the bar. "Let's talk in my office."

Jack takes his drink with him.

Boyle's office is nice and large, a combination living room, executive office, and fully-stocked mini-kitchen. The front sports a u-shaped couch and a flatscreen TV and stereo system. The middle of the room has his desk, a fancy one with a cherry oak top, with three comfortable chairs in front and a fancy executive chair behind. In the back of the room are a few heavy, metal filing cabinets set against the left wall. The mini-kitchen, which includes a small stove, sink, and a full-sized refrigerator, is set against the right. On the far wall is a large window covered with large, dark gray blinds.

Boyle sinks into the fancy executive chair. "Lock the door—deadbolt at the top—then have a seat."

The deadbolt slides into place with a satisfying *click* and Jack turns his attention back to the man sitting behind the fancy desk.

Boyle gestures to an empty chair. "Might as well make it official."

Jack nods, crosses the room and sits, placing his drink down on the desk. Boyle immediately picks up the drink, slides a coaster under it, and sets it down again.

Somebody's proud of that desk.

"So, Mr. Barrow, how can I help you today?" Boyle is looking even more like his old self—Jack can practically *feel* the wheels turning as the smaller man focuses on his new client.

"I need to know about a company that does business in New York. Nobody knows much."

Boyle nods. "And the name of this company?"

"Haruspex Analytics."

For an instant the old-Boyle facade crumbles. Boyle's eyes widen, his body goes rigid, and his jaw clenches as he sucks in air through his teeth, hissing loudly. The moment passes, and the old-Boyle facade returns: he leans back in his chair, his left arm folded around his chest, the right hand resting under his chin. His eyes narrow, his brow furrows, he purses his lips thoughtfully.

"You've heard of them," Jack says.

"Yes." Boyle opens a desk drawer and produces a bottle of scotch and a fresh yellow-tinted tumbler. He opens the bottle, fills his glass, and tops off Jack's. "Yes, I have. What are they to you?"

Jack frowns. The question is a little too casual given Boyle's initial reaction.

"They're mixed up in something I'm working."

Boyle grabs his tumbler and drinks quickly. He exhales, sets the empty glass down with a *thunk*, then grabs the bottle of scotch. "Go work something else."

Jack shrugs.

"I'm not kidding." Boyle fills the tumbler almost all the way to the top. "They are not good people."

"*We* are not good people," Jack says.

"*We* are far better people than most of the law-abiding public who ever pointed their fingers at us and called us 'villain,'" Boyle says. He sets the bottle down. "Haruspex, though... they *work hard* for that title."

"What do they do?" Jack asks. "So far all I've got is that they sell security software for computers."

"They do that." Boyle picks up the tumbler, drains it in seconds, then sets it back on the desk with another *thunk*. "That's their *cover story*. The truth... well, I don't know the truth."

He grabs the scotch and refills his tumbler to the brim.

Jack points at the bottle. "You're hitting that a little hard for not knowing what they do."

"I don't *need* to know," Boyle says. He drains the glass a third time; when he sets it back down on his desk—no coaster, Jack notices—his eyes are a bit glazed. "First time I ever heard about them, I admit I was curious. I was retired, but I still had contacts, you know? So I reached out to one and asked a few questions."

Boyle considers the bottle of scotch, then pushes it away.

"They killed him, Jack. They did it in a way they shouldn't have been able to, in a place they shouldn't have been able to *get* to. It was a mess—he didn't go easy. Then they sent me a goddamn sympathy card with a newspaper article covering the whole thing. They wrote 'thinking of you' at the bottom of the card."

Jack raises an eyebrow. "That sounds a bit loud for these guys."

"It's different for me," Boyle says. "I talk their language. They weren't interested in hiding from me, but they also weren't interested in killing me. It was too close to my retirement, back then. I had too many allies."

"You still have allies, Mickey." Jack leans forward. "If you need protection—"

Boyle's laugh is bitter and hollow. "No point. Don't get me wrong, Jack, I appreciate it. You're a stand-up guy, and a hell of an ally in a straight-up fight. But these guys are..."

He breaks off, shrugs, then sinks back in his chair, closing his eyes. "Tell me something, Jack—let me ask you a question. When we first started out, where did you think we'd be right now?"

Jack considers the question. "Ruling the world, I guess."

Boyle laughs again, the genuine article this time. "I guess that's what I thought, too."

"Didn't work out that way," Jack says.

"It did not," Boyle agrees. "Too bad for everyone. You know, I never believed in utopias until I met LaFleur..."

"He never promised us a utopia, Mickey," Jack says. "You remember the speech."

Boyle nods. "Yeah, yeah. 'There is no perfect way, only a *best* way. And the best way is still a road paved with suffering, and sacrifice, and men and women who will die before our struggle ends...' He was real good at killing the mood sometimes."

"He never wanted mindless support," Jack says. "He was always weeding out people who were in it for the wrong reasons. He wanted people in for the long haul. You know. Resolve."

"Yeah," Boyle says. "Grim, sober resolve... Well. *Dammit*. When you put it that way..."

He stands suddenly, pushing the chair away with enough force to send it a few feet out into the room. He goes over to one of his filing cabinets and pulls out the top drawer. It slides out until it reaches the end of the rails, then stops. Boyle tugs harder, and the entire drawer pulls out and *crashes* to the floor, banging and scraping against the cabinet all the way down. Files—real, honest-to-God paper files—fly into the air, fluttering around Boyle like oversized confetti.

"Jesus, Mickey..."

Boyle waves him off. "Nevermind that. Hold on a second." He reaches into the cabinet space with both arms and tugs. Moments later he pulls out two heavy metal boxes. "Here we are."

Boyle staggers, both from the weight of the boxes and from the scotch, as he makes his way back to his desk. He drops the larger box on the desk in front of Jack, then retrieves his chair and sits, the smaller box resting in his lap.

Jack looks at the large box. "What's this?"

"It's how you approach a problem sideways," Boyle says. "You know the difference between active and passive sonar?"

"I guess," Jack says. "Active sonar is more accurate, but it makes noise, so the Germans can tell when you're using it."

Boyle's mouth quirks. "Germans?"

"Old war movies," Jack says. "Anyway, passive just listens, right? If you listen long enough you can track the movement of whatever you're listening to."

"Good enough. Well I started listening to anything that might be Haruspex-related. I didn't hire anyone out, I didn't communicate with anyone, I didn't store anything on a computer. I just listened, and took notes, and eventually I started to get a feel for who the players were. It's all in that box."

Jack looks at the box again.

"Go ahead, Jack. Take it."

Jack picks up the box. It's a rectangular, light gray box with a flip-top hinge. The latch is a lever that flips right to lock, left to unlock. He flips the lever to the left and the top pops open a bit, as if the contents were under pressure. He opens the top and sees a stack of notepads. He pages through the first notepad—page after page is covered with Boyle's research, written in tiny black script.

"That's a lot of passive sonar," Jack says.

Boyle laughs.

"Thanks for this." Jack closes the box and flips the lever to the left, locking it in place.

"Don't thank me just yet." There's something funny in Boyle's voice—it's light and cheerful, in the way someone tries to sound when they're trying not to cry. Jack looks up and sees Boyle, staring at Jack intently. The smaller box in his lap is open, revealing a heavy caliber revolver.

Jack looks at the gun, then at Boyle. "Mickey..."

"Funny thing about those guys." Boyle's voice is still cheerful—forced-cheerful—but his attempt at a smile looks more like a grimace. "A week after I got that letter I found a bug in my office. A good one—I almost missed it. I tore the office apart looking for more, found a few... and then a week later I found the same bug, same make and model, in the *exact same location I found it before*. So I tore my office apart again, found a few more, and a week later, guess what I found?"

"Just put the gun on the table," Jack says.

"Nobody ever saw them come in," Boyle says. "Nobody was aware that anyone unauthorized had been here at all. There was nothing on any of my surveillance equipment—and that was stuff I installed myself, Jack. I'm a guy who knows what he's doing when it comes to things like that."

"Calm down," Jack says.

"I figured they were politely letting me know that they were keeping tabs on me," Boyle says. "They wanted me to know that they were listening, and there wasn't a damn thing I could do about it. Think about that, Jack. Think about what it means. It means *they're listening to us talking right now*."

"Mickey." Jack stops trying to be soothing and makes his voice as hard as it can go without shouting. "You know that gun isn't going to do a damn thing to me. So put it on the table and *calm down.*"

Boyle's eyebrows shoot up in surprise. He looks down at the gun in his lap. Then he smiles and shakes his head.

"Gun's not for you, Jack."

"Mickey—"

"You're probably going to want to go out the window. Just my advice."

"*Mickey—*"

"You're being played, Jack." Boyle picks up the revolver and calmly places the barrel in his mouth.

Jack is already moving, but he's not a speedster. He's sitting, the desk is in his way... there's too much between him, the man, and his intent. He's vaulting over the desk when Boyle pulls the trigger. The sound is enormous, deafening, just like every other time. Boyle's head jerks back as his body falls back into his chair. There is no exit wound.

The room smells like gunpowder.

"Jesus, *Mickey.*" Jack can't hear past the ringing in his ears. He stares down at the body a moment, then turns to grab the metal box off the table. He sees the doorknob on the office door moving; someone is trying to get in. He still can't hear anything, but he imagines people are shouting right now.

You're going to want to go out the window. Just my advice.

Jack runs to the window. He doesn't bother slowing down—a foot away from the wall and he jumps *through* the window, crashing through the blinds, shattering through the glass, and landing in a crouch in a narrow alley between the restaurant and another building. Glass tears at his clothing, but it does nothing at all to him, and after he shrugs the tattered remains of the blinds to one side he gathers his strength and *jumps.*

You're being played, Jack.

It's not flying, but it does what he needs. In seconds he's a block away from the restaurant. In a few more seconds he's further still. A few seconds later he stops running, orients himself, and makes his way back to the safehouse. He has reading to do.

PART FOUR: UNKNOWN LOCATION, TROPICAL CLIMATE

David Bernard finds the fishing cottage right on the treeline. It's old, but someone has lived there recently—the area around the house is clear of brush, the roof is in good shape, and the walls were painted within the last year. There doesn't appear to be anyone around at the moment.

David should leave the place alone—it's obviously still being used, and there's too much of a risk, given the lack of any other information, that whoever uses it will come by today. But David's head is throbbing harder than it was earlier, he's getting dizzier, and his vision is blurring with more frequency. The cottage is kept up. Someone lives there. It might have medicine.

He sways on his feet as a wave of nausea washes over him. He's going to have to risk it.

The front door is unlocked. A part of him finds that unusual, the rest of him is too relieved to care.

The cottage has four rooms: living area, kitchen, bedroom, bathroom, all furnished and fully stocked. It also has electricity and running water. This is not a shack that someone comes to on a fishing vacation, this is someone's *home*. David goes back to the front door, locks it, and slides a deadbolt across for good measure. That should give him some warning if the occupant returns at an inconvenient moment.

He goes to the bathroom and starts rummaging. The mirror over the bathroom sink opens up and David sighs in relief when he sees pretty much everything he needs: a thick roll of gauze, tape, rubbing alcohol, scissors, cotton balls, needle, thread, and—probably most important—acetaminophen. He was afraid he was going to find aspirin. He usually prefers aspirin, but he has a half-formed memory of a doctor lecturing him about aspirin and how it can make the bruising of a concussion worse.

He fumbles with the acetaminophen bottle, cursing the plastic child-proof cap as it takes him six tries to twist it open. He tries to read the recommended dosage on the back but he can't focus on text that small. He guesses the dosage, counts out six, and swallows them dry, two at a time. He gags the third time, but manages to force them down.

Next he sets about cleaning the wound. His eyes keep unfocusing, so it's hard to see what he's doing in the mirror, but leaning against the bathroom wall keeps him feeling steady, and his hands aren't shaking like they were earlier. He picks up scissors and starts cutting his hair, clearing it away from the wound so he can clean it more easily. There's no way he can do this with any precision, so he ignores his vanity and cuts off as much hair as he can. When he's cleared as much as he can manage, he turns on the spigot, grabs the cotton balls and the rubbing alcohol, and starts cleaning the wound.

The cut isn't deep, just bloody. Cleaning it stings like hell, but when he's finished and he covers it with gauze he feels better. He wants to sleep, but he knows he can't sleep here. The owner is going to return, and he needs to be gone by then.

His stomach growls. Maybe he'll raid the refrigerator first.

The kitchen is fully stocked, and whoever lives here eats well. The refrigerator is packed with healthy food, fresh fruit, and there's even a gallon jug of milk. He grabs the milk, finds a glass in one of the cupboards, and sits down at the kitchen table. He unscrews the jug, gives it a whiff. Smells fresh. He pours the milk into the glass, and it looks fresh. He drinks greedily.

It's not until he's finished pouring a second glass that he notices the expiration date on the jug. He starts, spilling a little milk over the side, and hastily sets the jug down on the table to get a better look.

EXPIR 7/22/92

That's when he notices the calendar hanging on the wall between the kitchen and the living room.

JULY 1992

Some of the spilled milk starts to seep into a newspaper folded up and sitting to the right of the chair. He picks it up.

PORT LIBERTAD DAILY

Saturday, July 18, 1992

He stares at the date for a moment. The paper doesn't feel that old—and the milk tasted fine.

You have a concussion. You can't be sure the milk tasted fine.

Except that he's pretty sure. What's more, he's pretty sure the milk wasn't *twenty years old*.

The bottom half of the newspaper falls down, revealing the entire page. David is immediately drawn to the large photo in the center: a white-haired man in gleaming metal armor, a cape bolted to his shoulders, a circlet or crown of some sort resting on his head. He has a noble and benevolent face. He looks familiar.

The caption reads: *Emperor LaFleur addresses the nation today. He is expected to make it clear that he will tolerate no attempts by so-called "liberation forces" to set foot on sovereign soil.*

LaFleur? David looks at the picture again. That face... he's seen that face...

He's sitting in the cargo bay of a plane, checking the straps to his parachute for the seventh time. LaFleur is sitting across from him, doing the same.

"After we jump it's likely we'll be separated." LaFleur has to raise his voice to be heard over the engines of the plane. "I'm sorry for that. It's going to be a difficult transition..."

The memory fades. David stares at the photo in amazement.

"Overmind." It's the first thing he's said since he woke up that morning. "This man is Overmind."

David stands up. He's feeling lightheaded again. He really needs to rest, soon.

"This man is Overmind... and *I know him*."

CURVEBALL
18
OCT 2014
CURVEBALL
A Prose Comic
A GAME OF SECRETS
STORY
CHRISTOPHER WRIGHT
COVER
PASCALLE LEPAS
LOGO
GARTH GRAHAM

PART ONE: FARRADAY CITY, DOWNTOWN

When it was still a thriving beach resort the Farraday City skyline *was* the beach: the largest buildings were the hotels, forming a wall of concrete and glass between land and sea. They were lighthouses in reverse, guiding travelers from the lands further in to the great waters beyond.

The old skyline remains, abandoned and weathered, long since fallen into disrepair. What had once been the reason for the city's prosperity is now left to rot, or collapse, or perhaps to one day be swallowed up by the sea itself. Until then the buildings have been claimed by two-bit slumlords and kingpins. The regular hotels are tenements, the luxury resorts have been claimed by petty crime lords with delusions of grandeur. Their fiefdoms exist only among the dregs—nobody but the Boardwalk cares about the Boardwalk, and lords of that part of the city have no standing anywhere else.

The new Farraday City skyline is downtown: the business district is new, and modern, and clean, and while the buildings of steel and glass aren't the tallest in the world, they're tall enough to say *now the center is here*.

Next to the business district is the casino district, Farraday City's new draw. The casino district isn't laid out like Vegas—it's not a single strip you drive down, with all the temptations lined up on each side as you pass. It's more like Disneyland: it's spread out like an amusement park for adults, with casinos and clubs and restaurants and hotels scattered across a wide campus, interspersed with parks and plazas and promenades. Lights flash on every corner, neon signs shine brighter than street lamps, and the unending thump of bass rolls across the grounds, bouncing off the walls and making the windows buzz.

It's garish and cheerful and brazen and manic, and from CB's perch atop the Denarius Financial Building it looks like an impressionist painting created by an artist who is constantly changing his mind. He looks down on the casino district, watching the cars race around the outer loop, watching groups of people go from casino to nightclub to hotel to casino. As he watches he smokes, and as he smokes he tries to focus.

He's very, very tired. He hasn't slept in days. His mind is a jumble of half-uncovered facts, rumors, agitation, and unanswered questions. He smokes his cigarette slowly, patiently waiting for the nicotine to do its job. Half a cigarette later he starts to calm down, starts to focus, and by the time he's finished his first, he's alert enough to sort through the puzzles one more time.

TriHealth. Plague. Richter. Haruspex Analytics. Senator Tobias Morgan. Magic, of all things. All connected, somehow.

All connected, though the connections aren't obvious. Plague and Richter aren't working through TriHealth—they're lying low, building their own network of suppliers and local goons. CB was able to find the "outer layer," the street thugs who acted as their eyes and ears in the city, and then after leaning on one a bit he traced their supply chain up to the Farraday City Police Department—but after that it disappears completely.

The way they've settled in is interesting: he doesn't understand why they aren't using TriHealth's resources. There is absolutely no activity or communication between TriHealth and Richter's group, yet somehow Richter has access to people in the FCPD—well-placed people, considering how thoroughly the trail vanishes at that point. You don't just waltz into town and start bribing cops, even if the cops are dirty—*especially* if the cops are dirty and *already working for someone else*.

"It doesn't make sense," CB mutters.

"No," a voice behind him says. "It doesn't."

CB tenses but doesn't turn. He didn't hear anyone approach, so he was either very sloppy—possible, considering how tired he is—or the person speaking is *very, very good*. In either case he needs to keep his cool. He forces himself to relax, takes a long drag from his dwindling cigarette, and turns around. Standing in front of him are *two* men, both wearing pinstripe suits and bowler hats. The smaller man is very thin, with a birdlike face, bright, sharp eyes, and a vague, empty smile. The larger man, solid and looming, looks on indifferently.

The small man tips his hat and bends into a half-bow. "Apologies." His smile sharpens for a moment, slipping from empty to predatory, then fading back to empty again. "We didn't intend to startle you. We simply thought this was the opportune moment to talk."

CB flicks the remains of his cigarette onto the rooftop and says nothing.

The predatory grin returns. "Yes," the smaller man says. "To the point. Indeed. If I may approach?"

CB shrugs. He watches warily as the small man walks up to the edge of the building and looks down over the multicolored spectacle of the casino district, just as CB had moments earlier. The larger man does not follow.

"My partner is a great believer in doing only what is necessary," the smaller man says. "I don't mean that he's lazy—far from it. A true professional, that man, and his dedication to his work is nothing short of *inspirational.*"

The large man doesn't react in any way to the smaller man's words.

"What I mean," the smaller man continues, "is that he believes in determining *exactly what is necessary* and in doing no more than that. You can think of it as conservation of energy, I suppose, though it's rather more than that."

"It's his schtick," CB says.

The smaller man laughs: high-pitched, full of mirth, deeply unsettling. "No! Not a *schtick*, as you call it. It's *him*. It is proof of who and what he is, the expression of his inner being... his *soul* at its most basic. Though I confess..." The man's voice lowers conspiratorially. "I confess that I once thought as you did. Not for the same reason. I thought it because of my vanity, because I believed that every part of the universe could be understood through *me*. You think it because..."

The small man turns to look at him then, his empty smile gone, replaced with a thoughtful frown. "Because it is *tactically sound*, I suppose."

CB suppresses an urge to take a step away from the strange man. "Who did you say you were, again?"

"Oh, my name isn't important." The small man banishes the notion with a dismissive wave of his left hand. "What is important, for you at least, is who my partner and I *represent*."

The small man turns toward the view once again.

CB regards him for a moment. "You represent whoever actually runs this city."

The empty smile returns. "Quite."

They say nothing else. The small man continues to admire the view. The large man continues to stand impassively at the center of the roof. CB watches both warily, waiting for something to happen.

"We're not here to fight," the small man says. "Not tonight. Someday we will—that is inevitable—but today, at our very first meeting, we find ourselves... allies, to a degree. Strange."

"Allies." CB doesn't bother to hide his skepticism.

"Oh, I know." The small man laughs, takes a step back from the edge of the roof and *spins*, throwing his arms wide as he twirls and laughs more, like a child discovering a new game for the first time. "Politics makes for strange bedfellows, but *religion*? It makes for the *strangest*."

"OK," CB says, "it's been fun. Really. But I'm getting a little tired of this game, and—"

"No games, oh Cat Who Observes Himself." The man stops spinning abruptly, facing CB and peering up at him with his bright, sharp eyes. "It's an imprecise term, to be sure, but what else applies? Politics is a clash of what people believe should be. *Religion* is a clash of what *is*, whether people want it to be or not. And we are at odds, you see—on a very fundamental level, on a level far, far beneath all the bits of matter that fly across the universe in their strange and intricate dances, you and I represent things that cannot share the same space. And yet here we are, you and I, on the same roof, breathing the same air, enjoying the same magnificent view."

"Uh-huh." CB fishes around in his pockets for his cigarettes. "It's a pretty good monologue, I'll give you that. I've heard a lot worse. You've got a knack for it."

The small man tips his hat again. "It's my vanity, I'm afraid. It makes me best suited for talking to the world, but it does lead me astray..."

"Just to recap." CB takes out a cigarette and sticks it in his mouth while he fishes for his lighter. "You're the arch enemy I never knew I had, on some kind of fundamental level of reality I'm not aware of, but just this once we're besties."

"Just this once," the small man agrees. "With so much at stake, how can we not be?"

"At stake?" CB shakes his head. "What's at stake? What's really going on?"

The small man lifts a single finger, bringing it up to his lips swiftly in a decisive shushing motion. "A dangerous question. The rules that govern our game do not provide answers to such questions—not without great cost."

CB lights his cigarette. "I'll bet. What cost is that?"

"'My tongue cleaves to my jaws, and you lay me in the dust of death.'"

"I'm pretty sure you're using that out of context," CB says. "Almost positive."

The small man ducks his head and shrugs. "The point, oh Cat, is that the rules of this game govern the consequences of discovering secret things. Learn such a secret and you will have power, but you will find yourself unable to share it with another."

"That doesn't make any sense," CB says.

"It does, actually. Just think of the stories." The small man chuckles to himself. "You find it used so often that it's practically a *cliché*. The old wizard gathers together a band of young, brash heroes. He doesn't tell them directly what must be done—he speaks in riddles. All through the tale, only in riddles, and the heroes must solve those riddles to learn what must be done. And each time such a story is told, someone invariably asks *why doesn't the old wizard simply tell them what to do?* The answer is that, on some level, the storyteller understands the price of such knowledge. The old wizard cannot say what is true because he is not permitted to do it. The cost of knowing a secret truth is that *it will remain a secret.*"

CB thinks back to his last conversation with Lieutenant Larry Hoydt. *Pay attention to what I'm saying. I.* ***Can't****. Tell you.* "This is getting a little too meta for my taste. Aren't you revealing a secret to me now? Shouldn't the rule apply here as well?"

The small man laughs again, obviously delighted. "Yes! Yes, it should! In most cases it would. But this is an unusual situation, and in unusual situations allowances are made..."

"What situation?" CB feels his patience starting to fray. There's something about the small man he doesn't like, something that goes beyond the obvious act of declaring himself an enemy. He feels *wrong*.

"You have asked," the small man says. The mirth drops from him like a falling curtain, replaced by an oddly respectful formality. "And so I will answer. Let us assume, for the sake of argument, that there is a war being waged between two armies. We will, for the time being, name these armies 'good' and 'evil.' They are clumsy, unwieldy terms, but within the limits of language they come close enough to the mark to be useful."

"A war between good and evil," CB says, voice flat. "That's what this is about."

"No," the small man says. "That is what *our* fight is about—the one that will come, in time, if this matter is resolved. But the war is more complicated than two armies clashing on the field at dawn. If you were to focus on a single army—let's focus on the 'good' army in our example—then you would find that there is as much fighting within as there is fighting against its foe. Each soldier in that army heartily agrees on the ultimate aim, you see, but they do not agree on the methods that should be used to achieve it... and many disagree on what should come after, if the fight is won."

The small man spreads his arms wide. "They argue over structure, you see. What should it look like? How much of it should there be? How does a world where 'evil' is defeated actually work? They argue without resolution, and eventually they come to blows, so now there are *two* wars, one without, one within."

CB regards the small man warily. "And on the other side?"

"The same. The same disagreements, the same fights. And one day, one of the factions on one side notices one of the factions on the other side, and they come to realize how very similar their views on *structure* actually are."

CB laughs—a short, barking laugh of surprised disbelief. "This sounds like a bad fantasy novel. What are we talking, Law versus Chaos?"

"No," the small man says. "Control versus self-determination."

CB doesn't reply.

"We are not, under normal circumstances, allies," the small man says. "But if there is one thing upon which you and I agree, it is that we believe, to varying degrees, that people must be free to choose their own way. You believe it because you think they will pick themselves up, I believe it because I believe they will drag themselves down. But the ones we oppose, oh Cat? The ones we must unite against, lest they claim the entire game for their own? They do not believe it at all."

PART TWO: BENJAMIN HOTEL, NYC

Martin Forrest knows his brother-in-law is waiting for him in his room before he even walks into the lobby: the Senator's car is parked on the street, a conspicuous armored black sedan with government plates. He forces himself not to roll his eyes as he nods to one of the Secret Service agents standing by the door—he's met enough of them to recognize their faces, even if they aren't forthcoming with their names. The agent doesn't reply, of course, but he has no doubt that his arrival is being passed on up the chain. He steels himself: meeting with Toby is never pleasant, always exhausting, and he's already tired.

The elevator is empty, and the trip to the fifth floor is far too short. Two of the Secret Service are stationed by the elevator, two more by his hotel room door. As he walks toward his room, one of the men steps forward, arm outstretched.

"*No*," Martin says.

The man stops for a moment, blinking in surprise.

"If you think for a minute that I am going to agree to be searched before being allowed in *my room* you are out of your damn mind." Martin hates lashing out at a guy who's just doing his job, but damn it all if Toby doesn't bring it out of him when he pulls stunts like this.

"It's OK." The voice is muffled through the door, but it's obviously Tobias. "It's all right. Just let him in."

The Secret Service agent returns to the side of the door. The other agent opens it for him. Martin walks through, muttering an apology under his breath.

The Benjamin is a fine hotel, but they needed a room in a hurry and couldn't afford one of the elaborate suites. The room is perfect for a vacation—one king-sized bed with everything arranged around it—but it's going to be another month before they can move back into the house, and Martin is starting to feel cramped. Senator Tobias Morgan sits in front of the room's one desk, set against the wall between the bed and window. His briefcase is open, stacks of paper spilling out over its edge and onto the desk itself.

"What are you doing here, Toby?" Martin goes over to the small closet, takes off his jacket, and puts it on a hanger.

Tobias stands. "I'm sorry. I should have told the men to just let you by—it didn't even occur to me. And I know it was a bad idea to come. I know that. Too much bad blood between you and me, and me and Julie, a lot of it my fault. But I'm stuck, Martin. People are trying to force me to take actions that are going to make matters between us so much worse than they are right now, and I really don't want that."

He sounds sincere, but that doesn't mean much.

"What are you talking about?" Martin demands. He goes over to the king-sized bed and sits on the edge, glowering at Tobias the whole way. "And where's Julie?"

"I don't know," Tobias says. "She was out when I arrived, which is why I... broke in."

Martin shakes his head.

"It's important," Tobias says. "Important to you. Jenny is in trouble."

Martin's heart skips a beat. He feels his blood run cold. "Jenny?"

"There's no easy way to say this," Tobias says. "Jenny... I have video footage of your daughter shooting a security guard with his own weapon."

The room sways for a moment. Martin places one hand on the bed to keep his balance. "What?"

"I'm sorry," Tobias says. "I was trying to think of a better way to tell you, but there's no good way to say that."

"Video footage," Martin repeats. His voice sounds hoarse and raw in his ears. "It's real?"

"I think so," Tobias says.

"Why would she shoot a security guard?" Martin isn't shouting, but he's working up to it. "That doesn't make sense."

"In her defense," Tobias says, "it looks like she was being held hostage by the guard. The whole situation is complicated."

"And why do you know this before I do?" Martin's voice is getting more and more shrill. "I'm her father for—"

Tobias raises one hand, and Martin breaks off. The sudden silence is startling—he didn't realize how loud he'd been.

"They told me because this is very much a federal matter." Tobias reaches into his jacket and pulls out a flask. He unscrews the top and offers it to Martin.

Martin smells gin. He takes the flask and drinks. "I think you'd better tell me everything."

Tobias reaches into his briefcase and pulls out a stack of papers. He sets them on the bed beside Martin.

"I'll need you to sign those," Tobias says. "What I'm about to tell you is classified. I'm reading you in."

Martin takes another sip from the flask.

"I told you this situation was complicated," Tobias says. "I wasn't lying. Just... hear me out before you start shouting, OK?"

Martin nods.

"It starts with the Pit," Tobias says. "I sit on a committee responsible for its funding and oversight. It's a mess. Due to our metahuman incarceration policies, it's filling up faster than it's emptying out. Due to the special equipment it requires to counteract metahuman abilities, it's much too expensive to just build another one. Essentially we're stuck: we need the one we have, we can't afford to build another, and in less than two years we're going to run out of room."

It's something Martin has heard before. The problem of overcrowding at the Pit had become a resource management nightmare for the warden and her people, and a civil rights nightmare for the ACLU. The part about it filling up in two years is new, though.

"Fortunately," Tobias says, "we haven't been sitting on our hands for this one. Ten years ago we stumbled across a potential solution for the problem we knew was coming. And now we're very close to making that solution real."

Martin hands the flask back to Tobias. "What solution?"

Tobias takes a drink. "It's called Project Rosegarden. It's a form of gene therapy—well, not exactly. I get the specifics wrong every time I sit in on a briefing. The big picture is that you can inject a metahuman with some kind of drug that alters a metahuman's DNA and chemically suppresses their abilities."

"Really?" Martin stares at Tobias in astonishment. "It can actually do that?"

"We are very, very close," Tobias says. "I'm told it's only a matter of months before we start formal trials. If we can get this to work we won't *need* a facility like the Pit, except for the most extreme cases... we can transfer prisoners to normal facilities. We can even start granting *parole*. If this works then the entire issue of managing metahuman criminal behavior changes forever."

Martin thinks about that for a second. "And someone won't like it."

"Hell, Martin, I'm one of its supporters and even *I* don't *like* it." Tobias sighs and rubs his temples. "It's a constitutional nightmare. People will compare it to forced sterilizations, and... well, it's not a bad argument. Right now we're looking at it as a more humane alternative to locking a metahuman up until they die, but... you know how these things go."

Martin looks at Tobias curiously. "What do you mean?"

"I mean eventually someone is going to get the bright idea to use it *more*," Tobias says. "They'll say 'let's mandate that it be used on metahumans who can't control their abilities,' and someone will sponsor a bill to do just that. And if it passes, then someone *else* will sponsor a bill giving parents the right to use the treatment on their metahuman children, if their children are found to be in medical peril. And then someone else will mandate that it be used on anyone not willing to register with the government. Eventually it's going to go too far."

"That sounds like Alex talking," Martin says.

"Yeah," Tobias says. "Granddad and I used to talk about this a lot. Argued, really. He didn't approve, but he also couldn't think of anything better..."

"What does this have to do with Jenny?"

"Right. Sorry." Tobias takes a breath. "We've tried to keep this research secret for a number of reasons, but there are two big ones. The first is purely PR—how it will be received, especially by some people in the metahuman community. The second is a bit murkier, ethically speaking. Rosegarden is based on technology we pulled out of PRODIGY."

"Ah." Martin nods slowly. "Yes, I can see how that would be a problem."

"It's a hard sell," Tobias admits. "PRODIGY focused on turning metahumans into remote attack drones. The technology involved was invasive, there's no other word for it. But the *research* that went into that tech... well, even Granddad said it would be a waste not to use it. And PRODIGY had set up an extensive network of medical facilities that it used to conduct this research, and all of those facilities were organized under a dummy corporation posing as an insurance company. TriHealth."

"Which is a legitimate business now," Martin says.

"Yes..." Tobias shifts uncomfortably. "It is, but we're still using it to continue the work on Rosegarden."

"I... guess that makes sense," Martin says. "Might as well use what's already there instead of building it over again. And?"

Tobias looks away. "The incident involving Jenny took place at a

TriHealth facility."

A sharp pang shoots through Martin's chest as he takes a ragged breath. "Tell me."

"They tripped an alarm at a TriHealth facility in Farraday City, of all places," Tobias says. "The guards all had digital video recording equipment embedded in their uniforms. Based on the footage we recovered, they attempted to subdue Curveball and failed—he took most of them out non-lethally. However, one of them was holding Jenny at gunpoint, and—well, the video doesn't show exactly how it happened, but we have a clear image of Jenny pointing the guard's own gun at him and firing twice."

"You said it was self defense," Martin says.

"I'm pretty sure it was," Tobias says. "It looks like the guard had her at gunpoint. But... that's tough to prove. And apparently the thing she did—the... move she used on the guard—I'm told that takes quite a bit of training to pull off."

"She trained with Alex," Martin says. "Since she was a kid. It was a thing they did, for some reason."

"Oh," Tobias says, then frowns. "*Oh*. Well. That explains it. But it gets more complicated, Martin. Don't get me wrong—I know we have our issues, but I also know you raised Jenny right. She's a good kid. And I may not like Curveball, but I made my peace with the fact that he was a legitimate hero a long time ago. But a few days ago *Crossfire* attacked the TriHealth building downtown, and we're pretty sure they're the ones who blew up my house in Schenectady."

Martin connects the dots. "Oh, no."

"Yeah," Tobias says. "Crossfire are officially classified as terrorists, Martin. And whatever the truth may be, right now it *looks like* Curveball and Jenny are colluding with them. People want to go after them, hard, and the only reason nothing has happened yet is because I'm spending a *lot* of political goodwill to hold that off. I can't do that forever."

"I have to talk this over with Julie," Martin says.

Tobias nods. "I understand. Look, sign those papers—there are some for Juliet as well—talk it over, decide what to do. But if you decide to try to contact Jenny, please let me know. If I can tell everyone that steps are being taken to extract her, we can make sure our people don't get in the way. Or even help, if you'll let us."

Martin nods. "We'll talk it over and call your office."

Tobias gathers up his papers, puts them in his briefcase, and closes it with a click. "I'm sorry. I know we don't—we haven't—what I mean is—"

"Yeah," Martin says. He smiles weakly. "I get it. Thanks Toby."

"We're family," Tobias says. "And honest to God... we've already been through enough."

They shake hands for the first time in years. Tobias leaves, taking the Secret Service with him. Martin is left alone with his thoughts, wondering what to believe.

PART THREE: FARRADAY CITY BUNKER

"Again," Red Shift says.

Jenny grits her teeth, narrows her eyes, and swings at him with all her strength.

She isn't trying for finesse, and Red Shift isn't trying to dodge. He's moving just enough to keep his force field active, but he takes the blow square in the chest. The force of the impact staggers him, but he recovers quickly.

"Again."

"Why?" She tries to conceal the frustration in her voice, but she knows it isn't working. She doesn't understand why he's making her do this. She's much stronger than she used to be, but that's not how she should be fighting. Her great-grandfather hadn't used brute force, he used discipline and finesse. That's how she was trained to fight. That's how she should be fighting.

"You need to know what it feels like," Red Shift says.

"What are you talking about?" Jenny's frustration boils over and her volume rises considerably. "What am I supposed to feel?"

"Your *limits*," Red Shift says. "You're in a new body, Zero. Cocooning helped you adjust to it for the most part, but the rational part of you is still thinking in terms of what you used to be able to do. You need to know what it feels like to really push your new body to its limits."

"By hitting you?" Jenny's still adjusting to her handle. It takes her a moment to register when Red Shift uses it—he won't call her anything else, now—and even when she recognizes it as hers she feels like an impostor, or a kid playing dress-up.

Red Shift shrugs. "If we had more time it'd probably be a good idea to train for all kinds of scenarios. Given our situation I think focusing on fighting is appropriate."

"My hands hurt," Jenny says. "A lot."

"It's only bruising," Red Shift says. "It'll heal. Hit me again. You haven't reached your limit yet."

"How do you know?"

"So far every time you take a swing you wind up hitting harder," Red Shift says. "Once you hit your limit that'll change. Hit me again."

"Masochist," she mutters, and hits him again.

Twenty minutes pass before Red Shift tells her to stop. At that point her hands are numb and her arms feel like rubber.

"That's your limit," Red Shift says. "For strength, at any rate. It'd be nice to test your top speed, too, but I don't know if we'll get a chance. We don't have the equipment we'd need to test you indoors, and Farraday City isn't a good choice for running laps."

Jenny laughs in spite of herself. "So how'd I do?"

Red Shift stares at her blankly. "This wasn't a test, it was an exercise."

"Not what I meant," Jenny says. "I know what going all out feels like now, but I still don't know what that limit is. I get it, that's not the point, but I'm still curious."

Red Shift shrugs. "That's fair. Can't help you much, though... we need equipment to measure that. I can tell you that you're stronger than the average human being—significantly stronger, actually. I'm basing this on having been hit by a lot of different people in the course of my career."

"Not, like, Regiment strong," Jenny says.

"No," Red Shift says. "Stronger than Curveball, though. You're strong enough to break bones and cause internal bleeding. You could inflict enough blunt force trauma with a single punch to kill a man, if you had to."

The briefest glimpse of a tight-faced, wide-eyed man staring at her flits through her conscious memory. Her mouth thins as she wills it back into a corner. "Okay. I'll keep that in mind."

Red Shift raises an eyebrow. "That doesn't bother you?"

"I'll handle it," Jenny says.

"I didn't ask you if you could handle it. I asked if it bothered you."

Jenny doesn't like the way Red Shift is staring at her. "I'm... no. It's fine. I mean, yeah, it's a little—"

"Let's talk about the guard you killed," Red Shift interrupts.

She sees the man's face again, just for an instant. "I'd rather not."

"He had a gun pressed up against your temple. You disarmed him and shot him in the face with his own gun. Twice."

Jenny winces as *that* image flashes before her eyes. "I'm not ready to talk about this. I already told CB I'll deal with it when I have the time to process it. Which I don't."

"Too bad."

She whirls on him, fists clenched, anger flashing in her eyes. "You don't get to—"

"I'm not a shrink, Zero." Red Shift's normally easygoing expression is gone. In its place is something grim and solemn.

"I'm not a shrink," he repeats. "And I'm not a priest. I admit I've been pushing your buttons a lot lately, but I really don't want to push this one. This is important, though, so if you don't do it on your own I swear to you I will push this button over and over again until either you deal with it or you break."

Jenny bites back what she *wants* to say. "Why?"

"Because waiting until you're in a position where you have to decide whether or not to kill someone else isn't the time to start working through that issue."

She doesn't answer.

Red Shift sighs. "The first time I killed a man was an accident, and it almost broke me."

Neither says anything for a moment.

Jenny takes a deep breath. "What happened?"

"I didn't know my limits," Red Shift says. "I was only starting to learn how to control my speed, and I didn't quite grasp the consequences of moving as fast as I could. I *thought* I understood it—I had a pretty good grasp of it on a theoretical level—but there's a gap between understanding it on paper and using it in the real world. The fight was... intense. It was the first time I'd ever faced someone deliberately trying to kill me, *specifically* me, so I was... well. There was a lot of adrenaline."

He pauses for a moment.

"I went supersonic when I hit him," Red Shift says.

Jenny's eyes widen. "Oh."

"Yeah." His expression grows distant. "Once I hit a certain speed my fist stops acting like a fist and starts acting more like a high-velocity projectile. It was... messy."

"What did you do? How did you deal with it?"

Red Shift shrugs. "I don't have any good advice. I was green working with two guys who weren't. They didn't have healthy coping mechanisms; their advice was 'drink a lot and keep going.' I don't recommend it as a long-term strategy."

"Yeah, I guess not." Jenny looks away. "I'll see what I can do."

He studies her for a moment, weighing his options. "Well, let's break for the day. We can try pushing more of your buttons tomorrow."

* * *

Jenny's bedroom is small, but it's so sparsely furnished—just an old army cot and a folding chair—that it feels larger than it is. She lies down on the cot and stares at a single spot on the ceiling—a tiny white chip in the blue-painted concrete—as she tries to force herself into a state of calm.

She doesn't want to think about this. She wants to think about anything other than this. So, for a while, she does: she thinks about how she hates being stuck in this bunker, how she's starting to get used to its smell, and how that bothers her. She thinks about her training, but that starts to lead her toward her recent conversation with Red Shift... so she steers back into more comfortable territory and thinks, once again, *holy shit, I'm a metahuman*.

She's still not used to that.

Someone knocks on her door.

"What?"

"It's CB." His voice is muffled through the door, but even so he sounds tired.

"Come in."

The door opens and CB steps in, smelling of car exhaust and cigarette smoke. Jenny suppresses the urge to cough, and doesn't bother sitting up.

"Hey." CB shuts the door behind him, moves the folding chair so it's sitting against the wall, parallel to the cot, and sits, sighing heavily. He looks tired—his eyes are red and watery, and his whole face droops. It's either lack of sleep or drugs. She's pretty sure it's lack of sleep. "Red tells me he pissed you off today."

"He pisses me off *every* day. I don't take it personally." Jenny thinks that over, then frowns. "Well, I do when he's actually doing it, but later when I figure out *why* he's doing it, I'm usually OK with it."

"Yeah. He likes that about you."

"Do you guys talk about me a lot? Because that actually pisses me off a little."

"Of course we do," CB says. "He's *training* you. Your first day out is probably going to involve a fight with Richter and Plague. So yeah, we talk about you a lot. You're the newbie."

Well, I can't argue with that.

"Anyway." CB leans back in the folding chair a bit, stretching his legs out in front of him. "Red told me about your last discussion. For the record,

I thought you were handling it OK."

"I wasn't handling it at all," Jenny says. "I was specifically not dealing with it."

"Well, yeah," CB says. "Not dealing with it is a legitimate short-term strategy."

"Bullshit."

"I'm serious. It's a *really bad* long-term strategy, but in the short term, grief is like fear—you can shove it aside and focus on something else. For a while."

"Thanks," Jenny says. "Seriously. It means a lot to know that you thought I was making a decent choice, at least for now. But I think he's right."

CB doesn't say anything.

"When that guard..." Jenny closes her eyes, takes a deep breath, and presses on. "When I knew he was the only one left, I made a decision and I acted. Logically, *tactically*, it was the right decision to make. I know that. But it was still a horrible thing to do, CB. It... there are things that happened—things I felt—that are going to tear me to pieces when I finally bring them out into the light. I'll never be OK with killing someone. It might be necessary. I might have to do it again, someday. But I'll never really be OK with it."

"Good," CB says. He sounds relieved.

"But it's all still there," Jenny says. She opens her eyes, focusing on the chip in the ceiling. "And the next time I'm in a life or death situation, what will I do if it all comes pouring out? Red Shift is right. The next time I'm in that situation I might freeze up."

"No he's not," CB says. "Really. He's not. Listen, Jenny, Red is doing good by you, OK? He really is. And everything he's doing, he's doing because he genuinely, one hundred percent believes it'll help. And ninety-eight percent of it is probably spot on. But he's wrong about this. I *know* he's wrong about this because *you've already been in that situation*. Richter had his fucking *gun* trained on you, and you decided to *fight*."

Jenny blinks in surprise. "Yeah. I did."

"Yeah, you did. So I don't see the problem. I mean, you *do* have to deal with it eventually, and the longer you put it off the harder it's going to get. But I already know what you're going to do when your back's to the wall. You're going to fight like hell. That's good enough for me."

She can't think of anything to say after that.

CB fidgets in his chair a moment, then stands. "I need coffee. I've got some things to take care of tonight. You OK?"

"Yeah." Jenny ignores the dampness welling in her eyes. "I'm OK. Are you?"

CB hesitates, considering the question. "Yeah. I guess. Why?"

"You look really tired, is all."

He sighs. "Yeah, well, that's true. Haven't been sleeping much."

"Have you learned anything?"

CB's eyes unfocus and he stares off into space for a moment. "Nope. Dead end so far."

"You'll figure it out eventually," Jenny says.

"I guess..." CB suppresses a yawn. "Right now I need coffee. Lots and lots of coffee."

He closes the door behind him as he leaves.

Jenny hears him stomp down the hall, then hears him rattling through the kitchen as he assembles the coffee maker to brew a fresh pot. She lies on her cot, staring at the chip in the ceiling, thinking about what he said.

I already know what you're going to do when your back's to the wall.

"I do, too." She speaks aloud, and she's surprised by the strength in her voice—not because it feels new, but because it *doesn't.* "I know what I'm going to do."

She sits up, swinging her legs so her bare feet rest on the floor. She feels the cold concrete floor seep in through the pads of her feet, and as her feet grow numb to the sensation she imagines that she is also growing numb, hardening her resolve and shoving aside her doubts and insecurities and fears and pains so that she can focus on what's coming. They're still there, on the periphery, and some day they'll have to be reckoned with... but not now. She has something else to do first.

"I'm going to *fight like hell.*"

PART FOUR: JULY 20, 1992

David Bernard wakes up remembering his last rational thought the night before: *don't sleep here, it isn't safe*. Everything after that is a blur, vague images obscured by ever-thickening layers of pain and exhaustion. He's lying on a mattress with clean sheets. The low hum of an air conditioner kicks in and cool air washes over his face. The constant, faint sound of tropical birds calling to each other can be heard just beyond the bedroom's window.

I guess I didn't take my own advice.

He sits up, surprised to feel neither pain nor dizziness. He obviously needed the rest, and it's done him good—his vision is clear and sharp, and he's thinking more clearly than he remembers in a long time. Even Crossfire's special medical treatment, as remarkable as it was, hadn't worked this well. That thought provokes a sudden surge of relief, as he realizes that the day before he couldn't actually remember that part of his life. His memory is back—he remembers getting hurt the first time, the second time, seeking out Crossfire, working with them, agreeing to help LaFleur in his investigation, and then they—

David frowns. Then they—there was a—

He's sitting in the cargo bay of a plane, checking the straps to his parachute for the seventh time. LaFleur is sitting across from him, doing the same.

"After we jump it's likely we'll be separated." LaFleur has to raise his voice to be heard over the engines of the plane. "I'm sorry for that. It's going to be a difficult transition..."

It's the same thing he remembered yesterday, after reading the paper, but nothing more. So his memory hasn't returned, not completely. He shrugs. Where he is today is remarkably better than where he was yesterday.

A little *too* remarkable, perhaps. An unspoken question begins to stir somewhere in the back of his head. He pushes it aside for the moment.

His pistol sits, still holstered, on a small nightstand on the left side of the bed. His clothes are neatly folded on the dresser to the left of the bedroom door. He checks his pistol, pulling it out of its holster, making sure it's loaded and the safety is set. He gets dressed quickly, stopping only for a moment as he catches the scent of his shirt as he pulls it over his head. It smells clean. All of his clothes smell clean, which doesn't make a lot of sense, because he distinctly remembers being pretty filthy when he stumbled into the house yesterday. He feels fairly clean too, for that matter—not what you'd expect from a guy who washed up on a beach the day before.

I guess I did the laundry before I passed out? And took a shower... yeah, that doesn't really make any sense.

His stomach growls. He's hungry: *that* makes sense. He finishes getting dressed, straps on his holster, then steps out of the bedroom and into the small living room. Everything is exactly the way it was the day before, including, he notices, the unlocked front door. He *tsks* in irritation as he locks it, and slides the deadbolt across. He must have been in really bad shape last night if he'd overlooked something like that.

If you were that hurt last night, why do you feel so much better now?

His growling stomach pushes the question aside.

Fresh fruit for breakfast—there's plenty on hand so he doesn't have to cook. The milk is still good, and there's more left than he remembers: he was sure the jug was half empty when he'd finished his second glass last night, but it's actually a little over three-quarters full. When he's finished, he goes over to the kitchen sink to wash his hands and splash water on his face.

It's at that moment he finally realizes he has a beard.

He's been superficially aware of it all morning, but it hasn't registered. It's not until he feels wet hair plastered against his face that he realizes he has hair on his face. The realization sends him running to the bathroom.

Before he was a cop, David was a soldier, and many of his habits come from that time. His hair has always been short, and he has always been clean-shaven. Even when his concussion was at its worst he managed to keep the hair off his face. As he stands in the bathroom, looking at his reflection in the mirror, he feels like he's staring at a stranger.

The terrible haircut he'd given himself yesterday—the one he gave himself while trying to clean the cut on his head—is gone. In its place is a thatch of medium-brown hair, thick and tangled, falling down past his shoulders. His beard is full and thick, making him look more like a Hell's Angel than a retired cop.

The part that unnerves him the most is how *natural* it feels. He's never had long hair before, never even *tried* to grow a beard before. He's gone without shaving for a few days at most, but after a few days his face starts to itch so thoroughly that he's driven to distraction until he shaves. But the length his hair is now, it would take—six months? Eight? A year to grow out? And it happened overnight?

He looks at his nails. They're still short. If his hair had magically grown out overnight, why wouldn't his nails?

The bathroom is too clean. Yesterday he was a mess, chopping off his hair, cleaning a head wound. He certainly hadn't bothered to clean up after himself in the state he was in, but today the bathroom looks as if nothing had happened there at all. He opens the medicine cabinet and sees everything he used to treat his wound—the gauze, tape, alcohol, scissors, cotton balls, all of it—in exactly the same place he found them, with no sign that they've ever been touched. He remembers tearing open the plastic bag of cotton balls, but the bag is completely sealed. It looks as if it was never used.

The sink is spotless. There is a thin streak of red at the bottom, where it looks as if some blood may have worked its way into the seam between the porcelain and the drain, but the rest of the sink is pristine and untouched.

This doesn't make sense.

Suddenly nothing makes sense. His clean clothes don't make sense. The full jug of milk doesn't make sense. The fact that he's no longer suffering from the effects of a concussion makes absolutely no sense at all. He's not a metahuman—there's only one way he'd recover from an injury like that. There's only one rational explanation for how his hair grew, his beard grew, and his concussion disappeared.

"Time," he whispers.

He goes back to the kitchen and looks at the calendar. *July, 1992.* He looks at the newspaper. *Friday July 18, 1992.* He opens the refrigerator and checks the expiration date on the milk. *EXPIR 7/22 1992.*

The house is exactly the way it was yesterday. He, however, is not.

He goes back into the bathroom and stares at his reflection once more. His hair is longer, and he looks healthier, but there's something about his eyes that isn't the same. They look older. It's not a scientific conclusion, there's no data he can think of to test that against, but when he looks into the eyes staring back out at him from the mirror he is absolutely convinced it's true. Much more time has passed than he's aware of, and looking at the length of his hair, and taking into account how much *better* he feels than he did, he's sure the progression of time can be measured in months rather than days or weeks.

But the house is exactly the same.

He goes into the living room and sinks onto the couch, staring at the house with a new level of suspicion and wariness. Suddenly the comfortable little house looks far more sinister than it did moments ago.

CURVEBALL
19
NOV 2014
CURVEBALL
A Prose Comic
THAT WHICH DOES NOT DREAM
STORY
CHRISTOPHER WRIGHT
COVER
PASCALLE LEPAS
LOGO
GARTH GRAHAM

PART ONE: JULY 20, 1992

David Bernard wakes up remembering his last rational thought the night before: *don't sleep here, it isn't safe*. Everything after that is a blur, vague images obscured by ever-thickening layers of pain and exhaustion. He's lying on a mattress with clean sheets. The low hum of an air conditioner kicks in and cool air washes over his face. The constant, faint sound of tropical birds calling to each other can be heard just beyond the bedroom's window.

I guess I didn't take my own advice.

He sits up, surprised to feel neither pain nor dizziness. He obviously needed the rest, and it's done him good—his vision is clear and sharp, and he's thinking more clearly than he remembers thinking in a long time. Even Crossfire's special medical treatment, as remarkable as it was, hadn't worked this well. That thought provokes a sudden surge of relief, as he realizes that the day before he couldn't actually remember that part of his life. His memory is back—he remembers getting hurt the first time, the second time, seeking out Crossfire, working with them, agreeing to help LaFleur in his investigation, and then they—

David frowns. Then they—there was a—

He's sitting in the cargo bay of a plane, checking the straps to his parachute for the seventh time. LaFleur is sitting across from him, doing the same.

"If it's become the thing I think it is, it will seek to minimize and assimilate disruption. After we jump it's likely we'll be separated." LaFleur has to raise his voice to be heard over the engines of the plane. "I'm sorry for that. It's going to be a difficult transition..."

It's almost the same thing he remembered yesterday, after reading the paper. A little more than that—he didn't remember LaFleur saying anything about minimizing and assimilating disruption. He wonders what that means. Still, it's progress—where he is today is remarkably better than where he was yesterday.

A little *too* remarkable, perhaps. An unspoken question begins to stir somewhere in the back of his head. He pushes it aside for the moment...

His pistol sits, still holstered, on a small nightstand on the left side of the bed. His notepad sits beside the holstered pistol. His clothes are neatly folded on the dresser to the left of the bedroom door. He checks his pistol, pulling it out of its holster, making sure it's loaded and the safety is set. He gets dressed quickly, stopping only for a moment as he catches the scent of his shirt as he pulls it over his head. It smells *clean.* All of his clothes smell clean, which doesn't make a lot of sense, because he distinctly remembers being pretty filthy when he stumbled into the house yesterday. He feels fairly clean too, for that matter—not what you'd expect from a guy who washed up on a beach the day before.

He picks up the notepad and flips it open. A folded-up piece of paper falls out onto the floor. He picks it up—it's heavily creased, as if it's been opened and refolded many times. He opens it and starts reading:

Hey David,

Yes, I'm writing a letter to myself. And chances are you've already read it, you just don't remember doing it. At the time I'm writing this I've been here for almost a year, I think, which means you've been here even longer than that. The concussion is gone, and I remember everything except what happened on the plane. I get flashes of that, nothing else.

You're trapped in some kind of screwed up time loop—that's the only way I can think of describing it. Everything that was on this island when it happened resets after twenty-four hours (working hypothesis only) and you are half-stuck in it. Your memory resets, but you keep aging. That's why you've healed, and why you have the beard.

He unconsciously reaches up to scratch his chin and pulls back his hand in surprise when he feels long hair. He runs to the mirror, stares at himself in shock, then glances back down at the note.

It's not as long as it was, it was getting in the way... but don't shave the whole thing, it's going to help convince you next time.

David chews over the phrase "time loop" and wonders why that tickles a memory. He can't place it.

I've figured out a few things:

1. Today's date: July 20, 1992. It's always that day—everything on the island is "stuck" in time. At the end of every day the island resets to however it was at the beginning of the day. I don't know when that twenty-four hour cycle starts, but I'm pretty sure it's some point after 10 PM and before you wake up, which is a little after 8. That's why the front door is unlocked: whoever left the house before this thing started didn't bother locking it. If you lock it now it'll be unlocked by morning.

2. You can't destroy anything on this island. At least, I don't think you can. Check the notepad—at one point you apparently burned the house down to see if it would take.

3. Everything you brought with you can change, however. Two of your magazines are empty. I don't remember why, but there are only a few reasons you shoot a gun these days, and it's a safe bet one of those reasons showed up. The inanimate objects you brought with you seem to be fully independent of whatever it is the island is doing. On that point, conserve your notepad, since it seems to have the only paper you can write on that stays after twenty-four hours. Only put down what you think is absolutely important.

4. Also—your pen is the only thing that works on the notepad. A pen from the island (including its ink) "resets" after twenty-four hours, all text is gone.

5. You are sort of half-in, half-out as far as the island is concerned. Your memory keeps resetting, but your body is aging. This is a mixed blessing—it means your concussion is gone (good thing) but if you don't figure out how to get out of this trap you're going to die of old age in 1992.

6. You're going to fall asleep by 10 PM. It's some kind of compulsion. Check your notes.

7. No sign of LaFleur, but if you wander into town (completely empty, as far as I can tell) and check out the newspaper archives you'll learn a lot that doesn't make sense. NONE OF IT HAPPENED.

8. Port Libertad might be empty, but there are signs of other people on the island. The house is safe. Stay there until you figure out how to remember.

Good luck.

David rereads the note four times before he folds it up and puts it away. He's certain it's his—it's definitely his handwriting—and what's more he *believes* it. He laughs when he realizes it's because of the beard: it's so completely out of character that it sells everything else.

Trapped in a 'time loop.' Wonderful.

David isn't a scientist. During his time as Sky Commando, he was introduced to some interesting concepts, including the existence of alternate realities with *diverging* timelines, but he never encountered anything that dealt with time travel.

He spends breakfast reading through his notepad, trying to keep his frustration in check. The first page contains the very brief and rudimentary notes he took on the plane. After that is a quick checklist of "to do" items. The original list is his handwriting, but very sloppy—it was written in the early days on the island, he suspects, when he was still affected by the concussion. Each item is followed by a notation in parentheses, and that handwriting is much more legible:

- Confirm date (7/20/92)

- Find a more secure hiding place (house OK for now)

- Determine location/scout surroundings (map of island in kitchen counter drawer, house in grid A, 14)

- Research LaFleur (newspaper in Port Libertad - Port Libertad Daily - archives in basement)

- Find LaFleur

"Find LaFleur" is the only entry that has no extra information.

The rest of the notepad mostly deals with his attempts to figure out how the island works. A few pages describe the experiments that appear to support everything listed in the note he left for himself, including a brief description of how he burned the house to the ground... an act that obviously didn't "stick." There are two separate entries describing a plan to head deeper into the island, to "visit the capital." There's no follow-up information for either.

He pays particular attention to the entries where he discovered the 10 PM sleep compulsion. One page is a log of his first attempt to stay up after 10, with a list of times and a brief status. He's apparently fine at 9 PM.

2100 - OK

2115 - OK

2130 - a little tired. Doing push-ups

2135 - making coffee

2141 - caught myself nodding off. Head feels weird.

2143 - overcome with desire to sleep.

2145 - coffee isn't helping. Feel like I've been up for days.

2148 - thought I heard a noise outside. Went outside to check; nothing.

2151 - I don't think I c

It ends there, abruptly, with a little wobble and a swoop at the end of the "c" that makes David think he actually fell asleep while writing.

His second attempt involved breaking into a pharmacy in Port Libertad and finding the raw materials to cook up dextroamphetamine—a crude form of the 'go-pill' that he'd used from time to time when he was in the military. That log was almost identical—half an hour before the "sleep wall" he took the drug, felt it kick in five minutes after ingestion, reported feeling as if he'd taken nothing at all at 2147, then no other entries.

He searches through the kitchen counter until he finds the map mentioned in his notes, then spreads it out across the table. ESPERANZA is printed across the top. That means... what, exactly? David frowns as he tries to remember his high school Spanish classes. "Libertad" is easy, but all he remembers about "Esperanza" is that it was the name of a girl in his tenth grade history class.

Still, at least he has a name, at least until tomorrow.

First impression: the map is censored. There are parts of the map that are blocked out in red, and the map key denotes those as "High Security Zones." Some of them are on the coast, and appear to be spaced at regular intervals, completely surrounding the island. Others are placed around a large city near the center of the island—Victoria, apparently the island's capital. Just north of the city is a swath of red that is much larger than the others.

Second impression: his suggestion to not bother exploring until he can break through this 10 PM barrier is tactically sound. The island is too big. The back of the map shows the island in relation to its neighbors, and it's almost as large as the Dominican Republic. If he could find a working car, he might get to the capital in three or four hours... assuming he wasn't trying to hide from anyone, but that's not a safe assumption. *Port Libertad is empty, but there are other people on the island.* And even if he got there, what would he do? There wouldn't be enough time to look around. Not when he'd forget everything the next day.

He drums his fingers idly on the kitchen table, alternating between studying the map and reviewing the notes. At least he knows where he is—a Caribbean island he's never heard of, set between the Dominican Republic and Bermuda...

His fingers stop drumming and he focuses on the map again. There's Miami to the west. There's Puerto Rico to the southeast. There's Bermuda to the northeast. And there is Esperanza, a Caribbean island he has never heard of before today, sitting right in the middle.

The Bermuda Triangle. It's right in the middle of the Bermuda Triangle.

PART TWO: 10 PM

David pushes the map away and laughs.

"Of *course* it is."

He hadn't really put much stock in LaFleur's explanation of "magic," brief as it was. He hadn't disbelieved it, exactly, but it was a level of detail he'd considered unnecessary. They already had people who could fly, manipulate the weather, run at impossible speeds... it was *all* magic, as far as David was concerned. The fact that some magic appeared to come from a complicated jumble of genetic sequences and some came from... well, spells, apparently—he'd considered that tactically irrelevant.

Now he isn't sure.

He tries to think back on what LaFleur said about it—not much, based on what he remembers. He still can't remember what happened to him in the few days before he woke up on the island, except for the fragment of the conversation he had with LaFleur on the plane. The only information that puts it in any kind of context is the explanation LaFleur gave when the topic first came up:

It's power. It's power that has existed for a very long time. It predates any civilization that we are aware of. It is not found in history books—the people who claimed to be magicians were, by and large, charlatans. The knowledge is not shared freely: the practice of magic is as much a religion as it is a discipline, and the power seems to represent a very specific point of view that is absolutely opposed to any other point of view. The belief system it represents is largely alien to our understanding.

Not a lot to go on. The only other significant thing he can remember is LaFleur's explanation of why it's so dangerous:

It harms the soul. The essence of your 'life force,' if the term 'soul' offends you. Most of us, metahuman or not, are equally vulnerable to it.

Still not entirely useful, but it's something. Magic isn't physical—or, at least, it doesn't *start* physical. If magic is what keeps the island trapped in a twenty-four-hour loop in 1992, then it obviously *becomes* physical at some point.

Maybe that's the problem. All David's notes are focused on dealing with the island physically—exploring, testing the boundaries of what he can change and what he can't. Even his attempts to get past the 10 PM barrier were acts of endurance. Maybe he needs to approach this from a different angle—one that's less physical. Assuming his notes are reliable—and he's assuming they are—he's going to fall asleep by 10 PM, whether he wants to or not. If he can't fight it, maybe he can work *around* it.

David spends the rest of the day relaxing. He reads through the newspaper, stretches out on the couch, enjoys the sounds of the tropical birds cawing outside, and soaks up the air conditioning: by the time the sun sets, he's thoroughly relaxed. He eats a light dinner, washes his clothes in the washer, showers, and at about nine in the evening he locks the front door and heads off to bed. He leaves a quick note for himself in the notepad, checks the time on the windup alarm clock by the bed, stretches out, and closes his eyes.

He starts moving the index and middle finger on his right hand: index finger down, middle finger up, then switch, as if he were alternating between two keys on a piano. Gradually the movements grow smaller and smaller, until finally his fingers aren't moving but his muscles are still contracting, ever so slightly, in that continuous pattern. Index up, middle down. Index down, middle up. Over and over and over, as his breathing grows regular and his eyes grow heavy. Over and over and over, until he finds himself lying down in a field near his parents' house—a lush, green field, far greener than he ever remembers seeing it. His fingers are still twitching, index up, middle down, index down, middle up, and he stays that way for a few seconds, taking in a clear blue sky and listening to the sound of ducks splashing around in a pond he knows is just behind a copse of trees to his left. Then, very slowly, he raises his left hand and pinches his nose, closing off his nostrils. He tries to inhale and is overpowered by the sweet smell of hay.

He can smell when he shouldn't be able to. He's dreaming.

David learned the trick to lucid dreaming while he was in the army. He got the idea listening to an interview with a professional athlete who used it to help her train. When he finally figured it out, he used it the same way: he'd go over whatever he was being trained in as he slept, practicing continuously, and when he woke up he remembered what he'd done. It worked, and he used it almost all the time until his concussion. The concussion made it hard to dream, lucid or otherwise. The concussion is gone now, and the lucid dreaming is back.

He sits up in the field, idly wondering what to do. Usually when he did this he had a specific goal in mind, but the only goal he has at the moment is running out the clock. He has to wait at least an hour before he tries to wake up—an hour to get past the 10 PM barrier at least, then maybe another two to break through into the next day. Would it be enough?

David assumes it all depends on how picky this "sleep wall" is. Right now he is fully in REM sleep, which is as deep as it gets—he just happens to be aware. How will that affect him? Will it affect him at all?

Something ripples on the horizon. David squints, and he sees it again—a momentary darkening of an otherwise clear sky at the edge of what he can see. A moment later he sees a more persistent change: clouds gather at the edges, and a low rumble echoes across the sky.

David stands, frowning as he watches the thin line climb up into the sky, now a proper wall of storm clouds rolling toward him. *This isn't supposed to happen. This is my dream. I control it.*

But he doesn't: the dream he's in is changing against his will, and while he's still *lucid* within it, he's no longer wholly *in control.* Something is invading, and he's fairly certain he knows what it is: it's almost 10 PM. The storm bearing down on him represents whatever is going to happen to the island when sleep falls.

He watches it warily, listening to the thunder boom like distant war drums. The ducks in the pond quack and honk nervously. The wind changes direction. David smells the ocean.

He takes a moment to change his dream. He's standing on the cracked stone floor of an open dojo in the middle of an endless grassy plain. This is a dream he used years ago, when he was trying to master staff fighting. The storm front is still there, closer now. He's not surprised by that: he didn't want it rolling over a place and a memory that was important to him. What will happen, he wonders, when the storm finally rolls over him? He's starting to see more than just the clouds—occasional flashes of lightning illuminate bits of a beach and the ocean beyond. Esperanza is coming.

David realizes he doesn't have to wait. The problem with his attempts to deal with the island in the past was that he tried to deal with it on its own terms, within the boundaries it set. This is different: he isn't entirely in control here, but neither is it. He can choose to resist it, to try to weather it... or he can simply *go there.*

This is a dream; he can fly.

He rises into the air, feeling a momentary thrill as the ground loses its hold on him. He soars into a still-blue sky, reveling for a moment at the sun on his face and the wind in his hair. Then, floating above the earth, he turns to face the storm. He sees it approach, acknowledges its strength. Then, marshaling all the will he can, he races toward it. The world blurs, the wind screams, and suddenly he is engulfed in darkness and fire.

Lightning tears through the sky, slicing past him and branding the ground below. He feels its power, but he isn't afraid. He's floating over the beach, now—the same beach he washed up on, as best he can tell. Trees whip back and forth in the wind, some bending over impossibly far without breaking. The ocean rolls up and breaks over the sand with enormous force: David can almost feel the island shake as the surf crashes down. He is soaking wet from the sheets of water pouring from the sky, but he's not cold. He is no longer in his dream, entirely, but he's not quite in the island's reality either. He still has control of his own persona, and his persona is unaffected by the weather.

He flies higher and turns inland. He catches his breath for a moment: though it's too dark to see much of anything other than shadow, bright white lights shine in the distance, swiveling to and fro like lighthouse beacons, cutting swaths into the darkness then winking out, only to return again moments later. The white lights are spaced evenly from each other, and David is reminded of the red, censored areas on the Esperanza map—specifically, the ones set along the coast. Is that what he's seeing?

There is another light, set very far inland—a thin green beam of light that rises into the sky. He stares at it in fascination, wills himself to move toward it—and is surprised to find himself thrown backward. He spins through the air, catching himself after a moment's disorientation, and in that moment he feels the full force of the storm bearing down on him—the sting of sand and rain beating against him, the deafening roar of the wind and thunder, the deep cold of the water washing over him. Then he has control again, and the ferocity of the storm slides away.

He stays where he is, hovering above the treeline, watching the storm rage on. The green line of light that disappears into the sky remains constant and untroubled by his presence, and he does not provoke it by trying to draw near.

A voice rises out of the storm. It's a familiar voice, but he can't remember where he's heard it. It crashes down around him louder than the wind and the thunder, strong and commanding and full of power. He doesn't recognize the words, but it sounds like a poem: four lines repeated, over and over again. Each time it repeats the voice grows louder, and each time the green light grows brighter, until at last he can see the silhouette of mountains around its base. The voice reaches a crescendo, and finally after uttering the last line it shouts a single word. In an instant the storm dies: the rain and wind cease completely. Only the clouds in the sky and the occasional rumble of thunder remain.

Moments later David hears a horn, followed by others. The sound comes from the direction of the green light, and it dives deep into his bones, stirring up memories that don't precisely belong to him. *The horns are not calling me,* he thinks, *but they are calling.*

Something replies: a low, rumbling pulse, deep and wet, rises out of the waters behind him. He turns to look and sees dark shapes emerge from the ocean. Distorted, snakelike salamanders crawl out of the water on long, grasping limbs, twisting in serpentine fashion as they make their way across the sand, disappearing into the forest. Their skin is rubbery and black, their heads are eyeless, little more than gaping maws filled with rows of teeth. They glow, ever so faintly, with green light, and as they walk their eyeless heads all turn toward the distant green beacon.

Wave after wave they come, out of the depths and ever inland, the horns blowing to call, their maws opening to bellow their strange, wet cry in return. There is no end to them—legions disappear into the trees as legions more emerge from the ocean. And then the horns falter. The creatures stop, muttering to themselves uneasily. And then, once again, David hears a voice—the same voice from before, strong and commanding, but now it's tinged with something else... something angry and desperate.

The voice shouts its words defiantly, and after the third repetition, the green beacon turns a deep, crimson red. The creatures make a new sound, now. Higher-pitched, urgent... angry. Afraid. The red light begins to pulse in regular intervals. After the second pulse, David sees a sphere of red beginning to form at the light's terminus. The sphere grows with each pulse, and finally it begins to pulse as well, expanding with each strobe. The strong, defiant voice grows louder, rising in pitch as it had before, until finally it speaks a final word once more.

And then the sphere explodes.

Red light washes over the island, twisting everything in its wake. David hears the creatures scream in terror, then realizes that he is doing the same. It rushes toward them, rushes over them, and for an instant David feels pain unlike any he's ever felt before...

He bolts upright, gasping for breath. The bedroom is silent, save for the ever-present hum of the air conditioner. He sits there for a moment, trembling, then remembers to look at the clock on his nightstand. It's a little after 2 AM.

He gets up, goes into the living room, and opens the now unlocked door, stepping outside into the warm, dry calm. There's no sign of a storm, the ground is not wet, there is no debris, the sky is clear and full of stars. He goes back inside, locks the door, then goes to the kitchen and looks at the three-quarters full gallon jug of milk sitting in the refrigerator. The island, it seems, has reset.

But he hasn't.

"I did it," David says, a grin slowly forming on his face. "I beat the island."

And then, moments later, he remembers everything.

PART THREE: AIRBORNE

David Bernard shivers in his seat and tries not to show it. The cargo plane isn't particularly well insulated or heated—enough to keep them from freezing to death, but not much more than that. LaFleur emerges from the cockpit, nods to David, and motions for him to follow as he passes. David gets up, stretches, and follows LaFleur into the cargo area. It's even colder here. LaFleur, characteristically, doesn't look the slightest bit uncomfortable.

"It's time to tell you what we're doing," he says.

David nods once and pulls out his notepad from his vest.

"We're going to try to get to Port Libertad," LaFleur says. "Unfortunately, there's no available map, and a compass is going to be useless, but it's on the west side of the island..."

"Why no map?" David asks.

"Because the island isn't actually here."

David looks up sharply. "It isn't here?"

LaFleur nods. "It's my fault, I'm afraid."

David stops writing and puts his notepad away. "Maybe you should talk a little before I start taking notes."

LaFleur nods. "Quite. Well, once upon a time there was a lovely island in the Caribbean called Esperanza—that means 'Hope' in Spanish. That's what attracted me to it. That, and a very unstable government..."

David shakes his head. "I've never heard of this island."

"There's no reason you would," LaFleur says. "I'll explain. Just... bear with me until then."

David shrugs.

"In those days I was... not the man I am today. I had the same ideal—the same desire to save the world from its own destruction—but I was willing to do whatever I deemed necessary to achieve it. In the 60s I decided the best way to show the world I was serious was to run my own country. So Overmind conquered Esperanza, and the United States found itself having to deal with Cuba and a country run by a 'supervillain.' They did not react well."

"I'll bet," David says.

"I managed to get a little breathing room in the beginning. I made public proclamations against communism, and for a while that was enough to keep the United States away. It wasn't hard to do—I had no particular love for the Soviet Union and certainly opposed its expansionist policies, not in the least because they conflicted with mine. I was content to wait, however—I focused on the country I had, worked on rebuilding it, modernizing it, educating the citizenry. I did well. Esperanza became a source of envy the world over... which wound up causing even more problems. The civilized world is willing to tolerate a despot, so long as he rules over squalor. If he should build anything of any lasting value... well, then he suddenly becomes dangerous."

When he was on the force, David had access to plenty of files on Overmind. His tactics were considered unusual—he showed a great deal of restraint for a criminal, always working to minimize civilian casualties, and on more than one occasion abandoning an operation when it became apparent that continuing would result in significant loss of life. There was significantly less information on what he, personally, could do: he was definitely a metahuman, and appeared to possess an abnormally high intellect. There were also reports of him being able to teleport (something David had seen first-hand) and alter his appearance (something David had not, at least to his knowledge). Little else was known, but in every report there was one point that never wavered.

"I'm pretty sure they always thought you were dangerous."

LaFleur smiles thinly. "Perhaps. They weren't wrong. But the timing was inconvenient—Esperanza was *working*. There were dissidents, but very few. People were genuinely better off. Disease was falling. Infant mortality was virtually non-existent. Most of the latest generation were well-educated. I was winning diplomatically, and I was making enemies determined to undermine all of it."

It's the first time David has ever seen LaFleur angry. His voice, usually mild and courteous, is hard and unyielding. All emotion fades from his face, but his eyes are very, very sharp.

"It wasn't only the CIA. They were quite good at destabilizing countries at the time, of course, but there were others who had a similar interest. I'd been expecting this, but I didn't expect all of them at once. Suddenly I found my country and my people—I'd starting thinking of them as *my people* at that point—engulfed in chaos and suffering. I took drastic measures: I offered amnesty to any metahuman criminal who was willing to fight for my country and follow my rules. This was an imperfect solution, of course—most criminals are criminals precisely because they possess qualities that make them poor employees—but for the most part I was able to direct their energies away from my people. Still, it wasn't enough. I needed more. That's when I discovered magic."

LaFleur sighs. "Rather, that's when it discovered me. I didn't really know what it was in those days. I didn't *believe* in it. I thought that old stories of witches and wizards and spells were the result of ignorant, fearful men and women persecuting metahumans who didn't quite understand what they were. There's probably more truth to it than not, but one day I was approached by a robed man who offered to give me access to powers 'unknown by mortal men.' I was intrigued, not the least since he'd somehow managed to slip past my security undetected. I agreed to become his student. I expected little of it. But he was right—he introduced me to power I have never seen equaled, either before or since."

"I thought you said people who use magic don't share their knowledge freely," David says.

"They don't," LaFleur says. "But I didn't know it at the time. The man who became my teacher claimed he wanted Esperanza to prosper. I believed him, and began to learn. I learned a great deal, became quite powerful, and suddenly the enemies who had tried to bring me down in secret were forced to step into the open. Almost thirty years after I had taken over that island and recast it in my own image, I learned that an invasion force was massing against me. I had little time to prepare or react—barely enough time to try to evacuate the island before the armies came down on us. That's when my teacher suggested a spell that would call forth an army out of the oceans—a spell that would unleash a power into the world that I could wield to defend my island."

He falls silent then, and looks away.

"What happened?" David prompts.

"I trusted him," LaFleur says. "So I cast the spell. It was... extraordinarily difficult. It didn't occur to me to be suspicious when my teacher just happened to have all the materials we needed for the ritual. It didn't occur to me to be suspicious when other 'students' of his appeared to assist us in the casting. I was too focused on saving my island. So I cast the spell, and then I went to my room and that's when the news came in."

LaFleur's gaze grows distant.

"Out of the oceans they came. Their numbers were legion. The first news reports were alarming, but people thought they could be contained. Initial forays by the military were encouraging. The creatures weren't immortal. They could be killed. But they could kill in turn, and they *kept coming*. That's what I had called forth: an unending wave of hungering things, intent on devouring the world. There were more of them than there were weapons. There were already reports of nuclear powers turning their arsenals on their own coastlines in a desperate attempt to stop them..."

His eyes glisten.

"I do not consider myself a good man, Lieutenant. I am not a hero. And then—in those days I was far worse than I am now. But even then, my overriding passion was to prevent the world from being destroyed by men who had the ability and willingness to create mustard gas and everything that followed. And yet, for all my desire to prevent that destruction, I had just destroyed the world myself. And in doing so, I finally recognized exactly what magic was: a power anathema to our world, a power that could not love, could not dream, could not know mercy or laughter or justice. It was not a tool that could be used to save the world, it was merely a weapon for destroying it."

"You talk like it's alive," David says.

"It is," LaFleur says. "Not in the way you and I live. It is far more alien than that. I told you once before, magic is as much a religion as it is a discipline—the magician wants magic to serve him, to be the tool he uses to get what he wants, but in order to do that he must find a way to get magic to serve him while remaining true to its own nature. To do this, the magician must study that nature. This often drives them mad."

David shudders.

"When I learned what I'd done," LaFleur says, "I set about undoing it. It wasn't easy. Magic does not like to be unraveled—the more powerful the spell, the more it resists unraveling. The spell we had just cast was... very powerful. The only way I knew to save the world was to escalate the atrocity against it."

"What did you do?" David asks.

"I had been a voracious student of magic," LaFleur says. "I was a fool, I didn't understand it, at its core, but I was very good at *using* it. And I'd long since been unwilling to restrict myself to my teacher's lessons. Once I learned about magic I made it my business to collect as much lore as I could. I had a spell so terrible I kept it in my private vault only to ensure nobody else ever used it. That is what I cast."

"But what did you do?"

"I unmade them," LaFleur says. He looks old, his face craggy with guilt and resolve. "The spell changed *time*. At the moment this universe came to be, something shifted in just the right way to prevent the island from even being formed. There is no Esperanza in this world, there never was. Only a remnant of that island remains—the last day of its life, looping endlessly, occasionally appearing in this world to trap unwary travelers. A boat disappears, a plane disappears, and they call it the Bermuda Triangle. But they don't remember Esperanza. I am the only man alive to remember the island that was there, and the people who were on it."

David turns away from the man's grief.

"We need knowledge," LaFleur says, pushing on. "Curveball's encounter with the rune-covered man is troubling. Healing is not normally within magic's nature. If it can heal a man, that effect is incidental to its true purpose, and if its *incidental effect* is as powerful as Curveball claims, then its true purpose must be terrifying. I have—had—an extensive library on the island. In my palace, in the mountains overlooking the capital. We need those books."

A buzzer sounds, and a yellow light set over the door begins blinking.

"We're almost at the jump point," LaFleur says. "Let's get ready."

They get into their parachutes and check their gear. LaFleur looks painfully frail in his parachute.

"You're a metahuman," David says. "The files I read on you say you teleport. Why don't you just teleport onto the island?"

LaFleur smiles lightly. "Physics, mostly. I can't shed velocity. If I'm traveling in a plane moving at two to three hundred miles an hour, and I teleport to a fixed point, I will still be traveling at two to three hundred miles an hour. It's a common limitation with teleporters. It wouldn't end well."

"No," David agrees. "All right. Anything else?"

"Yes," LaFleur says. He stares at David intently. "And it's very important. I've already said that magic is alive, after a fashion. It adapts. That means the spell that I originally cast—the one that sought to remove the island from reality altogether—has very likely changed, and has become the thing that is *preserving* what is left of it. That means it will react to intruders."

"Send goons after us?" David asks. "Cultists?"

"No," LaFleur says. "Too complicated. The simplest thing to do would be to absorb us into itself. Trap us in its world. You'll need to be wary of that possibility. Fight it."

"OK... sounds fun." David checks the straps to his parachute for the seventh time. LaFleur does the same.

"If it's become the thing I think it is, it will seek to minimize and assimilate disruption. After we jump it's likely we'll be separated." The plane labors suddenly as it gains altitude—setting them up for the jump. LaFleur has to raise his voice to be heard over the engines. "I'm sorry for that. It's going to be a difficult transition..."

David gives him the thumbs up to show he understands.

"Try to go to Port Libertad," LaFleur says. "From there, take the highway to the capital. Go to the public library. We'll meet there."

The flashing yellow light turns red.

PART FOUR: JULY 20, 1992

The silver-haired man hangs in the air, clothed in a thin white robe, suspended by a power that existed before time. The circle of power that imprisons allows nothing to pass through, in or out, unless willed by its master. He gave up trying to escape long ago, so long ago that he barely remembers the attempts, though the failures still haunt his dreams. He has had neither food nor drink in this prison—the power that sustains it also sustains him, nourishing him just enough to keep him alive and nothing more. Hunger and thirst are ever-present companions: even in sleep he dreams of food and drink.

He keeps his eyes closed, focusing on that hunger and thirst, acknowledging them, then pushing them as far back as he can. He does this every day. Some days it works, others it doesn't. Today it works, and the hunger and thirst recede to manageable levels. He sighs softly, allowing himself a measure of relief. Today he will be in control. Tomorrow will be another battle.

The large hall that holds his prison is empty now, but in a few hours that will change. In a few hours, the first of the acolytes will arrive, bringing in the artifacts and setting up the materials needed for the ceremony that will take place later that night. They will not see him, of course—they are locked in their predestined actions, caught in a time and a place where the silver-haired man and his prison do not yet exist. Later he will be forced to watch a shadow of himself perform a ritual that will doom the entire world, and even later watch that shadow perform a final ritual that will pull the world back from destruction by dooming every inhabitant of the island to non-existence.

All save him. Or so he thought.

The ornate double doors at the far end of the hall open, the sound echoing in the large space, and a man in a green silk robe strides purposefully into the room. The doors swing shut behind him of their own accord as he stares at the silver-haired man. That gaze was always unnerving; today it is almost painful.

Artemis LaFleur watches his teacher in silence. He watches as his teacher approaches, listening to the *wist* of the green silk robes brushing against the cold stone floor.

Artigenian appears to be a healthy, vigorous man in his early sixties. His hair is long, pulled back and held in place with an elaborate ivory and gold clip, revealing many gold and silver rings in his ears. He has no beard, which he claims is unusual for his people—instead, his chin and lower jaw are covered in tattoos. Each mark represents an aspect of the power he wields and serves. LaFleur knew what each mark meant, once. He can't remember any of them now.

Artigenian stops at the edge of the circle, watching him in silence. LaFleur closes his eyes.

"No." The man's voice is thick and harsh. His accent sounds Balkan, though LaFleur isn't sure which it is—Teteven, perhaps? Perhaps.

"No," Artigenian says again. "You will open your eyes and face me."

LaFleur feels his eyes open and his head swivel down to gaze on his teacher's face. It is hard and uncaring, a far cry from the friendly and wise mentor he had once cherished.

That friendship was a lie. This is his true form.

"Fate, it seems, returns you. Why is that, I wonder?"

LaFleur says nothing.

Artigenian waits a moment, then sighs in exasperation. "Would that I could compel you to speak. But even now, you are strong, my pupil. Even in your present state. So I must... *convince* you. This will take some time." He smiles savagely. "Fortunately, time is not a precious commodity in this place. Not for men like you and I."

He turns away from LaFleur, stalking the room, circling the place where, in a few hours, they will call forth untold horrors into the world.

"So close..." His voice is almost a whisper. "On this night I came so close. I thought you were the one. You had the power to tear the veil from this... *false* existence. We were very nearly on the brink of returning the one true empire to its rightful place in the spheres. But you betrayed us! Spit upon your purpose. Turned your back on all we had given you... and did *this!*"

He sweeps his hand angrily around him. "This... abomination. This prison, where I must watch myself taste victory for so short a time, only to see it all undone by your treachery! To relive that victory and defeat, day in and day out, to see what might have been for a moment, and what is for eternity! You! Traitor!"

LaFleur feels a release of pressure as Artigenian permits him to speak. He clears his throat, coughing up half-dried phlegm, mustering his strength. "That isn't how I remember it."

"No?" Artigenian laughs, full of scorn.

"I remember a teacher and a friend telling me of a spell that would *save my country from war*. I suppose that wasn't a lie, technically. But it was certainly a betrayal."

Artigenian shakes his head. "Not a betrayal. A *lesson*. A hard one, to be sure, but a necessary step for a power such as yours. You should have embraced your act and risen above us all. You would have become something wonderful. Terrible. A god, perhaps. Instead you emptied yourself in a fit of misplaced love for the lie that is this creation. And now you are a... shell." He spits the last word out contemptuously. "Empty. Hollow. Where is it? What happened to it?"

LaFleur doesn't answer.

"You *will* answer me." Artigenian's voice is thick with contempt. "You are not the student I loved like my own child. You are what remains. You are the dust that made up his form, the shadow he used to speak. The student I loved grew within you, and now he is gone. Where has he gone?"

LaFleur simply looks at him.

"*What has happened to your power?*" Artigenian shrieks in rage, fists balled, flecks of spittle flying from the corners of his mouth. LaFleur stares back in cold defiance.

Artigenian takes a deep breath, then bows once. "Very well. You refuse today. Tonight you will watch our victory and our defeat. Tomorrow we speak on this further. Eventually you will tell me where you hid your power, and when you do I will unravel this damnable prison, free my students, and finish what we started so many years ago. Goodbye, my student. Tomorrow the lessons begin anew."

He bows once more, then turns and walks to the double doors at the end of the room. The doors open before he reaches them, then close with an echoing *boom* when he passes through. When LaFleur is finally alone, he sighs in relief.

They have had this conversation more times than he can remember, and if the world is to survive he must continue having it for as long as he draws breath. Artigenian believes himself free of the island, but that is only partially true: he is powerful, and his power grants him some autonomy, but the island is always pulling at him, trying to bring him back into the pattern. So far, that has saved LaFleur's life, unpleasant though his current existence may be: Artigenian is completely unaware that he has been repeating the first day of LaFleur's interrogation for months, maybe even years. As long as he remains unaware of this, he will not resort to the methods that will break LaFleur's will. The moment he suspects...

LaFleur closes his eyes. He *will* suspect. Someday he will realize what LaFleur is doing, and all will be lost. But today is not that day... today there is still hope.

CURVEBALL
20
JAN 2015
CURVEBALL
A Prose Comic
THE DRUMS OF WAR
STORY
CHRISTOPHER WRIGHT
COVER
PASCALLE LEPAS
LOGO
GARTH GRAHAM

PART ONE: QUEENS, 7 PM

Roger Whitman stops at the end of his block, trying to figure out what's bothering him about his street. The sun is down, and the street lights shine dim white light that doesn't quite reach the far end of the sidewalks. The street is empty and silent; the only sounds come from the families in their houses: TVs blaring, music playing, people laughing and shouting. The sounds aren't overpowering—just there, familiar and comforting. Ten houses on each side of the street, cars in front of each.

That's it. That's what bothers him. There are too many cars.

His neighbors are creatures of habit—they park in the same spaces every night. Two cars parked along the street in front of the house on the left, one car and a motorcycle on the right. Station wagon, minivan, used Prius—Elly was so proud the day she bought that car. A clunker bought by the parents of an over-enthusiastic teenager who keeps talking about how he's going to convert it into a muscle car, but never does. Roger takes in each car, each in its proper place, until he comes across the car that isn't.

It's a red Ford Escape, parked a few houses down from his. It doesn't belong to any of his neighbors, but he recognizes it from another part of his life. He frowns slightly—he doesn't mind the visit, but given recent events he's not sure he's going to like why she's here.

He takes his time getting back to his house, enjoying the last of his walk, and notes the slim figure waiting patiently on his front stoop—an attractive, middle-aged white woman with blond hair, dressed in blue jeans and a black-and-white spring blouse. She waits patiently as he continues up the sidewalk, and says nothing when he finally stops in front of her.

"Hello Juliet," Roger says. "Hope you weren't waiting long."

Juliet Forrest smiles back. "Not too long. Hope you don't mind."

She looks very small standing in front of him. She was always small physically, but she was so fierce she seemed to tower over everyone else in the room. It was one of the qualities that made her such a good reporter, when she was still doing that. Everyone always underestimated Juliet, until she opened her mouth and suddenly she was the giant.

She doesn't come across as a giant tonight. Tonight she looks like a frail white woman who got lost and wound up in the wrong neighborhood. She's not, but she looks it, and that says a lot. He can't help but notice how tense she is. It's in her voice, the way she carries herself, in the tightness around her eyes. "Always good to see you. Sorry I was out. I was about to brew some coffee. Interested?"

"I'd love a cup," she says.

Roger's house is modest compared to the Forrests' brownstone. The ground floor has a small living room, a bathroom, and an eat-in kitchen. In the living room, stairs go up to the second floor. In the kitchen, stairs descend to the basement.

The kitchen was last decorated in the 70s. The floor is covered in faded orange linoleum tile, the countertops in green Formica, and the appliances are all brown and gold. Juliet sits at the dinner table and fishes through her purse, eventually pulling out a pen and a small notepad. Roger breaks into a grin—it's a holdout from her days as a reporter. She hasn't been one for some time, but she never goes anywhere without the notepad.

"I see your kitchen is still ugly," Juliet says, clicking the pen and starting to write.

Roger snorts as he rummages through his cupboard for the coffee tin. "I'm too lazy to renovate. It'll be orange and green and cheap linoleum until I move out. Or something interesting happens."

Juliet laughs softly. *Something interesting* has a very specific meaning to the surviving members of the Guardians. It usually involves smoking impact craters.

She puts her pen on the table, holds up the notepad toward Roger, and coughs softly. Roger looks over his shoulder and narrows his eyes as he reads the hastily-scrawled script on the pad:

I was followed but I lost them. Anyone listening in?

Juliet is still smiling, but once again Roger notices the tightness around her eyes. He puts the coffee tin down on the counter and concentrates for a moment. Then he shakes his head.

Juliet sighs, relaxing slightly. "You're sure?" The cheerful facade slips, and he can hear exhaustion and worry come to the forefront.

Roger nods. "Even the good ones make noise. When I'm listening I can hear it."

Juliet nods slowly. "I sort of forgot you could do that."

"It was never something I advertised," Roger says. "More useful that way. They haven't tried to bug my house for years, but occasionally I need to have stern words with someone in an unmarked surveillance van. Haven't had to do that in months. I'll keep an ear out."

"Thanks," Juliet says. "I'm sorry, Roger. I didn't see you much at the funeral, and it's been a long time since we—I just don't know who I can trust right now."

"You had other things to deal with at the funeral," Roger says. "And I like to keep to myself these days... but my door is always open to friends. How's the house? Moved back in yet?"

Juliet shakes her head. "It'll be another few months. We could buy another place, but we'd rather not... so we're still in the hotel."

"You both could stay here for a while," Roger says. "I have an extra room upstairs. There's not much space, but..." His voice trails off as he sees the expression on her face.

"That's probably not a good idea right now," she says.

Roger nods, and fills the carafe with tap water. "You look tired. Is this about CB?"

Juliet laughs—half amusement, half terror. "Yes. Not exactly. It's about Jenny."

Roger narrows his eyes. "Jenny?"

"She went with him, Roger. I didn't want her to—I don't think *he* wanted her to, to be honest—but she did. Just like I did, back in the day. And now she's..." She breaks off, draws a deep breath, steadying herself. Hardening herself, a little. "She shot someone, Roger. A security guard. He's dead, the government's involved, and they're seconds away from branding her a terrorist under Title XII."

Roger stares at Juliet for a moment, expressionless, before he pours the water into the coffee maker. "Think maybe I chose the wrong drink for this. Too late now. Start from the beginning."

He makes coffee while Juliet talks. When she finishes the pot is almost full.

"Shit," Roger says.

"Now they're following me, of course," Juliet says. "I don't know who. FBI. DHS. Someone attached to all those papers I signed. They obviously don't think I'm much of a risk, because they didn't put a tracker on my car and the people they assigned to follow me aren't that good. I was worried about electronic eavesdropping, but you cleared that up."

"Looks like someone underestimated you again."

Juliet smiles slightly.

Roger pours the coffee into two mugs and sets one in front of Juliet.

"There's cream and sugar if you want it, but I seem to remember you preferring it black."

Juliet nods. "Still do. Thanks."

Roger takes a moment to enjoy the smell of coffee filling the room. Caffeine has no effect on him at all—the only reason he drinks it is because he likes the smell. "So. Does the government know about Richter? That he killed Alex, I mean."

Juliet shakes her head. "We haven't told anyone. We have a copy of that file, but we're sitting on it."

"So all they know is that CB and Jenny disappeared after those guys attacked your house, and then they wound up in Farraday City attacking a... health insurance building?"

"I have no idea what they were doing there," Juliet admits.

"Dammit, CB..." Roger shakes his head. "And *Travers*? Wow. OK. So you're here because you don't trust your brother."

"Do you?" Juliet asks, sounding surprised.

"No. But he's not my family. Where does Marty fall on this?"

Juliet hesitates. "He... he believes CB and Jenny are innocent. But he also thinks Toby is being reasonable. He's doing exactly what my grandfather would do in a situation like this."

"Cooperate with the authorities as much as he can, but keep CB and Jenny safe as long as he can," Roger says. "I assume he doesn't know you came here."

"The less he knows, the less he has to walk that line," Juliet says.

They lapse into silence. Juliet hunches over her coffee, not bothering to drink it, just soaking in the heat. Roger leans back in his chair, staring at his orange kitchen ceiling.

"CB told me he was going to get in touch," Roger says.

"When?"

"At the funeral. I guess he hasn't had much opportunity to call..."

Roger pushes back from the table and gets to his feet. "The neighborhood is quiet. Give me a second to take a look outside, just to make sure, then go home."

"What are you going to do?" Juliet asks.

"It's like you and Marty," Roger says. "The less you know the better. But

I'm on it, OK?"

Juliet stands, and hugs him. A flash of that old fierceness returns, and she fills the room again. "Thank you."

Roger laughs. "I knew I'd have to pull CB's ass out of the fire eventually. I didn't think your daughter would be part of that, but I guess it runs in the family."

Juliet tries her best to look disapproving.

Roger opens the front door and looks around. "It's clear."

"You have X-ray vision, too?" Juliet sounds more playful now, the way she did in the old days.

Roger snorts. "You're just like CB. Trying to get me sued."

He waits until her car drives down the street before he closes and locks his front door, empties Julie's coffee into the sink, then takes his own mug with him upstairs. His computer sits on a small desk next to his bed. He turns it on, leans back in the chair, props his feet up on his bed, and sips at his coffee until it boots up.

He spends a few minutes checking his regular email, then he opens up his other email. No messages—he didn't expect any. He creates one of his own:

To: rt@thorpe.tti

Subject: Something interesting

Alex, CB, Crossfire. Thought I'd stop by.

- Roger

He hits send, then returns to sipping his coffee. Five minutes later, he gets a reply.

To: roger@regiment.tti

Subject: Re: Something interesting

I'll leave the door unlocked.

Roger spends an hour writing letters on his computer, printing them out, and stuffing them into envelopes. Then he goes back downstairs.

He does the dishes by hand, including the coffee pot, and puts them away before they're dry, ignoring the mental image of his mother scolding him for doing so. He empties his refrigerator, putting most of the perishables in a trash bag, putting the more useful items—eggs, milk, butter—in a small cardboard box. He takes out the trash—a few days early, but it should be OK—then starts unplugging everything, and turning everything off.

He takes his printouts and the cardboard box filled with perishables as he steps outside and locks his front door. He walks over to the house on the left and knocks. The thunder of footsteps booms through the door, and the sound of laughter and excited shhshing and whispering, along with the twitching of the living room curtains, tells Roger that Esteban's kids have decided to ignore their bedtime in favor of spying on their late-evening caller.

A small, thin, clean-shaven Hispanic man with salt and pepper hair opens the door a crack, then all the way when he sees who it is.

"Roger?"

"Hi Esteban. Sorry for coming by so late."

"We were just getting ready for bed..." Esteban frowns slightly and looks over his shoulder. He shouts something in Spanish, and Roger catches a glimpse of Esteban's kids as they race past the doorway, up the stairs.

Esteban stifles a yawn. "Anything wrong?" He eyes the cardboard box.

Roger holds it out. "From my refrigerator. I'm going to be traveling for a while, I figured your family could use it. Also I wanted to leave you my key. Can you keep an eye on things?"

"Sure." Esteban takes the cardboard box and sets it down on the floor, then takes the keys.

"One more thing," Roger says. "I'm sort of in a hurry, and I need to leave some messages with some people. It's... work related."

Esteban raises an eyebrow. "You mean...?" He makes an up, up and away motion with one hand.

Roger nods. "I wrote some letters. Put names and addresses on each one. Could you deliver them? I hate to ask, but—"

"No problem, Roger." Esteban doesn't hesitate. "We'll be OK. Nobody's gonna mess with a guy doing Regiment's business."

"Thanks." Roger hands the letters over.

"So you're going to make trouble, eh?" Esteban's grin is uncharacteristically impish.

Roger can't help but grin in return. "Sort of. I'm getting the band back together."

PART TWO: FARRADAY CITY BUNKER

By the time Jenny is up and out of the shower CB and Red Shift are already dressed and staring down at the dinner table, where an actual fold-out map of Farraday City is spread over the top.

"Wow," Jenny says, looking at the map. "I didn't think they made those things any more."

"So *where* did they trace it?" CB looks down at the map in irritation. "Saying 'it's in Farraday City' isn't very specific. We need something more specific."

Red Shift shrugs. "Street Ronin thinks Zero can probably figure it out. They have to make some preparations before the move. Scrapper Jack hasn't checked in yet, and Overmind and the Lieutenant are still looking into the magic thing. They have to make sure they can leave messages that won't get intercepted."

"I can figure *what* out?" Jenny goes over to the coffee and pours a cup. "What the hell are you talking about?"

"Crossfire did something clever the other night," CB says. "I'm trying not to sound impressed, so I'm complaining instead."

"Oh?" Jenny wanders back to the table, looking down at the map with interest. "What'd they do?"

"Vigilante attacked the TriHealth building in Manhattan." CB shakes his head, trying not to laugh.

Jenny arches an eyebrow. "That's *clever*?"

"I know, right?" CB grins. "It doesn't sound clever at all, which is why it's *so damn pretty*."

"Maybe you better explain it to me," Jenny says. "I just woke up."

"Vigilante burst into the building from the ground floor, made a lot of noise, attracted a lot of attention," Red Shift says. "So TriHealth enacted its security protocols, and Street Ronin was on hand to monitor all the data traffic flowing out of the building. He traced a huge dump of data here."

"Oh," Jenny says, surprised. "The security protocols were set up to archive important data off site, then wipe it locally to prevent it from being stolen."

"Apparently," Red Shift says.

"So they *forced* a situation that would trigger those protocols, with no intention of actually getting the data—they just wanted to see where it went."

"Like I said," CB says, "damn pretty."

"Can you figure out where the data went?" Red Shift asks.

Jenny shrugs. "Won't know until I try. Give me the data."

"Already on your laptop," Red Shift says.

Jenny looks around. "And where is that?"

"Moved it into the monitor room," CB says. "To make room for the map."

"We have about a day before they get here," Red Shift says. "Another two if we wait for Scrapper Jack, which we probably should. We should use that time to—"

"Wait, *what*?" Jenny's eyes widen. "They're coming *here*?"

"It's going to be a little cramped in the bunker," CB says. "Might be a good idea if I picked up some air freshener. I'm thinking the little pine-scented tree things..."

Jenny doesn't pay any attention to CB. She looks at Red Shift uneasily.

"Problem?" Red Shift stares back, expression bland.

"Uh... not exactly. It's just... if they're on their way here then training is over."

Red Shift nods. "It's a little sooner than I'd like to see you in the field, but there's not much more we can do in here and it's too dangerous to train outside. To be honest, I'm looking forward to doing something productive."

"So I'm in on this? You're not making me stay here?"

CB looks up in irritation. "Why would we do that?"

"Because I'm green."

CB shrugs. "Everyone starts out green, *Zero*, and we don't have a lot of allies right now. Right now I figure you and Street Ronin are our best shot at recovering whatever data this place is storing... assuming we can find it."

"Right," Jenny says. Her eyes unfocus.

"Jenny." CB squints at her. "*Jenny.*"

She blinks. "Right. I guess I better get started on that."

She walks into the monitor room and finds her laptop, already set up next to one of the monitors. She turns it on and waits for it to boot. She takes slow, deep breaths.

"You're going to do OK."

She turns in her chair and sees Red Shift leaning against the doorframe, arms folded.

"You sure about that? I don't have a bulletproof force field."

"Oh, you might get killed. But you'll be OK."

Jenny frowns. "That's not funny."

"I'm not joking," Red Shift says. "You might get killed. It happens. But if you do, it won't be because you lost your head and panicked."

"I notice you didn't say 'it won't be because you did something stupid.'"

"In my experience it's actually pretty hard not to do something stupid," Red Shift says.

"Not encouraging," Jenny mutters.

PART THREE: DOBRETTI'S PIZZA, GREENWICH VILLAGE

Special Agent Phillip Henry is sitting in a wooden booth covered in graffiti, staring down at a pizza set on their wooden table, which is also covered in graffiti.

"I can't eat all this." His voice carries a mixture of amusement and genuine alarm, causing the man sitting across from him to burst into laughter.

"They don't sell by the slice, boss." Special Agent Alan Grant shakes his head, grinning at Henry's discomfort. "Anyway, you don't have to eat all of it. I promised to save Hu a slice, and I'm pretty sure our guest is going to be hungry. Assuming he shows up."

They look slightly out of place—both men dressed in black suits, the shorter dark-skinned man wearing sunglasses indoors, the taller pale-skinned man wearing a black trenchcoat along with the suit. Everyone else is wearing t-shirts and jeans, with maybe the occasional polo shirt sprinkled in the crowd. But this is New York City, and nobody pays much attention.

Agent Henry sighs and carefully extracts a slice from the pan.

"Think he'll show?" Grant sounds skeptical.

Henry nods. "It was his idea."

"Yeah, but you're not alone, and you're not exactly hiding that."

"That's true," a familiar voice says. "But it's the company he keeps that's important."

Peter Raphael Travers looks down at the two of them, smiling his trademark polite, mildly friendly smile as he takes in their looks of surprise. His smile is the only thing recognizable: his head is shaved, he sports a thick, unkempt beard, and he's wearing blue jeans and an unbelievably garish orange and red Hawaiian shirt. He holds a New York Mets baseball cap in his left hand, and a lime green backpack—the kind a pre-teen student might carry—hangs over one shoulder.

"Love the look," Grant says. "Very inconspicuous."

"In this city? You'd be surprised." Travers slides into the booth next to Agent Henry, nodding to Grant amiably. "It's not whether Phillip comes alone. In a situation like this it would be stupid to come alone, and your boss isn't stupid. If he looked like he *was* alone, I'd assume he wasn't and wonder who he was trying to hide. He didn't bother doing that—instead, he put *you* in plain sight, and if *you're* here, that means Hu is probably around here somewhere..." He scans the room, then shrugs. "If he'd brought Frank, Mallory, or Collins... I'd be expecting a trap. He brought Collins and Frank when he came to arrest me. But you and Hu... that means he thinks we're about to go off script."

Agent Henry doesn't bother to protest. Travers helps himself to a slice of pizza.

"I am *wounded*," Grant says. "Cut to the quick."

"I'm sure. Phillip, is it safe to talk here?"

"Until Grant tells us otherwise," Agent Henry says. "I won't say you look well, because you don't."

"Field work doesn't suit me," Travers agrees. "As long as you don't say 'I'm placing you under arrest,' I'll manage to carry on." Travers' expression doesn't change, but Agent Henry can hear the caution creep into his voice. "You aren't going to do that, are you?"

Agent Henry shakes his head. "For the time being, the video you sent us of Clive Darius contaminating our crime scene has convinced me that our chain of command has become... unreliable."

"Unfortunately," Travers says, "insider threat in the DHS is not what you need to focus on right now. At least, not entirely."

Agent Henry raises an eyebrow. "All right. Tell me what I *should* be focusing on."

Travers opens his backpack, pulls out a thumb drive, and sets it in front of Agent Henry. "This."

Agent Henry glances at Grant, who nods once. He stares at the thumb drive thoughtfully. "What's this?"

"I have given copies of this to two other people," Travers says. "Curveball got the first copy, back when the Forrests' home was attacked. The second was given to one former police lieutenant David Bernard."

"Which is what led to your current status," Agent Henry says.

"That's right," Travers says. "That has everything I know about PRODIGY. And I'm more certain than ever that there's an important connection there. One that your unreliable chain of command is trying very hard to prevent you from finding."

Agent Henry picks up the thumb drive and sticks it in his jacket pocket. "Anything else?"

"There's something happening in Farraday City," Travers says. "I don't know what, but I'm pretty sure it has something to do with—"

"We gotta go." Agent Grant stands and heads toward the back, expression grim. "Now."

Travers follows immediately, relaxed and alert. Agent Henry slides out of the booth without comment, straightening his jacket as he stands.

"Come on." Grant makes his way past the restrooms to a heavy security door that opens into the alley behind the pizzeria. He steps through, looking around warily. There's not much to see—the backs of stores, mostly, all looking pretty much the same: cinderblock walls, heavy metal doors with industrial lights set into the wall above them. A large green dumpster sits to the right of their exit. It's half filled with trash, and the smell of rancid pizza sauce fills the air.

"What's going on?" Travers doesn't sound worried, but his eyes linger on doors and rooftops.

"There's a van prowling around out front," Grant says. He unbuttons his suit coat, revealing a shoulder holster. He unsnaps the thumb break on his holster, fingering the handle of his Glock service pistol. "Hu doesn't like it. If she doesn't like it, neither do I..."

Travers looks puzzled. "How is she telling you this? You're not wearing an earpiece."

"Well, we have really good communication ski—whoa, dumpster! Now!"

Agent Henry shoves Travers behind the large metal dumpster and draws his weapon just as Agent Grant dives onto the ground. Brakes squeal as two unmarked vans race around a corner and come to a stop at the end of the alley.

"Grant?" Agent Henry sounds a little annoyed.

"Yeah," Grant says. "We didn't notice *them*. Uh... oops?"

"Right," Agent Henry says. "Travers are you armed?"

Travers pulls a .45 semi-automatic out of his backpack.

"OK," Agent Henry says. "Grant. This is not where I want to be."

"Only cover I could find on short notice."

"Nevertheless..."

"Yeah," Grant says. "I know. Hu is on her way. I'll try to make a path."

He grips his pistol, reaches into his coat pocket, and pulls out two extra magazines, setting them in his lap. He takes several deep breaths in rapid succession.

"One... two..."

Five shots fire in the distance *(bam, bam, bambambam)* followed by shouts of alarm, followed immediately by two more *(bam, bam)* sounding much farther from the dumpster than the first set and then all they can hear is chaos. Men shout incoherently. Automatic weapons start firing in short, controlled bursts, though none appear to be firing at their position behind the dumpster. It sounds to Travers as if they're not trying to advance on the dumpster at all, but to respond to an entirely different ambush.

(*bambambam, bambambam*)

Grant releases the magazine in his Glock. It slides smoothly out of the grip and falls to the ground. He grabs one of the magazines in his lap and slides it into place.

"How are we doing?" Agent Henry can't see anything—the dumpster blocks everything.

"Uh, well, OK..." Grant's voice is strained. "I'm just waiting for Hu to—"

More shots fire, this time farther back.

"—get here so we can get some proper—"

Someone decides to switch their weapon to fully automatic (*dakkadakkadakkadakkadakka*) and Grant yelps in surprise.

"—*shit*, where'd he come from—"

(*Bam, bam, bambambambambambam*)

"—and they're wearing body armor, what the *fuck*—"

(*Bam bam bam bam*)

He releases the magazine in his pistol a second time, and grabs the third.

"Where's Hu?" Agent Henry sounds as he always does—detached and calculating. Travers knows it's a facade—the man who can always detect a lie has the best poker face Travers has ever seen—but it's a very effective facade at the moment. He appears completely unfazed by current circumstances.

Grant shrugs as he slides the third magazine into his gun. "She was on her way last I checked. Look, they're distracted, we might be able to make it back into Dobretti's."

"No," Agent Henry says. "Too many civilians. Need backup?"

"I'll need ammo pretty soon."

Agent Henry reaches into his jacket and pulls out three more magazines.

"It's shame we didn't get access to the armory today," Grant says. "That'd make things a little easier."

"I didn't think we'd need it. Sorry."

(*Bambambambambambambam, bam, bam, bambam, bam, bam*)

The alley is silent.

The last of Grant's magazines slides out of his pistol. He picks them up (all empty, Travers notices) and puts them in his suit jacket pocket.

"I think that's all of them." Grant takes one of Agent Henry's magazines and reloads. "Let's go find Hu."

They walk around the dumpster. Two black, unmarked vans block the end of the alley. Bodies are everywhere—ten in all, all armed with rifles and wearing body armor. None of them move.

"Fucking body armor," Grant says. His voice shakes with adrenaline.

Travers look at Agent Grant steadily. "I never did learn what it was that got you placed in Division M, Agent Grant."

"My *winning smile*," Grant says.

Agent Henry says nothing. He's staring at one of the vans and frowning. Travers looks at him questioningly.

Agent Henry nods at the van. "It's one of ours."

Grant looks at the van. "Seriously?"

"Definitely one of ours," Agent Henry says.

"We just got swatted by our own guys?" Agent Grant's face starts to twist into a scowl, then his eyes go wide. "Did I just...?"

"Hold that thought." Agent Henry runs to the closest van. The windshield has three bullet holes in a tight grouping on the driver's side, angled as if the shooter was standing on the hood of the van, shooting down. The windshield is tinted, but he can see a vague silhouette slumped over in the front seat.

The side door is open. Agent Henry pokes his head in and immediately notices the surveillance gear. He swears, which surprises both Travers and Grant more than anything else that's happened so far.

"They were tracking our phones," Agent Henry says, looking at Grant. "Mine, yours, Hu's. They weren't after Travers. They were coming for us."

"But that doesn't..." Grant's voice trails off. "Fuck. Where's Hu?"

The alley opens into a narrow street that doesn't look as if it gets much use, other than to provide access to the alleyways that empty onto it. Grant looks down both directions, frowning, unsure which way to go.

"She was supposed to—"

A gray Cadillac DeVille skids around the corner, the back fishtailing up onto the too-thin sidewalk and smacking into the corner of a red-and-tan brick building, smashing the right rear taillight as it tries to straighten out and keep moving. Another black van, identical in every way to the two parked in front of the alley, smashes into the side of the car, engines roaring. Glass breaks, the back doors crumple, and the DeVille is hurled into the brick wall, tipping sideways from the force of the collision.

"Hu!" Grant starts running down the street, weapon drawn. His outline blurs slightly, then he's at the end of the street, closing in on the van and the car.

Fire erupts from the DeVille's driver seat. The windshield and the top of the car vanish as a column of liquid heat shoots into the sky. Grant staggers back, covering his eyes, and the column arcs up and bends back toward the wreckage, hanging in the air over the van. The column coalesces into the shape of a woman—no distinct features, only unending flame.

Fire roils around the form, then streams down into the van. Agent Grant blurs again, and this time he reappears halfway up the street just as the van explodes, sending metal and glass in all directions. None of it seems to affect the burning woman in the least.

Agent Henry and Travers run over to Agent Grant.

"Thank God," Agent Grant says. "For a second there, I thought she was in trouble."

The burning silhouette floats over to them. The heat rises rapidly. The silhouette stops a few feet from Grant.

"Sorry I'm late." The silhouette speaks with a woman's voice. "I had a thing."

"Yeah," Grant says. "We saw the thing. We had a thing too. Glad you're OK."

Special Agent Lijuan Hu laughs. Flames trail off into wisps of smoke where her mouth should be. "These guys were not here for surveillance. They must want Travers pretty bad. Hi, Travers."

"Agent Hu," Travers says. "Always a little terrifying to see you work."

"They weren't here for Travers," Agent Henry says. "They were tracking our phones."

Hu turns in midair to face Agent Henry. "*Our* phones?"

Agent Henry nods. "I assume yours is no longer an issue." He takes out his and places it on the ground. "Agent Grant."

Grant stares at him blankly, then understanding dawns. "Right." He reaches into his trenchcoat pocket and pulls out his cell phone. He sighs, then throws it on the ground next to Agent Henry's.

Agent Henry steps back. "Agent Hu, if you would be so kind."

Fire surges around her, and a stream of white-hot flame smashes into the phones. When the flame retreats, all that's left is a bubbling puddle of plastic and glass.

"We need to leave," Agent Henry says. "I expect police soon."

"Or their backup," Travers says, gesturing to the burning van.

"Police would be better," Agent Henry says. "I'd rather be somewhere else, whichever the case."

Agent Hu floats a little closer to Agent Grant.

"Alan..." Hu shifts uneasily. "I... um..." She gestures toward his coat.

Agent Grant sighs. "Oh come *on*, Hu. You didn't wear your bathing suit? Again?"

"I didn't know today was going to be so *active*," Hu snaps. "Also, it's not a bathing suit. It's uncomfortable as hell, it's made of fucking *asbestos*, and I'm not real keen on cancer."

"Yeah, OK." Still grumbling, Grant takes off his trenchcoat and holds it out. He turns his head. "Avert your eyes, gentlemen!"

Travers and Agent Henry comply. Immediately the wave of heat dissipates. Cloth rustles briefly, then Agent Hu sighs in relief.

"Thanks," Hu says.

In place of the figure of pure flame is an attractive Asian woman with an oddly reddish tint to her skin.

"I was trying to bring the car around," Hu says. "That van started pursuing. I tried to ditch it, didn't work. When it sideswiped me I decided their intentions weren't honorable so I lit up. Uh... sorry about the car, boss."

"Later," Agent Henry says. "Come on, let's go."

Travers feels himself starting to relax, and turns to look down the other end of the street. "Agreed. I know a few places where we might—"

"Gun!" Agent Hu shouts the warning, and Travers turns to see a figure rising from behind the twisted wreckage of the burning van, a pistol bearing down on—someone, but it's all happening too fast, he can't really tell where it will—

His vision blurs, then Agent Grant is in front of him, knocking him to the ground. A single shot is fired, and Grant jerks to one side, grabbing his head, face twisted into a mask of pain. The attacker falls back as Agent Henry fires four shots (*bam, bam, bam, bam)* waits to make sure he doesn't move, then turns to kneel in front of... Agent Grant, lying motionless on the ground, blood pouring out of the back of his head.

Travers looks at the dead body of Agent Grant in front of Agent Henry, then back down at the writhing form of the still-living Agent Grant at his own feet. He's not screaming any more. Just muttering *no, no, no, fuck, fuck no, no* to himself as he clutches at the back of his untouched head.

"Alan. It's OK. Alan, *listen* to me, it's *going to be OK.*"

Agent Hu kneels in front of *another* Agent Grant, curled up in the same position, clutching at the back of his head.

Agent Henry is looking at Grant as well. "Hu. He's gotta leave the corpse."

Agent Hu looks up, shocked. "Boss, this is going to be hard enough—"

"I know," Agent Henry says. "Believe me, I'm not happy about it."

She nods once, clearly frustrated, then returns her attention to Grant.

Agent Henry looks around the scene one last time, then holsters his gun. "Come on, Travers. Hu is taking care of Agent Grant. We need to take care of everything else, and we don't have a lot of time."

PART FOUR: FARRADAY CITY BUNKER

"Found it!"

Jenny leans back in her chair, staring at her laptop screen in satisfaction.

CB's head appears past the edge of the doorframe. "Yeah?"

Jenny nods. "Yeah."

Moments later CB is standing over her shoulder, peering at the screen. "Where is that? Can you zoom it out?"

Jenny does. "It's past the north end of the boardwalk. You see that cluster of buildings there? Looks like old warehouses and office buildings."

"Oh," CB says. "I know where that is. It's a Superfund site. Nobody goes there because of all the poison."

"Somebody does. That's where the trace stops." She points at a spot on the monitor. "I'm guessing from there it switches to some other kind of network. I can probably find it and give you a more specific location, but there's a pretty good chance someone will notice."

"Can you do it in the field?" CB asks.

Jenny shrugs. "I guess. If there's a place for me to hook up."

"Street Ronin can take care of that." Red Shift is in the room now, peering over her other shoulder. "Can you automate it? And can you make it look like someone is actively trying to hack the network?"

"I like that," CB says. "If we can find out where the network begins it'll give us a starting point when we storm the castle. And if we can get them to think it's a remote threat at the same time, they'll be focusing on trying to track that down instead of paying attention to us. Might be a nice distraction."

"I probably could," Jenny says, "but I don't know what I have to work with. I kinda don't want to use my laptop. I already had to give up my car because of these assholes, I don't want to lose my baby."

Red Shift chuckles softly. "Street Ronin can help you with that, too. I'm not familiar with all his toys but... well, you two should talk when we get started."

"OK," Jenny says.

"Also, I'm breaking curfew," Red Shift adds. "I'll be careful, but I need to talk to your friend Elliot about getting some of those things we talked about."

"Oh..." CB nods. "Right. *That*. Well, be careful. They obviously don't know where we are, and I want to keep it that way."

"What things? What *that*?" Jenny looks from Red Shift, to CB, then back. "What are you talking about?"

"You're going to need a..." CB reaches for the right word and stumbles over it.

"The traditional term is *costume*," Red Shift says, "though I had something a little more practical in mind."

Jenny blinks. "Costume."

"'Uniform' is probably more accurate, these days." Red Shift shrugs. "You're definitely going to need something that can handle more wear and tear than street clothes."

Jenny narrows her eyes. "No heels. Also, if my *costume* winds up doing anything cute like flashing cleavage I *will* find a way through that force field of yours..."

CB laughs. "No spandex, no boob window. We promise!"

"Back in a bit," Red Shift says. A moment later Jenny sees him on the security monitors as he emerges from the safehouse and heads off into the city.

When she looks up she sees CB staring at her thoughtfully.

"What?"

He shrugs. "Just... sorry you've been stuck in here all this time. It's a little unfair."

"It *sucks*. I get it, though. It wasn't the most convenient time for me to go all metahuman on everyone. It would have been better if I'd done it in New York. At least I know where everything is up there."

"I was thinking more about what would happen if Richter or Plague had found you wandering around topside," CB says. "But yeah, Farraday City is its own brand of special. Not the place I'd have chosen for your cotillion."

Jenny snorts. "A *cotillion*?"

"This is the South," CB says. "That's apparently what you do."

Jenny smiles mischievously. "So should we send out invitations? It sounds like the kind of thing you RSVP."

"I like that," CB says. "Something along the lines of '*Zero requests the honor of your presence on the occasion of her Inaugural Farraday City Metahuman Cotillion for the benefit of shooting, punching, and otherwise royally kicking your sorry asses into next week.*' We'll print it up on fancy paper, with calligraphy done in gold ink."

"Excellent," Jenny says. "And on top of it all you're getting me something pretty to wear. What girl could ask for more?"

"Red is handling the pretty," CB says. "Crossfire has a lot more experience with body armor than I do. He's going to frankenstein my old suit and add a few extras. Uh, that reminds me."

He reaches into his trenchcoat pocket and pulls out a carpenter's tape measure. "Stand up, let's get this over with."

Jenny eyes the tape measure doubtfully. "I'm pretty sure that's not what you're supposed to use."

"So am I," CB says, "but it's what I've got. Stand up, hold out your arms in a 'T'."

Jenny stands. CB awkwardly starts taking her measurements.

"So what are they like?" Jenny asks. "Crossfire, I mean. They're not really who I thought I..." Her cheeks color slightly, and she laughs, embarrassed. "I mean, when I was a kid, and pretending I was... what I am, now, when I pictured the kind of people I'd be working with, they were never..."

"Yeah, your cotillion is going to be *really* fucked up."

"First, let's not call it that any more," Jenny says. "Second, I'm serious. I'm the newbie, remember? All I know is what I get from the news and the Internet."

CB shrugs. "You've met Red Shift."

"Yeah, so, friendly, laid-back killing machine. They're all like him?"

"Look, Jenny, I've been out of this life for a while. The last time I had anything to do with Crossfire at all was before 9/11, and we were *fighting* at the time. The Guardians won, for the record."

"How does that work, anyway? One day you're fighting them, and a decade plus later you're best friends? And working with *Overmind*? Isn't he one of the most dangerous men on the whole damn *planet*?"

"It's complicated," CB says.

"Come on, CB, do better than that." Jenny looks at him pleadingly. "I don't know how to do this. I know *you* trust these guys, for whatever reason, but trusting them because you do isn't enough. I want to know why *I* should. I *need* to know."

CB doesn't say anything at first. He's staring at her, but it seems to Jenny that he doesn't actually *see* her. He's somewhere else, lost in a memory—a bittersweet one from the smile she sees play across his face. The memory passes, the smile fades, and he focuses again.

"Yeah," he says. "That's fair. Sorry. You're getting the crash course on the hero biz, and you're getting it from the grays. It's a hell of a thing."

"Grays?"

"Yeah. Unofficial term. Groups like Crossfire—groups that operate outside the law and make everything complicated. A lot of 'em showed up in the 90s, and someone called 'em 'grays' because trying to place them on a side was a real problem. We like our lines clear and unbroken, and they make drawing those lines a real bitch."

"No black or white, only gray," Jenny says. "That kind of thing?"

"Yeah," CB says. "The thing is, though? It's bullshit. The dirty little secret about Crossfire: they're not shades of gray. They're *true believers*. They have a vision of how the world should be, and they bring war to anyone who gets in its way. They're a lot like me, back in the beginning."

"When you were a villain?" Jenny shakes her head. "How is that a good thing?"

"*Before* I was a villain. Before I crossed the line."

"Oh," Jenny says.

"Look, they're not saints," CB says. "They're criminals for a reason. They kill people. If they think the law is protecting one of the bad guys, they ignore the law. If they think the 'good guys' are protecting the 'bad guys,' they'll fight the good guys. I wouldn't want them on my side if I was trying to negotiate a cease fire, but for something like this? Yeah, I'll take 'em in a heartbeat."

"OK," Jenny says. "What about Overmind?"

CB grimaces. "That's more complicated. He is legitimately trying to take over the world, and all that. But LaFleur is the devil you know: as bad as he wants to take over the world, he's not going to kill everyone to get there."

PART FIVE: JULY 20, 1992

The old man hangs in the air, frayed white linen hanging from his gaunt, feeble frame like the last drooping fronds of a dying willow. He's lost track of how long he's been there—months? Years? Long enough that he can barely remember anything else. The power that suspends him also sustains him—it is a prison, not a tomb—but it provides only enough sustenance to prevent his death.

Each day he struggles to master his hunger and his thirst, steeling himself to meet his captor, and each day they go through the same ritual. His former mentor and friend accosts him, threatens him, makes demands he cannot possibly fulfill—and, when the day nears its end, he threatens to do worse the day that follows. But for his captor that day never comes: he's still trapped in the death-throes of the island, and when the island resets, so does he. And so the next day the old man is forced to do it all again, and the next day, and the next, a never-ending stream of being reintroduced to the man who betrayed him and the entire world.

Except that each new day brings even greater hunger and thirst, and each day it becomes harder to master. It cannot last.

His captor *(Artigenian, a tiny voice whispers)* is locked in time and half-blinded by his rage, but he is not a stupid man. The old man is *not* locked in time, and he is changing. His hair grows, his beard grows, and he grows ever thinner, ever weaker, ever more gaunt. The pain of hunger and the agony of thirst make it hard to focus on his task... and if he fails at his task, the entire world fails with him.

He tries, as he always does, to focus on his hunger and his thirst, to recognize their strength and find a way to turn that strength aside. Day after day he wrestles with the gnawing teeth in his stomach, the fire in his throat, and so far he has won. Day after day, but not today: today he feels the power of hunger and thirst and he cannot cast them aside. They are too strong; he is too weak.

The ornate double doors at the far end of the hall open, the sound echoing in the large space. A man dressed in green silk *(Artigenian! a tiny voice screams)* strides purposefully into the room, the hem of his robes trailing along behind him. The doors swing shut of their own accord as he stares at the old man.

As he always does.

The old man closes his eyes.

"No." Artigenian's voice is thick and harsh. "No. You will open your eyes and face me."

As always, the old man feels his eyes open, his head swivel down to gaze on his captor's hard and uncaring face. And in a moment his captor will say *fate, it seems, returns you. Why is that, I wonder?* And so the cursed dance will continue as it always has.

"Who are you?"

The old man's heart skips a beat as he stares at his captor. Artigenian stares back, frowning in suspicion, as if seeing him for the first time.

"You are *not* the man I put in this prison last night. You are the desiccated remnants of a man, perhaps, if ever you were a man at all. Nothing like the—"

Artigenian breaks off and steps forward, just to the edge of the circle that imprisons him. "You will look into my eyes." He speaks with such absolute certainty that it's not even a command, and the old man immediately meets his gaze. It's a terrible gaze, full of power and anger and purpose and the end of all things. It scrapes its way past his eyes and gouges into his soul. Artigenian's eyes widen in surprise.

"It *is* you. But how...?"

The old man hopes against hope, but he sees the suspicion flickering in his captor's eyes.

"You are not as you were, my student. You *were* an empty shell devoid of its glory, yes, but the shell was strong when it arrived. Strange how in the passing of a single night you have become... *this*." He gestures contemptuously.

Artigenian turns away from him and begins to pace, taking long strides down the great hall, hands clasped behind his back, head bowed in thought. Nostalgia washes over the old man as he sees this—it is, perversely, an image he remembers fondly. When he believed this man was his friend, the sight of him so deep in thought was comforting. He knows the man is not his friend, yet the image still conjures that warmth.

Perhaps he is finally about to crack wide open. Perhaps he is finally going mad. The thought is almost comforting—if he can't save the world, it might be better to be oblivious of its end...

Artigenian stops mid-stride, straightens, and turns. "How long?" He glares at the old man, the veins in his neck bulging with anger. "How long have we played this game? How long have you allowed me to believe that this was your first day of captivity?"

The old man says nothing.

"You are no longer strong, my student." His captor's voice sheds its anger and takes on an icy calm. "The circle sustains you, but not well, I think. Your shell is paper thin. And would tear just as easily. And yet..."

He turns away and resumes pacing. One length of the hall, two, three, five, eight... on the eighth he slows to a halt, head held high. Artigenian turns to face the old man.

The old man shudders in horror. Artigenian is smiling.

"I am, it seems, trapped in time. I am more aware of it than the others, but still *bound*. And it raises an interesting dilemma for me."

He advances slowly on the old man. The feeling of horror deepens.

"The dilemma, stated simply: what I have learned *right now* will be forgotten come morning. I wonder if I've made that discovery before. How many times have I discovered my captivity, only to realize that there was no way to retain that knowledge? I have the power to carve my story into the very foundation of this place, to gouge my words in the marble and tile... even the steel, if I chose. But come morning the words would be gone, because they would never have been written. Nothing here *persists*."

Artigenian stands just outside the circle again.

"Nothing persists but you."

The old man begins to tremble as his captor passes his hand across the plane of the circle, disrupting his prison. The old man falls to the ground, groaning in pain as his feeble limbs collapse beneath his weight. He tries to crawl away, but Artigenian is *not* weak, and he steps on one thin arm with his foot—not enough to break bone, but enough for it to *hurt*.

"I cannot use paper," Artigenian says. "So you, my student, will serve in its place."

The old man shakes his head, but can't bring himself to speak.

Artigenian leans over him, tearing away at the linen covering his chest. "Here beats your worthless heart. You, who betrayed us all, *cause est proditor*, you alone are free of this prison. You *persist*. And so tomorrow, when we speak for what I will believe is the first time, I will see the memories I have set into your skin, and I will know it to be a lie. And thus will the prison be broken, and thus shall I be made free."

Artigenian speaks words in an ugly, vicious tongue—words that make the old man's flesh crawl. *Did I speak these words once? Did I blaspheme this world so, and believe that I was doing good?* Before he has time to remember, Artigenian's hand touches his chest. The old man screams as the tip of each finger presses down, and fire bores into his skin. He gags from the smell of his own burning flesh, then screams a second time, like an animal, terrified and desperate. And then, just as the pain threatens to overwhelm him, it changes: the tips of his captor's fingers turn icy cold, and waves of power flow into him. He shivers; his eyes roll back in his head. It cuts and burrows. When Artigenian draws his hand away a complex symbol of black, spidery lines is embedded in the old man's chest. It isn't *part* of him—not like a tattoo, or even a common brand. It simply sits within him, glistening, waiting patiently to be removed.

His captor straightens. He steps back, utters a word, and the old man's prison is restored. Once again he hangs in the air, tattered linen streaming down like dead branches.

"Tonight I will forget you exist," Artigenian says. "Tomorrow, I will remember." He gives a curt, mocking bow, then strides out of the room.

Left to the silence of the room, the old man can do nothing but weep. He has lost. He was not strong enough to resist, and if Artigenian can free himself it will only be a matter of time before he finds a way to undo everything and swallow the world in an ocean of grasping, slithering horror...

"LaFleur?"

The voice comes from behind him. The old man twists helplessly, trying to turn toward the sound, but he has no control over his prison.

"Sorry."

He doesn't hear movement—strange in this hall, where every breath is magnified by its echoes—but he sees a man step into his view. He looks familiar: a young man, in his late twenties or early thirties. Clean-shaven, short, light brown hair, clear blue eyes. He is certain he's met this man before. He reaches for a name...

"...Bernard?" His throat is so dry he can barely get the name out before he dissolves into a fit of hacking, retching, and coughing.

David Bernard. Lieutenant, NYPD (Retired). The first Sky Commando.

"God, LaFleur, what happened?" Bernard stares at the old man in shock.

The old man takes a deep, rattling breath. "Prove it's you."

Bernard blinks in surprise. "I don't... I mean. How?"

"Prove to me you are not one of his lies!" It is painful to speak, but even now the old man must be certain. He doesn't have the strength to win, but he must still fight.

Bernard grimaces. "OK, I get that. But... we don't really know each other. That kind of stuff requires..." His voice trails off and he frowns, thinking quickly. "OK. Back in New York when you first asked for my help, Scrapper Jack acted like he knew what you were planning to do. I didn't understand the context at the time, but I noticed it. He knows, doesn't he? You told him about what happened here. You told him what you told me on the plane—probably more than that, since you trust him more—which is why he didn't want you to come."

The old man sighs in relief. "Thank you. I thought you were lost to the island."

"I was for a while. I cheated. Look, I heard a little of the conversation you had with that guy. I'm pretty sure you don't want to be here tomorrow."

"No," the old man (*LaFleur—my name is Artemis LaFleur*) says. "I don't. Can you free me?"

Bernard hesitates. "Maybe. Hold on."

His expression unfocuses, as if he's staring at something a long way off, and then the old man (*LaFleur, damn it! My name is Artemis LaFleur!*) feels the prison cease to exist. He crashes to the ground in a heap.

"Are you all right?" David kneels next to him, peering at him in concern.

"I need a moment." Artemis LaFleur is weak, but he feels something of himself return. "I need a moment to make sure I'm not dreaming."

"Oh, I'm pretty sure you're not dreaming," Bernard says. "But I am..."

CURVEBALL
21
FEB 2015
CURVEBALL
A Prose Comic
THIS MORTAL COIL
STORY
CHRISTOPHER WRIGHT
COVER
PASCALLE LEPAS
LOGO
GARTH GRAHAM

PART ONE: JULY 20, 1992

Artemis LaFleur stares at the young man kneeling beside him and realizes he's staring at a ghost.

He's certain he's talking to David Bernard, but he's not sure that the man is actually here. Artigenian should have sensed him—the physical presence of an unknown should have set off all manner of wards laid across the stone, and even in this fragment of time they would function. So Bernard's presence is not what it appears.

"You're not really here," Artemis says. "How are you doing this?"

David shrugs. "I don't know how to answer that. I really am asleep right now, if that helps."

"It doesn't," Artemis says. "I'm not even sure how to put that in context."

"That's not encouraging," David says. "I was kind of hoping you'd be able to explain it to me. Can you stand?"

Artemis raises a hand. "Give me a moment."

The power that contained him is gone now. His hunger and thirst is still there, threatening to overwhelm him, but the surge of hope that accompanies his new-found freedom gives him the strength he needs to rein them in, at least for now. He forces himself onto his hands and knees, and is thankful that nothing broke when he fell.

"I... will... manage..." Artemis grits his teeth and forces himself to his feet. His balance is still unsteady, and he's not ready to try walking, but for the first time in a very long time he is standing on his own.

"It was hard to break down that circle," David says. "That's not going to be a problem, is it? Will it alert that man? The one questioning you?"

"Artigenian," Artemis says. "No. The prison was bound to me, not him. If it had been bound to anyone but me, it would have vanished when the island reset."

David nods. "We need to move, then. Can you walk?"

"Not yet." Artemis sways again. "I've been in that prison for quite some time."

"You don't look well," David says.

Artemis closes his eyes and takes a deep, slow breath. "I am very weak. I am very hungry. I am very thirsty. I don't know how far I'm going to be able to go on my own."

"Can you teleport?"

Artemis opens his eyes and stares at David's image. "I might."

David nods once. "When we were on the plane you told me to meet you in a library. Do you remember? The public library in the capital city."

Artemis frowns. "Vaguely. I do know the place."

"Can you teleport there?"

He considers the question. "Perhaps. It would be difficult to manage, but not necessarily impossible. Is it safe?"

"Safer than here," David says. "I watched the place for a few days before moving in. Nobody comes anywhere near it."

"How long will it take you to get there?" Artemis asks.

David shrugs. "I'm there right now. All I have to do is wake up."

Artemis hesitates before answering. He's weak, weaker than he's ever been, and he hasn't been able to use any of his abilities for the past year. He doesn't know if he has the strength to do it. On the other hand, he doubts he has the strength to leave on foot.

"I will try." Artemis' voice is faint, but steady. "I think I can do it."

"When?" David looks around. "I don't know how much time we have."

"We have plenty of time," Artemis says. "No one returns to this hall for hours, and of the people who return, the only one who will notice my absence is Artigenian. And by then he will have forgotten."

"OK." David appears to relax slightly. "Do you want to rest a little before you try?"

Artemis shakes his head. "That will be counterproductive. I must rely on adrenaline, for as long as it lasts. Which may not be long. I'm going to try now."

"All right," David says. "I'll wait until I see you disappear *here*, then wake up there. I'll be a little groggy when I wake up so it might take a minute to get to you."

"I will be at the front desk," Artemis says.

"OK. Good luck."

Artemis closes his eyes. In the past, teleportation has been an almost effortless affair, with very few exceptions—but in the past he was healthy, and in much better shape than his apparent age suggested. He is operating at the very limits of strength and endurance now, and his famed concentration eludes him.

It's because you're doing it wrong.

He's been in that prison for so long that he's nearly forgotten who he is. His gifts were mostly suppressed in there, and now, in his desperate state, he's grasping at them clumsily. He *tsks* to himself in annoyance.

I am my only master.

Immediately the feelings of hunger and thirst vanish. This is a dangerous state to stay in for any length of time, but it is, for the moment, a blessing. He stands straighter, clears his mind, and concentrates. He feels his power stirring, then—his *real* power, not the magician's crutch he'd relied on when Esperanza was his home. He focuses on the memory of the place he wants to be and wills himself to be there.

The power that surges through him brings with it a pain so great that he cannot suppress it. This mode of travel requires energy, and he has so very little. It burns through him as the world shifts around him; moments later, when he collapses on red-and-brown industrial carpeting, he loses all semblance of self control.

PART TWO: BASEMENT OFF ALLEY, NYC

Peter Travers peers through dirty curtains at the crime scene beyond. It's now swarming with NYPD police and emergency rescue personnel, and he can see the beginnings of what will eventually be swarms of federal agents beginning to arrive. Special Agent Phillip Henry is in the middle of it all, giving everyone something to do, and—more important—keeping everyone away from the basement where Travers and Special Agent Alan Grant are hiding.

Their basement is in an alley adjacent to the crime scene, and Travers can see enough from their street-level window to get a general sense of what's going on. He sees Agent Hu sitting in the back of an ambulance, still wrapped in Grant's trenchcoat but now also wrapped in a large, heavy blanket. A police officer is asking her questions. That was Agent Henry's idea, Travers is certain, and it's smart: her statement will become part of the police report, and it'll be harder for whoever directed the DHS agents against them to suppress it.

Not impossible, but harder.

Agent Henry is constantly in motion as he interacts with every group that arrives. He doesn't bother with diplomacy—he just flashes his badge and starts giving orders. What's interesting is that it *works*—people respond as if it's only natural that he be in charge. Maybe it has something to do with his delivery, the way each order feels as if it was given to someone because that person was the only one who could get it done. Maybe it's the unflinching confidence he exudes when he talks to the other law enforcement and emergency response teams as they arrive on the scene. Maybe it's the sunglasses—whatever it is, everyone responds to it, and in short order he has them working together—securing the crime scene, keeping the gathering crowds back, and working with the forensics teams and Fire and Rescue so each group can do their jobs without getting in the way of the other.

Travers sighs as he carefully arranges the curtains so no one will be able to look into the room, then turns to Agent Grant. The tall, dark-haired man is sitting on a crate, leaning against the wall, eyes closed, head tilted up. He looks exhausted.

"What?" Agent Grant's voice slurs slightly.

"I didn't say anything," Travers says.

"You say nothing pretty loud." Grant rubs his eyes, then shakes his head, as if to clear it. "Might as well ask. I know you're curious."

"You look like you're going to fall over," Travers says. "I don't want to—"

"I'm OK." Grant laughs hollowly. "Well. I'm *kind of* OK. It's complicated. I'm OK *here*, but out *there*..."

Grant's gaze travels past Travers to the curtains, and the crime scene beyond.

"The experience is creeping me out, OK? I don't like knowing what dead feels like."

Travers raises an eyebrow. "What *does* dead feel like?"

"Not a goddamned thing," Grant says. "And it's real aggressive about it."

Travers tries to put that into some kind of context, fails, and moves on. "All right. How long do you figure we need to wait here? What are the chances of someone peeking in on us during the inevitable canvass?"

Grant shakes his head. "They won't look here if Agent Henry is directing traffic. Which I'm pretty sure he is. I'm looking into maybe getting us out through the front of the building."

"Oh?" Travers looks at Grant curiously. "There's... another you out there?"

Grant looks a little annoyed. "No, just the same me. I had to go home and change clothes. I figure I don't have a lot of time before the DHS sends a team to search my house, so I'm also packing a few things. Gimme thirty minutes and then I'll be knocking on the front door of the building, trying to see if I can get us out that way."

"So I guess you can't teleport me out," Travers says.

"Sorry, Travers," Grant says. "Can't flip people."

"Is that what you call it?" Travers turns back to the window, and fights the urge to peek through the curtains again. "I know some teleporters have their own nicknames for it, but I've never heard it called that."

"I called it 'flipping' before I really knew what teleportation was," Grant says. "Feels like a backflip each time."

"And you can also copy yourself," Travers says. "That's interesting."

"That's *wrong*," Grant says, annoyance creeping into his voice again. "That's not what I do."

"That's what it looks like you do," Travers says.

"Sure," Grant says, "and if the DHS ever finds out about it I'm gonna swear on a stack of Bibles that that's all it is. But it's more complicated than that."

"Is it?" Travers feels his curiosity shove his anxiety off to one side. "So what is it, exactly? And why doesn't the DHS know about it? What do they think you are?"

Grant sighs. "I don't really like to talk about it much. Reverse order: DHS thinks I'm a teleporter, which is enough for them because the way I do it breaks the rules. They don't know about the other part because I never told them—told the team, eventually, but that's different."

Travers nods.

"As to what it is..." Grant thinks it over. "Keep in mind I'm not an egghead, so my explanation is gonna come up a little short."

"I'm also not an 'egghead,'" Travers points out. "So I probably won't notice."

Grant snorts. "Fair enough. Look, every time I flip there's a moment where I'm in the place I started and also in the place I'm flipping to. At the same time."

"OK," Travers says.

"OK, so the moment passes, I disappear from where I was, and that's that. Except that if I want I can maintain both locations. Simultaneously."

"You can..." Travers frowns. "You can—"

"Be in more than one place at the same time. Yeah. It's not copies, Travers, it's *me*. I can manage five, though I think I'll be down to four for a while, because..." Grant nods to the crime scene. "Unpleasant events can knock me back a location for a while."

"It's actually *you* in all those places?" Travers asks.

Grant nods. "Actually me."

"OK," Travers says. "It's a little hard to process, but OK. Why aren't you crazy?"

Grant laughs. "Who says I'm not? I'm really good at multitasking, and I've been doing this a long time. I learned how to flip in elementary school. I figured out how to go multi-location in middle school. Managed to work up to five locations and... well, I never got past five."

"Interesting," Travers says. "And still incomprehensible."

"Yeah," Grant says, "it's a real mindfuck."

"But how did that happen?" Travers jerks his thumb toward the crime scene. "You got shot in the head, and you're still talking to me. I could put that in some kind of context if you were creating duplicates of yourself, but you say it's you in every location. So why didn't you die when you... er... died?"

"Paradox," Grant says. "Physical stuff is localized. Look..."

Agent Grant's silhouette blurs for a moment, and then a second Agent Grant stands to his left.

"I'm beside myself," the first Agent Grant says. The second just smirks. "So here's the thing... if I break my arm in this spot..."

"It won't affect me over here," the second Agent Grant says.

"So whatever happens to you while you're here, you don't feel it over there," Travers says.

"Oh, I'd *feel* it," Grant says. "It's a little hard to explain, since I'd *also* feel *not* having my arm broken. It'd hurt. But I'd only have the broken arm in the location where it broke."

"What happens when you stop being in more than one place?" Travers asks.

"Depends how I do it," the first Grant says. "If I break my arm in this location, and I decide to leave, the broken arm just disappears..."

"And I'm fine," the second Grant says. "But if I decide to leave *this* location..."

"Then I still have a broken arm," the first Grant says. "And from that point forward, I have a broken arm. Until it heals."

"Oh," Travers says, then his eyes go wide. "*Oh.* That's why Agent Hu was trying to get you to focus on her voice, right after you were shot..."

The first Grant nods. "In situations like that I really have to pay attention. If I'd left every location except the one where I was a bloody corpse on the ground... well. I don't want to think about it."

The first Grant's outline blurs for a moment, then he disappears. The second Grant—the only Grant—shrugs. "I owe Hu big for that."

"You realize what you're describing is impossible," Travers says. "Completely impossible."

"Yeah? Have you met my partner? She *bursts into flame*."

"Yes," Travers says, "but there's a scientific hypothesis for that. I've read it. It doesn't make any sense to me, but someone, somewhere has written a paper describing her unique cell structure and has a peer-reviewed narrative of how her abilities might work. Has anyone ever done that for you? What's the theory behind you violating the laws of physics by being matter that can exist in more than one place at the same time?"

Grant shrugs again. "Because? I dunno, Travers. Call it a quantum whatsit. Quantum whatsits are real popular these days. It doesn't matter:

whatever you call it some scientist is going to say you're wrong. And then he'll probably start shouting really loud. For a really long time."

"Not necessarily," Travers says. "I know a scientist who would be positively giddy at the thought of the accepted laws of physics being so *wrong* on such a fundamental level."

"Well I'm not really too keen on giddy, either," Grant says. "First they're giddy, next I'm strapped to a table having my organs removed while Mozart plays in the background."

"Why Mozart?" Travers asks.

"I dunno," Grant says. "I always picture Mozart."

"I see," Travers says. "Do you think about this often?"

"Yeah," Grant says. "I'm a glass-half-full kinda guy."

PART THREE: ESPERANZA CAPITOL LIBRARY

All the thirst and hunger and pain and desperation crash down on him at once. His eyes are open but unfocused, unable to perceive anything but the color of the floor, and all he hears is a strange grinding, croaking noise coming out of his own throat. His body goes rigid, the world fades to white, and he is dimly aware that his head is repeatedly striking a brick wall.

A different sound filters into his awareness—muffled, but agitated. Someone yelling, perhaps? The white-on-white vision darkens momentarily, then he can feel something pressing against his head, keeping it from striking the wall. The sound returns, less agitated, more soothing. It means nothing to him, but it is calming, and a part of him, the part that is trying to return to rationality, focuses on it. Eventually the seizure passes. Eventually his body calms down. And, eventually, the sounds he's hearing start to make sense.

"...not sure I want to risk feeding you just yet."

A man's voice. Familiar.

"You need it though. What happened to you? I thought I was in a tough spot, but I had food..."

The policeman's voice.

"Well, I've got some food with me. Water, too, which is probably more important right now. I need you to be a little more focused, though. I don't want you to choke on it..."

The mention of water causes him to gasp, then cough.

"There we go. You with me? LaFleur?"

Artemis forces himself to nod.

"OK, good. Can you sit?"

Artemis nods again.

David grabs him by the shoulders and helps him sit, positioning him so his back is against the brick wall he'd been slamming his head against only moments before. Artemis' vision starts to clear, a little. He can see shadows and outlines—an expansive room filled with large, rectangular shapes.

A shadow dances out of sight, and Artemis hears running water—what's more, he can *smell* water, which is an unusual and altogether unpleasant sensation as the feeling of thirst that he'd managed to put off returns with a vengeance. The shadow—a man-sized shadow—returns, kneeling next to him. A cold, wet cloth is pressed against his lips.

"I don't really know what I'm doing," David says apologetically. "I think you're supposed to be on fluids right now, but I don't have any on hand and I don't know what I'd do with them if I did. I'm assuming that as badly as you need food and water, you need to start slow. So... this towel is clean. I brought it from, uh, the place I was staying before I got here, and I haven't had to use it yet."

Artemis forces himself to patiently suck at the water, throat burning as he swallows.

"I've also got some protein bars, when you're ready."

Artemis nods, but doesn't say anything. He keeps sucking at the corner of the towel. His head starts to clear, and in a minute he sees well enough to confirm he is, indeed, in the main lobby of the library. He'd been very fond of the place, once. He would alter his appearance and come here to read, and to watch people reading.

David watches him closely. Artemis raises an eyebrow as he notices how very different the man looks from his projected self.

"You have a beard." His voice is raspy and harsh, and he returns his attention to the towel.

"Yeah..." David scratches his chin sheepishly. "We've been here for a while. Ten months to a year and a half, as near as I can guess."

"Slightly more than a year," Artemis says.

David unhooks a canteen from his belt, unscrews it, and hands it to Artemis, who abandons the towel and starts drinking greedily.

"Somewhere along the line I got the idea to grow it out," David says. "I'd figured out what was going on—wrote a note to myself and everything—and told myself not to cut it, to make it easier for me to accept the situation next time."

Artemis lowers the canteen for a moment. "You'd forgotten," he says. "That was a risk."

"Got myself another concussion somewhere between the plane and the island," David says. "That didn't help. I'll have to be careful about that. They're easier to get after the first."

Artemis nods. "How are you now?"

"Oh, I've had plenty of time to heal," David says. "I found an abandoned house, fully stocked. It was a very comfortable twenty-four hours."

Artemis screws the cap back on the canteen and sets it on the floor. "On that note... I'd like to try some food."

David reaches into a vest pocket and produces a wrapped bar. He unwraps it for Artemis and holds it out for the older man to take.

Artemis breaks off a small piece of bar and puts it into his mouth. Almost immediately he tries to throw up, but he's regained enough self control that he puts a stop to that.

"Tell me how you escaped," Artemis says.

David shrugs. As Artemis eats food for the first time in a year, he describes how he woke up on the beach, made his way to an empty house, and gradually learned that he was trapped in time.

"I figured my best shot at getting out was to stay awake during the reset." David looks away sheepishly. "I didn't really know if it would work. I don't understand how *any* of this works, really... but I figured if the island didn't want me to stay awake, staying awake was something to shoot for. It worked a lot better than I thought it would."

"Yes," Artemis says. "It appears you have discovered something new."

"It can't be that new," David says. "I mean, all those stories about 'astral projection' have to come from somewhere, right?"

Artemis shrugs. "Perhaps. But being able to *interact* with magic while you dream—I don't believe I've ever heard of that."

"Maybe it's in one of your books."

"Yes," Artemis says. "The books. Now that we are both free of our prisons and in the same place, we have the luxury of planning how to get those."

"Your friend isn't going to raise the alarm?"

Artemis smiles thinly. "Come tomorrow, Artigenian won't even know who I am."

PART FOUR: FARRADAY CITY BUNKER

"So," Jenny says, "you're a villain."

Scrapper Jack doesn't look up from his cards. "I figured the scar gave it away."

"It is suitably villainous," Jenny admits. It is—it's a nasty, jagged thing that travels down the length of his left cheek, and it pushes the left side of his mouth down into a slight frown.

They've been playing cards all afternoon. Crossfire and CB are out running errands, and playing cards is better than just sitting around, awkwardly making small talk. It turns out Jack is a lot more amiable than he initially appears, and Jenny has found herself slowly warming up to him.

He's also not a bad card player, which means Jenny doesn't feel obliged to pretend she can't play.

"Ex-villain, though," Jack says. "I retired."

"How does that work in the villain world?" Jenny studies her hand carefully, trying to decide whether to play it safe or go for the long shot.

"Tricky," Jack says. "People show up on your doorstep and remind you about 'that time when...' and suddenly you're back in because you owe them a favor."

"Like the Godfather," Jenny says. "Just when you're out, they find a way to bring you back in."

Jack laughs. "Yeah. Sorta like that. But most of my career I worked for Overmind, so there wasn't a whole lot of that, and when there was it wasn't... it didn't get ugly. My reputation was a problem though. I was always worried about someone new on the block who figured they'd try to make a name for themselves, track me down, call me out, that kind of thing."

"Did anyone ever try?"

"Twice," Jack says.

"Do I want to know what happened?"

Jack glances up at her for a moment, then very deliberately places two cards in the discard pile.

Oh. Jenny slides two new cards across the table, and decides to change the subject a little.

They play two more hands before Jenny works up the courage to ask him about the scar.

"How'd you get it? You're invulnerable, right? Like Regiment."

"Regiment?" Jack looks up from his cards, surprised. "Uh. I guess. He's actually a little higher on the scale than I am."

"You heal, too," Jenny says. "So you shouldn't have any scars at all."

"It's complicated," Jack says. "I got the scar the same time I turned into a Very Special Boy."

"Do I want to know how *that* happened?"

"It's your basic trauma-triggering-metahuman event," Jack says. "A bunch of guys thought it would be a great idea to push my face into a table saw. As soon as it broke the skin I got real special, real fast. Not sure why the scar didn't heal."

Jenny wins two hands in a row.

"Glad we're not playing for money," Jack says. "Where'd you learn to play?"

"Cops," Jenny says. "And CB. Cops and CB."

"Right. Forrest. You're Marty Forrest's kid."

Jenny stares at Jack in surprise. "You know my dad?"

Jack makes a face. "Not socially. He arrested me a few times."

That's a little too awkward, so they play a few more hands. Finally Jenny folds her cards on the table and stares straight at Jack. "I'm sorry, I have to ask this. It's making me crazy."

Jack raises an eyebrow and waits silently.

"Look, before I was like this—a metahuman—God, it still feels weird to say that out loud. Before, I didn't really pay a whole lot of attention to it. I mean, not the big picture. I knew about various heroes, and my family was friends with all the Guardians, and I liked watching the news and reading about them as much as anyone else, but I didn't really pay attention beyond the big issues."

"Big issues," Jack repeats.

"Yeah. Who's trying to blow up the world, what laws are metahuman-related, that kind of thing."

Jack nods.

"There was all this other stuff that I sort of noticed, but I didn't really dwell on, and now that I'm... well... now that I've *joined the club* I'm noticing things that don't make sense. And there's a big one that I want to ask you."

"OK," Jack says.

"What the hell is the deal with women in this gig?" The question has been building for weeks, and Jenny is dimly aware that she's shouting when she asks it.

Jack looks surprised. "What are you talking about?"

"Women," Jenny repeats. "Half of the world's population. Also—according to science—half of the world's *metahuman* population."

"Sure," Jack says. "That works out about right, by my experience."

"Not by *mine*," Jenny snarls. "How many women *hero* metahumans can you think of?"

Jack frowns. "Well, there was Mental Marvel. She's crazy now, right? And Desire..."

"Oh, *Christ*!" Jenny throws her hands in the air, shaking her head. "That's exactly what I'm talking about. *Two*. Watch the news, read the newspapers, you're lucky to hear about three or four. But on the *villain* side? Right off the top of my head I can think of Requiem, Nightshade, Earsplitter, Sidestep, Lotus, Darkmoon... I'm not even trying, and that's just New York State!"

"Oh," Jack says. "Yeah. Hero-side's a sausage-fest. That's true."

"Why?" Jenny stands and starts to pace. "That's the part I can't understand."

"Easy," Jack says. "Women are evil."

Jenny gives him a flat look.

The non-scarred side of Jack's face twists into a grin. "Sorry. Couldn't resist."

"I'm serious," Jenny says. "It makes no sense."

"It makes perfect sense," Jack says. "There's still a glass ceiling. If you're a villain, a glass ceiling is just one more thing to break on the way to getting what you want."

"OK," Jenny admits, "that does make sense. If you're a sociopath."

"That's got nothing to do with it," Jack says. "Look, I wasn't especially open-minded when I was growing up. I didn't specifically *hate* blacks, Latinos, women, gays, or anyone else in particular, but I sure as hell looked down on them. It wasn't personal. Just the way I grew up."

"And being a villain turned you into the progressive standard-bearer you are today?" Jenny asks, sarcasm oozing from every word.

"Cute. No, but one day I called Lotus 'honey' and she broke my damn jaw."

Jenny's eyes go wide.

Jack laughs. "Yeah. That got my attention. She was actually trying to do a lot more than that, so I got off pretty easy. I did what came natural, which was to jump in with both fists, and I got my ass handed to me. I was tougher, but she was stronger, and she was a *lot* better at fighting. I mean, *scary* good. Eventually I swallowed my pride, apologized, and asked her to teach me. She's the reason I got so good at fighting speedsters."

"So the trick to getting ahead in the villain world is to beat up anyone who crosses you," Jenny says.

Jack shrugs. "That's sort of how it works, yeah."

"That's got to be exhausting," Jenny says.

"Look," Jack says, "my perspective is kinda screwed, OK? So take it with a grain of salt... but however tiring you think it might be, it's a lot more straightforward than how it works on the hero side. Think about Liberty—I got no problem saying he's one of the good ones. Hell, a lot of us respected him, even if we didn't particularly *like* him. He walked the walk. But think about what that meant."

"What did it mean?" Jenny asks.

"He was standing up for truth, justice, apple pie, puppies and kittens, all the good things America is supposed to be," Jack says. "In order to do that, he had to *be* all the good things America is supposed to be, which meant he had to *toe the line*."

"He spoke out," Jenny says defensively. "He admitted when he was wrong. He called out the government when it was wrong. He got put on Nixon's shit-list because of some of the things he said. It was his duty as a citizen. That's how he described it."

"Good for him," Jack says. "Seriously. He was a stand-up guy. But *his duty as a citizen*... that's where it sticks. He was part of the *thing*. And when the thing went wrong, he couldn't go outside of it and fix it from there—he had to *use* the thing to *fix* the thing. What would happen if he didn't? He wouldn't be Liberty any more. He'd be like Crossfire."

She doesn't answer.

"Look, I'm not attacking the guy," Jack says. "Changing something from the inside, I can respect that, if that's actually what you're doing. But it's *slow*. And what about the people who are around now, getting screwed over? That's my point. The bad guys have a lot of genuine psychos, sickos, and assholes. But there's also people who go bad because they don't see a place at the table anywhere else. They keep getting told to be patient, wait their turn, all that crap, and one day they decide 'no, fuck that.' So they go to the other side. And the other side is more than happy to give 'em a shot."

"Yeah?" Jenny shakes her head. "What about groups like the Reichstaadt?"

Jack makes a sour face. "Yeah, well... yeah. That's the problem with the bad guys. There's all kinds of assholes in there."

PART FIVE: ESPERANZA IMPERIAL PALACE

Artemis LaFleur stands in a room he has not thought of for a very long time.

When he'd commissioned the construction of the Imperial Palace, he'd made it a grand and public affair. Set into one of the few mountains on the island, it would look out over his tiny nation, serving as both beacon and reminder of its new way forward. His quarters, it was reported, would be at the lowest levels—no dungeons here, just a secure suite for the island's leader. This was in stark contrast to the previous "leader," a despot who took pride in the dungeons and torture chambers of his own palace. It was also considered a reasonable nod to security, since the United States and Soviet Union had been locked in a desperate cold war, and the threat of nuclear Armageddon was ever-present.

There was another reason Artemis had wanted his rooms there, however. As soon as he moved in he began carving out a series of secret rooms beneath his own—a sanctum where he could plan in private. Rooms that, eventually, only he could open—he could thank Artigenian's tutelage for that, for the spells that recognized their master and opened only upon his command.

There is a moment, just before he reaches out to a specific point on a specific panel on a wall, that he fears he will fail. Perhaps the magic that seals the portal is not keyed to him, but to the magic he once possessed. Perhaps, as far as magic is concerned, the power he possessed was the only part of him that mattered. But when he reaches out to the panel on the wall it opens, and behind it the broad stone stairway leading down is immediately illuminated by light from an unseen source.

He descends in silence, lost in memories. This had been a sanctuary, a place where he could work alone, free from the attention and expectations of friends and enemies alike.

The stairs open into a comfortably-furnished sitting room. Bookcases and cabinets line the walls—the bookcases full of trivial but entertaining books, the cabinets full of liquor and drinking glasses—and in the center of the room are two overstuffed chairs and a love seat arranged around a simple wooden table. The only thing the room lacks is a fireplace. He never did figure out how to ventilate the room properly for that.

The cabinets are well stocked, and when he finally catches up to old habits he's sitting in his favorite chair, a copy of *The Decline and Fall of the Roman Empire* in his lap and a snifter of brandy in his hand. It's been a long time since he's been *here*, and he realizes that this room, more than any other, was home to him. For a while he sits, and wallows in the memory of a happier time. A time before he realized the extent of Artigenian's betrayal. A time before he had to unmake the only part of the world he'd ever come close to saving.

Perhaps now is not a time for drinking, he thinks. He sets the brandy aside, and waits.

Half an hour later the dream-form of David Bernard floats down the stairs. Artemis smiles at the image of the clean-shaven man, dressed crisply in black fatigues, shirt, and utility vest. This is still how he sees himself—not the bearded man currently sleeping in the library.

Artemis stands. "I'm glad you made it."

"I'm glad *you* made it," David says. "I was afraid you might have a relapse, after what happened last time."

Artemis smiles reassuringly. "I've recovered fairly quickly, since then."

The truth is, it was close. He *is* much recovered, but being in a state of near-starvation for almost a year isn't something you shake off in a matter of days. Teleporting to his chambers had seemed the most logical method of approach for him—he doesn't have the ability to move about unseen, as David's dream form does—but it was tiring.

"Well, you give good directions," David says. "You should close the outer door now, though."

Artemis nods, walks over to the stairs, and passes his hand across a carving set into the wall. The light on the stairs dims, and he can hear the *click* of the upstairs wall as it swings shut.

"We will not be disturbed, now. Not without a great deal of warning."

"Your friend won't bother us?"

"He doesn't even remember me, at this point," Artemis says.

"You mentioned that before," David says. "Why is that, exactly? I mean, good for us, but it's curious."

Artemis unbuttons the top of his shirt—taken from one of the abandoned clothiers in the city—and reveals the very top of the glistening symbol Artigenian embedded into his chest five days ago.

"The day you found me Artigenian realized he was trapped in time. And he suspected, based on my physical frailty, that I was not. He needed a way to escape, and as far as he knew I was the only 'new' thing on the island—and I was helpless."

"Sure," David says. "He had you trapped, he didn't know I was there."

"Exactly," Artemis says. "So he made a very daring and clever decision. One that would, had you not intervened, have freed him from the island's grip. He took every memory he had of me—from the time we first met, right up to that very day when he realized he was trapped and I was not—and bound it into a sigil which he then bound to my flesh."

"I get the daring part," David says. "Not so sure how it's clever."

"The problem with the island is that memory is not persistent here," Artemis says. "When you are in its grip, whatever you do in the last twenty-four hours of its life is erased from your mind. Unmade, just as most of the island's history is no more. The process of this unmaking places the victim in a deep, dreamless slumber first, which is where the memories are undone."

"That's how I got out of it," David says. "I was asleep but aware, and the magic didn't... know what to do with me, I guess."

"It seems as good an explanation as any," Artemis says. "It would never occur to Artigenian to try that. But he knew—suspected—that I was free of the island entirely. So he fused his memories of me into my flesh. When the island began anew, Artigenian would wake up with no memory of me at all, but when he inevitably found me hanging in my prison, he would recognize that symbol, realize its purpose, and retrieve those memories. And because those memories would have persisted past the island's cycle, he would be free of it from that point forward."

David looks at the edge of the symbol snaking out from the top of Artemis' shirt and shudders. "So his solution was to rip out a piece of himself and burn it into your chest."

"It seems so."

"Magic is a sick business, LaFleur."

"It makes monsters," Artemis says.

David looks around. "So if every memory of you is trapped in that thing, then any knowledge he'd have of this place would be trapped with it."

"Which means we can take our time." Artemis stands, and gestures for David to follow. "Let's get what we came for."

The sitting room is attached to a small office with a rolltop desk. Just beyond the office is a trophy room—sculptures, works of art, strange objects kept in glass cases. Artemis stands before one of the sculptures—a small statue of a semi-formed humanoid with a face that looks reminiscent of the larger sculptures on Easter Island—and places his hand, fingers outstretched, over the top of its head.

"What's that?" David's voice is sharp and wary.

"What?" Artemis keeps his hand over the statue, waiting patiently.

"I feel something..." David reaches for the right word. "Moving, I guess. I don't know how else to describe it."

"Ah..." Artemis glances up at David and nods. "I expect that's the ward reacting to my presence. You seem to have an uncanny awareness of magic in your dream-state. It shouldn't be long now."

As if on cue, the statue twists in place. Artemis takes a step back as the statue and the pedestal beneath it rise out of the floor and slide to the left, revealing a staircase going down.

David exhales sharply. "You have a secret room inside your secret room?"

"Layers within layers," Artemis says. "I assumed someone would learn of the existence of these rooms, or that I would eventually trust someone enough to tell them myself. So I set aside a place for the things I wished to keep to myself. A vault of secret and dangerous things. The books we need are here."

"The magic books," David says.

"The magic books." As his foot touches down on the first step, he sees the chamber beneath him fill with a soft, dim light. It is a large rectangular room of rough-hewn stone, completely empty and unadorned. Stone doors without visible hinges or latches line the far wall, eight in all.

"Is it safe down there?" David asks.

"Only I will be able to pass through the vault doors," Artemis says. "But the foyer is fine, and I may need your assistance in a bit."

Artemis steps down into the foyer and stands before the second door to the right. He is dimly aware of David standing at the bottom of the stairs, watching him silently.

"This is where I placed forbidden knowledge," Artemis says. "That sounds excessively dramatic, when said aloud, but I don't think it's wrong."

He runs his hands across the door. It seems almost foolish to call it a door, since it is nothing more than a stone fitted perfectly within the stone wall.

"When Curveball described the runes on the skin of the man he fought—Plague—he said they seemed to move. To ripple across his skin. That tugged at an echo of something. I'm certain I read about something very similar in one of the books sealed behind this stone."

"But you don't remember what," David says.

Artemis shakes his head. "No." He doesn't bother disguising his frustration. "I wish I remembered how to describe the relationship between a magician and the magic within him. The best description I can manage is that of a symbiote in a host. It grows within, is nurtured, its strength becomes the host's. And the knowledge of magic is contained within magic itself. It is *remembered* by the magician because the relationship between them is symbiotic, but the actual knowledge is not stored in the mind."

"That sounds more like science fiction than magic," David says.

"Yes," Artemis says. "Any magic, insufficiently explained, is indistinguishable from technology."

David snorts.

"It's time to open this door." Artemis places both palms on the surface of the stone door.

"How are you going to do that?" David asks.

"If it were anyone else," Artemis says, "it would take someone with the strength of Jack to move this stone. And if they did, it would trigger a number of... other, deeply unpleasant things. But this place still recognizes me, and all I need to do is..."

A light tap on the stone causes it to sink back and slide to one side, revealing a darkened room beyond.

Artemis smiles in satisfaction. "Now we just need to figure out how to get them..."

His voice trails off. His eyes widen in shock.

"LaFleur?" David remains at the foot of the stairs, unsure how close he can get before he triggers whatever protects the room. "LaFleur? Is everything OK? Can you see it?"

Artemis turns to David, face ashen, his expression one of bewilderment and fear. "Gone..."

"What?" David takes a step forward. "What's gone?"

Artemis leans against the stone wall and gestures to the room. "Empty. The entire room. Every book is gone. *Every last one.*"

PART SIX: THIS MORTAL COIL

David stays against the far wall, but moves over so he's facing the door. Through it he can see a long room that reminds him of the old workshop his dad had in the basement of their house—narrow, full of shelves, with a table set against a wall that lacked only a vise to complete the picture. And it is empty: every shelf, every surface. Completely bare.

"The books are *gone*?"

Artemis nods.

"How?"

"I don't know," Artemis says, voice hollow. "It's... it's not possible. The wards are intact—they *must* be intact, because the door *opened*. And if the wards are intact, then I am the *only person allowed in this room*."

"Obviously that isn't true," David says.

"Obviously..." Artemis takes a moment to compose himself.

I am my only master.

"Still, it's appropriate to take a moment to reflect on the sheer impossibility of this."

"It's not impossible if it happened," David points out.

"That's not what I mean," Artemis says. "When I originally left this island, I deliberately left these things behind. The power that had been mine was gone, sacrificed as part of that final spell I cast, so I could no longer really understand them in any practical way. As a result of the spell, I wasn't sure if they were the originals. Technically, in this world, Esperanza never existed, so I never claimed it as my own, Artigenian never sought me out, and I never sought *them* out. It was possible they existed both in my vault and out in the world."

"Maybe that's a good thing," David says. "Maybe that means we can still find copies of—"

"No," Artemis says. "The books existed here alone. That was one of the first things I looked into. Each of the books mysteriously disappeared at about the time I procured them in the old reality. Artigenian did the same—I was able to track down his history almost to the day when he showed up at my doorstep. Reality becomes a bit of a mess where Esperanza is concerned..."

David says nothing.

"So *in theory*," Artemis says, "my decision to keep the books *here* was sound. My vault was more secure than any of the places I'd taken them from, and the vault was on an island that exists as a single day in the entire expanse of time... barring destroying them—which I wasn't sure was possible—there was no safer way to keep them out of the hands of others."

"I hate to sound like a broken record," David says, "but however safe it was in theory, it looks like someone proved you wrong."

"I agree," Artemis says. "Placing that reality beside the theory gives us an idea of who is capable of doing so. Someone who knew the island existed. Someone who could *find* the island. Someone who could *escape* the island. Someone who could retrieve the books without triggering the wards that protected them. There is only one other person, besides myself, who has the ability to do such a thing."

David raises an eyebrow. "Only one? Who?"

Artemis looks at David, expression grave. "Me."

David frowns. "You said *other* than you."

Artemis starts to reply, then he looks around and sighs. "Let's go back to the library. There's nothing for us here, and there's no reason to continue talking here. Wake yourself up. I'll be there soon."

* * *

David is groggy when he wakes up. He's not used to that—before the concussion he was always alert and moving the moment he opened his eyes. Even with the concussion he was able to rouse himself relatively quickly. Here on the island, however, things are different. Especially since he started interacting with it in his dreams—there seems to be a recovery time as he transitions from the weirdness he encounters in his "dream form," as Artemis calls it, to the physical world.

It takes him a few minutes before he's aware enough to stand, clear his head, and walk out of the utility closet and into the main floor. When he does he's not surprised to see Artemis waiting for him. He is surprised to see a bottle of brandy and two snifters sitting on the table they've been using.

"From my private stock," Artemis says. "I think we can both use a drink at this point."

David doesn't disagree. Artemis pours; they both drink. David waits long enough for the brandy to take the edge off, then he gets to the point.

"You were about to explain how you were the only other person who could have taken those books."

Artemis stares at the brandy as he swirls it around in his snifter, frowning deeply. "The final spell... the spell I cast that unmade the island. It required a sacrifice."

"Sacrifice," David says. "We talking stone table, bound virgin, heart on the altar?"

"That could have worked," Artemis says. "That's not what I did."

David feels a surprising surge of relief. "Glad to hear it. It's not really your MO."

Artemis smiles. "Thank you. I chose to sacrifice myself. At the time I believed the sacrifice would be literal—that I would indeed die when the spell was cast. Obviously that didn't happen. Instead, I woke up on the island devoid of power. The magic inside me was gone."

"Which is why you don't really understand magic any more," David says. "Not like you did. Symbiotes and whatnot."

"Yes," Artemis says. "I assumed the magic was the sacrifice. That it was consumed by the spell. But every day—every day but the day you witnessed—Artigenian would say something to me that makes me question that assumption."

"What'd he say?" David asks.

"He said '*You are not the student I loved like my own child. You are what remains. You are the dust that made up his form, the shadow he used to speak. The student I loved grew within you, and now he is gone.*'" Artemis looks at David gravely.

David's brow furrows. "He was referring to your magic as a... person."

"I thought he was speaking in metaphor," Artemis says. "That I had betrayed my purpose. But he was *convinced* that my power still existed. He demanded to know where it was..."

David can see where the conversation is going. He doesn't want to go down that road.

"I told you once that magic was a living thing." Artemis looks exhausted. As if the mere act of speaking the words is sapping his strength. "Alien, utterly alien, but *alive*."

"And you think it's still alive," David says. "Right now. Out there, somewhere. That it—you, or a piece of you, enough of a piece of you to get past those wards, took those books and... went somewhere."

"That is what I think," Artemis says. "I think that during the casting of that spell, something... happened. I have no idea what. But if Artigenian is convinced that my power must still exist, and if I am the only one who could have removed the books in the manner they were taken..."

"Damn," David says. "Damn it all to hell, LaFleur, one of you is bad enough."

"It gets worse," Artemis says. "I'm fairly certain I'm the *good* twin."

CURVEBALL
22
MAR 2015
CURVEBALL
A Prose Comic
KING'S GAMBIT
STORY
CHRISTOPHER WRIGHT
COVER
PASCALLE LEPAS
LOGO
GARTH GRAHAM

PART ONE: HARUSPEX ANALYTICS, TOP FLOOR

"Thank you all for coming. I regret the necessity."

Though he is, as always, covered in shadow, the tension in the Chairman's posture is unmistakable. The boardroom is silent, all eyes on him. Jason Kline shifts uneasily in his seat, instantly regretting it as it squeaks in protest.

"As you know," the Chairman continues, "we have been operating under the shadow of a very serious security breach. Someone has betrayed us, quite overtly, on at least two separate occasions. We still don't know the extent to which they have betrayed us *covertly*. The damage may take years to undo. This is especially worrisome in light of our decision to suspend Project Recall until this matter is settled. We've made great strides there, and now that progress is in danger of unraveling completely."

A low, worried murmur fills the room. The Chairman lifts one hand, motioning for silence, and it quickly fades away.

"To counter this danger, I have tasked Mr. Kline and his group with discovering the identity of this mole... this *traitor*." The Chairman's voice hardens, then smoothes over once more. "Today he will report on the progress of his investigation."

Showtime.

Jason stands, clears his throat slightly, and nods respectfully to the Chairman. "My team and I have been analyzing the known security breaches. So far, there have been *at least* two, and we are strongly considering adding a third."

Jason holds out one finger. "First: someone leaked information to Captain Alexander Morgan, aka Liberty, about the existence of Project Recall."

He extends a second finger. "Second: after Crossfire assaulted the TriHealth facility in downtown Manhattan, someone ensured that our standard protocols were *not* followed and a Code Ultraviolet was issued by the police, calling Sky Commando and other unvetted forces to the scene."

He extends a third finger. "Our third potential breach was the attack on the Forrest Brownstone. While Ms. Ioannou has taken responsibility for that breach—" he pauses a moment to nod toward the striking woman sitting to the Chairman's left. "While she has taken responsibility for it, a closer examination of the events behind the attack led us to believe that she did so mistakenly."

Mara Ioannou, a tall, slender woman with coppery skin and dark black hair, tilts her head to one side, listening intently. The thick curls of her hair part at her neck, revealing a large silver earring cast into the shape of a double epsilon.

"What we learned," Jason continues, "is that the original order she authorized was *altered* and *manipulated* by a third party intent on ensuring that the response would be inadequate. When Curveball's email was answered, the assumption should have been that he was on the scene. The team that was sent in was not rated for metahuman engagement."

"Question," the Chairman says. "What about the event in the Bronx? Sky Commando appeared on the scene there as well."

Jason shakes his head. "Unrelated to the security breach. However, the fact that it *wasn't* part of the security breach gave us some important data that allowed us to improve our model, which helped us determine who the mole actually was."

He starts to pace around the table, causing the board members to shift and squirm as they all turn to follow him.

"The first breach was the riskiest—actually delivering information to Liberty, information unknown in scope that Liberty has, we assume, passed on to Curveball in encrypted form. The individual must have had easy access to the information. Someone who was expected to have the information. Someone who would be able to oversee the sabotage of a response protocol. Someone who would have learned about the Bronx incident, and seen an opportunity to sabotage us further to ensure that the next time our organization tried to suppress a Code Ultraviolet, it would fail. In short, it had to be a member of the board, sir. Someone sitting in this room."

The reaction is pretty much what he expects: some of the members of the board already know this, since they've been pre-vetted. They either sit stoically, holding their cards close, or they steal glances at the unvetted board members, wondering if one of them will betray themselves. The unvetted members look around in alarm, some of them immediately asking questions or voicing their objections, some of them even rising out of their seats to object. Jason keeps walking around the room, largely unnoticed as the attention turns to the *confirmation* that one of their number is a traitor.

The Chairman allows the tumult to continue for a few seconds, then once again raises his hand for silence. It takes a bit longer this time, but once again the room settles down. When silence returns, the Chairman turns his attention to Jason once again.

"Mr. Kline. Have you determined who the *traitor* is?"

"I have, sir." Jason stops pacing and turns to face him. "I can, without reservation, identify the traitor sitting in this room."

The Chairman nods once. "Proceed."

The silencer attached to the pistol he's been hiding beneath his suit jacket prevents everyone in the room from going deaf, but in the enclosed space the shot is still incredibly loud. The moment he pulls the trigger, everyone in the room jerks back, involuntarily flinching away from the sound. Everyone, that is, except for the distinguished-looking white-haired man sitting in the chair in front of Jason. He topples forward, blood spraying out of the back of his head, covering Jason and spattering across the men and women sitting beside him.

The immediate reaction is one of alarm, and some cries of fear and pain from the sudden noise. That reaction is quickly mastered as the surviving board members realize what happened, and what it means.

The Chairman doesn't recruit fools.

The room falls silent as everyone looks at the corpse of the white-haired man bleeding on the table.

"Andrew Estovich," the Chairman says, "was a traitor. He betrayed me, and he betrayed all of you. He was very good at going unnoticed—Mr. Kline, I believe you had originally cleared him of suspicion?"

"Yes sir," Jason says. He switches the safety on his gun and returns it to his jacket pocket. "He was in the first group we vetted."

"Mr. Kline came forward with their findings earlier today," the Chairman says. "I can't dispute the facts. Mr. Kline, if you would summarize."

Jason manages to keep his voice steady as the dead man's blood runs down his neck and pools in the collar of his shirt. "I ordered a closer look at the initially vetted pool of candidates, and we noticed discrepancies in Mr. Estovich's activities—both personal and financial. His job performance had slumped. He had personal accounts, accounts he believed were untraceable, that contained large deposits made by an unknown third party. This led us to examine his personal computers more thoroughly, where we found the program that was used to modify the protocol that triggered the action on the Forrest Brownstone. Once we found that, we were able to tie him to everything else."

"What else did you learn?" the Chairman asks.

"He was the only one," Jason says. "The way he set up his security shows that he was too paranoid to trust anyone. He was working for someone on the outside, but he was the only one they had on the inside."

"I see," the Chairman says. "Do you know who he was working with on the outside?"

"No sir," Jason says.

The Chairman nods. "Well. I won't pretend I'm happy to learn of Andrew's betrayal... he'd been with us for a very long time. But thank you for your work. I expect you'd like to clean up, you're excused with my thanks."

"Yes sir," Jason says. "Thank you sir."

Board members shy away from him as he heads to the exit.

"As for the rest of you," the Chairman says, "I suspect some of you would like to clean up as well. We're going to take a two-hour break. When we return, our first order of business will be getting Project Recall back on schedule."

Jason steps out of the boardroom, leaving behind the cramped, stuffy room and stepping into cool, fresh air. He forces himself not to shudder as he rolls back his blood-soaked jacket sleeve, exposing the transmitter embedded in his cufflink. He raises his wrist to his face and activates the transmitter.

"Go Phase Two."

He hurries down the hall, eager for a long shower and a change of fresh clothes.

PART TWO: NEW YORK CITY MORGUE

Special Agent Alan Grant is dead. His body is placed on an autopsy table, his upper torso split open, the gaping crack in his chest held apart with an old, dented rib spreader. Plastic bags filled with his organs, each clearly labeled and marked with permanent black marker, sit in a pile on a small wheeled table to the left of his head. His lifeless eyes are still open, and wide dark stripes—something called *tache noir*—spread across the whites of both eyes.

"Jesus."

Special Agent Alan Grant is alive. He's a tall, thin man, clean-shaven, dressed in a black suit (rumpled), white shirt (rumpled, collar unbuttoned), black tie (pulled open and hanging loosely around his neck), and a long black trenchcoat (strangely unrumpled) that comes down to his ankles. His dark hair is slicked back away from his face, revealing dark eyes that narrow as he stares at his corpse on the autopsy table. His mouth, usually turned up in a smirking, crooked half-smile, shows no trace of mockery or amusement. A fine layer of sweat covers his forehead.

"They really did a number on me, didn't they? I mean never mind shooting me in the back, these guys *scooped my organs out of my body*. And put them in *little baggies*."

"How does it feel?"

The woman standing to his right is shorter, Asian, with slightly reddish skin. Her long black hair is pulled back into a simple ponytail, but strands have fallen out and hang along her face on both sides. She pays them no mind. She is also dressed in a black suit (not at all rumpled), white shirt (neatly pressed, collar properly buttoned), and black tie (pulled up tight and hanging properly), though she doesn't wear a trenchcoat. She is not sweating. She never sweats.

She is also a Special Agent. She is, in fact, Alan Grant's partner.

"It pretty thoroughly sucks, Hu." Grant shakes his head. "It makes me want to drink. A lot."

Special Agent Lijuan Hu smiles slightly. "You *always* want to drink a lot."

"Point," Grant says. "But... oh, *Christ*."

He turns away from the body and rubs his eyes. Hu frowns slightly. This isn't Grant's usual behavior. She's been his partner for years, so she gets to see a few more sides of him than most of the rest of the world, but this is more than he likes to show *willingly*, even to her.

"Grant... *Alan.*" Hu doesn't like using his first name. It's too formal.

Grant half-turns toward her. "Sorry. This is just... fucked. It's fucked."

"Obviously. I'm not gonna get you to stop thinking about it, so at least think about it out loud."

Grant laughs, and to Hu's relief the side of his mouth curls up, just a little bit. "Yeah, OK. I ever tell you about the first time I actually died like this?"

"A little," Hu says. "You were sixteen or something? It's why you can't go past five locations."

"Ah, the stupidity of youth..." Grant's mouth twists into a sneer. "Yeah. So... when I was thirteen I figured out how to flip into two places at the same time. There's a trick to it—it's all in the timing—and after I did it I was knocked on my ass, because I couldn't understand what I was seeing. I mean, I was seeing two different places at the exact same time. Think about when two people are trying to have a conversation with you at the same time—in a really noisy room—and both of them assume *they're* the one you're paying attention to. It's like that, only with everything."

"I want to hit someone just thinking about it," Hu says.

"That's why I like you," Grant says. "Anyway, it took some time to figure out how to process everything. Even when I thought I'd have a handle on it, there'd be situations where I'd turn to walk through a door only to realize—after I ran into a wall—that the door was in the *other* location."

Hu snorts.

"Yeah. That kinda shit is great when you're thirteen. I was The Kid Who Ran Into Stuff For No Reason."

Hu laughs out loud.

"It got a lot better as soon as I sorted it all out. I don't ever want to go back to being stuck in one place, Hu. I don't know how the rest of you do it. It would make me crazy."

"Too late," Hu says. "So you're thirteen and you're in two places at the same time."

"Yeah," Grant says. "And it's *fun*. I mean, talk about having the perfect alibi, right? But I'm an ambitious kid—under the right circumstances—so I want to see how far I can go. I try to figure out how to be in *three* places. Takes a while to get the timing right, and then, just like before, I need to take a while to process the third location. It takes longer, because I'm processing three separate locations instead of two, and there's an even *longer* period where it feels like I've got it but I keep getting my wires crossed. Finally I get it sorted, and it turns out that being able to be in three places is *even more awesome* than being in two."

"I see where this is going," Hu says.

"Yeah, I kept pushing myself to add more locations. Thing is, it took longer each time. So three years later I'm trying for location number six. I manage to get all six locations sorted, and I convince myself I've got a handle on the disorientation... but I'm dead wrong. One day I turn in the wrong location. In one place I run into a telephone pole. In another... I trip over the side of an overpass and fall in front of a tractor trailer."

Hu's eyes widen.

"The driver *freaks*—I can't blame him, you don't expect a kid to drop from the sky right in front of your rig—and he tries to turn, but all that does is jackknife the truck and cause it to roll on top of me. That's what kills me. And Christ, Hu, that *hurt*. A lot more than getting shot in the back. To have this thing roll on top of you and tear you to pieces... I don't really know how to describe it. I wasn't *thinking* any more, but my nervous system hadn't cut out, so I could still kind of feel what was going on, and I was aware in five other places. I could actually feel this huge metal thing grinding me to pieces."

"That's... sick," Hu says.

"It gets worse. At that point I'm really disoriented, and then I start to feel myself *letting go*. Not the dead place—it's like I'm holding on to that location with all my might. But one second I'm in my bedroom, and then I'm not there any more. A second later I'm doing laps in the community swimming pool, and then I'm not there any more. Public library—gone. Alley behind the supermarket—gone. Suddenly it's just me in the high school bleachers with a bunch of friends, and dead-me crushed under tons of rolling metal, and I can feel myself *starting to let go of the me that's still alive*."

"But you didn't," Hu says.

Grant shudders. "It was really, really close. I don't know, chalk it up to being stubborn, but I forced myself not to let go at the bleachers, then forced myself to let go of the corpse. And I *fought myself* the whole way. It was like the only place I really wanted to be was the place where I wasn't any more."

"Why would you want that?" Hu asks.

Grant shrugs. "You know how Collins is with heights? Put her on a balcony and she's five steps away from the rail, because if she gets any closer she's got this little voice in her head saying 'jump.' It was like that. But it wasn't whispering, it was shouting at the top of its lungs. Man, that screwed me up. My friends on the bleachers thought I was having a *really bad trip*."

He turns back to his body, gazing at his dead face.

"I had to start all over after that. Relearn two locations. Then three. Then four. Then five. Never did make it to six—mental block, or something..."

Hu looks down at the corpse of her partner and tries to imagine what he's feeling. She's so used to seeing Grant all over the map—*literally* all over the map—that the corpse on the table doesn't affect her any more than any other random cadaver on a slab. As far as she's concerned, that's not Grant, because he's standing right next to her, talking to her. But to *him* it *is*.

"How bad is it, really?" She doesn't bother to make it sound like a joke.

Grant laughs, voice sounding hollow and thin as it echoes off the autopsy room walls. "It's pretty bad. I haven't slept in two days."

"Why?" Hu asks.

"I'm afraid if I fall asleep I'll..." Grant points to himself, then makes a *poofing* gesture with his hands. "It almost *itches*. I mean death shouldn't feel like anything, right?"

Hu shrugs. "Depends on what you believe, I guess."

"Well I don't see a white tunnel. Or a red one, either. It feels like *nothing*, but... nothing feels like something. Christ, that sounds really stupid."

"Grant." Hu looks straight at him. "Just let it go. You've already been tagged and declared dead. Just... let it go."

"Boss wants me to wait a little longer," Grant says.

"*Too fucking bad for him*." The anger in her voice is unexpected, and Grant blinks in surprise. "He doesn't understand. If he did, he wouldn't have asked."

Grant looks at his corpse again. "Yeah?"

"Jesus, Grant, you are the weirdest mix of maverick and good soldier..." Hu grabs his hand and squeezes. "Focus on that. Don't screw this up. Hold on to the hand. Hold on to the place where you feel the hand. Let go of the place that *doesn't* feel the hand."

Grant stares at her for a minute, hope and fear flashing across his face as he wrestles with himself.

Maybe literally, Hu thinks. *I have no idea how that works with him.*

Finally Grant nods. He turns back to his corpse and regards it for a moment. “I am never gonna get tired of not looking at you,” he says.

His hand squeezes hers, just for an instant, then the corpse on the table blurs and disappears, followed by the quick patter of empty plastic bags falling as the organs they once held disappear as well, knocking them off balance and sending them to the floor.

Alan Grant sighs, shuddering in relief. “Thanks,” he whispers. He doesn’t let go of her hand. “I owe you. Big.”

Hu grins. “You’re good for it.”

He lets go of her hand, looking a bit sheepish, and then tugs at his already-too-loose tie. “I need a drink.”

“You always need a—” The door to the morgue opens and Special Agent Phillip Henry, their boss, walks into the room. He stops in the doorway, words dying on his lips, as he stares at the empty autopsy bed. He looks at Grant, who stares at the floor guiltily.

“I told him to,” Hu says.

Special Agent Henry frowns. He’s a tall man, almost as tall as Grant. His skin is very dark, and his hair is cut down almost to his scalp. He’s *also* dressed in a black suit (crisp), white shirt (crisp), black tie (crisp), and on top of that he wears a pair of dark-tinted sunglasses. The sunglasses make him look like the ultimate G-Man stereotype, though they’re actually an act of courtesy on his part. Like Hu and Grant, Agent Henry is a metahuman: he can instantly tell when someone is lying... and when he makes eye contact, the person is incapable of lying at all.

He nods once. “I’m sorry, Alan. I shouldn’t have drawn this out as long as I have.”

Grant shrugs.

“It shouldn’t be too hard to sell the idea that someone wanted to steal the corpse of the agency’s most powerful teleporter,” Agent Henry continues. “That may actually work to our advantage. I’m convinced there’s a mole in Division M.”

Both Grant and Hu look alarmed.

“It’s not on our team,” Agent Henry continues. “I’m sure of that. It’s part of the support staff, but I can’t look too closely without people asking questions. This gives me an opportunity to dig deeper.”

"How is the team?" Hu asks.

"They know everything," Agent Henry says. "I'll fill in Sky Commando next. As far as the rest of the world is concerned, Special Agent Alan Grant is dead, and his partner, Special Agent Lijuan Hu is on leave due to trauma."

"It's because you're a *girl*," Grant says.

Hu snorts. Grant is definitely feeling better now.

"OK, boss," Hu says. "You got us out of the public eye. So what exactly is it you want us to do?"

"Help Travers," Agent Henry says. "He thinks he knows where the Next Big Thing is going to happen, and he wants to be there when it does. I want you with him to keep him safe, and to make sure the right side comes out on top."

"Which side is that?" Grant asks.

"That's your call," Agent Henry says. "I trust you and Hu to figure it out."

"OK," Grant says. "Where exactly is Travers going?"

"Farraday City."

A long silence follows.

"Shotgun," Grant says.

PART THREE: ONE DAY EARLIER

"Which is why we're certain it isn't a member of the board."

Jason Kline stands in the Haruspex Analytics Situation Room, facing a large flat screen monitor displaying the shadowy silhouette of the Chairman. Simon Yin is working on a laptop to his right. The rest of the team is in other parts of the building making discrete alterations to the network that will make things a little easier to manage in the future. The only other person in the room is Mara Ioannou, sitting off to the side, listening intently. She hasn't involved herself in the discussion so far, but she's been paying close attention.

"Why not?" The Chairman isn't dismissing the notion out of hand, but he's resistant to the idea. "Whoever it is, they have access to information that only board members can access."

"Not entirely," Jason says. "The board members have access to all of it, but other people have access to *pieces* of it. They have to. You need staff to maintain the machines that store the information and monitor communications. You need more staff to man the systems that trigger armed responses to threats. Our technology is constantly being tweaked and adjusted by personnel. Nothing here runs itself, and the board members aren't directly involved in any of the operations and maintenance activities that go on."

"In fact," Simon adds, not looking up from his laptop as he speaks, "that's the main reason why a board member would be in the worst position to do this."

"Who was that?" the Chairman asks.

Simon's eyes widen as he realizes who he's talking to. He's a slightly overweight man, about Jason's height, and has thick, straight black hair that shoots out in all directions, making it look perpetually spiky. He stands, wiping his hands on his jeans as he turns toward the Chairman's monitor. "Uh... Simon Yin, sir. I'm on Jason's team. I apologize for speaking out of turn."

The Chairman waves his hand dismissively. "Don't worry about that. Mr. Yin, why would a board member be in the 'worst' position to do these things?"

"Board members are too visible," Simon says. "They don't usually interact directly with the systems that needed to be manipulated to—for example—override the NYPD Code Ultraviolet alerts. A board member certainly has the *authority* to access those systems, but standard procedure is to issue a directive and have someone else take care of it. When they do something *directly*, people notice."

Jason notices Mara nodding to herself thoughtfully.

"My point is that while, from a power and authority perspective, a board member would theoretically be the best position to be in, if a board member tried to do any of these things on their own almost everyone would notice, because it's an extreme aberration from how things normally work."

The Chairman is silent for a moment.

"We also need to take into account the depth of system knowledge required for some of these breaches," Jason adds. "The board is full of very capable people, sir, but their skills focus on analysis, planning, and management. All of those skills are necessary to pull off any one of these security incidents, but on top of that you also need in-depth knowledge of our systems. We're looking for a second-tier employee, or group of employees. People who work directly *for* members of the board."

"I see," the Chairman says. "Someone they trust."

"That's right," Simon says. "One of the people who carry out the directives. Someone who can go into a data center and say 'the board needs you to pull these files in the next hour' and nobody will even think twice about it. Preferably someone who has the expertise so they can say 'I need to get this information for the board' and someone will offer them a seat, because everyone knows they're qualified to do it themselves."

"You've been looking for a Brutus in your organization," Jason says, "but what we need to focus on is *Brutus'* Brutus. Someone who works for one of the board members, an employee they trust *implicitly*."

"I expect that describes everyone we rely on," Mara says, breaking her silence. "There are at least two or three such people for every board member. I'm afraid you haven't narrowed down your search at all."

"It's a wider net," Jason agrees, "but it'll be easier to narrow down as time goes on. The trick is figuring out how to narrow it down before there's another incident. At the moment, with Project Recall on hold and our investigation being conducted openly, the mole—or moles—will be in hiding. We don't have many options."

"What options do we have?" Mara asks.

"Well," Jason says, "Simon came up with an interesting play, and we've stumbled across something that—"

The door to the situation room opens, and a distinguished-looking white-haired man, dressed smartly in a three-piece suit, walks in.

"Mr. Estovich," Jason says. "Thank you for coming."

"Andrew," the Chairman says.

Andrew Estovich looks from Jason, to the image of the Chairman on the monitor, then over to Mara, who gives him a small nod. "How can I be of service?"

"Have a seat," Jason says. Andrew hesitates a moment, nods, then sits next to Mara.

"What's going on?" He doesn't bother disguising the apprehension in his voice. "Is anything wrong?"

"You're being set up," Jason says.

Andrew stares at him blankly.

"We found some files on your computer," Simon says. "Files we know aren't yours. It's a... virus, of sorts."

"Which computer?" Andrew asks.

"The one in your office," Jason says.

"Someone put a virus on that one?" Andrew frowns and shakes his head. "I don't know what for. I just use that one to keep track of meetings. Everything important I do is... in the boardroom. Or in a SCIF. If they're trying to spy on me..."

"Not spy," Jason says. "Frame. Simon?"

"The program waits for an external command," Simon explains. "When it receives the right trigger, it will build a fake digital trail implicating you in every security breach we're investigating."

Andrew blinks. "What?"

"It will also—we think—link to a few financial accounts that have apparently been set up to look like they're yours. Accounts that will make it look like you're being paid by someone outside the organization."

"I'm not," Andrew says.

"We know," Jason says. "We're telling you this because we want you to know, ahead of time, that we know you're not involved. However, Simon thinks we're about to hit a point in the investigation where the guilty party is going to activate this program in order to deflect attention away from him or herself."

"Or themselves," Simon adds.

"Or themselves," Jason agrees. "We're not sure why they've targeted you specifically—"

"I know why," Andrew says.

Jason raises an eyebrow. "Why?"

Andrew's smile struggles between amusement and bitterness. "My value to Haruspex is that I'm a company man, Mr. Kline. I'm not a stupid man by any means, but I'm not one of the bright, rising stars, either. I'm valuable because I put the company first, keep my eye on the end goal, and I'm not concerned if someone else comes up with the brilliant idea that moves the project forward. It's not a glamorous track, and there are a lot of people on the board who think I'm more than a bit past my prime."

Mara shakes her head and *tsks*. "Andrew..."

"No, Mara, it's OK. I'm not insulting myself, and I'm not being self-deprecating." Amusement wins out, and Andrew chuckles softly. "It's the way business works. It's hard to avoid, even in places like this, it's hard to avoid. Human nature is what it is, and ambition... well, it's always there, and there are always people—even loyal people—who will play the game for personal gain instead of looking at the big picture."

No one says anything. Mara sighs and nods, sadly.

"I don't do that any more. I did, once, when I was younger, but since coming here..." Andrew's cheeks redden slightly. "Well, I found something here that's bigger than myself. It's huge and terrifying and absolutely necessary and it takes putting aside your own goals in order to get it done, and I've found *seeing it happen* a lot more rewarding than getting the praise for something less effective. And let's be honest, Mara, I don't really understand the technical side of things nearly as much as a lot of the rest of you. And that's where so much of our work is headed, these days..."

"I've never questioned your dedication," the Chairman says. "Nor has your place in this company ever been in doubt."

Andrew's cheeks redden more noticeably. "Thank you, sir. But I sort of wandered off point. My point is, I'm considered a bit out of touch by some of the other board members, and more than a few of the staff. That makes me an easy target on one level. And my... perceived ineffectiveness makes for a perfect manufactured alibi. 'Old Man Estovich knew he was being boxed out, so he decided to sell his services to the highest bidder.' That kind of story. It's the kind of thing the more ambitious kids would accept without so much as a second thought."

Jason shifts uncomfortably. It occurs to him that it's exactly the kind of motive he would have assumed, if he hadn't known Andrew was being framed.

"So, yeah, I know why they chose me," Andrew says. "I'm the dinosaur. As far as everyone knows, at any rate. There's no reason for them *not* to choose me."

"Well," Jason says, trying to move past his discomfort, "since we know in advance you're being set up, it should be pretty simple to fake an accusation. We'll have to keep you hidden for a while, but as soon as we flush these guys out—"

Andrew shakes his head. "It's not gonna be that simple, Mr. Kline. I assume you've ruled out the other board members at this point?"

Jason blinks. "We have. How did you know?"

"A member of the board, going into my office, messing with my personal computer?" Andrew laughs. "The number of systems they'd have to disable to avoid being logged just for stepping into my office... no, it's easier to put someone one or two levels lower. Staff go into our offices all the time, whether we're there or not."

Suddenly Jason doesn't feel quite as clever as he did a few minutes ago. Simon shakes his head, trying not to grin.

"That's true," Jason admits. "We think it's probably an aide or attaché to a board member. At least."

"Well, that's where my problem comes in," Andrew says. "If it's one of our assistants, that means they know how this place works as well as any of us."

"I don't follow," Jason says.

"They know how we deal with traitors," Andrew says. "The *real* way."

"I..." Jason fumbles for words and loses. "Mr. Estovich, we're not planning to *retire* you."

"Then you're going to screw the whole thing up!" Andrew's voice takes on the distinct tone of a disapproving parent. "This is more than just setting me up to take the fall, Mr. Kline. I'm not just their patsy. I'm their canary in a coal mine. If they trigger that program and *I don't die* they'll know you're on to them."

Jason doesn't know how to reply to that. He hadn't considered it. He looks at Simon, who is gaping at Andrew in open astonishment. He looks at Mara: she's looking down at the floor, expression troubled. The Chairman simply looms, his silhouette unmoving, offering no comment or advice.

Andrew sighs. "You should do it in the boardroom. Don't tell anyone what you're going to do—you need to shock the board, really make them believe that you think I'm guilty and you're making me pay for it. I'd appreciate it if you made it as quick as possible. I know there are no guarantees."

Nobody says anything.

Andrew stands. "As soon as it's done... well, act like the matter's settled. The board will go back, tell their staff what happened—the important ones, anyway—and the real traitors will think they dodged the bullet. Then you stage something. Give 'em something irresistible to go after. Then you catch those sons of bitches and you make sure you get every last one."

"That's close to what I was suggesting," Simon says. "Though... in my plan we just hid you for a while."

Andrew smiles. "That's awfully nice of you, young man. I like your plan better. It's a shame it won't work."

"I agree," the Chairman says. "I'm very sorry, Andrew."

"I'm a company man, sir," Andrew says. "I know what that means."

"Andrew, it occurs to me it's been a long time since we've had dinner." The Chairman's voice radiates warmth. "I wonder if you'd stop by tonight?"

"Thank you sir," Andrew says. "But if you don't mind... I'd prefer to spend the evening with Carol and the boys tonight."

"Of course," the Chairman says. "I'm sorry. That was thoughtless of me. Breakfast, then?"

Andrew nods, eyes glistening. "I'd like that, sir. Thank you."

"I think you should take the rest of the day. Surprise Carol."

Andrew nods again. "Well. See you tomorrow then."

Mara stands and places her hand on Andrew's cheek. Andrew smiles and squeezes her hand. Then he wipes his eyes with his thumb, straightens his tie, and walks out of the situation room, straight-backed, head held high.

Everyone watches the door as it closes behind him.

"I want to make something very clear." The Chairman's voice has changed again—cold, with a hint of raw fury seething just beneath the surface. "I am not angry with anyone in this room. But I am very... very angry."

PART FOUR: ESPERANZA, JULY 20, 1992

Artemis and David have been at the small house on the beach for four days, trying to decide what to do.

The library was acceptable as a base of operations when the focus of their activities was the palace, but when it became clear that was no longer the case David decided Artemis needed access to a real bed and a refrigerator stocked full of healthy food. Artemis didn't object—he was subdued for most of the short trip back, brooding silently over the discovery that the books he'd counted on retrieving—the purpose of their trip to the island to begin with—were gone. And that they were taken, apparently, by a copy of himself.

An *evil* copy of himself.

Artemis spends the first three days at the house sleeping, for the most part, and eating ravenously when he's awake. His appetite is a good sign: David guesses whatever it is that makes Artemis a metahuman helps him bounce back from trauma more quickly than most. A lot of metahumans are like that, to one degree or another. David finds it intensely frustrating.

On the fourth day Artemis wakes up by mid-morning and shuffles out to sit at the small kitchen table. He pages through the newspaper, sighing softly as he reads the headlines.

"LaFleur." David stands in front of the table, arms crossed. Artemis glances up at David briefly, then returns his attention to the newspaper.

"Snap out of it," David says. "We need to come up with a plan."

Artemis sighs and pushes the paper away. "I know. I'm afraid I'm not quite myself at the moment."

"C'mon, LaFleur, setbacks aren't new. You've even been soundly defeated, from time to time. That never kept you down before."

Artemis frowns slightly. "I hadn't suffered torture for a year before being defeated by myself. Or a part of myself. Or a... I don't even know what it is. I'm not giving up, David, but I need some time to gather my strength."

"Tough." David hardens his voice just a bit—adopting a little of the hardass persona he used when he put Alishia through her paces in the early days, before he even deigned to call her *rookie*. "We don't have time for it. Look, LaFleur, I know you're hurt. I also know about working hurt. I followed you into this mess with a concussion—my second—and I got a *third* my first day on the island. Too many more and I won't be able to tie my shoes without help. I'm not asking you to do jumping jacks, I'm asking you to help me come up with a plan. Strategy is kind of your thing, being a big-time supervillain and all."

Artemis raises an eyebrow. "Very well. Let's summarize our current situation."

David leans against the refrigerator, arms still folded.

"First," Artemis says, "I was tasked with trying to determine what kind of magic we're dealing with. I no longer have any direct, in-depth knowledge of magic because of the strange symbiosis magical power shares with its host, so I brought us here—this island was the only place where I knew I could find reliable texts about magic. We need *reliable* texts because most of the books you'll find that purport to have anything at all to say on the matter are rubbish."

"OK," David says.

"Second," Artemis says, "the texts I was looking for are gone. However, the wards I created to protect those texts are still present. I have forgotten most of what I know when it comes to magic, but I remember enough to know that if someone *else* had removed the books, it would have destroyed the wards. The only logical conclusion is that *I* removed them... but I have no memory of doing so. Thus I conclude that the magical power I once had—the power I thought I had sacrificed in order to cast my final spell—somehow survived, and the wards recognize it as 'me' because it was that magical power that erected the wards in the first place."

"What would a sentient mass of magical power want with a bunch of books?" David asks. "Doesn't it already know magic?"

"It knows magic as well as I did, when it was a part of me," Artemis says. "Or perhaps a little less, if it exists without a human host. It would certainly have use for the books if it intended to... I don't know what it would intend to do."

"All right," David says. "We'll table that speculation for another day. Where does that leave us?"

"Nowhere," Artemis says. "We have nothing. There's little else to do but attempt to return home, to our time, and tell Curveball and the rest that we've failed."

David shakes his head. "You're forgetting something important."

"Oh?" Artemis looks skeptical. "What am I forgetting?"

David points at Artemis' chest. He's wearing a loose-fitting golf shirt—something taken from the original owner's closet—but his hand automatically goes to a spot just beneath his right collarbone, where the beginnings of an intricate and wholly unnatural rune are buried in his flesh. David has seen the entire symbol, and he knows it covers the older man's upper torso.

"We can't use it," Artemis says.

"You said the crazy wizard put his memories into it. Every single memory he had of you."

"He did," Artemis says, "but *we* can't use it."

"Just humor me for a second," David says. "You said he bound the memories to *you* because you weren't trapped by the island. The idea being that bound to you, his memories of reappearing on the island wouldn't reset, and if he could reclaim them, the fact that he had memories the island couldn't reset would free him from the island."

Artemis nods.

"Why *all* of his memories of you? And why did they have to be about you anyway? Why not just bind a trivial memory of what he did that morning?"

"In reverse order: It had to be a memory of me because he was binding it to me," Artemis says. "I don't remember enough to properly explain it, but it's a kind of sympathetic magic. Because this symbol contains memories of me in it, it stays in my flesh. If it were a memory of something else the spell would have nothing to attach itself to."

"OK. Why *every* memory of you he's ever had?"

"To make sure the island wouldn't unravel it. This is another area where I... can't be as specific as I'd like. But by putting every memory he had of me in this symbol, he increased its strength. It draws strength because it is attached to someone who is free of the island. It draws more strength because the memories are *about* the person it is attached to. And it draws even *more* strength because it is *all* of the memories about the person it is attached to. It has... mass, I suppose is the best term. Enough mass to survive the island resetting itself day in and day out."

"OK," David says, "here's my point. This thing on your chest contains every memory this guy, Artigenian, ever had of you."

"Yes," Artemis says.

"So it has every memory he's ever had of *teaching you magic*."

"That's true," Artemis agrees.

"What's more, it has every memory he's ever had of *not* teaching you magic. Every time he made a conscious decision *not* to teach you something, to hold something back... that's a memory of you. That's something he'd put in there. So the big double-cross with the world-ending spell, that's in there."

"A reasonable assumption," Artemis says. "But it doesn't matter, because we have no way of accessing it. You need *magic* to access it. I don't have magic. I can't interact with the thing on my chest in any way."

"Maybe not," David says, "but I bet I can."

Artemis opens his mouth to protest, then stops, frowning as he thinks it over.

"I don't really understand it," David says, "but you and I have both seen it. When I lucid dream on this island, the island interferes with it, and I can interfere right back. I'm not actually casting spells, but I *am* interacting with magic somehow. I'm pretty sure that'll only work here, and I'm pretty sure it only works here because reality is... not entirely real here."

Artemis nods thoughtfully.

"So I figure this is an opportunity," David says. "I fall asleep, start lucid dreaming, then project myself over here and my dream-self tries to absorb all those memories."

"What you are suggesting is... *irresponsibly dangerous*," Artemis says.

"It's not my favorite plan," David admits. "Look, LaFleur, before we got to this island I thought magic was basically just another metahuman ability. I was wrong. I thought Curveball was freaking out about magic because it was his... weakness, the same way Permafrost freaks out about heat. I was wrong. The truth is, magic is exactly the way you described it at Crossfire's safehouse: it's *alien*. I saw what happened when you cast the spell that ended the world and I still can't really wrap my brain around it. If that's actually part of what we're fighting... we don't have a choice, LaFleur. *Somebody* needs to know about it. I'd rather it be almost anybody other than me, but... it's gotta be somebody."

Artemis studies David carefully. "Answer a question first."

David's taken off-guard by the request. "OK..."

"Your last fight as Sky Commando," Artemis says. "I read the report on it shortly after you were put on medical leave. I like to keep tabs on New York City for a number of reasons, and you being sidelined was a not insignificant development."

"I don't hear a question," David says.

Artemis smiles slightly. "Your last fight was with a villain calling himself *Leviathan*."

David winces involuntarily.

"Yes," Artemis says. "He hit you with a bus. Knocked you through a cinderblock building. Both sides. That was the fight that ended your career."

"Thanks for reminding me," David says.

"What interested me," Artemis says, "is that as far as I could tell, based on the reports I read, you had time to avoid it, and you didn't. You made the *tactical decision* to be hit by that bus. I want to know why."

"I was tanking," David says.

Artemis shrugs. "I don't understand the reference."

"It's a video game thing," David says. "In multiplayer games you'll get one guy who armors up and tries to keep the bad guy occupied so the more fragile players don't go down. Normally emergency response crews hang back until an active threat is taken care of, but when I arrived on the scene they were trying to get civilians out of the area because Leviathan decided he was gonna pick up a bus and start pulping anything that moved."

David shakes his head. "I don't know how a guy that big managed to get so many drugs in his system, but he was obviously gone. He just wanted to kill things. And I didn't have many options. I couldn't use the stuckeys because there was too much debris, too many civilians trying to get away—rapidly expanding and hardening foam is dangerous when rocks and bits of twisted metal can fly in every direction. The asshole already had the bus, the only thing I could do was get his attention and keep it long enough for some of the others to respond."

"A sacrifice play," Artemis says.

"It's part of the job," David says. "Sometimes you have to take the hit."

Artemis considers David's words. Finally he stands.

"We don't know how you will react," he says. "When you try to absorb Artigenian's memories, anything could happen, but I *strongly suspect* that you will find the ordeal excruciatingly unpleasant, and even if it goes well you'll probably be disabled for a while."

David nods. "Sounds par for the course."

"The other thing to consider is what will happen to the memories when they are released," Artemis says. "Will you actually absorb all of them? If they're released, will they return to Artigenian? Artigenian getting his memories back is the worst-case scenario, so we have to plan for it. As soon as this happens, we'll need to get off the island, regardless of your condition."

"Can you handle that?" David asks.

Artemis shakes his head. "Not at the moment. But if you give me a week to rest—actual rest, not listless despair masquerading as recovery—I will be strong enough to make sure we leave this island before anyone can stop us."

"OK," David says. "One week. Then we leave."

"One week," Artemis agrees. "Then we leave."

CURVEBALL
23
APR 2015
CURVEBALL
A Prose Comic
AEINTERLUDE
STORY
CHRISTOPHER WRIGHT
COVER
PASCALLE LEPAS
LOGO
GARTH GRAHAM

PART ONE: ESPERANZA, JULY 20, 1992

David Bernard and Artemis LaFleur stand in the living room of a small house near the shore of an island that only barely exists. Through the curtained windows the bright glow of lightning flickers, followed shortly by the low rumble of thunder. It's getting close to the moment when a pale copy of an Artemis that was—a byproduct of the island's unique condition—will finish casting a spell that dooms the world.

David's body sleeps fitfully on the couch beside them, and his consciousness—what he's started thinking of as his "dream form"—stares down at it uneasily. The sleeping figure looks almost nothing like him—the full beard and long hair frame a face that is considerably more gaunt than it was when he arrived at the island. He's never lacked for food, but the diet isn't what he's used to, and that combined with a severe concussion at the beginning of his stay contributed to a lot of weight loss. He looks like a man who has been stranded on an island for a year.

Which, in almost every sense, is true.

His dream form reflects the way he still thinks of himself: as a Lieutenant in the New York Police Department. His hair is short—not as short as it was in the army, but that distinction would be lost on anyone who wasn't—and he's still in shape. It's pre-concussion David all the way, without a trace of the wear or exhaustion on his body. He looks old, sleeping on that couch. Much older than he should.

"You look at yourself like you're seeing a stranger," Artemis says.

"I am, I guess," David agrees. "Not too many people get to see themselves quite like this."

"And not many have been through what you have, in the past year."

David nods, then turns back to face the older man. "And what we're about to try is going to be a hell of a lot worse."

"We don't have to do it. It will probably be much better for you if we don't."

David shakes his head. "We need the intel."

"Do we?" Artemis raises an eyebrow. "Is it really so important that you're willing to put your *soul* on the line for it? Don't fool yourself into believing the stakes are any smaller than that."

"LaFleur, do people dabble in this stuff?"

Artemis frowns. "I don't understand your question."

"I mean when people practice magic, is it the kind of thing they do on the side, or do they go all in?"

"It's not something you can *dabble* in," Artemis says. "It takes time and dedication to learn to control the power, to figure out how to communicate with it without it destroying you."

"That's what I thought," David says. "So if this guy Curveball fought—Plague—if he's covered with spooky runes all over his skin, whoever put them there didn't do it as a weekend job. Someone on that side has all the skill and dedication your teacher has, only he's not trapped in 1992."

Artemis sighs. "Very likely."

"Yeah. We're wasting time."

"I should point out," Artemis says, "that even if this works, the likely side-effect will be that Artigenian is also freed from this island."

David shakes his head. "I think I figured out a way around that. C'mon, things are happening out there. If the point is to take advantage of everything getting stirred up outside, we need to get started."

Artemis hesitates, then nods, unbuttoning the front of his shirt to reveal the symbol embedded in his flesh. It covers his entire torso, traveling from shoulder to shoulder and crisscrossing his chest in multiple places until it ends halfway down his abdomen. It's glowing slightly, and the glow pulses rhythmically, matching the swells and eddies of the power raging outside.

"Does it hurt?" David asks.

"No," Artemis says. "It is unpleasant. But it's not precisely pain."

"All right."

"How are you going to do this?" Artemis asks. "You have no more training in the art than I."

"Yeah, but I'm dreaming," David says. "I don't know anything about magic, but I can still do things. I just need to will it to happen. And... uh... formalize it, I think. Look, Artemis, this next part is a little embarrassing, so just... try not to comment, OK?"

Artemis raises an eyebrow. It's the first time David has called him by his first name.

"I don't really know how magic works," David says, "but I know how I *think* it works. I mean, in terms of fantasy stories and stuff like that. I can manipulate the environment around here, but it's clumsy, because I don't have a point of reference to work with. So I'm going to—uh—invent my own magic in order to work with the real stuff."

Artemis' eyebrow remains raised, but he says nothing.

"I'm not going to recite mumbo jumbo, or say 'a la peanut butter sandwiches,' or anything like that, but I am going to vocalize what I'm doing. It'll help me focus."

Artemis nods.

"OK. So don't move." David's dream form reddens slightly as he stretches out his right hand, fingers splayed open.

"I define the man before me as 'Artemis LaFleur,' also known as 'Overmind.' I further define that the man before me has a soul, and that the soul of the man is also the man."

Artemis blinks in surprise.

"I further define that dwelling within the flesh of this man, but not part of this man, is a power that is not this man. It is a mark left by a man I define as 'Artigenian.' I further define that this mark is both a source of power and a shell for that power, and that until defined further the shell of that power shall not be broken."

Artemis feels the mark embedded in his chest pulse, as if responding to David's words.

"I further define that in this space 'Artemis LaFleur' and 'the mark left by Artigenian' are complete and distinct entities, and that nothing apart from these entities, here or in any other space, shall be affected by my words and deeds."

Against his will, Artemis feels his eyebrow start to rise again.

"In light of the truths I have spoken and defined, I declare that Artemis LaFleur and the mark left by Artigenian are imprisoned by an act of my will, and that only by an act of my will shall they be released."

In the passing of a single heartbeat the air darkens around Artemis, and a globe of shadow surrounds him. This is not the prison Artigenian had placed him in, when he was trapped in the palace—this is... something else. Similar, but considerably more substantial. He can barely see it, just a shadow bending around him, but he can feel it pressing against him, making him unable to move. He fights back a sudden surge of panic.

"This is just temporary," David says. "Bear with me while I set up the next part."

Artemis nods quickly, trying to force the claustrophobia down to a manageable level.

"OK," David mutters. "Time for the next bit." He stretches out his left hand, fingers splayed open, mirroring his right.

"In light of the truths I have spoken and defined, I declare the entities Artemis LaFleur and Artigenian are separate and whole, each unto themselves, and that *they shall be separated*."

David spreads his arms wide.

The burning in his chest intensifies for a moment, and Artemis cries out as he feels the symbol tear away from him, ripping itself out of his flesh. Almost as quickly he feels the pain recede, and he can move again. When he touches where the symbol was he finds his flesh is smooth and unmarked. The symbol floats in the air before him, seething angrily in the dim light.

"Sorry," David says. "I'd hoped that wouldn't be as rough."

"I'm fine." Artemis' voice sounds hoarse to his own ears. "Please continue."

David nods. "In light of the truths I have spoken and defined, I declare that Artemis LaFleur is released by an act of my will, and that he may pass beyond the bounds of the prison I have made."

Artemis no longer feels the shadow pressing against him.

"Get out of there," David says. "You should just be able to step through."

Artemis steps forward and passes through the wall of shadow. It tingles slightly as he crosses the barrier, and then he's out.

"Take a step or two back. This part gets a little harder."

Artemis hurriedly steps back.

David steels himself. Hands still outstretched, he focuses on the symbol floating in its shadowy prison. "I define the entity Artigenian to be of two parts: that of power and that of shell. I define that the shell contains the power, but the shell is not the power. I further define that the power, unbound by the shell, shall continue to be the entity Artigenian, and shall continue to be imprisoned by an act of my will, and that only by an act of my will shall it be released."

The symbol continues to hang in the air, apparently unaffected by David's words. Artemis supposes there is no reason it would be, since the words take no specific action against it.

"In light of the truths I have spoken and defined," David says, "I declare the part of Artigenian that is shell to be no more, while the part that is power shall remain."

At this David closes his fists. Artemis hears something cracking, then the symbol changes—it flickers, grows brighter, and finally expands to fill the entire prison. It is no longer a symbol, but a whirling mass of energy—a miniature storm trapped by a wall of shadow that suddenly seems much too thin.

David nods in satisfaction. He closes his eyes, steadies himself, then walks through the wall of shadow and into the center of the prison.

It reacts almost immediately, swirling around him instead of simply swirling, flattening out into a disk, rotating like a hurricane with David's dream-form in the eye. Occasionally strands of energy leap out of the mass, leaving shimmering trails behind them as they arc up as far as David's face, or down to his shins, leaving corkscrew patterns in the air around him as they eventually wind their way back.

A horn sounds in the distance, followed by another, and another. Artemis closes his eyes for a moment—*this is when the world ended*—then opens them, focusing on David. "You're running out of time."

David nods. "In light of the truths I have spoken and defined..." His arms stretch out, as if to embrace the power swirling around him. "In light of the truths I have spoken and defined... where this power is caged by my will and subject to it... *I claim it as my own*."

The room falls silent. David's dream-form stands motionless in the shadowy cage as the light surges around him. Then the horns blare again, all at once, urgently, triumphantly, and the power collapses in on him. It tries to *destroy* him, and David begins to scream.

Not his dream self: the physical body of David Bernard bolts up from the couch where it sleeps, eyes open but unseeing, as it screams in fear and agony. The t-shirt he's wearing begins to smoke as the pattern of Artigenian's rune burns its way through the fabric. Artemis pushes David's body back down on the couch, grabs a heavy blanket folded over the back of a nearby chair, and tries to stifle the flame. He can smell flesh and fabric burn as David continues to scream.

Artemis looks over his shoulder. David's dream form is suspended in the shadowy prison, engulfed in energy. His face is expressionless, almost serene. It's a stark contrast to the expression of terror and agony etched in the face of his physical form.

"David," Artemis says, "wake up."

The body continues to scream and thrash. The smell of burning flesh grows stronger. The dream-form doesn't move.

"*David*." Artemis raises his voice. "It's time to *wake up*."

No response. Artemis turns to face the dream-form again, and notes its face—eyes wide, mouth open, as if about to speak. Frozen in an unmoving mask of... surprise.

Artemis hurries into the kitchen, opens the refrigerator, and pulls out the gallon jug of milk. He removes the top as he hurries back and dumps the contents of the bottle on top of David's head.

Almost immediately the dream-form disappears, and David bolts upright, sputtering and clutching his chest.

Artemis sets the jug on the coffee table and kneels beside the younger man. "Are you all right? Can you hear me?"

David tries to speak, but the best he can manage is a nod.

"I apologize for the rude awakening. I thought it best."

David nods again, still clutching at his chest.

"I'll get the first-aid kit," Artemis says, and turns toward the bathroom—then stops as he sees the shadowy prison, still set in the middle of the living room, still encasing the pulsing, swirling energy released from Artigenian's rune.

"It's still there," Artemis says.

"Good," David manages to say.

Artemis steps around the prison, into the bathroom, and moments later emerges with gauze and first aid cream. He hands them over to David, who has shed his shirt and is gazing down at his torso in dismay. The same mark that Artigenian had embedded into Artemis' flesh is now seared into his own.

The two men work in silence as they clean and dress the wound. Outside they can hear the inhuman sounds of the creatures coming out of the ocean, slithering past the tiny house, silhouetted by unearthly green light as they pass. When the wound is treated as best they can manage, they continue to sit in silence as the monsters move past. And they continue to sit in silence as the horns call, then falter, then the crimson light washes over the island and everything *twists* in every wrong way and suddenly the day has reset.

It's the morning before the end of the world. David, Artemis, and the trapped, swirling mass of energy remain where they were, but the empty gallon jug of milk and the first aid kit—including, unfortunately, the dressing on David's wound—are gone.

"I should have thought of that," David says.

"We'll do it again," Artemis says. "Did it work?"

David closes his eyes. "Something happened. Something's there. There are words..." When he opens his eyes they don't focus.

Artemis carefully goes through the process of treating and dressing David's wound again. "This should hold long enough to get off the island. Once we're out of its influence I expect the bandages will remain."

David nods. His eyes still aren't focusing on anything.

"David," Artemis says. "David, can you hear me?"

David nods.

"The process you devised to free me and trap the rune..." Artemis waves his hand in front of David's face. The young man doesn't blink, his eyes don't track the motion. "It was inspired. How on earth did you come up with it?"

David mumbles something indistinct.

"Come again?" Artemis snaps his fingers in front of David's face. He still doesn't blink, though he tilts his head slightly at the sound.

David closes his eyes and takes a deep breath. "Requirements."

"I... don't understand," Artemis says.

David opens his eyes again and turns his head to stare at Artemis. His eyes manage to focus on him for a moment, then his gaze slides away into nothing.

"Federal requirements," David says. "Ever read them?"

"No," Artemis says.

"Lucky you," David says. "It's like what I just did, only it makes less sense..."

"I'll take your word for it," Artemis says.

"There are words," David whispers. "In my head. Swirling, just like that light. Terrible, sharp, burning words that want to devour... everything."

"Not you, I hope."

David shakes his head. "They don't have the purpose for that. They have no volition. But they burn and hunger just the same."

Artemis frowns as he stares at David, trying to determine how best to help him. Ultimately he decides he can't—not directly. The best he can do is try to get them both away.

"How do you feel?" Artemis asks. "If we're going to get away, now is probably the best time."

"I feel different," David says. "I can't see. Or... I can see too much? Either way it's the same thing."

"Can you walk?" Artemis asks.

David thinks about it, then nods.

"Then grab my arm," Artemis says. "We can't afford to have you and Artigenian on the same island, not when you're like this. We'll leave Esperanza, and once we have a safe place to rest we can figure out our next step."

David nods and reaches out. Artemis guides David's hand to his arm, then helps him to his feet. David stumbles once, rights himself, then follows as Artemis opens the front door, and steps out into the night.

There are words.

PART TWO: RALEIGH, NC

It's Friday afternoon and the bank lobby is crowded. Special Agent Alan Grant sighs in irritation as he glances at his watch, noting with displeasure that they've only moved up two spaces in the last thirty minutes.

"You're not supposed to be the fidgety one, Grant." Special Agent Lijuan Hu suppresses a grin as she stares at her partner. "You can be doing other things while we wait."

"I *am* doing other things while we wait," Grant says. "But none of them are 'getting closer to Farraday City,' which is what I *want* to be doing."

Agent Hu is out of uniform, dressed in dark blue jeans, a light gray tank top and a tan purse that looks so new it still squeaks when she shifts her weight. Agent Grant remains steadfastly *in* uniform: black suit, white shirt, black tie, and a long, black trenchcoat that doesn't quite fit with the approach of summer in North Carolina.

"We need cash," Hu says. "And it's on me, so..."

She didn't bother to add *because you're officially dead and Travers is wanted for terrorism*. Grant nods, still annoyed but conceding the point.

Hu drops her voice lower and leans in to her partner. "You could try dressing a little less... conspicuously."

Grant snorts. "I'm a guy in a suit standing in line at a bank. Trust me, everyone's paying attention to the hot Asian chick with red skin."

Hu scowls. "My skin isn't that red."

"Red enough." Grant rocks back on his heels, looks around the lobby again, and sighs. "I think there's only one teller on duty. Hu, can't you use a bank card or something?"

Hu raises an eyebrow. "Not really."

Grant mutters something obscene under his breath. Of *course* she can't use her ATM. They're trying not to be traced.

"Hurray for computers," Hu says.

"I know, right?" A thin, balding man with a patchy red beard turns to look at Hu and grins. "I've been trying to get off the grid for *years*, but there's always something that keeps pulling me back in. At least this branch uses older tech. It takes them a few days to report all their transactions, so I've got a little time to do things with my money before Big Brother finds out about it."

"*What* things?" Grant asks.

The man blinks in surprise and shifts his attention to Grant. His eyes narrow. "Who wants to know?"

"Well it ain't Big Brother," Grant says. "I'm more like that *other* uncle—the one who always gets drunk on Thanksgiving, then tries to pick a fight with your dad."

"Grant..."

"Hey, *pal*," the man says, raising his voice a little. "I don't think I appreciate your tone."

"Well I'm hurt," Grant says. "I was just asking a question. You seemed awfully pleased that you had a few days before Uncle Sam figured out what you were doing with your money, and I wanted to know why you needed those days."

"I don't *need* them," the man says. "I *want* them. On *principle*. And don't act innocent, Mister Man in Black, because I'll bet you two chose this branch for exactly the same reason."

"Not exactly the same," Grant says. "I don't have principles..."

"Grant!" The exasperation in Hu's voice is readily apparent. She turns to the other man and smiles. "I'm sorry, mister. He gets jealous."

"What? We're not—ow!" Hu steps squarely on his foot. She knows how to make it hurt.

"She's right," Grant says through clenched teeth. "She has a thing for squirrelly guys. So naturally, when you started talking to her..."

The man turns away, body rigid. Hu looks reproachfully at Grant. Grant rolls his eyes.

"Be nice," Hu whispers.

"Not my strong suit," Grant says.

Two minutes later he says "Oh, fuck!" Then the front wall of the bank explodes.

* * *

Peter Travers tries not to fidget as he pretends to be asleep. The passenger seat is tilted all the way back, and his loosely-woven straw hat covers his face. People walk by the car, glance down and move on without so much as slowing. There's nothing unusual about a man sleeping in a car, or a man covering his face with a hat to keep the sun out. The fact that the weave of the hat is loose enough that he can easily see through it—and keep an eye on anyone who might be a little too interested in him or his nap—is one of the reasons he bought it, Agent Grant's ridicule notwithstanding.

The caution is sensible, given his fugitive status, but so far it's been unnecessary. Nobody pays him a second thought. It's starting to get warm in the car, but not uncomfortably so. The windows are down halfway and a pleasant breeze wafts through, just strong enough to keep the air moving. Travers is on the verge of succumbing to his own deception—of actually falling asleep in the car—when he hears a high-pitched shriek fill the air. He almost has enough time to form the thought *that sounds like a high-speed missile* when the car rocks as something hits something else, and then explodes.

Any consideration of sleep is promptly abandoned as Travers sits up and scans his immediate surroundings. The people on the sidewalk are staring at something behind him—he turns and sees a thick, black column of smoke rising from a few blocks away.

From the bank, it's from the bank.

Travers has his hand on the door-handle when the air blurs in the back seat, and the agitated form of Special Agent Alan Grant appears.

"We got a thing," Grant says. "We're gonna need you to move the car."

Travers nods once, then reaches for the car key in his shirt pocket.

* * *

Grant had been keeping an eye on the building from across the street, but he hadn't thought to add *missile attack* to his list of things to look out for. He recognizes the sound as soon as he hears it, but by then it's too late.

The initial surge of panic inside the bank lobby quickly lapses into confusion when all of the expected side effects of an explosion—searing heat, carnage, debris—fail to appear. There's plenty of smoke and dust, as bits of the wall are pulverized and sprayed across the room, but there are no large chunks of rock and glass strewn about the floor. People are not trapped under collapsed portions of wall or roof. When the smoke and dust clears, Grant sees why: it's not an ordinary missile.

"Hu..."

"I see it."

There's a hole in the side of the wall, pretty much where they expect it should be. There's debris from the wall, too—suspended in midair, lodged in an unknown substance that has hardened into a strange umbrella-like second ceiling.

"What. The. *Fuck.*" Grant stares at the strange shape in disbelief. "How is that even *possible*?"

"Focus," Hu says.

"No, seriously." Grant shakes his head. "In order for the bomb to catch the debris like that, it would have to... parts of it would have to move faster than the actual explosion. That's impossible, right? I mean, I should talk, I guess, but I expect tech to obey the laws of physics at least a *little*..."

"Grant," Hu's voice sharpens. "Company."

The air smells faintly of ozone as a blinding yellow light flashes just beyond the strange hole in the wall. As the light fades, three humanoid figures wearing gold-plated body armor and helmets, each carrying a rifle of unknown but clearly advanced design, step through the hole into the bank lobby. The yellow light flares up again, and again three gold-armored figures step through the wall.

"Teleportation," Hu murmurs.

"That doesn't make any goddamn sense," Grant says.

The light flares three more times, until a total of fifteen soldiers have stepped into the bank lobby, their weapons trained on the crowd. As they advance the crowd presses back against the walls—Grant and Hu following along with the rest—until finally the center of the lobby floor is clear of everyone but the soldiers.

The soldier in the middle of the group steps forward. The voice that comes out of its helmet is perfectly modulated in tone.

"You will all move over to the right side of the room. You will all sit on the floor. Anyone who fails to comply will be shot. There will be no other warnings. Move now."

Immediately the bank patrons start to move to the right side of the room. Grant and Hu follow, making sure to stay on the outer edge of the group, closest to the soldiers. Two soldiers go to the far end of the room and start demanding identification.

"I think we're going to have to blow our cover," Grant whispers.

"No shit, Sherlock." Hu's expression is sour. "But I'm going to need a little more space when I light up."

Grant looks around. They're definitely too close to the civilians.

"OK," Grant says. "When I find the right opportunity, I'll create a distraction..."

The thin, balding man with the patchy red beard is in the same part of the group they are.

"Hey. Red. *Pssst.*"

The man glances at Grant nervously. "Leave me alone."

"Shut up and listen. In a few minutes I'm going to be loud and charming. You know. When that happens, I need you to try to get the crowd away from me and my friend here. Understand?"

"You're crazy," the man says.

"No, I'm *charming*. Keep it straight. What's your name?"

"Lester," the man says.

Of course it is. "Well, Lester, I'm Alan. Look, remember a few minutes ago when you thought maybe I was a Fed?"

Lester nods slightly.

"Well you're right. I'm a Fed. But I'm more than that, Lester, I'm a Fed with a *plan*, and part of the plan involves making sure nobody but the bad guys get hurt. That means you need to make sure everyone takes a few healthy steps back when I start making friends and influencing people. Got it?"

"I'm not squirrelly," Lester says.

"*What*? Look, this is not the time to—"

"I'm not *squirrelly*."

Grant grits his teeth. "Pal, if you do your part you won't only not be squirrelly, you will have helped take down a bunch of asshole terrorists robbing a bank."

Lester thinks it over, torn between a genuine desire to help and a genuine desire to not get shot by soldiers in gold armor.

Grant curses silently. It's only a matter of time before the soldiers notice them talking and make them stop. "Also, if you do your part I will personally take you off The List."

Hu raises an eyebrow.

Lester's eyes widen. "Seriously?"

"Hell, we do more for people who never stick their necks out. All it takes is a phone call."

"OK," Lester says. "When you start being an asshole, I'll get everyone back."

He knows me. He really knows me.

Hu inches closer to Grant, leaning her head in so only he can hear her.

"What list?"

"I dunno," Grant says. "Worked though. Look, he's gonna give you enough room to light up. I'm gonna make sure they're not looking at you when you do. All we need is the opportune moment for me to—"

The smell of ozone fills the room again, and another flash of bright yellow light fills the gap in the bank wall. When it fades, what stands there isn't a gold-armored soldier, but something much larger. The heavily-armored figure stands at least ten feet tall, as wide as at least three of the gold-plated soldiers standing shoulder-to-shoulder. Affixed to its right arm is a massive cannon, similar in design to the rifles the soldiers carry but obviously *so much more*.

Everyone stops what they're doing—soldiers and captives alike—as they watch the huge armored form step through the hole and tromp into the lobby, the floor shaking with each step. When it finally speaks, its voice is lower and deeper than the soldiers, but it has the same modulated tone.

"I am Doctor AEvil," the armored figure says. "You are all my prisoners."

"You have got to be fucking kidding me," Grant mutters.

"What?" Doctor AEvil's form turns toward the crowd of prisoners. "Who dares?"

Hu nudges Grant, the expression on her face clearly saying *I think you found your opportune moment*.

Grant looks at the armored figure and his mouth twists into a sneer. Finally he shrugs, stands up, and steps forward.

"Yeah, you caught me, boss," Grant says. "That was me."

Immediately four guards line themselves between Grant and Doctor AEvil, each pointing their strange rifles directly at the man in the trenchcoat.

"And what," Doctor AEvil says, "did you think was so important that you dared speak before being spoken to?"

"Just this," Grant says. "Studio 54 called. *They want their cage dancers back*."

PART THREE: DIPLOMACY IN ACTION

Nobody moves.

The only sounds come from outside the building—those sounds are louder than they would normally be, due to the gaping hole in the concrete wall. Agent Grant hears sirens, *many* sirens, as police frantically converge on the scene. He wonders if there are any metahumans in Raleigh who will also respond. He assumes there has to be at least one, what with all the technology in Research Triangle Park, but he's not familiar with the area.

Doctor AEvil stares at him impassively—he supposes it's impossible for a hulking suit of powered armor to do anything *but* stare at him impassively. Grant glares back at the tin suit for all he's worth.

"Bring him to me," Doctor AEvil says.

Two of the soldiers step forward, each grabbing one of Grant's arms, and they drag him over. Grant doesn't bother resisting. Doctor AEvil is *considerably* larger up close, and Grant tries to look nonchalant as he glances at the cannon welded to his arm.

Grant thinks he can probably fit his entire arm inside the barrel.

"So..." Doctor AEvil's voice drops to an even lower pitch. "We *amuse* you."

"No," Grant says. "You don't *amuse* me. If you *amused* me I'd be laughing, *slapping* you on the back, maybe offering to buy you a drink. What you do is *embarrass* me. What the fuck are you doing? This is all kinds of stupid."

"Your laws mean nothing to me," Doctor AEvil says. "FOR I AM—"

"*Jesus*, chief, I'm not talking about the *laws*. You're a supervillain, I get it. But *COME ON*. This is penny-ante, romper-room *bullshit*. You've got something that can blow shit up and *freeze the tiny bits in midair*, teleporter beams, what I can only assume are *laser guns*, and the best you come up with is a *painfully stupid name* and a plan to *go rob a bank?*"

"There is nothing wrong with my name!"

"My ass there's nothing wrong with it," Grant says. "It's the kind of name a precocious twelve-year-old kid picks for an MMO because someone already registered the name he wanted. *Fuck you* there's nothing wrong with that name. It's embarrassing. I gotta believe the guy who got 'Doctor Evil' laughs his ass off every time he hears your name."

"I AM A GENIUS," Doctor AEvil says. "AND SOON THE WORLD WILL KNOW MY—"

"If you're such a goddamn *genius*," Grant says, "why the fuck did you blow off the side of a building to rob the bank? You've got *teleporters*."

Doctor AEvil thinks it over.

"I wanted to field test the bomb," he says.

"You wanted to—" Grant stops, frowns, then shrugs. "OK, that makes more sense than I expected it to. Except that it's not a *bomb*, you dumb fuck, it's a *goddamn missile*, because it *flies through the air under its own power*."

"No," Doctor AEvil says. "The missile is the delivery system. I didn't want to field test the delivery system. I already knew that worked. I wanted to test the part that explodes, and that is a bomb."

Grant opens and closes his mouth multiple times before he gives up. "I guess I gotta let you have that one."

"Now let us move away from the topic of my name, or my methods," Doctor AEvil says. "Let us instead discuss why you thought it would be a good idea to mock a heavily armored and heavily armed man who has just taken you captive."

"OK," Grant says, "but to do that we're going to have to go back to the topic of your name and your methods, and probably throw your sense of style into the whole goddamn mix, because it's exactly this kind of two-bit, half-assed job that *really pisses me off*."

"How *dare* you—"

"Oh *shut up*. I don't know how many times I have to say this until you get it. *You're robbing a goddamn bank*, sport. That kind of shit went out of style in the 70s. Big leaguers don't rob banks. People with your kind of tech? If they need money, they hack a system and transfer it into a private account in the Caymans. Or create quantum supercomputers to mine Bitcoin. The point is, the only people who actually *rob* places these days, are meth addicts and high-class jewel thieves. You cooking in that armor, sport? Because you ain't a high-class jewel thief."

"I have my reasons!" Doctor AEvil says. "And I don't need to explain them to a nobody."

"Denial. It's sad to see in what I *assume* is a fully grown adult," Grant says. "Though for all I know you really *are* a precocious ten-year-old. That would definitely explain the name..."

"Enough!" Doctor AEvil's voice booms through the room, causing Grant to wince and take an involuntary step back. "I will not be mocked by someone who is clearly my inferior in every way! Choose your next words carefully, sir—they may be your last."

Grant looks around the room. All eyes are on him. He turns back to Doctor AEvil and shrugs.

"Fire in the hole?"

The room explodes. Again.

* * *

"Seriously, Pete, *Doctor AEvil*? Who the fuck names themselves that?"

Their car is parked in a dead-end alley twelve blocks away from the bank. They can hear sirens rush past as law enforcement races to the scene, but the alley is practically hidden from the rest of the world. Travers isn't happy about it being a dead end, and Grant can't really blame him for that, but it means that people who know their way around the city—specifically cops—won't bother using it.

Grant and Travers are quickly unloading the trunk, dumping luggage as they try to clear enough space to open the spare tire well.

"Hu certainly packed a lot of luggage," Travers says.

"Most of that is mine," Grant says.

"Oh..." Travers coughs, embarrassed. "How many black suits do you need?"

"All of them, Travers... but that's not the point. Have you ever even *heard* of this guy?"

They finally get to the tire well. Grant starts unscrewing the heavy iron screw that keeps it shut.

"No," Travers says. "Believe me, if I ever heard of a guy calling himself 'Doctor AEvil,' I'd remember it."

"Well I can't figure it out," Grant says. "The tech he has... teleporters aren't cheap, and these weren't run-of-the-mill. Plus the weird-ass missile that shouldn't work? And the Buck Rogers laser gun shit? The guy probably isn't in the highest tiers—not like Gladiator or Sentinel or Overmind, or anyone like that—but he's still a notch or two above Sky Commando, which is pretty sweet in its own right."

"What's to figure out?" The screw finally works free, and Travers helps Grant pry open the lid that separates the trunk from the spare tire well. "This Doctor AEvil is unknown, but smart."

"Come on, Pete, you're not thinking this through." Grant reaches down into the tire well, grabs the side handle of a large, rugged crate, and starts pulling. "Gimme a hand here. No, the problem isn't his gear, it's what he's doing with it."

Travers puts his knees up on the rear bumper to allow him to lean farther into the trunk so he can help Grant pull. "Ah. The bank robbery."

"Yeah..." The edge of the crate clears the spare tire well, and they quickly pull the rest out and open the top.

The crate is full of weapons.

"It doesn't make sense," Grant says. "It's not even a main branch. Hell, Travers, it probably cost more to build one of those crazy impossible missiles than the bank has on hand. There's no practical reason for him to show up and stir the shit like that."

"Maybe that's not the practical reason," Travers says.

"I don't follow." Grant starts pulling out various weapons—nothing lethal, Travers notices—and stuffing them into his pockets.

"Maybe it's a distraction. Maybe he wants everyone looking at him while something important happens somewhere else."

"Maybe," Grant says, "but he gets really pissed off every time I make fun of his name."

"Ah," Travers says. "Well, maybe he's just an idiot."

Grant laughs. "That's where I'm putting my money down. OK, I gotta go. Looks like the fun is about to start."

With that, the outline around Grant blurs, and Travers is alone in the alley.

* * *

When Agent Hu first discovered her abilities, she mastered most of the aspects of control relatively quickly. Once she entered her burning state, most of her ability to control the flame she generated was instinctive—it was part of her body, and was no different to her than flexing an arm or a leg.

The process of moving from a non-burning state to a burning state—a transformation she refers to as "lighting up"—was another matter entirely. The first time she triggered her powers she *exploded* like a fuel-air explosive, incinerating most of the junkyard she was standing in at the time. Controlling the overpressure she generates when she lights up is something she struggled with for a long time.

She doesn't struggle with it now.

One second she's an Asian woman sitting alone cross-legged on a cold tile floor. When Grant says "fire in the hole," she explodes into a being of living, solid flame. The blast immediately knocks three soldiers off their feet, and staggers two more. Everyone turns to face her as she rises into the air, the flames around her burning white-hot as she surveys the room.

That's when Grant drops the flashbang grenade.

His form blurs for a moment, then he drops something to the floor, then he blurs again as he disappears. The painfully bright light and sound cause the four soldiers who were guarding him to stagger, one falling to his knees and one completely losing his balance and falling over. Doctor AEvil appears unaffected, and turns away from Hu to see his men falling over each other.

"Stop them!"

Grant appears behind three soldiers, dropping a cylinder to the floor.

Grant appears in front of a soldier standing guard at the fire exit.

Hu reaches out with one hand, and a bright thread of fire corkscrews through the air.

The mini-stuckey spreads out across the floor, miring the soldiers in knee-deep, fast-drying polymer. Grant jams a cattle prod into the side of the soldier at the fire exit—the armor is apparently not grounded, and the soldier slumps to the ground, twitching.

Hu guides the thread of fire as it cuts a line from her position to the fire exit, separating most of the soldiers—all but the one guard Grant took down—from the civilians. She concentrates, and the thread grows into a thin, burning wall of flame.

One of the soldiers caught in the stuckey drops his rifle. The other two raise theirs, aiming at Hu. Grant appears in front of them, shoves each in the chestplate, then disappears again. They both topple over backward.

The sudden appearance of a flaming wall causes panic to set in on both sides. Grant throws open the fire exit, yells "This way!" and the civilians surge toward him, not quite trampling each other in their effort to get out. Lester, of all people, tries to keep them calm and organize their evacuation. The soldiers who are still on the floor scramble to get away from the flame. Even the soldiers who are still untouched are distracted by it.

But there are more than just soldiers in the room.

Oh, crap. I forgot about

A flash of blinding light and heat *thoooms* through the air as energy from Doctor AEvil's gun smashes into Hu's burning form, sending her flying into the ceiling. Broken bits of charred ceiling paneling fall to the tile floor as Hu melts a trough across the ceiling that reaches the far wall, where she finally falls back onto the tile floor.

The wall of fire disappears, of course. She has to concentrate to maintain it. It doesn't matter at this point—it bought Grant enough time to get the civilians moving.

Doctor AEvil's gun is powerful—she actually *felt* it, and it *hurt*. It could potentially cause her significant damage, if he manages to hit her like that a few more times. She picks herself off the floor, then races through the air, straight at him.

The soldiers who aren't incapacitated focus on her as the threat, and start shooting their fancy rifles in her direction. This is good—it means they're ignoring the civilians. They don't shoot lasers, but they do shoot energy of some kind. They do nothing while she's in her fire form—the hits barely register as she smashes into Doctor AEvil.

Hu's moving fast, but she still has her original mass—Doctor AEvil staggers back, but doesn't fall. She grabs the cannon strapped to his arm.

Bang

Another flashbang goes off to her left, and

Bang

another to her right, as Grant steps up his game. She hears the cattle prod again, and a perfectly modulated shriek as another soldier falls.

She focuses on the cannon, pouring heat into the point where the gun connects to the arm.

"Stop!"

Hu thinks she hears a note of panic in Doctor AEvil's perfectly modulated voice. She ignores him, focusing on the cannon.

"I said STOP!"

Hu flies through the air as Doctor AEvil throws her off. He raises his cannon.

"Not this time," Hu snarls.

Fire erupts from her and rushes toward the armored figure, engulfing him. Doctor AEvil backs up quickly, trying to evade the flame, but Hu simply wills it to follow him. Finally in desperation he raises the cannon again and...

...then he stops, stumbles once, and falls over. He doesn't move.

Hu floats over to Doctor AEvil's unmoving form. "Need to check the heat tolerances on that armor."

"They also need to put more padding in their helmets," Grant says, walking up beside her to look down at the scorched armor lying motionless on the floor. "You know every time I hit one over the head it was instant lights out? Like pressing a magic button. If I'd known that I wouldn't have brought the cattle prod."

"Only counted you in three places," Hu says. "Slacking off?"

Grant shakes his head. "I was also getting the security footage and making a safe path for the civilians. And I'm down a point."

"This is the police!" A megaphone blares from somewhere outside, just out of sight of the gaping hole in the bank's wall. "Come out with your hands up!"

"Oh for..." Grant shakes his head, blurs for an instant, then throws a fireproofed duffel bag on the ground at Hu's feet. "Robert Palmer." Then he's gone again.

Robert Palmer. They relocated to the alley. Hu picks up the bag, looks around the bank once, then flies through the hole in the wall, over the heads of the growing police presence, and far enough away to foil pursuit. It's going to take a while to properly sync up with Grant and Travers. A lot of walking...

It'll have to be walking, Hu thinks. *I never did get the money*.

PART FOUR: HARUSPEX ANALYTICS

They've been gagged and bound for nearly two days, hands stretched over their heads, feet tied together and tethered to the floor. All three figures—two men and a woman—bear their incarceration stoically. There were initial attempts to work free of the restraints, but they proved fruitless, and eventually all three resigned themselves to waiting.

And so they wait, in a darkened room, with nothing but their own thoughts and the occasional muffled sounds of their fellow captives to keep them company. They wait, grow hungry, grow *thirsty*, and continue waiting.

Finally, toward the end of the second day, someone turns on a light.

The light is painful at first, but as they gradually adjust they see they are in a very empty, unfurnished room. Unfurnished, but fancy—the walls and floor are granite, and the ceiling is covered in baroque plaster tiles. At the very end of this empty room is a simple door, so plain it looks almost shabby by comparison.

It is another hour before the door finally opens. When the man walks in, the three recognize him immediately.

"I apologize for the delay," the Chairman says. He crosses the room slowly, deliberately.

"That is pure artifice, of course. I apologize for nothing of the sort. Not in this room. Not to any of you."

He stops in front of them, noting with amusement that they have all averted their eyes.

"This won't do at all. Very few people are given the opportunity to look at me directly. I suggest you take advantage of it."

One by one they look up. His face looks as if it had been kind, once.

"Better. Let's review, shall we?" He turns and begins to pace the width of the room, hands clasped behind his back, like a prosecutor presenting his case before a jury.

"All three of you have been with us for some time. We don't know how long you've been working for someone else, and we don't know who you are working for..." At this he stops and turns to face them. "Though I have my suspicions."

He resumes pacing.

"We know one of you—though we don't know who—is responsible for contacting Alexander Morgan and telling him about Project Recall. We know all three of you were involved in framing Andrew Estovich—yes, we *always* knew he was framed, I'm afraid, and this, I think, was your biggest mistake. Andrew was not a stupid man by any means, but he was certainly not one of our brightest. He was, however, without question one of our best. I feel compelled to tell you, right now, that it was at his insistence that we carried through with our little charade the other day. The man you identified, so dismissively, as a *patsy* died a hero's death in order to root out your corruption and expose it for all to see."

Two of the three gazes drop. The woman stares back defiantly, eyes hard.

"Of course, you've still managed to do quite a bit of damage to our organization. It will take some time for us to trace your activities to learn the full extent of it. But one thing that *fascinated* me were your efforts to learn more about me, personally."

He stops in front of the woman with hard eyes, looking directly at her, ignoring the others for the moment.

"Gathering intelligence on the leader of the organization you are trying to take down is not in itself unusual, of course. What interests me is that despite the substantial collection of intelligence you already had on me, it appears you have yet to send any of it on."

He locks eyes with the woman. The woman struggles valiantly, but her gaze breaks.

The Chairman smiles. "It tells me that you have correctly deduced that the intelligence you have is not only incomplete, but it lacks something that will place it in the appropriate context. That everything you have is meaningless, perhaps even detrimental, if it were passed on without the context you lack."

He begins to pace again.

"I can't pretend to like any of you, of course, but I find myself strangely grateful. I wasn't prepared for how keenly I would feel Andrew's death. One of the dangers of being in command *behind the scenes* is that it is easy to forget what sacrifice entails. I require my people to make sacrifices every day, and they make them. Seeing Andrew make his... reminded me of what, exactly, that entails. Of what I *owe* the people who work to make my vision—*their* vision—come to fruition."

He stops in front of the woman again—the two men are much closer to breaking than she is—and offers her a thin smile. "You have, if anything, made me more committed to my task than ever."

The woman narrows her eyes.

"In light of that," the Chairman says, "I have decided to help you. After a fashion. I will give you the one thing you tried, and failed to find. I will give you *context*."

He turns away from them, reaches into his jacket, and pulls out a small cell phone. He presses something on the screen, holds it up to his ear, and waits.

"It's me," he says. "Yes. I just wanted to congratulate you and your team on a job well done."

Pause.

"Not at all," he continues. "You were brought in under difficult circumstances, and you handled the matter exceptionally. Each of you should be proud of what you've accomplished. That matter is out of your hands, of course, but I would like you to be more involved in the day-to-day business of Project Recall going forward. We are facing unprecedented threat and scrutiny, and I believe your team's involvement will go a long way in mitigating much of it. Please report to Mara in the morning."

Pause.

"Of course. Thank you. Enjoy the rest of your evening."

The Chairman puts his phone in his jacket, then turns back to face the prisoners.

"That's done," he says. "Where were we? Context. I promised to give you context."

All three are staring at him. One of the men is clearly on the verge of breaking, his eyes wide with fear. The other still resists, but he has accepted the inevitable outcome. He is simply trying to cling to himself for as long as he can before he succumbs. Only the woman tries to fight back with the only weapon she has—her eyes. But now there is a hint of uncertainty behind her gaze.

"Context," the Chairman repeats. He frowns, considering, then nods to himself as he reaches a decision.

"I don't believe we've been properly introduced. Let us start by telling you my real name..."

CURVEBALL
24
JUN 2015
CURVEBALL
A Prose Comic
... AND JULY. IF WE'RE BEING COMPLETELY HONEST.
TRIPLE HELIX
-SIZED ISSUE
TRIPLE
STORY
CHRISTOPHER WRIGHT
COVER
PASCALLE LEPAS
LOGO
GARTH GRAHAM

PART ONE: ATLANTIC OCEAN, NIGHT

It was a stupid oversight. It looks like it might get them killed.

Steal a boat seemed like the most reasonable approach to escaping the island. Sea travel had been the most common way to get to and from the island for most of its history, after all. But Artemis had ordered the civilian population to *evacuate*, and as a result most of the seaworthy boats were gone. The one they'd chosen—an old seiner fishing boat—had looked like the best of the few boats still moored in the Port Libertad docks, but a few hours in and Artemis can tell they're in trouble.

He's not sure how fast they're sinking. Every calculation he attempts produces a different result, and eventually he admits he simply doesn't know enough about the condition of the boat to predict when the leaking will stop being manageable. A few days at most, is his most optimistic guess—and that's assuming the weather stays calm, which is far from guaranteed. He doubts there's enough time for them to actually get anywhere.

"What's going on?"

David Bernard slumps in a corner of the wheelhouse, sweating and shivering in turns, trying desperately to stay awake. The immediate effects of his encounter with Artigenian's rune wore off hours ago, so he's no longer blind, but something else is clearly affecting him. Artemis notices a slight tremor in the younger man's hands.

Artemis tries to look unconcerned. "Everything's fine."

David laughs weakly. "We are too deep into this for you to lie to me right now."

Artemis sighs. "We're taking on water. I've sealed the offending section off below-decks as best I can, but it's only a matter of time."

David frowns. "I don't remember any of this."

"You were nodding off," Artemis says. "I thought it best not to wake you."

"We escaped the island, though?"

Artemis nods. "We're in no danger of being pulled back in. Not at this point. But it hasn't quite released its grip, I'm afraid. The on-board compass is useless, as is the two-way radio."

"Bermuda Triangle strikes again," David says.

"It seems so. We'll have to travel a bit longer before we're free of it. Once we are... well. I don't think we'll make it to land. We'll have to radio for help, and hope for a rescue."

"Oh," David says. "That's not good, is it? That's going to attract attention."

"Rescues at sea do tend to invite scrutiny." Artemis turns on the radio again. White noise crackles. He turns the volume down, but leaves the radio on. "That said, I've made some arrangements that will, I hope, allow us to escape notice."

"Arrangements," David says. "Members of your organization?"

Artemis shakes his head. "I don't altogether trust my people."

"Crossfire?"

"Not this time. Though I doubt they will object. How are you doing, David?"

David shrugs. "I don't feel so hot. And I have a lunatic's memories floating around in my head—Artigenian was a real nasty piece of work. Still, it's better than having a concussion."

"Hmmm." Artemis isn't entirely sure he agrees. Absorbing the memories of a madman—not just a madman, but a man who is as close to a very particular brand of evil as it's possible to get and still be human—isn't a trivial act, and he wishes David would stop treating it so trivially. How much of Artigenian is in his mind? Did David absorb any of the man's *will?* Are the memories *aware?* David claims they aren't, and Artemis would like to believe him. Experience, however, has taught him to mistrust everything having to do with magic... and it doesn't explain David's current condition. He obviously absorbed something *more* than memories. He's feverish, drifting in and out of consciousness. If Artemis didn't know any better, he'd say the man was on the verge of—

Yes. Yes, of course.

Artemis locks the wheel in place, then turns to face David. He kneels, placing his hand on David's forehead.

"Shouldn't you be steering?" David moves to bat the hand away, but Artemis simply grabs his wrist, feeling for his pulse.

"The boat will be fine for the moment," Artemis says.

"What are you doing?"

"I'm trying to take your pulse. Are you cold?"

"I'm fine." David crosses his arms and tries to suppress a shiver.

"The question is important. Give me your flashlight."

David removes the LED flashlight from a vest pocket and holds it out. The tremors in his hands are increasing.

"I wouldn't mind a blanket," David admits. "I don't remember the ocean being this cold, this time of year."

"The ocean is almost always cold," Artemis says. "But at present, I find the weather quite warm."

He takes the flashlight, draws back David's left eyelid, and shines the light into his pupil, watching it contract. David flinches, but waits patiently as Artemis repeats the process with his right eye. "I should have seen this sooner. You're *cocooning*."

It takes a moment for the words to sink in.

"That's not possible," David says.

"*Very* possible." Artemis stands, brushing the dirt from the floor off his knees. "You need a space to lie down. You'd probably be more comfortable in one of the cabins—at least at first—but I think it's better if we both stay in the wheelhouse. I'll be back in a moment with some bedding."

It only takes a few minutes to collect what he needs—one very worn pillow and two wool blankets. When he returns, David is still sitting in the corner, arms wrapped around his knees.

"I'm serious, Artemis. I'm just sick."

"You are not sick," Artemis says. "You are in the early stages of cocooning, and you're struggling against it. Your fever, tremors, nausea... these are a result of you fighting against what your body needs to do."

"It's not *possible*," David insists. "It's just *memories*."

"It's far more than that. Lie down." Artemis forces David to lie down against the far wall, placing the old pillow under his head and covering him in the blankets. "Think about what you said when you were performing your—your *ritual*. You didn't define it as 'memory.' You defined it as *power*. You were claiming *power*."

David's eyes narrow. "I only did that to—"

"I know why you did it," Artemis says. "You had to release the memory from the force that bound it. I understand your reasons. But it *affected* you, and your body is adapting to it the same way a metahuman adapts to the manifestation of his or her gifts. You aren't stupid, David, and I recommend you move past denial as quickly as you can to prepare for what happens next."

David starts to retort, hesitates, then his expression sinks into a scowl.

"At the moment, the most important thing for you to do is sleep," Artemis says. "Your body needs it. It's... well, essentially it's recalibrating itself to a new set of specifications."

"Specifications," David says. "What specifications?"

"An excellent question," Artemis says. "One we will have to explore, in depth, at a later date. For the moment, *stop fighting it*. Stop struggling to stay awake. I realize this isn't the most convenient time or place, but there's nothing to be done for that. Trust me, if you can, and allow me to make sure we get out of here alive."

David exhales through his teeth, the *hiss* of his breath a sound of pure frustration. "I don't really understand. But I don't have to, I guess. All right, Artemis. I'll trust you, and... take a nap. I guess."

"Good," Artemis says. "I will keep us safe."

David closes his eyes. It doesn't take long after that—his breathing steadies into the rhythmic cadence of sleep.

"Sleep well, David."

Artemis stands, straightens, and returns his attention to the endless gray water.

PART TWO: FARRADAY CITY SUBURBS

"Well it doesn't *look* like a cesspit." Special Agent Alan Grant stares out the passenger-side window, staring at his surroundings with a mixture of curiosity, skepticism, and mild disappointment. "It does look evil, I guess. But suburbs always look evil to me."

Special Agent Lijuan Hu rolls her eyes, slowing the car down as they drive past children playing basketball in the driveway of one of many ranch-style houses lined up along the street. "*Everything* looks evil to you. You're a misanthrope."

"Am not. This isn't hate, it's *tough love*."

Former Special Agent (now wanted terrorist) Peter Travers chuckles in amusement from the back seat.

"Sure it is," Hu says. "Gimme a break. Do you know how many assholes I've met who use 'tough love' as their excuse to just be an asshole?"

Grant flashes her a wolfish grin. "At least one."

"Don't sell yourself short," Hu says. "It would take ten of those guys to come close to what you do."

"I only want you to notice me," Grant says.

Hu punches Grant in the arm. "There, I noticed. Stupid *boy*."

Grant rubs his arm. "Ow."

"But you have a point," Hu says. "Any time I read about this city it's always about drug problems, prostitution, corruption, human trafficking, the slums—I mean it sounds like a real shithole. This isn't anything like that. This looks like where my parents live."

"Farraday City is... unique," Travers says. "It's so unique that it's considered an outlier by sociologists and routinely excluded from studies and reports. Even the Census Bureau excludes Farraday City from the rest of Georgia."

"Seriously?" Grant turns away from the window, glancing over his shoulder to regard the older man. "I didn't know that."

"It has incredibly high crime rates in specific areas of the city. But as soon as you move out of those areas, crime drops off sharply, to the point where it's no higher than any other thriving city in the US—actually, somewhat lower than average. As far as anyone who's studied the matter can tell, there's almost no crossover between the areas that are safe and the ones that aren't."

"That doesn't sound strange at all," Hu says. "You're always safer where the rich people live."

Travers shakes his head. "It's not like that. The 'safe' areas aren't exclusively rich. There are middle-class and poor neighborhoods that are similarly crime free. And there are upper-class neighborhoods that appear to be rife with criminal activity. This assumes the research is accurate, of course, but I think it is."

"So you're saying there are good and bad parts of the city, but nobody knows why one part's good and another is bad?"

"That's about right," Travers says.

"That's fucked up," Grant says. "And a little disappointing. I was expecting the entire city to be a post-apocalyptic war zone, full of burning trashcans and people dressed in animal skins. Or human skins, maybe. I don't know. So how do they get away with no federal footprint in the city?"

"Good question," Travers says. "There were a few attempts to open DHS field offices over the years. All of them were rejected. I ran across a few of the rejected proposals. Apparently someone was able to convince someone else that the offices weren't necessary because neighboring cities already had them."

Grant raises an eyebrow. "Someone? Someone else?"

"There were no names," Travers says. "Just a brief statement, explaining the rejection..."

"Wow," Grant says. "So the only police are local."

"Yes," Travers says. "And, I assume, quite corrupt."

"We wouldn't be able to work with them anyway. I'm on leave, grieving over the death of my beloved partner." Hu hits Grant in the arm again.

"Hey." Grant rubs his arm again. "What'd I do this time?"

"It's for later. Anyway, Travers is a wanted man, and you're *dead*. So I don't see any way flashing a badge and asking for assistance is going to work, even if they were legit. But that leads to a fun question: now that we're here, what exactly are we going to do?"

"Ah," Travers says. "Yes. That. Well it's hard to explain."

"Hold on a second." Hu pulls the car into a convenience store parking lot, kills the ignition, and turns in her seat to face Travers. "I hope you have a little more detail than that. Grant and I are used to working need-to-know, but usually we know a little more than this."

Grant nods in agreement.

Travers nods slightly, smiling politely. "I'm not keeping anything from you. I'm just not exactly sure."

Hu and Grant exchange glances.

"Not exactly sure *what*?" Hu tries to say it without growling.

"What happens next," Travers says. "This is one of the... challenges of working with someone like Curveball."

"*Curveball*?" Grant laughs in disbelief. "Didn't he break your jaw once?"

Travers sighs. "That is one of the *other* challenges of working with someone like Curveball."

"Shut up, Grant," Hu says. "Go on, Travers."

"There's not much else. Curveball is investigating Liberty's murder. Shortly after I was forced to leave my office in such a *theatrical* fashion, I was contacted by a mutual friend because he was in trouble. I did what I could, and I've come to the conclusion I can probably do considerably *more* if I work with him directly. So we're going to meet him, join his group, and help uncover a conspiracy that is very likely poisoning our country from within."

Hu and Grant exchange glances again. They're not telepaths, but they've been partners for a long time—long enough to read the tics and micro-expressions that most people would overlook. Travers had a partner, once, and he knows what's going on, he's just not privy to the conversation. He waits patiently, hands folded in his lap.

Hu faces forward and starts the car. "Where are we going?"

"Into the city," Travers says.

Hu nods, easing the car out of the parking lot and back into the street. "What then?"

"I'm not sure," Travers says. "Just... drive around. Head for the ocean—apparently the city gets progressively seedier the closer you get to the beach. As I said, this is one of the challenges of working with someone like Curveball."

"So, what?" Grant turns his attention back to the passenger-side window. "Is he just gonna randomly crash through our windshield, or something?"

"I hope not," Hu says. "If I have to file for metahuman coverage again, my insurance will go through the roof."

Travers coughs apologetically. "It, ah, wouldn't be the first time."

Hu scowls.

PART THREE: WAREHOUSE COMPLEX

The room is dim, narrow, long, and cold.

Cold in every sense of the word: it is physically cold—cold enough for Plague to see his own breath when he exhales—but it's also cold in the abstract. The floor is bare concrete, the walls and ceiling metal—dull, brushed metal, treated to prevent frost.

The medical gurneys are set lengthwise against the longest of the walls, twelve to a side. The test subjects on the gurneys sleep—Plague prefers to think of it as sleeping—and equipment *beeps* and *hisses* softly as it monitors the vitals of each man, pushing more drugs into their bodies as needed.

"Poor bastards."

Plague's voice echoes slightly, bouncing off the walls as it travels down the long room. The technicians monitoring the equipment don't bother to look up. He walks down the length of the room, looking at each subject in turn. There are no names, only numbers: Test Subject #1, Test Subject #2, Test Subject #3, and so on. There are twenty-four in this room, and two more rooms just like it. They tell him it's the largest group yet. They tell him that's why he's here.

One of the reasons, anyway.

"So we got, what... seventy-two today?"

The technician leaning over Test Subject #14 looks up. She's in her mid-40s, streaks of gray showing in dark hair pulled into a tight braid. Her ID badge displays the name ELENA LOPEZ. Hispanic—that would have been a problem for him, once upon a time. Her eyes focus on him, and she nods briskly. "That sounds right."

"How's the weather?"

Her mouth twists in annoyance. "Clear skies so far."

"*Clear* skies? You gotta be kidding me."

She shrugs. "They told us to get everything set up anyway. They said they'd deal with the talent."

"Talent my ass," Plague mutters. "How long do we got before they freeze to death?"

"We're bringing in electric blankets."

Plague stares at Test Subject #14 for a moment. He's in his late fifties, early sixties—strong, though, still in shape. Not metahuman levels, but impressive for a man his age. The tattoo on his arm suggests military service, and the calluses on his hands suggests he didn't have a desk job.

"Who is this one?" He shouldn't care. He doesn't, exactly, but something about the man strikes a familiar chord.

"Test Subject #14," she says. "Someone has their names somewhere, but they don't tell us."

"Ah." Plague stares at Test Subject #14 and tries to figure out what it is that pulls at him. The working-class roots, perhaps: Plague grew up poor, always looking for a way out, always looking for something better. Fourteen's tattoo suggests he enlisted—maybe he thought that was his way out. Plague was never in the military, but he considered himself a soldier in his younger days.

"It's better that way," Elena says. "No point getting to know them. They'll all be dead by evening, one way or another."

"Yeah," Plague says. "I get that. It's easier not to know."

He flinches at the unbidden image of a dying woman sitting on a cheap couch. He doesn't want to remember the slow, rasping sound of her final breath, but the memory wraps itself around him like a noose.

"Are you all right?" Elena looks on with a mix of curiosity and alarm.

"I'm fine." His voice is hoarse. "I'm going to find the *talent* and deal with him myself."

* * *

The man is bound, wrapped tightly in his straitjacket, curled up in the corner of a bare metal room. They don't have proper psychiatric facilities here, so they're using one of the holding cells, with guards on hand to make sure he doesn't try to use the hard, bare walls as a weapon against himself. He's tried, twice, and the walls are still stained from each attempt.

Johann Richter stands in the observation room overlooking the cell and watches the man in silence. He barely recognizes him. Horace Preston was once competent, focused and self-assured, considered reliable by his superiors. Now he barely exists; he has dissolved into a bundle of tremors and nervous tics, given to bouts of anger and self-inflicted violence. He mutters to himself, apparently without end: fearful, incoherent ramblings that don't connect to anything tangible.

He turns his head slightly as the observation door opens. A muscular, white-haired man, dressed in blue slacks, thick-soled work boots, and a blue denim button-up shirt, stands in the doorway, scowling.

Richter nods in greeting. “Plague.”

Plague walks up to Richter, falling in beside him, gazing through the observation window. His eyes lock on Horace, and his expression changes from anger to shock.

“What the hell happened?” Plague’s voice is rough and uncultured. It’s easy to dismiss him as stupid, but Richter knows better.

“No one knows.” Richter’s own voice is smoother, more educated, with the slightest hint of a German accent. “A few days ago he began his work. Yesterday he suffered a breakdown. We’ve kept it quiet—no sense in alarming personnel.”

Plague’s scowl returns. “One of the lab techs says it’s still clear and dry outside.”

Richter nods. “That will change soon enough. We have a Prodigy Harness. If he will not cooperate willingly...”

Plague shakes his head. “Kinda dangerous, putting a guy like him in one of those.”

“We have no choice,” Richter says. “Weather manipulators are very rare. The harness will do what must be done. It will be messier than I’d prefer, but it will give us what we need.”

They stand in silence, watching Horace mutter, and twitch, and rock back and forth. Occasionally he cries out, as if he were a young child suffering through nightmares.

“Jesus,” Plague says. “A few days?”

“Four, to be precise.”

“Nobody knows why?”

“Unfortunately.” Richter sighs softly. “Mr. Preston complained of fatigue on the first day. He said the process was more difficult than it usually was. But he assured us everything was on track—it was requiring more effort to get the weather to respond, but it wasn’t taking any more *time*. Everything was on schedule. On the second day he was withdrawn. Only spoke when spoken to, and then only to say he was still on schedule. Everyone around him assumed he was simply focused on the task at hand. On the third day he attempted to harm himself.”

“So you put him in a straitjacket and took the harness out of storage.”

“It seemed prudent,” Richter says.

"How long?" Plague asks. "I get that this is a problem, but nobody told us to stand down."

"Once he is in the harness, we will proceed as planned," Richter says. "Once the test is complete we will evacuate the facility. A search is currently underway for our new location."

"In Farraday City?"

Richter hesitates. "Unlikely. Once we use the Prodigy Harness to get what we need... well, I suspect we will have *crossed a line*."

"What about the *other* reason we're here?"

"Yes..." Richter's brow furrows. "Curveball and the girl. Unfortunately, it will be difficult to—"

He is interrupted by a sharp knock on the observation room door. The door opens, and a man wearing body armor over medical scrubs enters the room.

"We have it." The man looks from Richter, to Plague, unsure which of them he should be focusing on. "It's right outside the cell door."

Richter turns to face him. "And you are?"

The man fumbles for a moment. "Wallace, sir. Doctor Michael Wallace. My team is responsible for Prodigy Harness operation and maintenance."

"Very good." Richter looks through the observation window at the huddled form of Horace. "Dr. Wallace, I will assist you in securing him to the harness. Plague, stay here. We can't risk you being injured before the test."

"I *can't* get injured," Plague says. "Not any more."

"That is not universally true."

Plague scowls as he remembers the blonde girl who broke his jaw. "Yeah, OK, that one surprised me. But I can handle this."

"I don't doubt your willingness or your ability," Richter says. "But without you we have no test. Stay here, while we deal with Mr. Preston."

"Fine." Plague looks away.

Richter turns back to Dr. Wallace. "Let's go."

The team waiting outside the cell door is larger than Richter expected. The harness is in multiple parts, each part has its own team of technicians, and an armed guard accompanies the group.

"We recommend assembling the harness in the cell," Dr. Wallace says. "I think it'll be faster to assemble it in there than it will be to attempt to transport him to another location."

"There are no outlets in the room," Richter says.

"Not needed. We brought a generator. We checked the charge before bringing it up—it'll operate for days."

Richter thinks it over. "Very well. We will secure him in the main harness first. Then we can assemble the pieces around him."

Dr. Wallace nods and turns to his people, giving out orders. Richter motions for the armed guards to follow him into the cell.

* * *

Horace Preston doesn't react when the cell door opens. When Richter puts his hand on the man's shoulder, however, the reaction is immediate.

"NO!" The howl is barely recognizably human as Horace jerks away, falls on his back, and starts lashing out with his legs. Richter immediately grabs the man's legs, as two guards grab the straps on his straitjacket, lifting him into the air. Horace flails desperately, trying in vain to shake his way free.

"We have him!"

The cell door opens again, and four men roll in what appears to be a bed surrounded by a half-formed cocoon. Horace stares at it, uncomprehending, then his eyes go wide.

"No." His voice is just a whisper this time. "No, no, Richter, *Richter*, please, *no*."

"Bring it here." Richter's voice is cold and unmoving.

"*Richter*." Horace lifts his head to focus on the man holding his legs. "Richter, *listen to me*. You can't do this. You can't... don't do this." His eyes are clear, as if the shock of seeing the harness has, for a time, dispelled his madness.

Richter doesn't reply.

"You don't *understand*." Horace is pleading now. "It's... no good. I tried, I *tried*, but the city. The *city*, Richter. The city."

He has Richter's attention now. "What are you talking about?"

"The *city*," Horace repeats. "I started moving the air and the city moved it back. It fought me. It's *fighting* me. It doesn't like anyone else to decide. Only it. Only it decides."

"Decides what?" Richter's voice is sharp. "Horace, what are you talking about? What does the city decide?"

Horace looks away. "When to make it rain."

Richter considers his words. “Put him under.”

“NO!”

A strong gust of wind surges through the room, coming seemingly from nowhere. Two of the doctors wheeling in the base of the harness are knocked over, and the harness itself rolls to the right as one of the guards is forced back three steps, knocking into it. Richter and the two men holding him up hold fast.

“*Do not put me in that thing!*”

Lightning explodes from the center of the room, arcing into the harness. Richter smells ozone and scorched plastic as everyone scatters, some throwing themselves against the walls of the cell, others diving through the door.

“*I will not defy the city again! Never again!*”

The wind grows stronger. Richter is forced to let go of Horace as he’s pushed out toward the wall. Horace’s legs drop to the ground, and suddenly he’s standing on his own as the two men holding his straitjacket lose their grips, and are flung, hard, up and into the ceiling. They drop to the floor, unmoving, and are pushed to the walls like detritus in a storm.

In the center of the room, Richter can see the vague outline of a funnel beginning to form. A tornado. Horace Preston is creating a miniature *tornado* in the middle of his cell.

And then, all at once, it stops. Horace doubles over, gagging, then sinks to his knees as he begins to retch.

“Quickly,” Richter says. “Sedate him *now*.”

Dr. Wallace rushes into the room, carrying a hypodermic needle filled with a dark, cherry-red liquid. He steps around the harness, over the guards, and kneels next to the still-retching form of Horace Preston. Richter pushes him onto the floor, pressing down on his back to keep him from moving, as the doctor injects the liquid into his neck. In a matter of seconds, Horace begins to calm down. By the count of twenty, Horace is asleep.

Richter sighs in relief.

“What happened?” Dr. Wallace looks around in confusion. “What set him off? What made him stop?”

“I don’t know what set him off,” Richter says. “As to what made him stop...” He looks over to the wall he knows separates the cell from the observation room, and nods once. “Plague.”

Dr. Wallace takes a half-step away from Horace's unmoving form—an unconscious, reflexive, unscientific reaction, but one easy to understand.

"Take these guards to the infirmary," Richter orders. "Make sure the harness is undamaged, then put Mr. Preston within. Revive him as soon as it is operational. We need him conscious for what comes next."

"What does come next?" Dr. Wallace asks the question aloud, but everyone in the room is wondering the same thing.

Richter's smile is cold and thin.

"Change."

PART FOUR: FARRADAY CITY BUNKER

Jenny shifts in her body armor, wishing she'd just hurry up and settle into it so she'd stop obsessing about it. It's not exactly uncomfortable—it's not even particularly heavy, thanks to her now-above-human-norms strength—but the extra layer of bulk is new, and it's throwing her off.

"You'll get used to it." Street Ronin makes a few final adjustments to something on her back. "Faster than you think. I figure by the end of your first fight."

They're in her room in the bunker. It's still *her* room, despite the fact that the bunker is now putting up six people and was really only designed for two. CB claims he's lived in smaller spaces with more people, and the other guys claim they don't mind. She figures it's mostly macho sexist bullshit, but at the same time she finds herself wanting to spend more and more time by herself, so she takes advantage of it. She's jumped into something she can't jump out of, and the enormity of it is terrifying.

I'm not backing out. I don't ***want*** *to back out. I'm going to do right by these guys.*

God, I hope I don't screw up.

"I haven't trained in it," Jenny says. "I mean, when I was sparring with Red Shift I was focusing on being agile—dodging, weaving, not getting hit."

"That's good," Street Ronin says. "I recommend you keep doing that. This armor won't turn you into Vigilante or Scrapper Jack. It's mitigation, not absolute protection."

"I get that." Jenny tries not to sound impatient. "I do, but... won't it slow me down?"

"A little, at first, but not nearly as much as you think. And once you adapt? You'll need to adjust your balance and your stance, but you've got Liberty's strength and reflexes. Give it a while and it'll be like wearing clothes."

"If you say so," Jenny says.

"Don't worry, Zero. I don't have super powers, and my armor is heavier than yours, but I can still duck and weave with the best of them." Street Ronin claps her on the shoulder.

The shoulder pad rattles slightly. He frowns.

"Hold still, I need to tighten that. This is supposed to be stealth-friendly..." He tightens something between the plate and the shoulder and claps her on the shoulder again. This time it just thuds, no rattling.

"That's good. OK, try on the helmet."

He holds out what looks like a black paintball helmet, complete with built-in goggles and face grille. She stares at it, not sure what to think.

"Put it on," he urges. "It's stronger than it looks. The grille will obscure your features—that's good if you don't want anyone to know who you are—and it won't constrict your breathing. It also won't protect you from gas, though, so keep that in mind."

Jenny takes the helmet and puts it on. She immediately regrets having long hair.

"Try a ponytail," Street Ronin says. "Braiding your hair would be better. Keep it low, right where the back of the neck joins the skull."

"Braid. Yeah, OK." Jenny nods. "Gimme a few minutes."

"Tell you what," Street Ronin says. "I'll go back out with the others—I still have to tweak some of the rest of our gear. Why don't you take off the armor and get back into it on your own, just to get used to that part of it. Get your hair straightened out, and then come out when you're ready to tune the helmet. It's as good a time as any to show the team."

Jenny reddens slightly. "They'll laugh."

"They're not going to laugh," Street Ronin says.

"CB is going to laugh."

"Well, yes," Street Ronin admits. "Curveball is probably going to laugh." He grins, turns, and shuts the door behind him as he leaves.

* * *

Crossfire's equipment, fully unpacked, won't fit in the monitor room, and the common room is starting to look like a military command center. Red Shift sits in front of Crossfire's "mobile network"—the computer rig they take with them when they're on the road. Four long metal crates, probably filled with weapons, are stacked in the center of the room, and a fifth has been placed in front of the couch for use as an ad-hoc coffee table. Jack Barrow sits on the couch, feet propped up on the crate, reading a dog-eared copy of *The Long Goodbye*. Vigilante is in the kitchen making coffee. Street Ronin is in Jenny's room helping her with her new armor. CB stares at all the equipment piled around him and feels a brief surge of hardware envy. Then he looks over Red Shift's shoulder, examining the images of the warehouses they'll be attacking only a few hours from now.

They've had to be very careful with their reconnaissance. They're operating under the assumption that the bad guys are well-equipped and extremely paranoid, so they've been relying on long-range surveillance. Crossfire has a few floating spheres—Street Ronin gets upset when CB calls them "drones," but he can't think of anything else to call them—that they occasionally send on long-distance flybys, taking pictures of the warehouse area in an attempt to determine where the actual hideout is.

It's an inconvenient process that requires a great deal of patience. In order to minimize detection, the drones don't transmit anything—they have to be physically deployed and retrieved, their data recovered and processed, and only then can the images be studied. The images are taken at long-distance, so they don't reveal a great deal of detail. They do, however, show activity, and the batch of images taken the day before show a number of trucks pulling up to one of the warehouses and unloading cargo.

The drone was too far away to pull a license plate, but CB recognized the trucks: Elmuth Shipping. The trucks are unloading cargo, but the pictures aren't clear enough to determine what that cargo is—crates of some sort, long, rectangular crates.

Or coffins. Crap.

"Could this be where they're collecting all that medical data?"

Red Shift shrugs. "It's possible. We don't know what data the New York office sent them. But I thought you said there wasn't any tie between the local TriHealth office and this group."

"I didn't find one when I went out looking," CB says. "But I'm looking at one right now." He points at the yellow-and-orange trucks in the photo they're studying. "Elmuth Shipping."

"Oh," Red Shift says. "That's interesting."

"Interesting," CB says. "Yeah. Also worrying. I'm pretty sure Elmuth isn't 'in' on whatever's going down—if they're being used, it's because they don't care and don't ask questions, which is a short-term advantage. But it's *only* short-term."

Vigilante is standing next to CB now, holding three mugs of hot coffee. He sets two down in an empty spot, and takes a sip from the third as he stares down at the blurry image. "You said their security wasn't great."

CB picks up one of the mugs and fights back the urge to light a cigarette. "I said it was a *joke*. These guys aren't big players. If they're being used it's because our Very Special Friends are short on time and couldn't wait to do it the right way."

"So they're planning something big," Vigilante says. "Big enough that they need to risk being noticed."

"That's not good." Jack doesn't look up from his book.

"I can't think of a situation where it would be," CB says.

Jack looks up from his book. "It means they'll bolt when they're done. They're not bozos. They're high-level players. They're... well. They're operating at Artie's level. *At least* at his level."

CB tries to ignore the strangeness of someone calling Artemis LaFleur, one of the world's most dangerous villains, "Artie."

"Oh," Vigilante says. "I get it. It's a calculated risk."

Jack nods. "They've decided the payoff is worth losing the base. Whatever happens, as soon as they get what they want, they're gone."

"We'd better get going, then." Street Ronin stands in the doorway dividing the common room from the hall. "Zero's almost ready. Armor fits pretty well."

"Yeah, but what's it look like?" CB asks.

"She'll be out in a few. You can see for yourself."

Vigilante looks around the room. "So this is it, then? For real, this time?"

"Now or never." Jack turns his attention back to his paperback.

CB turns to Street Ronin. "I think I'm gonna want some hardware for this. Hook me up?"

Street Ronin raises an eyebrow, then waves to the crates on the floor. "Help yourself."

"We better suit up," Vigilante says.

CB walks over to one of the long metal crates and starts unlatching it. "Use my room if you want some privacy."

Vigilante nods, picks up a bulky rucksack sitting to one side of the couch, and disappears down the hall. Red Shift stands, stretches, and follows.

"I'll change after I finish with Zero's armor," Street Ronin says.

CB glances at Jack, still buried in his paperback. "Jack?"

Jack shrugs. "Not my style. Pissed about my boots, though."

"Why?" CB looks at Jack's boots. "They're fine."

"Give it time."

CB and Street Ronin unstack the crates in the middle of the room, and CB goes through each until he settles on two custom automatic pistols.

"Excellent choice," Street Ronin says. "You'll want the holster for those. The belt's rigged to hold high-capacity magazines."

"You're right," CB says. "I *will* want that."

"Might also want to consider this." Street Ronin hands him a black metal baton about six inches long.

CB takes the baton and flicks it downward. The baton extends swiftly, locking into place with a crisp *clack*. "This have a holster too?"

"Clips on to the gun belt."

"Works for me," CB says. "Put it on my tab."

"I guess I need a tab, too..."

Everyone looks up as Jenny steps into the room. Her body armor is patterned after body armor made for snowboarders: a series of plates set over more flexible material, providing protection while still allowing for maximum flexibility. The difference is that sports armor is usually hard plastic over nylon, and this armor is metal composite plates over a steel chain mesh—essentially chainmail for the 21st century. The armor plating locks into sockets set directly into the mesh, removing the need for extra straps, and over the armor is a vest harness with pockets and hooks and pouches. Her gloves are heavy nylon and fingerless, and a metal plate is attached to the back of each, coming just past her knuckles. Her hair is braided and coiled into a short bun at the base of her neck.

"Huh," CB says.

Jack sets his paperback down. "If I were going to have a costume, that'd be a good one."

Jenny smiles slightly. "It's not a costume. It's *body armor*."

Jack laughs. "It's body armor for you. It'd be a costume for me."

"Now try the helmet," Street Ronin says.

Jenny walks into the center of the room, grabs the helmet, and puts it on.

"Goodbye Jenny," CB says. "Hello Zero."

Jenny cocks her head to one side, which looks a little odd with the helmet. "Yeah?" Her voice is still Jenny's—the mesh does a good job of obscuring her face, but it doesn't muffle her voice at all.

"You look like a Stormtrooper and a SWAT Commando had a one night stand," CB says. "In a good way."

Street Ronin grins. “I was going for Stormtrooper/Ninja, but I’ll take it. Zero, the helmet has a tactical earpiece so you’ll be able to maintain radio contact. Other than that, all it really does is protect your head. It doesn’t do anything fancy. I didn’t have enough time.”

“It’ll be fine,” Jenny says. “Thanks for all this. I’m sure I’ll be the prettiest girl at the cotillion.”

“You’ll...” Street Ronin trails off, confused. “What?”

CB bursts out laughing.

PART FIVE: ATLANTIC OCEAN, DAY

By day the ocean is an endless blue expanse, flecked with shades of darker blue as the waves roll up, casting shadows over its own surface. There are no clouds today; the sky is as unblemished as the ocean is mottled.

There is no sign of land, nor sign of any ships. The compass has started working again, but the two-way radio is still just a constant stream of static, white noise turned so low it barely registers against the sound of the engine as it labors to keep the boat moving. Artemis turns it up higher, listening for breaks or variations in the endless wall of sound.

They've taken on a considerable amount of water in the past few hours, and the boat is definitely lower in the water than it should be. There's too much water below. He's not sure how much longer they have before the boat gives up entirely, but he's certain it's "hours" instead of "days."

Artemis makes plans.

The boat has a life raft, and he devotes some time to getting it ready. It auto-inflates without issue, and the survival kit, while basic, appears in good order. There are life jackets on board, and David is so deep into cocooning that he doesn't react when Artemis puts one on him. An hour passes, and they have an exit strategy. It will give them more time, but not enough.

Radio reception is starting to improve. The static is no longer unbroken: he can hear pops and squelches, interrupted occasionally by the distorted sound of speech. He fiddles with the channels, trying to find one clear enough to listen to, and ten minutes later he stumbles across a weather forecast in Spanish. The voice is mostly clear, fading out occasionally but only for a moment or two. Relief floods through Artemis as he realizes they finally have a chance at getting out of this.

He adjusts the radio to a very specific channel, then begins to transmit.

"Oscar, Zoroaster, Phadrig, Isaac, Norman, Henkle, Emmanuel, Ambroise, Diggs. This is Yellow Brick Road. Oscar, Zoroaster, Phadrig, Isaac, Norman, Henckle, Emmanuel, Ambroise, Diggs. This is Yellow Brick Road. Oscar, Zoroaster, Phadrig, Isaac, Norman, Henkle, Emmanuel, Ambroise, Diggs..."

He repeats the message five times, then waits five minutes. Then he repeats the message five times, and waits five minutes. On the third broadcast he gets a reply.

"*Yellow Brick Road, Yellow Brick Road, do you copy?*"

Artemis allows himself a moment's satisfaction before replying. "Oscar, Zoroaster, Phadrig, Isaac, Norman, Henkle, Emmanuel, Ambroise, Diggs. This is Yellow Brick Road."

"Yellow Brick Road, I am Oz, the Great and Terrible. Who are you, and why do you seek me?"

"Oscar, Zoroaster, Phadrig, Isaac, Norman, Henkle, Emmanuel, Ambroise, Diggs, this is Yellow Brick Road. Requesting *silver shoes*."

The line is silent a moment. Then, in a stronger, clearer tone: "Yellow Brick Road, we have your position. Delivering silver shoes in three hours."

Artemis does some quick mental calculations. "Acknowledged. We may be in a life raft by then."

"Understood, Yellow Brick Road. Oz out."

The channel falls silent. Artemis heaves a sigh of relief.

"Thank you, Dr. Thorpe. A pleasure, as always."

PART SIX: WAREHOUSE COMPLEX

In hindsight there had been no need to ask about the weather—Plague knows the moment the storm starts. He stands in the observation room, looking into the now-crowded cell block as doctors and lab techs crowd around the Prodigy Harness, going through the steps to revive the man imprisoned within. He can see Horace Preston within, lying on something that looks like a coffin bed, and as he stirs he feels the temperature drop, ever so slightly.

Dr. Wallace looks up from a small hand-held computer, currently attached to the harness by a tether. He holds it out in offering. "He's keyed to your voice, Mr. Richter."

Richter takes the computer and hesitates. "How do I...?"

"Just speak," Dr. Wallace says. "He's keyed to your voice."

Richter nods. "Mr. Preston."

Horace Preston's eyes snap open immediately. They do not focus.

"Mr. Preston. I need you to complete your mission. Now."

Given how violent his reaction was before he was put in the harness, Plague half-expects a repeat performance. But he doesn't respond at all: he simply stares blankly into space.

The air grows colder, however, and Plague's skin tingles as he feels power surging through him. His arms itch. Rolling up his sleeve, he sees oily runes flowing over his skin. He runs out of the observation room and into the cell, holding up his arm for all to see.

"It's working," he says. "He's doing it. I haven't done anything, and it's already started."

Richter looks at Plague's arm, face unreadable. Finally he nods.

"Go."

"Showtime," Plague mutters, and hurries out of the room.

Richter watches Plague leave, then turns back to regard the man in the harness.

"We are now on a very compressed schedule. Stay here, monitor Mr. Preston. I will be in OLC. Contact me if anything... unexpected occurs."

"Yes sir," Dr. Wallace says.

* * *

Operations, Logistics, and Control is the second largest room in the facility. It serves, in no particular order of importance, as the primary communications center, security center, and command center for the complex. The largest room in the facility is the server room next door, and it has been unusually busy of late.

Richter is immediately greeted by a nervous communications tech.

"We have a call from central. I put them on hold."

Richter nods and sits at the communications station. The monitor shows that an encrypted outside feed is queued up, awaiting activation. Upon activation, the image of a sandy-haired man with a very serious expression fills the screen.

"Herr Kline. This is an unscheduled call."

Jason Kline nods. "I apologize for that, but this is important. We recently resolved the security issue at the home office. I thought you'd want to know."

"Oh? Who was it?"

"Assistants to some of the senior partners. They're being dealt with."

Richter nods approvingly.

"But that's not my primary reason for calling. A week ago the TriHealth facility in New York was attacked by members of Crossfire."

"Yes," Richter says. "We received the data without incident."

Jason shakes his head. "Not quite without incident, I'm afraid. My team thinks the attack was staged."

"Staged?" Richter finds the notion amusing. "From what I understand, Vigilante did quite a bit of damage to the eighth floor."

"To trigger the data transfer protocols," Jason says. "They followed the data to Farraday City."

"That is... very inconvenient," Richter says.

"Yes it is," Jason agrees. "You need to clear the facility as quickly as possible."

"We are already preparing an evacuation," Richter says, "but we are also minutes away from the final test."

Jason looks surprised. "Oh. I didn't realize... yes, I see the problem. Hold please."

The screen goes blank.

Richter turns to a subordinate. "Begin issuing transit bracelets to all personnel."

The subordinate nods once, then hurries off.

Richter turns back to the screen and waits. A few minutes later Jason's image returns.

"In light of your specific circumstances, we've been authorized to provide additional support."

* * *

Plague stands in front of Test Subject #14, staring down at the tattoo on the man's arm. He had plenty of tattoos of his own, once. Tattoos on his arms, on his back—even one on his face. Getting them removed had been a painful process, but he'd done it willingly. It was a small sacrifice, compared to what he was getting in return.

Or so he had thought at the time.

He rolls up his sleeve and looks down at his left arm. The oily runes swirl and flow over his skin, much faster now, responding to the fury of the storm outside. It must be terrifying out there, considering how much power he can feel coming out of the ground. That's the strange part, though—the power isn't coming from the air, it's rising out of the ground. He doesn't understand that part.

A loudspeaker *clicks* and suddenly Johann Richter's voice fills the room. "*Plague. Are you ready?*"

Plague raises his voice so it can be picked up clearly by the intercom system. "Ready."

"*Good. Have you chosen the index case?*"

Plague looks back to the old man, focusing on the faded tattoo on his arm.

"Test Subject #14."

All twenty-eight subjects are fully prepped and ready now. They've been moved from their gurneys and strapped into transparent, hermetically sealed caskets, each with an LCD monitor displaying vital functions and other medical data. They tell him that's the most important part of the experiment: the subjects must be completely sealed off from each other, and from the rest of the world.

"*All right, we're entering Test Subject #14 into the record.*" Richter's voice pauses for a moment. "*You should know we've been told to expect interference.*"

Plague's vision dims. He feels heat rise into his face. His fists clench tightly, and when he speaks, his voice is full of venom. "Curveball."

"Quite possibly. Crossfire as well. This experiment is your primary responsibility, but once it's complete—"

"Yeah, I understand. I'll be ready."

Plague unbuttons his shirt, letting it drop to the floor behind him. The runes are everywhere now, flowing across his arms, chest, neck and face in endless, indecipherable patterns.

"I'm starting now." Plague focuses on Test Subject #14 and taps into the power surging around him, allowing it to pass *through* him as he brings his own gift to life.

Plague's ability is simple: he can create any illness he's personally encountered, and inflict it on anyone he wants. There are limits—the effects are temporary, not everyone is affected by his power, and some illnesses are far more difficult to create than others, requiring more time and energy—but it's a simple, instinctive process. What he's doing now is a departure from that. Instead of imagining an illness, he conjures the image of a very specific symbol and keeps that image in his mind.

The symbol is the culmination of decades of scientific research: a double helix, with a very specific set of nucleotide pairs at each helical turn. He builds the mental image carefully, forcing himself to remember each paired base in turn. And then, once the image is complete, he changes it further.

Plague starts at the bottom of the chain, mentally adding a symbol above the first covalent bond. He goes up the chain, like a man slowly climbing a ladder, adding a different symbol above each bond. He's sweating by the time he finishes—recalling each symbol is a difficult and taxing process. When he finishes, the double helix structure he'd built so painstakingly has become something else entirely: a triple helix, each nucleotide pair warped into a triad.

It is no longer a thing of science. It has become something far older.

He's shaking from the sheer force of will required to keep the image in his head. He pours his gift into it, wraps it in the power surging through the room, and sends it through the sealed casket, into Test Subject #14.

"We got a jump."

Plague doesn't know who said it. He doesn't bother to look. He focuses on Test Subject #14, focuses on the faded tattoo on the helpless man's arm, gathers every bit of power he has, every scrap he can grab from the room, and pours it into the thing he made.

Fourteen twitches.

"Fever spike. 103 and climbing."

"Test Subject #12, we got a jump."

"Test Subject #7, we got a jump."

Plague focuses only on feeding his creation the power it needs to grow. He can hear, as if from a great distance, the excited reports of the lab techs each time it jumps into a new test subject: *Five, thirteen, ten, six, nineteen, twenty-three, twenty-four.* The loudspeaker comes on, and he can hear reports from the other rooms: *Thirty-five, forty-nine, sixty-two, seventy.* Then the sound of test subjects flatlining: one by one, the continuous tone of death fills the room.

He focuses on his creation. He *feeds* his creation. He feels his creation *grow*, gaining in strength, lengthening its reach, ever searching for new hosts. His skin burns as the power surges through him, almost more than he can handle, and he wonders how much longer he can do this before it starts to burn him alive...

Someone is shaking him, hard. His concentration falters, and suddenly he's staring at Johann Richter. His mouth is moving, but he can't—

"*Plague! Stop!*"

Plague blinks, sways to one side, and grabs Richter's arms for support. He looks around. The flatline tones are gone, now, and the techs are all staring at him in a mixture of awe, fear, and exhilaration.

"Huh?" Plague looks back at Richter. "What..."

"The test is *over*," Richter says. "It's done."

"It is?" His voice is hoarse. "What happened? How did we do?"

"Every subject." Richter is almost beaming. "Every test subject, in every room. All infected. Well done. Well done."

Every subject. Plague steadies himself and lets go of Richter's arms. Richter releases his shoulders and stands back. "Every subject. How many dead?"

"Everyone in this room," Richter says. "Except for fourteen, for some reason. That will need to be investigated. Ten in Room B. Three in Room C."

"Oh..." Plague nods slowly, feeling let down. "So we failed."

"No!" Richter shakes his head vehemently. "Not at all! The test was to *transmit*. And you did, successfully, to all subjects and to *no one else*. They will need to study the data more closely in order to refine the transmission process, and *then* they can work on the virus in its final form, but this was an *unqualified success*."

"Unqualified success." Plague takes a moment to let the words sink in. He feels himself starting to smile. "We did it."

"We did," Richter confirms. "Today, Project Recall officially enters Phase Three."

A cheer goes up around the room. Someone is clapping Plague on the back, someone else is calling for drinks, someone else is actually starting to *sing*.

And then the walls shake. The lights flicker. The walls shake again. And then an alarm sounds, and the lights change from white to red.

The intercom crackles to life. "Security breach, upper level. Armed guards responding. Metahuman agents confirmed."

Richter and Plague exchange glances. Without speaking, both turn and run for the door.

PART SEVEN: FARRADAY CITY, MIDTOWN

"Christ Almighty. What the fuck happened to the sky?"

Agent Grant stares in amazement as rain pounds against Hu's car. The city is a mess: cars are abandoned in the road, along the side of the road, sometimes even on sidewalks as streams of people slog through the rain, heading for any building they can find. The only people actively driving on the road are Hu—who is clearly unhappy about it—and, based on occasional glimpses of flashing red light, a few emergency response vehicles.

Most of the time all Grant can see are solid sheets of water crashing into Hu's windshield. It looks like someone has pointed a garden hose directly at each window in the car—all he sees is water spilling over more water. When lightning flashes he can see a little more: endless black clouds roiling in the sky, wind whipping sand and garbage through the air, tiny streams coursing down streets and pooling at intersections. Then the light fades, and once again all he sees is sheets of water against the windows.

"Wasn't it sunny ten minutes ago?" He squints, wondering if the vague shapes he thinks he sees through the rain are really there, or if it's just the rain screwing with him. "I distinctly remember there being sunlight."

"Sure wish somebody thought to tell us we'd be driving through a hurricane today," Hu says, voice tight.

"There's not supposed to *be* a hurricane." Travers holds up a newspaper. "Their front page story is 'DROUGHT THREATENS WATER RATIONING.' This was not on anyone's radar. Literally."

"I think it's cute that you bought that," Grant says. "Really, newspapers are *adorable*. Me, I'd just check the Internet, but apparently *it can't swim*. Still, if you wanna be retro, at least try something with a little less delay..."

He turns on Hu's car radio and almost immediately they hear the electronic warning tones of the Emergency Broadcast System.

"*Warning. A significant weather event has occurred over much of the Farraday City Metropolitan area. You are advised to remain indoors at this time. Sustained winds of up to ninety-eight miles per hour have been reported in some areas. Do not remain outside. Do not remain in your car. Do not attempt to drive at this time. Please seek the nearest storm-ready shelter and remain there until the storm subsides. The boardwalk and surrounding regions are considered especially unsafe. Do not attempt to travel at this time. Warning. A significant weather event has occurred over much of the Farraday City Metropolitan area...*"

Grant turns off the radio. "There you go. Ninety-eight miles per hour. We just wandered into a category two hurricane. *Jesus*."

"Yes," Travers says. "I think this storm is significant."

"It's about to wash the whole fucking city out to sea," Grant says. "I'm pretty sure *everybody* thinks the storm is significant."

"That's not what I mean. This storm is obviously unnatural."

"What are you saying?" Grant asks. "Weather machine? Weather death ray?"

"Maybe a manipulator," Hu suggests.

"I don't know," Grant says. "I never heard of a manipulator who could do something this big."

"Whatever the cause," Travers says, "it's not natural. Someone—something—*created* it. It sounds like the source is near the boardwalk, and if we can find that, I'll bet we find Curveball as well."

"How are we going to do that, exactly?" Hu asks. "We can barely see the street. How do we find the center of the storm when we can't even really see the part we're in?"

"Good question. It's not like we can—well. Huh." Agent Grant frowns thoughtfully.

"It's not like we can *what*?" Hu asks. "Is this gonna piss me off?"

"Maybe," Grant says. "Probably. I know how to find the center of the storm. Well. I know how *you* can find it."

Hu narrows her eyes.

"You won't find it *under* the storm," Grant says. "You gotta go *over* it."

Now it's Hu's turn to frown thoughtfully.

"Can you do it?" Travers asks. "I assume all this water would work against you."

"Not too much," Hu says. "I can burn underwater no problem. The wind's tricky, though. Grant, I've never tried to fly in wind this strong before."

"Yeah, that's... yeah," Grant agrees. "But you don't have to fly against it. You know how they tell you not to swim against a current, but to swim at an angle? Well this is the same thing, only your angle is *up*."

"Oh *really*," Hu says. "And this comes from how many years of experience as a flier?"

"Got me there," Grant says. "Still, it sounded good. Come on, Hu. I got shot in the head, died, then had my organs scooped into tiny bags by the coroner. This is *nothing*."

"After today, you don't get to use that line on me any more."

"Yeah, I figured," Grant says. "Really, the window was closing on it anyway."

Hu pulls over to the side of the road. "Shut up, Grant. Travers, hand me my carry bag. It's on the floor behind my seat."

Travers grabs the heavy fireproof bag and sets it on the armrest between the driver and passenger seat. Hu opens it up, rummages through the contents, nods in satisfaction, and throws her phone on the top.

"If I find what we're looking for, I'll try to call. Of course if there's something *exciting* going on..."

Travers leans forward slightly. "If there's something exciting going on, and you happen to run into either Curveball *or* Crossfire, please tell them I sent you."

"OK," Hu says. "What if they don't believe me?"

"Then don't let CB break your jaw."

"Hey Hu," Grant says. "Are you wearing your—"

"*—yes*," Hu snaps. "I am wearing my 'bathing suit.' I figure if we're in Farraday City, I'd better be ready to burn things down..."

She stares out the windshield, watching the rain, listening to the wind shriek.

"I better get this over with." She unhooks her seatbelt, grabs her bag, and grabs the door handle. "See you boys later. Grant: don't drown, don't make trouble, don't drive my car."

She shoves open the driver's-side door and tumbles out of the car. Even that brief moment of exposure to the storm drenches the interior; the wind whips the rain so fiercely that it stings when it hits skin, and Grant flinches as the first spray hits his face. Then Hu slams the door shut, and Grant and Travers watch, soaking wet, as Hu disappears into darkness.

"Do you think she—" Travers begins, then a fireball explodes in the intersection, shooting up into the sky.

"Yeah," Grant says. "I think she did."

The car falls silent. The rain sounds like hail.

"OK," Grant says, "time to motor."

His edges blur for a moment, then he disappears from the passenger seat and reappears in the driver's seat. He turns the ignition.

"What are you doing?" Travers asks.

"Driving us to the boardwalk."

"Agent Hu told you not to drive her car."

"I know," Grant says. "She's gonna be *pissed*."

PART EIGHT: WAREHOUSE COMPLEX, ABOVE

The Sorrel-Eades warehouses, a small complex just north of the Farraday City Boardwalk, have been abandoned for years. They were declared an EPA Superfund site a decade ago, when a truck dangerously overloaded with industrial chemicals exploded outside the center warehouse building. It's well known among the locals that anyone who goes into the S-E complex dies, and some of the earliest examples of that death were graphic and frightening. But the EPA never actually sent anyone to clean it up—whether they forgot, or the lords of the city forbade it, nobody knows. The end result was the same: nobody went there unless they actually wanted to die.

The truth of the matter is that the chemicals have been gone from the complex for years. When Haruspex Analytics wanted to find a place where they could operate in anonymity, they chose the most environmentally inhospitable location they could find, cleaned it up, and made sure nobody knew it was clean. In the end, it was simply one contaminant being replaced with another, and it still killed anyone who came too close or stayed too long. In the last few days, however, locals have noticed things happening there—specifically trucks driving up to the center building, and armed guards unloading sealed containers. So far no one has worked up enough curiosity to start poking around, and the storm currently engulfing the city is a far more pressing concern.

A storm, it should be noted, that has left the Sorrel-Eades complex relatively untouched.

All eleven buildings sit comfortably within the storm's eye. The old chain link fence that closed off the complex from the rest of the city is gone, ripped to shreds and flung across the city by the eyewall separating the complex from everything else, but the warehouses themselves are untouched, an oasis surrounded by a swirling wall of screaming clouds. The clouds themselves are terrifying, moving at such speeds, with such a small circumference, that they resemble the inside of a tornado—smooth, almost marbleized. At the higher elevations, lightning sparks so furiously that the light filters down through the clouds, so that even at ground level they glow with a faint green light.

It is into this scene that Jack Barrow emerges from the eyewall next to the southeast warehouse, soaked to the bone, carrying Red Shift and Jenny Forrest, one under each arm. He hops up onto an old loading platform as if the weight of the two were nothing, and sets them down against the warehouse cinderblock wall. Red Shift immediately staggers to his feet, using the warehouse wall to steady himself. Jenny stays where she is, fumbles with her chin strap, and removes her helmet. Her braided hair is soaked, and she wordlessly turns her helmet over, watching the water spill out.

"That... was undignified," Red Shift says.

Jenny snorts, taps the back of her helmet a few times to make sure the water is gone, and with a sigh puts it back on her head.

Vigilante appears out of the clouds a few seconds later, between the southeast and east warehouses, carrying CB and Street Ronin, one under each arm. He takes a moment to get his bearings, sees Scrapper Jack and the others, and moves quickly to join them. Only when he reaches the loading platform does he set his passengers down, at which point Street Ronin sits up and removes his helmet, emptying it of water in much the same way Jenny did. CB simply rolls over on his back, reaches into a trenchcoat pocket, and pulls out a half-empty pack of cigarettes and an old Zippo lighter.

"Well," CB says, "*that* part of the plan was shot all to hell."

Jack grunts in agreement as he shakes the water out of his leather jacket.

"No time to rest," Vigilante says. "If they haven't spotted us yet, they will soon. Everyone in position."

Jack nods. "Luck." In a single, smooth motion he leaps into the air, disappearing from sight. Vigilante runs east, disappearing from sight.

Street Ronin stands, pulls down his visor, and reaches over his right shoulder to detach his rifle from its mount. "Ready Zero?"

Jenny stands, testing her balance, then nods. They run around the opposite corner of the building, heading north.

Red Shift taps his visor once, then sighs. "At least it's dry in here. I hate hydroplaning."

CB says nothing. He pulls out an earpiece from a trenchcoat pocket, placing it in his ear with his right hand as he lights his cigarette with the zippo in his left.

Red Shift's mouth twitches slightly, then in a blur of speed he's gone.

CB takes a drag from his cigarette and feels the world spin around him, much like the storm they just fought their way through moments ago. It spins and tiny pieces swirl around him, like parts of a puzzle scattering through the air. He takes a second drag and the whirling stops, the world snaps into focus, and he can see all the angles.

Time to play pool.

He flips up onto a small awning partially covering the loading platform. From there it takes two broken windows and a rusted air conditioner to get to the roof. He crosses the roof quickly, and looks down at the rest of the complex. All of the buildings are dark. All of the spaces between are empty.

He taps his earpiece once. "In position."

One by one, the rest of the team answers in kind. Red Shift, Street Ronin, Jenny, Vigilante, Jack. Everything is set. All that remains is the opportune moment.

"All the pieces on the board," a voice says.

CB spins around, pistols in hand. There, in the middle of the roof, stand two men. Men he has, in fact, met before: one large, one small, both wearing pinstripe suits and bowler hats. The large man stares at him impassively, betraying no emotion at all. The smaller man is very thin, his eyes are very bright, and his smile carries all the warmth and sincerity of a rictus grin.

"All the pieces on the board, waiting for the bell to ring. Who shall live to be the pawn? Who shall die to be the king?" The grin sharpens to match the eyes.

CB exhales sharply, then returns his pistols to their holsters. "I'm more of a checkers guy."

"I think you are not," the small man says, and doffs his hat, bowing low. "But I am not offended by the deception. Quite the contrary, in fact. Oh Cat Who Observes Himself, we truly must stop meeting like this."

"Fine by me." CB watches the small man warily. "We still besties?"

"Indeed. Our alliance must, it seems, continue apace. We have gone so far as to attempt to intervene on your behalf. The results were somewhat disastrous, unfortunately." The small man gestures wide, indicating the shrieking wall of clouds.

CB looks at the clouds. "You did the storm? That's your idea of helping?"

The small man gives a slight shrug, his smile rueful and mocking at the same time. "It wasn't what we intended. *They* wanted the storm. We attempted to stop them. They countered with something... unexpected, and now we have this..."

The small man stares at the roiling clouds.

"It will continue to grow, of course. It's hard to believe the little man had so much power, in the end. There are very few on this earth who can do what he is doing right now. Perhaps only one other. Had we known what he was truly capable of... well."

"Wait." CB focuses intently on the smaller man. "A *person* did this?"

"Oh yes, a person. Horace Preston. Do you know him? They needed him to create a storm. He could have done it, in time, had we let him. Not one like this, of course. Probably little more than a monsoon. But we wouldn't have it, and we broke him. It should have ended there."

"Where did it end instead?"

The small man laughs. "That's the problem, oh Cat. It isn't ending. It isn't ending *at all*."

He spins, arms wide, just as he had on their first meeting. "They put him in an iron box, and sealed him shut with mighty locks, and when the king made known his will, the jester danced, and dances still." He stumbles at the end, almost losing his hat, and he laughs like a child. But when he stops spinning he stares at CB with uncharacteristic calm and gravity.

"He's somewhere underground. Buried in a burrow, a box within a box, set beneath a box. There's nothing left of him now, I'm afraid. Nothing but his power, unfettered by his flesh. As long as he is trapped within that box he is power without constraint, and the power he channels is more than enough to destroy this city. He will bury it in water, destroy it with wind, bring lightning and fire from the heavens, and it won't stop here. It will continue to grow... and grow... and grow... the devastation will be immense. He's become quite the prodigy, our Mr. Preston."

CB turns to look at the other warehouses. Somewhere underground... that was what they'd suspected to begin with, but it was good to have some kind of confirmation that they were on the right track.

"Hold on. He's become quite the *what*?"

No one replies. The men are gone. CB is alone on the roof.

"Great," CB says. "One of *those*."

He looks at the eyewall and wonders if it's grown *taller* since they arrived. Is the patch of blue sky overhead smaller, or is that just his imagination?

He's become quite the prodigy, our Mr. Preston.

...quite the prodigy...

CB's eyes widen.

"Oh. Oh *shit*."

PART NINE: ESCALATION GAMES

Phase One.

There are eleven buildings in the warehouse complex—four to the south, four to the north, one east, one west, and one much larger building at the center. To simplify communication, they refer to the buildings by number. The southeast warehouse is one, and moving west are two, three, and four. Four is the first building they came to when they emerged from the storm—the one CB is standing on. The next row, east to west, is five, six, and seven. Six is the large building in the center of the complex, and that's the building all the trucks had stopped in front of the day before. Finally the north side, from east to west: eight, nine, ten, eleven.

Street Ronin and Zero crouch against the west wall of Eleven. Zero is typing furiously on a small, ruggedized laptop connected to a thin cable that travels down the length of the warehouse wall and into the ground.

"Status?" Street Ronin's voice is calm and steady.

"Almost there." Zero's voice is anything but—a mixture of excitement, anxiety and adrenaline makes her voice shake so badly she laughs just to cover it up. "I've connected to the remote server, I'm sending it instructions now. When it finds the location it'll send it straight to your helmet."

"Good," Street Ronin says. "How long before they trace it back to us?"

"They won't," Zero says. "In theory they *shouldn't* trace it back to us—they should only be able to trace it to the remote server, and they won't be able to tie that to us unless they tear it apart and find the code that has your 'phone number.'"

"How long will it take?"

"Not too long," Zero says. "We're not really trying to hack in, right? Just figure out where they are? It'll be pretty fast. If you want something more specific than 'pretty fast' I can't help you."

Street Ronin almost grins—it's exactly the same thing he's said to Vigilante on more than one occasion.

"Sent," Zero says. She unceremoniously yanks the laptop connection out of the cable and snaps the laptop shut.

"Come on." Street Ronin runs to the west warehouse, crossing the open space as fast as he can. He hears Zero right behind him, easily keeping pace. As soon as they reach the corner, they press flat against the wall.

Farther into the center of the complex they hear a noise that sounds like an electric razor pressed against the grille of a fan. Light flickers, the smell of ozone fills the complex, and Street Ronin's earpiece crackles to life.

"Eight guards just ported in between Six and Seven," Curveball sounds distracted. Street Ronin wonders if he's worrying about Zero. *"They're headed toward Eleven."*

"Are they looking around?" Street Ronin keeps his voice low.

"They're looking around, but they're not putting a lot of effort into it. They're sure as hell not looking up."

"OK. Tell me when they go inside." Street Ronin lets his rifle hang from its strap as he removes the remote detonator from his belt and arms it. He glances at Zero—she's staring at the detonator.

"You know what's going to happen next?" he asks.

He can't see her expression through her helmet, but she nods.

"This won't be a pretty fight."

"I know the plan," she says. "And I understand the consequences." Her voice still shakes from the adrenaline, but there's no hesitation in it.

His earpiece crackles again. "Six guards went into Eleven. There are still two by the door."

At that moment, a location appears on the HUD in Street Ronin's visor.

"Warehouse Two," he says, then presses the remote.

Phase Two.

CB takes an involuntary step back as the explosion incinerates Eleven's west wall as well as the internet connection they'd used to track the bad guys to this location. The two soldiers standing guard at the door—just your basic heavily-armed commandos in light body armor—instinctively throw themselves to the ground.

Almost immediately a streak of black and red smashes through Six's east wall. Concrete shatters inward as the entire complex rocks from the sound of the impact, and then the western wall explodes *outward*, sending rock and glass and bits of twisted metal into Seven's west wall. Red Shift streaks away, passing Eleven as he disappears around Seven. The guards on the ground don't move. They will never move again.

"I have two," Red Shift says.

The streak of black and red returns, smashing into Six's southern wall and out the north. A good third of the southern wall is gone, and more concrete cracks and shatters as the entire second floor begins to sag. The next pass takes out the southeast corner; the next, the southwest. This is too much for the rest of the building to bear, and the southern side of the second floor collapses with an ear-splitting crash. A cloud of dirt and pulverized stone rises into the air and billows out over the rest of the complex. Moments later Eight's southern wall shatters, and the streak of black and red begins the process anew.

CB draws his pistols and waits.

The strange metallic screech fills the air again.

"More incoming," he says.

A pale light flickers all around him, and as ozone fights with dust, four soldiers *(Alpha, Beta, Gamma, Delta)* appear on his roof.

They're not the lightly-armored guards from before—these are shock troops, wearing battlesuits that add at least half a foot and a hundred pounds. Their helmets are smooth, the faceplates made out of some kind of reflective material that covers the entire front of the head, and they carry heavy, strangely-shaped carbines with barrels that glow green at the tip. The one CB tags as "Alpha" immediately brings his carbine to bear.

"Four on the roof!" CB dives to the ground as the carbine fires. A streak of bright green heat flashes above him as he hits the roof, rolls up, and opens fire with both pistols. Bullets ricochet harmlessly off the armor. He's dimly aware of Street Ronin shouting something over his earpiece, and the sound of weapons fire in the distance.

Push. Escalate.

CB drops his pistols and runs forward, head low, as Alpha fires again. Green heat tears through the end of his trenchcoat and burns through the spot where he stood. He's now two steps away from Alpha—too close for Beta, Gamma, or Delta to risk using their guns.

He winks. Somewhere off in the distance—barely audible over the shrieking clouds and other noise—something goes *pop*.

Push. Escalate.

Alpha's carbine immediately begins to emit a high-pitched whining sound, causing him to hesitate and look down at his gun. Beta, Gamma, and Delta spread out, their carbines sliding up their arms, locking in place farther up the arm where they're out of the way. CB leaps forward, using Alpha's own body as leverage to run up, push off, and kick the soldier's faceplate with the heel of his boot. The short, sharp kick fractures the reflective material in a spiderweb pattern, and Alpha staggers as CB somersaults backward down to the rooftop in a crouch.

Beta flicks his right arm downward. A high-tech baton with a glowing green tip slides out from beneath his arm and into his waiting hand. Gamma and Delta follow suit. Beta, Gamma, and Delta close in.

Push. Escalate.

Delta jabs with his baton. CB steps beneath the swing and grabs the arm, hauling himself up and using his weight to make Delta stumble forward into Beta, closing from the other side. The tip of the baton touches Beta's armor and a *hisssss* fills the air as green light arcs over the alloy. Beta goes rigid; Gamma steps back hastily.

Push. Escalate.

Beta falls to the ground as CB grabs the baton in Delta's hand and jerks sharply to the left, putting his entire weight behind the force of the motion. The baton rips from Delta's grasp, and CB jabs down into Delta's knee. Green light arcs over armor; Delta goes rigid, and topples over.

Push.

CB turns to face Gamma. Gamma drops his baton as his carbine slides back down into the active position.

Escalate.

CB throws the baton; it flies through the air like a spear, ripping through Gamma's faceplate and embedding itself in the helmet. Gamma sinks to his knees, clawing at his helmet with flailing arms, before he topples forward and to the side. CB tries not to think about what he just did.

Push.

Alpha has regained his balance and some semblance of vision. CB leaps, hands outstretched, reaching for his pistols, lying discarded on the rooftop.

Escalate.

Alpha fires, the flash of green heat from his carbine becoming a solid green line, cutting through the rooftop. CB hits the ground, reaching.

Push.

His hands close around the pistols as the furious green line sweeps closer.

Escalate.

He sits up, firing round after round after round at the soldier's already-fractured helmet. The third shot finally gets through, the solid green line of heat swings wide, then ends abruptly. Alpha falls over and does not move again.

CB activates his earpiece. "Four down. All wearing some kind of enhanced combat armor. Go for the mirrored faceplate, it seems to be their weakest—"

The metallic screech comes from *everywhere*, all at once; a flare of light as bright as the sun envelops the complex, and when it fades there are soldiers in battle armor everywhere. Every rooftop, road—squads of soldiers with weapons at the ready.

"Hey guys..." CB takes a ragged breath and forces himself to relax, waiting for what's about to happen next. "I think they finally figured out who we are."

Phase Three.

Warehouse Seven is cluttered and covered in layers of dust. Zero sneezes once as she opens the laptop on a stack of sealed, rotting warehouse crates and mutters something about mold allergies. "Gimme the thing," she says finally.

"Hold on," Street Ronin says. "Blanket first."

He can hear Zero sigh in exasperation, but she unrolls the thermal blanket and pulls it over herself and the laptop. "Happy?"

"Ecstatic," Street Ronin says. He lifts up a corner of the blanket and hands her the two oversized smart watches Red Shift dropped off before he resumed destroying Warehouse Six. "These are all we have. If we need more we'll need to sift through Eleven and find the bodies."

"We won't need more." Zero's voice is muffled from beneath the blanket, but that does little to mask her confidence. "If it's networked, I'll get us in. Then it's up to you."

"If you can get us in, I can handle the rest," Street Ronin says. "Maybe."

"I'll take your word for it."

Street Ronin takes up position near a dirty, cracked window that gives him a good view of the ruined Warehouse Six. Most attempts to access Seven will require moving through that area.

"Clear so far," Street Ronin says. "I thought they'd respond by now."

A metallic grinding sound cuts through the air. He sees a flash of light on the roof of Warehouse Four—Curveball's position—then he hears Curveball over his earpiece.

"More incoming."

Short pause.

"Four on the roof!"

Street Ronin sees a flash of green, hears the hiss of burning steel and stone, then Curveball's pistols, firing rapidly.

Four on the roof.

Street Ronin looks up. His visor shows the dim outline of four heat signatures filtering through the rock. They aren't human heat signatures—most of the heat comes from the joints. Either robots or men in armor. Either way...

"Keep working," Street Ronin says. He walks quickly to the far end of the warehouse, putting as much distance between himself and Zero's work area as he can. Sure enough, the four signatures on the roof reposition themselves, tracking his movement. He activates his headset and aims his rifle at the ceiling.

"Seven, four on the roof."

He pulls the trigger four times. He sees three of the heat signatures scatter; the fourth signature distorts, but doesn't otherwise move.

One down.

The IR display shuts down as something generates enough heat to render it useless, and Street Ronin dives to one side as a streak of green energy *hisses* through the ceiling and cuts a swath across the floor where he stood. The line on the ceiling widens, and the structure sags slightly as it cuts through what appears to be a support beam. Street Ronin finds himself thinking "what the hell kind of weapon is that?" followed by "and where do I get one?"

He can't track them with heat, but there's a chance that's working both ways.

"Back in a sec!" he shouts, and starts to run.

"...what? Where are you going?"

He doesn't bother to answer as he leaps through the window. His armor protects him from the glass, and he assumes they're expecting him to use the door. As soon as he hits the ground he turns and looks up. He can see an armored figure—big, with a glassy, reflective faceplate—starting to turn toward the noise. He switches his rifle to burst mode and pulls the trigger. The burst impacts solidly on the shoulder and appears to do nothing more than get the soldier's attention. He switches back to semi-automatic fire and aims for the reflective faceplate.

One shot later, and the armored figure slumps and falls over.

Curveball cuts in on the line. "*Four down. All wearing some kind of enhanced combat armor. Go for the mirrored faceplate, it seems to be their weakest—*"

Another metallic screech rings through the air, the air is filled with light, and suddenly there are armored troops everywhere.

"*Hey guys... I think they finally figured out who we are.*"

He prepares for a very bad day. Then, over the earpiece, he hears Zero announce excitedly: "*I did it! I'm in!*"

Street Ronin smiles. Zero just hacked a teleportation network.

PART TEN: RIDING THE WAVES

Jack Barrow and Vigilante stand in front of Warehouse Two's heavy outer door, arms crossed, wearing almost exactly the same frown.

They completely ignore the sound of Red Shift destroying Warehouse Six. They react only when it finally goes down and dirt, stone and dust roll over them in an immense cloud—even then, all Vigilante does is wipe a layer of grime off his visor, while Jack shakes some of the dirt out of his hair.

They ignore CB's warning of the soldiers on the roof, listening to the sound of energy weapons discharging as they continue staring at that door.

"It's not a regular door," Vigilante finally says.

"Really isn't," Jack agrees.

The door looks like a blast door—a solid piece of metal without any visible handle or hinge. There isn't even a control panel on the side to allow fingerprint or card key access.

"You don't put a door like that on a brick building," Vigilante continues.

"Brick's a facade," Jack says. "My guess is, they gutted the building and built their secret villain base under it."

"Yeah..." Vigilante moves two steps to the side, as if the change in perspective might reveal something new. "So what do you figure happens after we bust it down?"

"Seven, four on the roof."

Vigilante and Jack continue to ignore the sounds of gunfire and discharging energy weapons.

Jack sighs impatiently. "Look, we're short on intel for this part. That's why you and me are going in first. So as far as I can tell, there's really only one way to find out."

Vigilante nods, expression sour. "I know. It's just... something's off. I mean, if this were my secret underground base, I'd have, I don't know, more surveillance. And if I found us standing outside the front door, I'd probably try to—"

Curveball breaks in over the line. *"Four down. All wearing some kind of enhanced combat armor. Go for the mirrored faceplate, it seems to be their weakest—"*

Curveball's report is interrupted by a metallic screech that fills the entire warehouse complex, followed by a quick, blinding pulse of light. When the light recedes, there are armored troops everywhere: battlesuits with polished, reflective faceplates and carbines attached to their right arms.

"*Hey guys... I think they finally figured out who we are.*"

Vigilante turns to Jack. "This is closer to what I'd try to do."

They scatter as beams of green energy flash through the air, cutting through the ground and walls. Chunks of brick are sliced away from the wall, revealing a silvery alloyed metal beneath. A beam of green energy hits Jack squarely in the chest, causing him to grunt in surprise and burning away his shirt. He looks down and sees that part of his leather jacket has also been sliced away. He swears, drops the remains of the jacket to the ground, then steps into the fray.

Jack has been fighting all his life. He got his nickname before he even knew he was metahuman—as a kid he had a bad habit of never backing down, even when he knew it would hurt, and once people started calling him "Scrapper" they never really stopped. His instincts were always good, and he never stopped trying to get better. He's mostly a boxer, focusing on short, fast strikes (with the occasional low kick—he's not a *fair* boxer) while keeping his arms close to his body to avoid telegraphing his moves. A jab to the chest caves in the upper torso completely. A strike to the arm shatters the arm. Occasionally he'll aim a low kick at a shin or kneecap, with similarly devastating results.

Vigilante never had the constant exposure to fighting Jack did. He's also not as strong, or as immediately durable. But he fights with a tightly-controlled fury that seems to fuel every blow. He leaps for a soldier, ignoring the pain of energy hitting, then ultimately punching through his skin, he grabs, throws, twists, tears at his enemies. He pulls no punches, and gives no quarter. The trail of mangled alloy and steel he leaves in his wake is a testament to the effectiveness of his rage.

Together they battle their way across the complex, nearing the collapsed remains of Warehouse Six, and through it all they catch glimpses of the others fighting as well. Curveball has descended from his perch on Two, weaving between multiple targets, engaging them all at once, lining them up in such a way that they can't actually attack him without risking friendly fire. Red Shift tears through the melee, a blur the human eye can barely follow, leaving a trail of carnage very similar to Vigilante's, only *faster*.

Individually, the soldiers are outmatched. Together they are *still* outmatched, at the moment, but thirty seconds into the fight Jack hears another metallic screech and sees another flash of white.

"They're porting in more!" He doesn't bother using his earpiece. Vigilante and CB are right next to him at the moment, and for all he knows Red Shift might be too. He snarls as one of the soldiers manages to get him in the side of the head with the glowing green tip of a melee baton. He's dimly aware of the discharge of energy, but he doesn't feel anything more than a tingle. He grabs the soldier's arm and squeezes at the elbow. He feels it shatter, and can dimly hear the soldier screaming as Jack throws him into another a few feet away.

"Well that's just *great*." CB steps to one side, lighting a cigarette as a wall of green energy washes over him, somehow missing him completely. The soldiers standing on the other side aren't so lucky. "I know the whole 'fight the minions first' thing is kind of traditional, but I was kind of hoping we could skip the grind and cut ahead to the boss fight."

Jack has no idea what he's talking about.

"Street Ronin!" Vigilante cuts in over the line—an unsettling effect, since Jack can also hear him shouting not fifteen feet from where he's standing. "What's your status?"

"We're working on it." The response is clipped and hurried. "We could use some backup though. We need a little room to breathe."

"I'm on it." Red Shift's voice is heavy with fatigue. "The rest of you keep fighting by Two, hopefully most of the soldiers will head over there."

"We'll be OK." CB flicks some ash at one of the soldiers and winks. Jack hears something *pop* off in the distance, and suddenly the soldier's joints lock in place. Then he uses the frozen soldier as a springboard, vaulting over the heads of two more as pistols suddenly appear in his hands. He fires as he somersaults over the heads, almost exactly the way some guy did in a ridiculously over the top action flick Jack saw once, and both of their faceplates crack and splinter. He moves casually, even lazily, but Jack can see a sheen of sweat on his forehead.

He's pushing it hard. Whatever "it" is.

Jack doesn't really understand what CB does, but he knows he's good in a fight. But CB gets tired. Red Shift won't last long, either—Jack saw how fast he was going, and he'll literally burn himself out if he keeps going like that. He and Vigilante can last a lot longer, stamina-wise, but if they can't actually bring the numbers down—

Another metallic screech cuts through the air, another flash of light fills the sky, another legion of soldiers joins the fray.

"This is *pissing me off.*" CB spins, firing his pistols a few more times. The bullets begin to ricochet from one soldier to another, like an elaborate pool shot. They don't really do anything other than startle the ones they hit, but by the time they recover CB has moved somewhere else, and either Vigilante or Jack has taken them down. "Street Ronin, look, not to be pushy but they've got stormtrooper in a can down there, so either find a way to turn that off or—"

A column of white-hot flame crashes out of the sky and engulfs three soldiers, their battlesuits fusing instantly from the heat. Jack looks up, surprised, and sees a humanoid surrounded by flame, floating above them. The figure—vaguely female, though it's impossible to be certain—extends its hands, and a thick wall of flame surrounds another ten. The soldiers focus on the figure and begin to return fire. Four beams appear to hit, and the figure flies back.

"*Ow!*" The voice is definitely female. She dives toward a large group of soldiers, and as she nears the ground the flames around her appear to contract, almost disappear, and then with a sudden *boom* they flare up, brighter than ever. Jack can feel the concussive wave that emanates from her and armored soldiers go flying everywhere.

There's a brief break in the fighting. She flies back to where CB, Jack, and Vigilante have regrouped, all watching her warily.

"Federal agent," the burning woman says. "Travers sent us."

"Travers?" CB's eyebrow shoots up in surprise.

"He's here," the woman says. "I'm not entirely sure where, at the moment, but—"

The air fills with a metallic screech, a flash of light fills the sky, and legions of soldiers appear out of nowhere.

"I really hate this," CB mutters, and pulls out his pistols again. His hands shake for a moment.

"Let's go," Jack says, and leaps toward the nearest target.

"So you're a Fed?" CB ducks as a soldier swings a glowing baton at him. It goes over his head and hits the soldier closing in behind him. Jack can't count the number of times something like that has happened during this fight, but it seems to be a recurring theme.

"DHS," the flaming woman shouts. She shoots up into the air again, drawing their fire as her flames grow more intense. The light she radiates plays off the cloud wall, leaving red-and-orange patterns over the eerie green glow.

Something blurs out of the corner of his eye. Something blurs into view near two soldiers, then disappears. Jack turns his head to focus on the spot, and suddenly the soldiers are surrounded by goo that quickly solidifies into a hard shell. He activates his earpiece. "Red Shift, are you using *stuckey*?"

"What? ...no..." Red Shift sounds very tired. "Are we... done... yet?"

A soldier forgoes his weaponry and punches Jack squarely in the face. He isn't hurt, but he wasn't expecting it, and the battlesuit outweighs him considerably—the force of the blow knocks him into the Warehouse Two wall, and he stumbles as he lands, falling over on his side. The air blurs above him, and a man with slicked-back dark hair, wearing a black suit and a matching long black trenchcoat appears between him and the soldier. He fires an automatic pistol three times, and scowls as the shots bounce harmlessly off the armor.

The battlesuit is engulfed in a sheet of flame as the burning woman floats down to hover next to the man in black.

"Grant? How the hell did you get here?"

"Don't ask." The man grins, blurs, then disappears.

Jack gets to his feet. "He with you?"

The woman nods, then flies back into the sky.

In a few minutes the area is cleared *again*.

"We did it!" Street Ronin's voice is relieved and triumphant in equal measure. "We blocked the teleporter. They won't be able to send in any more soldiers for a while."

CB lets out a long breath and bends over, hands on his knees. "I need another cigarette."

Vigilante eyes the flaming woman and the man in black warily. "Good news. Get over to Warehouse Two. We have some new arrivals. From the DHS. They say Travers sent them."

In the few minutes it takes for Street Ronin, Red Shift, and Zero to arrive, the others regroup and the new arrivals introduce themselves. The flaming woman lands, her flames wink out, and standing before them is a slim, athletic Asian woman with slightly reddish skin, wearing a leotard that appears to be made out of stiff, uncomfortable material. She introduces herself as Agent Hu, and the man in black as Agent Grant.

Jack nods. Vigilante says nothing, and watches them warily.

CB laughs, and fumbles through his pockets for another cigarette. "So

Travers is here, and he brought the Feds? I'm surprised. I didn't think he was a field agent."

"Yeah, you can keep not thinking that," Agent Grant says. "I'm dead, she's on vacation, and Travers is a wanted fugitive suspected of collaborating with *known terrorists*." He jerks his head in Vigilante's direction.

Vigilante relaxes slightly.

"I can't believe I'm using vacation for this," Hu mutters.

"Hey, at least you're getting paid. I'm just doing this out of the goodness of my shriveled little heart. And also because I'm a goddamn patriot."

Street Ronin, Zero, and Red Shift appear around the rubble of Warehouse Six. Street Ronin's armor is scorched, but otherwise he looks OK. Zero's helmet is missing, and a purple bruise blooms just under her left eye, spreading downward onto her cheek. Red Shift is limping—from fatigue, apparently, rather than any visible injury. A small, rugged IV is attached to his suit, and he occasionally taps at it, as if he's trying to get it to work faster.

Hu and Grant introduce themselves all over again.

Zero stares at Jack. "You're naked."

Jack looks down. His clothes are never as resistant as he is. "I'm not naked."

"OK," Zero says, reddening slightly.

"I'm *not* naked," Jack insists.

Hu looks Jack over. "Is your secret identity a lawyer? I feel like you should be on a calendar right now."

"Or shouting '*this is Sparta!*'" Grant chimes in.

"Shut up, Grant," Hu says. "Where is Travers right now?"

"We're close," Grant says. "It's, uh, slow going. It's getting a lot worse out there."

Hu narrows her eyes. "And how are you actually getting here?"

"Ask me no questions, Hu."

Hu's voice raises in volume and sharpens considerably. "Grant, if I find out you've been *driving my car*—"

A metallic sound fills the air—similar to the sound before, but accompanied by a bass rumbling that makes it feel larger, even though it isn't louder. The flash of light is purple—not as intense as the white light, but it fills the air around them, blocking out all sight for an instant. The group scatters instinctively, and when the light leaves they see something new.

Standing in front of them is a metal construct, humanoid in shape, standing fifteen feet high. A line of symbols written in an unknown script trails down the length of each arm and leg, and a single massive rune glows purple on its chest.

"Oh look," Grant says. "A *convenient distraction*."

PART ELEVEN: GOING THE DISTANCE

Whatever the thing is, it isn't obviously mechanical. While it appears to be made of metal, it has no seams anywhere—no joints to allow the arms and legs to move. But it does move, and it moves with unexpected fluidity and speed: it leaps away from the group, landing in front of the ruins of Warehouse Six, and sinking low into a battle-ready crouch.

It moves like a living thing, CB thinks. The arms and legs don't just move back and forth, they rotate like actual limbs, and even the torso bends and sways and twists for extra balance.

"I thought you said you blocked their teleporter," Jack says.

"I *did,*" Street Ronin says. "It *is.* I don't understand what's going on."

"It's not teleportation," Jenny says. CB wonders how she got that bruise. "At least not exactly. The sound and color were different. This is magic, isn't it? CB?"

CB stares at the big purple rune on the thing's chest.

Fuck.

"Yeah... it's magic."

The thing remains in its crouching position, waiting.

Jenny nods slowly. "That means we're probably screwed, right?"

"Not quite." Vigilante keeps his gaze locked on the thing. "Jack, our objectives just changed."

"I noticed." Jack's voice is very dry.

"Street Ronin, Zero, and Curveball need to get into that base and get whatever information they can before the base gets cleaned out. That means you, me, and Red Shift need to fight the magic robot."

"It's not a magic robot," CB says. "I think they call it a *golem.*"

"It's a big metal thing," Vigilante says. "I'm calling it a robot."

"I'll stay up here," Hu says. "Not that you invited me or anything, but I think you could use the extra firepower."

Vigilante nods.

CB looks over at Agent Grant. "What about you, G-man?"

Agent Grant stares at the golem skeptically. "I ain't gonna do jack shit against that thing. Put me on the B team. Any thoughts on how we're going to get through this door? Because it looks pretty—"

Jack turns around and hits the door hard. His fist sinks deep into the metal, causing the door to buckle and warp, one edge peeling out of the frame entirely. Jack grabs the edge, places a foot against the wall, and pulls. The door tears out, revealing a dimly lit room within.

The golem swivels its head to focus on Jack.

"B team," CB says. "Yeah, that's fair."

"Move," Vigilante says, and starts running toward the construct.

"Come on," CB says, and ducks through the door, pistols drawn. Street Ronin and Jenny follow.

Agent Grant shrugs and follows them in. "I guess we're splitting the party..."

* * *

The golem reacts quickly to Vigilante's approach, and with devastating effect. It reaches forward, and as it does its arm lengthens, its hand enlarges, and it grabs Vigilante off the ground.

It closes its hand into a fist and squeezes.

The pressure is immediate and immense. Vigilante feels his organic armor fail almost immediately, and after that it's hard to focus. Bones shatter and reform, muscles tear and reattach—he's pushing against the closing hand, but he's barely strong enough to slow it down.

The world rocks and spins, and the hand opens. Vigilante gasps in pain as his mangled body hits the earth. The golem is face down on the ground, and Red Shift is racing away, dodging a second elongated arm. Jack leaps on its back and starts hitting it for all he's worth. At the same time, Agent Hu shoots a stream of white-hot flame that engulfs both the golem and Jack.

Jack sighs in frustration as the flame sweeps over him. *Well, now I really am naked.*

"Sorry!" Hu calls out. "I didn't know you were going to jump on its back... like a crazy person..."

He's not sure how much progress he's making, but he's doing something. He can see the back of the golem getting more and more deformed with each blow. He's about to land another blow when he sees the upper back shimmer, as if the metal were actually a liquid, and then he sees an *arm* emerge from the back. The arm grows, thickens, and then it grabs Jack by the face and pulls him face-forward into the golem's body. Jack hits the metal with a loud *clang* and is then cast aside as the golem stands up again.

Jack is actually a little dizzy from that last blow.

"Oh, *shit...*" Agent Hu streaks higher into the sky as the golem focuses on her. It extends an arm, and the arm shimmers and telescopes forward, the hand transforming instantly into a keen edge. Hu flies to the side, just barely avoiding the razor-tip as it shoots past her. She rises higher into the air, shoots another blast of fire down at the golem, and manages to avoid a second strike as the arm extends even farther.

"This is not possible!" She flies even higher, and still the arm follows, thinning as it elongates. It doesn't need mass to cut her open—she's a lot tougher than most people, but she saw what it did to Vigilante and she's not interested in testing her limits like that. She keeps flying up, and the arm keeps following.

This is getting ridiculous. I don't care how magic it is, this shouldn't be possible.

The pursuing arm wavers, then retracts so suddenly it looks like it disappears.

She examines the scene below. Jack is back on his feet, and Red Shift is harassing the golem yet again. They're not doing much to hurt it, though—just distract it.

Fire blasts don't seem to be doing much. Time to try something else.

She focuses on generating heat, and *radiating* heat, and she dives. She flies as hard and as fast as she can as she puts all her strength into gathering heat around her. The air shimmers in her wake, her form grows brighter and brighter, and finally she slams into the back of the golem with all the speed and heat she can muster.

The golem is heavy—it doesn't fall—but it's rocked by the force of the blow. Hu feels herself burning through its right shoulder, and then a moment later she's through the other side. She hits the ground, sending rock and dirt in all directions, and as she slides across the asphalt she returns to her human form. She skids to a stop next to the broken form of Vigilante and tries not to whimper from the pain.

"Nice one," Vigilante says.

Hu turns to look at him. He's not nearly as bad as he looked when he first hit the ground. His uniform is torn, his visor is shattered, and what she can see beneath it is a bloody mess. But it's a bloody mess going in reverse, as if someone were rewinding a slasher flick: his right leg, broken in at least three pieces, is actually *straightening out*, aligning itself, bones knitting back together on their own. Half of his chest looks caved in, but it's filling out, and bones crack and snap as they put themselves back in place.

"I read your file," she says. "I thought it was bullshit."

"Occupational hazard," Vigilante says. "Look at its arm."

Hu tries to focus on the golem, still being harassed by the remaining two members of the "A team." The arms, like the legs, lack any noticeable hinges, but they seem to bend and flex as if they were covered in living tissue. A long line of strange symbols runs down the length of its arms and legs, starting at the shoulder and ending at the—

"Hey," Hu says. She squints, trying to make sure she's really seeing it.

"It's not an illusion," Vigilante says. "When the fight started the symbols went all the way down to the wrist. Now they stop halfway down the forearm."

Jack hits the golem in the knee hard enough to bend it backward. The golem backhands him, sending him flying, then the knee turns to silvery liquid and the leg rights itself. The rune on its chest glows purple, and that's when Hu sees it—one of the symbols on the arm smooths over and disappears.

"Holy shit," Hu says, feeling a sudden surge of elation. "It has *charges*."

As her gaze runs down the length of each arm and leg, her elation quickly subsides.

"Holy shit. It has a *lot* of charges..."

* * *

The first thing CB thinks when he steps into the room is that it looks like the NASA Mission Control room—at least, it looks the way NASA's Mission Control is portrayed in movies. Row after row of desks and computers, all facing the same direction, with a large display screen placed on the opposite end.

The room, like everything else in the complex, is empty.

"This place gives me the creeps," Jenny says. "Where is everyone?"

The base appears to be fully functional—the overhead lights are on, the computers are all still on, the ventilation system is working—but so far they haven't encountered a single person in the facility.

"Looks like they left in a hurry," Agent Grant says. "Someone didn't finish their coffee." He points to one of the terminals, where an unfinished, still-steaming mug of coffee sits next to the keyboard.

"Well that's just *wrong*," CB says. "Sure, evacuate if you have to, but take the coffee." He picks up the mug and takes a sip. "Well... OK. It's instant."

He keeps drinking.

"You're disgusting," Jenny says, and sits down at the terminal.

"They must have teleported out," Street Ronin says. "The soldiers were sent to keep us busy while they evacuated."

"That was a hell of a distraction," Agent Grant says. "They sent a fucking army."

"I'm not sure they teleported *before* you blocked them," Jenny says. "This terminal hasn't locked itself out yet, and the buffer shows whoever was using it was issuing commands five minutes ago."

"That's after the magic robot showed up," Grant says.

"Golem," CB says. "What were they doing?"

Jenny frowns. "They were wiping their data."

"Did they finish?"

"I... don't know," Jenny says. "Looks like something interrupted the process. We need to find the server room."

Street Ronin points to a heavy door just to the right of the large screen. "Through there. I found a map."

He points to another terminal, displaying a schematic of the facility.

"Two levels under this one. Looks like there are some holding cells and a medical facility."

CB nods. "We should probably check that out. How about you and Zero get to the server room and see if there's anything you can recover. I'll take G-man to the lower levels and see what we can find."

"OK," Street Ronin says. Jenny nods in agreement.

"G-man?" Grant's eyebrow shoots up.

"Crossfire likes code names," CB says.

"That's a dumb code name."

"Well," CB says, "I don't like you yet. Got a problem with that?"

"I'll cry later," Grant says. "Let's go."

* * *

Vigilante has been crushed, disemboweled, and nearly decapitated. That was in the last five minutes.

There's nothing he can do about it: that thing is larger, stronger, tougher, and faster than he is. The only advantage he has is that it can't *kill* him, and every time it tries it winds up erasing one of those weird symbols running down its limbs. The symbols on its arms are completely gone, and it's just started on the left leg. They're wearing it down—but they're wearing themselves down as well.

Red Shift is the worst of the bunch—he's been pushing himself too hard, and Vigilante's worried if he tries to go supersonic again he'll wind up killing himself. Agent Hu's flames don't have the intensity they used to, and while she's still in the game, she's not flying as fast as she was. Jack's OK, and will be for a while. Vigilante's in trouble, though. It's getting hard for him to focus.

Vigilante's problem isn't fatigue. He's almost immune to that. The problem is that coming back from a certain level of injury is an excruciating process, and he's been reaching that level of injury over, and over, and over again throughout this fight. It hurts, and it hurts to the point that it triggers a very primal fight or flight response.

Vigilante isn't running, and his rational mind is losing its grip on his instinct to kill.

He picks himself off the ground yet again and tries to focus on the situation. The damn robot—golem—*whatever*—is still moving just as fast and just as powerfully as it did when it first showed up out of nowhere.

Not fair. Really not fair.

Vigilante clenches his fists and gets ready to leap back into the fray.

"Hold on." Someone places a hand on his shoulder, and he spins around, fist flung up into a backhand. He stops his swing just inches before it hits Red Shift.

Red Shift looks bad. His eyes are sunk into his face, his cheeks are hollow. He looks like he's been eating himself alive.

"You need to calm down, Tommy." He looks half-starved, like a gust of wind could knock him over, but he sounds just as calm and easy-going as ever.

Vigilante doesn't bother chastising him for using his real name. He knows why.

"I know. But I don't have a choice right now."

Red Shift nods slowly. "I understand, but let me take this one. I got one more in me. Let me knock it over, take off a pip, give you a breather."

Vigilante frowns. "You're sure, Greg? You don't look so good yourself."

Red Shift grins. "'course I'm sure. I've still got half an IV pack. I'll be OK."

Vigilante sighs. "Fine. One last time. Promise?"

"Promise," Red Shift says. "After this, I—"

It's a testament to exactly how tired Red Shift is that he doesn't even flinch when Vigilante hits him. Red Shift is knocked off his feet from the blow, and when he hits the ground he doesn't move. Vigilante kneels over him to check him out. His face is a mess—his jaw is smashed to bits—but his pulse is still strong.

Passed out from shock. Here's hoping that lasts.

"Sorry, Greg." Vigilante stands, and drags Red Shift's unconscious form off to the side of Warehouse Two, away from most of the fighting.

* * *

"What the hell just happened?" Agent Hu dodges another swipe of the golem's arm—not a razor this time; it's getting stingier about how it spends its energy.

"Pay attention!" Jack manages to jump to one side, narrowly avoiding the golem as it tries to kick him. The golem's blows are starting to hurt: there are only a few people on the planet tougher than he is, but there's no such thing as complete invulnerability, and the fact that this thing is powered by magic probably gives it an unfortunate edge.

"I *am* paying attention!" Hu weaves and shoots a low-level blast of heat at the thing, more to distract it than as an attempt to do any serious damage. "Your friend just knocked the shit out of your other friend."

"Which friend did what?" Jack glances over in the direction of Warehouse Two and sees Vigilante dragging Red Shift's limp form around the corner.

The golem takes that opportunity to hit Jack hard in the side of his head. His vision goes white. He's dimly aware of flying through the air and impacting the side of a wall. When his vision clears, Vigilante is standing over him, helping him up.

"You look worse than I thought," Vigilante says.

Jack doesn't say anything. Vigilante's visor was destroyed very early in the fight, and his face, exposed to the world as it is, looks... off. His eyes are wild—too wide, blinking too fast, staring too intensely at nothing in particular.

"I had to take Greg out of the fight," Vigilante says. His voice trembles with barely-suppressed rage. "Hit him too hard, but he's alive. He heals, he'll be OK. He'll be OK..."

Jack doesn't say anything.

"He wanted to go supersonic. It was going to *kill* him," Vigilante insists.

Jack holds up his hands. "Take it easy, Thomas. I'm not disagreeing with you. But you have to admit, you sound a little—"

"—crazy." Vigilante nods. "I know. I get it, Jack, I *get it*, but hear me out. We don't have a lot of time."

He turns toward the golem, watching Hu focus on playing defense, flying high enough to dodge the golem's attacks, but keeping low enough to keep it from going after the men on the ground. "She's tired, you can't last forever, and I'm losing it."

"Well, at least you're aware of it," Jack says. "That's a good sign."

"One more time around the block and I'm gone," Vigilante says. "I figure we have to make that count."

Jack's eyes narrow. "What do you mean?"

"Every time we hurt it and it uses up one of those... pips. Charges. Symbols. Whatever. Every time it heals itself, or grows a new limb, its skin does something."

"Yeah," Jack says. "Goes all shimmery and liquid. Then it hardens and looks like new. *Very annoying*."

"Get it to do that," Vigilante says. "Then throw me into it."

"Throw you into the—" Jack's mouth drops open. "Are you out of your—"

"Just do it, Jack. We're running out of options here."

"That's your plan," Jack says. "The naked guy throws the crazy guy into the magic robot. *That's* your plan."

"That's my plan," Vigilante says. "If you have a better one, I'm ready to hear it."

Jack scowls. "Fine. Follow me."

He leaps back toward the golem, closing the distance quickly. Hu circles away as she sees him close, forcing the golem to turn away from Jack's approach.

"Hu!" Jack shouts up, hoping she can hear him. "We have a plan!"

Hu creates a wall of fire around the golem—something that usually confuses it for a while, but never seems to do much more than that. She flies over to the two of them, hovering just overhead. "A plan?"

"Yeah," Jack says. "It's... not so great."

"That's OK," Hu says. "I work for the government. That sounds better than the plans we usually get."

PART TWELVE: CIRCUMSCRIPTION

"Good news and bad news," Street Ronin says.

"Yeah?" Jenny peers over his shoulder, staring down at the screen on his ruggedized laptop. She's a little relieved he decided to do the work himself, because she finds using it frustrating. It doesn't come close to the power of her own rig.

On the other hand, my rig won't resist energy weapon fire...

"Well it looks like their delete protocol started with the most important files first, so that's bad. But something interrupted the process, so I'm going through copying all the half-empty and corrupted directories first."

"So at least we know where to look," Jenny says.

Street Ronin nods. "That's the good news. The bad news is, we're copying half-empty directories and corrupted files."

"That's not so bad. Not all corrupted data is created equal. With the right tools you can recover almost anything."

"With the right tools, and with time." Street Ronin shakes his head. "It's the time I'm worried about. There's a lot of stuff to go through here. I don't think I have access to the raw processing power I'd want to chew through so much junk."

"Maybe I can find some backups," Jenny says. "If they left in a hurry, they might have overlooked the backups."

"That'd be nice," Street Ronin says. "Be careful. The place looks empty, but don't assume it is."

"OK, Dad," Jenny says, and starts wandering down the aisles.

* * *

"The schematic says the medical wing is at the lowest level," CB says. "So we start there."

Agent Grant raises an eyebrow. "You want to start at the bottom? You don't want to work our way down?"

"Not enough time," CB says. "Medical is our best bet."

"Time for what? Best bet for what?"

CB doesn't reply.

"Hey, Old Man..." Grant's voice takes on a subtle, needling edge. "I appreciate the whole man of mystery/lead people by their nose act as much as anyone, but it'd help if I knew what I was looking for."

"Can't say," CB says.

"You don't *know*? Well that's just—"

CB whirls around and stares Grant in the eye. "I didn't say that. Listen to me very carefully. I. *Can't.* Say."

"You *can't* say..." For the *very* short time CB has known him, Agent Grant hasn't done much to give the impression of being particularly thoughtful, but there are wheels turning in that head.

"You heard me."

The wheels turn faster. Something clicks, and Agent Grant shrugs, his expression smoothing into one of casual disinterest. "OK, Boss. Travers said we could trust you, so that's what I'm gonna do. But that's a hell of an NDA you signed."

CB laughs sharply. "Come on, G-Man. Let's get this done."

* * *

The backups won't be stored in the server room, of course—that would be stupid, and whatever these guys may be, Jenny's pretty sure they aren't stupid. She goes back into the Mission Control Room—or whatever it is—and calls up the schematic Street Ronin found.

The safest thing to do is store them off site, but they probably didn't have that luxury. If you're going to store them on site, you need a room that's isolated from everything else. Something that would survive if the whole place burned down. A vault...

There's one room on this floor that looks like it might fit the bill. The schematic doesn't give much in the way of details, but it's at the far end of the complex, separated from everything else by a long hallway. That could be it.

She ducks back into the server room and finds Street Ronin still hunched over the tiny laptop. "I think I found backup storage. Back in a sec."

"Hold on a moment," Street Ronin says. "I'll go with you."

"Nah, it's OK. I'm just going to make sure it's the right place. I'll come back as soon as I have it figured out—I'll need help transporting the backups anyway."

Street Ronin's gaze drifts back to the laptop. "...OK. I think I'm almost finished here anyway. Be careful, all right?"

"You already said that," Jenny says, and heads off to the far side of the complex.

* * *

The room is full of coffins.

They're caskets, actually—hermetically sealed caskets, like incubation chambers. But the first thing that leaps into CB's mind when he enters the room is *holy shit it's full of coffins*, and even when they discover that most of the people inside are still alive he can't shake it. A room full of coffins, all numbered, three occupants dead—and from the looks of their bodies, their deaths were not at all pleasant.

"This is sick," Grant says. He's not smirking right now. He's not doing much of anything, other than staring in shock at the coffins and their contents.

"Let's check the other rooms," CB says.

The second room is almost identical to the first. Ten victims dead this time, all looking roughly like the three victims in the previous room. The third room is more of the same, but only one survivor.

CB looks down at the unconscious form of the lone survivor in the third room. *Test Subject #14.*

"This is all kinds of fucked up," Grant says. "Is this your NDA?"

CB shakes his head. "It isn't here. I'll have to check the next level."

"What about these people? We can't leave 'em."

"We don't have a choice," CB says. "We can't let them out of those things until we know what happened to them. They could be infected with a super-virus and kill us all the moment we cracked the seal... or maybe their immune systems were stripped away, and we kill them the minute they're exposed to us. We don't know. And we can't wheel them out until the A team takes care of that golem."

"Right," Grant says. "Well today's a great day to be one of the good guys."

"Come on, G-man. We need to get to the holding cells."

"G-man," Grant mutters. "You know that's the FBI, right?"

CB shrugs. "I always called Travers a G-Man."

"Didn't you also break his jaw?" Grant asks.

"*Let's go.*" CB tries to keep his impatience in check and fails. "We don't have a lot of time."

Grant forces himself not to ask the obvious question, shrugs, and follows CB to the next floor.

* * *

As she peers down the long hallway separating the backup vault from the rest of the complex, Jenny sees that the reinforced steel vault door is open at a ninety-degree angle, and that an armed guard stands in the doorway. He's not one of the battle-armored soldiers they fought earlier: he's dressed in a black commando uniform and body armor, and wears a gas mask. He's armed with an assault rifle—a good one, from what she can tell, but nothing on the level of those energy carbines.

He looks like one of the people that attacked Dad's house.

She ducks out of sight the moment she sees him, and for a few tense seconds she holds her breath, trying to hear whether or not he reacts. The seconds pass, the guard makes no unusual noises, and she exhales slowly.

There are sounds coming from the hall: people talking. She can't tell exactly what they're saying, because they're keeping their voices low, but she's pretty sure it isn't small talk.

*They stayed behind to get the backups. No, that doesn't make sense. They stayed behind to **destroy** the backups.*

She weighs the options in her head. It'd be good to have Street Ronin here, but if they actually destroy the backups before she gets back...

You're a metahuman now, Jenny. Time to step up. What would your great-grandfather do?

He would stop the bad guys. That's what he'd do.

Jenny takes a slow, steadying breath, then steps out into the hall.

* * *

"So this is, what, some kind of detention center?" Agent Grant looks around the room, clearly not impressed. "Looks more like my office building."

They're standing in what appears to be a waiting room of some sort. Cheap carpet covers the floors, cheap plastic chairs line the walls, and a receptionist's desk stands in the center of the room. Four office doors line the back wall, and heavier doors sit to each side.

"Not quite what I expected," CB admits. He walks up to the receptionist's desk and starts flipping through the logs. "Oh, but look—Richter was here. He actually *signed in.*"

"Seriously?" Grant wanders up and looks at the ledger CB is reading. "J. Richter. Well I'll be damned. He checked in this morning. Don't see a sign-out time, though."

"Yeah..." CB stares at the name scrawled beneath *J. Richter*. "Looks like he wasn't alone."

"Doyle?" Grant looks at CB. "Any reason I should know that name?'

CB shakes his head. "Not really. I guess he's my arch-enemy."

Grant snorts. "I thought that was Liberty."

"My *first* arch-enemy," CB says. "Nasty piece of work. He was a Neo-Nazi skinhead back in the day. Now he's... I don't know what he is. Still an asshole."

"You know how to pick 'em," Grant says. "What's he do?"

"Makes people sick," CB says. "Also he has lots of weird magic runes tattooed all over him. Heals him real fast. Look, if you start to feel sick, dizzy, get a headache, even if you think maybe you're going to sneeze—do your teleporting thing. Get out, get help. Look for Zero. She seems to be his Achilles' heel."

"OK." Grant pulls out his service pistol and loads a fresh magazine. "I'm ready when you are, chief."

CB looks down at the log again. "They checked into Cell E. Come on, that's through here."

The hall is long and narrow. The cell doors are reinforced, with biometric keypads set into the wall beside them. Each cell door has a large letter stenciled on it: A, B, C, D, E, and F on the left; G, H, I, J, K, and L on the right. Between each pair of cells is a much simpler door with OBSERVATION stenciled on the front.

They hear the hum of a generator. Looking down the hall, they actually see the generator—not your standard gas-powered generator that you'd get from a hardware store, this runs quieter and cleaner—useful when you're underground and proper ventilation is a concern. The generator sits right outside Cell E. The door to Cell E is open, and a rugged cable leads from the generator into the room.

CB looks at Grant and motions for him to hang back. Grant nods, and crouches, gun at the ready. CB slowly draws both of his pistols, and creeps down the hall.

He passes Cells B, H. D, I. He stops at the generator and peers around the corner, into Cell E.

There it is: the Prodigy Harness.

It's pushed against the far wall and set upright, like a sarcophagus. The top half is transparent, giving him a clear view of the victim trapped within. Whoever he was once, he's barely recognizable as alive. His skin stretches tight across his face, his muscles are atrophied so severely that CB can see every contour of the skull beneath. His mouth hangs open, and a long line of dried spittle trails down one corner. His eyebrows are gone, and his hair is nearly gone—only a few strands at the top and a few tufts around the ears remain. His eyes are open, but they do not see. Occasionally he blinks.

CB steps into the room. "I found it, Agent Grant."

A few seconds later Agent Grant appears in the doorway. "You found wha—oh *Christ*, what the fuck is that?"

"That," CB says, "is my NDA."

"Jesus, what happened to—what did they do to—who is that?"

"A guy named Horace Preston," CB says. "He's a weather manipulator."

Grant looks at what's left of the man. "The thing he's in. Is that what I think it is?"

CB nods. "Prodigy Harness."

"Fuck. *Fuck*. I thought we confiscated all those. Travers is going to shit a brick." Agent Grant pauses for a moment. "Yep. A brick."

"Look, Agent Grant, I don't know the specifics of how you came to be involved in this, but I gotta know where you stand."

"I don't understand," Grant says.

"Preston is causing the storm," CB says. "Those bastards left him behind because they don't care what he's doing, and if we don't stop him the storm is gonna wipe Farraday City and a good chunk of Georgia off the map."

"So unplug it." Grant looks at the cable running from the generator, attaching to the base of the harness. "No more harness, no more storm, right?"

CB sighs. "No. The harness already did its part: it wound him up and turned him loose. If he wasn't this far gone we could probably give him a new command—tell him to stop—but *look at him*. All it's doing now is keeping him alive, and it's doing a piss-poor job at that."

"Yeah," Grant says. "Yeah."

There's a brief silence as CB and Grant stare at the desiccated man in the harness. Finally Grant turns to CB, expression grave.

"You want me to take a walk, chief?"

CB hesitates, then nods once.

"OK..." Sympathy flashes across Grant's face as he turns away from the harness. "Guess I'll go find the others and tell 'em about the people we *can* save. Back in fifteen." His outline fuzzes out for a second, then he disappears.

CB stares at the empty space where Grant stood moments before, then forces himself to turn back to the harness. He walks over to it and releases the electronic latch that keeps the top closed.

"Sorry Horace. For all I know you were an asshole... but you didn't deserve this."

He opens the lid. Pressure releases with a hiss, and the first thing CB notices is the *stench* rising out of the harness. Whatever it did to the man, however it's keeping him alive, he still smells like a rotting corpse.

CB's stomach churns, and he takes a moment to collect himself. That's when he feels a sharp, stabbing pain in his gut, and the next thing he knows he's on the floor, swimming in sweat, shivering with cold, trying to keep the world from spinning away.

Oh... oh fuck.

He tries to get to his hands and knees, but every time he moves he loses his sense of equilibrium. He barely manages to turn his head down before he vomits. He shudders as another wave of cold runs through him. The pain in his gut increases, and he curls into a ball for relief.

Someone steps into the room. CB forces his eyes open, and sees the blurred form of a man in canvas pants and heavy work boots walk up to him. The man stops in front of him, kneels, and grabs CB by the hair, forcing his head up. CB recognizes him immediately.

"Heya CB," Plague says. "Glad you decided to stop by. Kinda hoped you might."

PART THIRTEEN: EXERTION

He stares straight up at the triangular lights, unable to blink. He can feel—the hard back of the gurney, the sting of the leather straps as they cut into his flesh—but he can't move. He's not sure the straps are necessary: whatever they gave him has paralyzed him completely. He can't even move his head.

"Jack." His voice is hoarse. He barely recognizes it as his own.

"Save your strength, Thomas." Jack sounds tired. Defeated.

"What the hell is your problem?" He tries to get his voice to sound more like his own—the way he remembers it—but he can't clear his throat. "They're not cutting you."

Jack doesn't answer.

"Jack, so help me, if you don't say something I'll—"

"You're a good guy, Thomas. I never thought I'd say that to a cop, but you are. And you're ***tough****. Honestly, I thought you'd be dead a week ago... and so did they. That's the problem. They're not interested in whatever their original experiment was. Now they're just trying to see how far they can push you before you die."*

He tries to strain against his bonds. He doesn't even twitch. "I guess I should be flattered."

Jack laughs. "Christ, Thomas, just ***die****."*

"What?"

"I'm not saying that because I want you to. I'm saying it because you ***should****. Because at this point, they're hoping you* ***won't****. They're hoping you'll keep fighting them, and hanging on, so they can keep torturing you. They're really getting off on it, man. Just give up and die, so you won't have to scream like that any more."*

"No." He's surprised by the vehemence in his voice. "Not gonna happen."

"Thomas, I'm not saying it because—"

"—I know why you're saying it. I don't care. I'm not going to die today. I'm not going to die tomorrow. I'm going to take everything these guys throw at me, and eventually I'm going to escape. And when I do, I'm going to kill every asshole in this place, and then I'm going to kill every asshole just like them. They're doing this because they think they can get away with it. Well they can't. They can't because I say so, and if I have to scream to get through this, then by God I'll scream until my throat splits open."

"You're gonna scream," Jack says. "God... I wish you'd just decide to die."

Vigilante is screaming.

Liquid steel washes over him, crushing him, trying to expel him. He can feel it breaking his body apart, just as he can feel his body knitting itself back together, and somewhere in all that pain he loses himself to blind, feral rage. His screams—silent as they are, engulfed as he is in an ocean of metal—are not screams of desperation, but screams of pure, defiant rage.

He kicks. He claws. He lashes out with everything he has, churning, twisting, trying to find purchase. It connects with nothing—it's like being tied to concrete while fighting in a swimming pool—but he fights nonetheless. He fights purely on instinct, indeed there are times when instinct is the only part of him that is actually alive—but the instinct is not *get out, get out of this before you drown*. The instinct that drives him on is an echo of his last sane, conscious thought:

Don't let it win.

He doesn't know why he needs to do this. He doesn't know what "it" is. He knows only that it wants to stop him, that it will hurt him until it does, and that he will fight it until he can do nothing at all.

And so Vigilante fights... and as he fights, he is screaming.

* * *

The minute Jenny steps into the hall she starts running. The guard turns toward her, surprised, and she can hear him shout a warning from beneath the gas mask as he raises his rifle and fires quickly. The first shots ricochet off the left wall, causing the soldier to flinch and take a step back into the room, using the doorframe as cover. Jenny falls back into a slide just as she crosses the doorway, and more bullets fly overhead from other assailants as she reaches out, snags the soldier's ankle, and pulls hard.

She stops sliding abruptly, and the soldier slips forward, letting go of his rifle as he tries to keep his balance. The rifle swings wildly from its shoulder strap as the man grabs the doorframe for support. Jenny hooks her legs around the vault door and pulls again. It's no contest: the soldier is ripped away from the doorframe, falling on his back with a thud as she pulls herself and her captive around the heavy steel door. She hits him in the face a few times, trying to ignore the sickening crack of the gas mask *and other things* as the guard stops moving.

She hears the other people in the room shouting now, and hears them scuffling about as they choose their positions. Three in all, she thinks. She looks at the soldier, looks at the assault rifle still tangled in its strap.

What do I know about these things? I've never held one in my life.

Gritting her teeth, she snaps the strap in two and grabs the rifle.

You don't have to be Street Ronin, Jenny. You just need to know which end to point. You know you can do that much...

Something clatters into the hallway and bounces off the wall—a small, round object that looks like a bumpy green

Grenade, oh Christ it's a

She's off the floor and halfway up the vault door when it explodes. The door sways slightly, and she hears something tear into the other side of it, but she's unharmed. Another goes off seconds later, then another. Each time the door sways, and the third time she can feel the outer skin buckle and warp as shrapnel almost tears through. Ears ringing, she throws herself over the top of the vault door, rifle firing as she lands. The hallway is smoky and her ears are ringing, but she can see three more soldiers hiding behind half-empty shelving. She crouches and rolls into the room, still firing her rifle, not bothering to aim.

It's a large, rectangular room, full of shelves and crates and filing cabinets. There's a main aisle in the center, running from the vault door to the very back of the room, where the wall is filled with a row of wide metal lockers. Twelve rows of heavy shelving units, each five shelves high, sit on each side of the aisle. The bottoms of the shelves are stacked solid with metal crates, but they thin out by the third shelf, and Jenny can see the tops of three heads, crouching behind shelves toward the back.

She runs, hearing bullets strike the floor, the shelving, the walls, even one or two bouncing off her armor. She discards the assault rifle as she races across the aisle, speeds down the length of the shelving unit on the opposite side, and finally leaps into the air when she reaches where the shelf meets the far wall. She grabs the top of the shelf and pulls, places her feet against the wall and pushes, and though the shelf wobbles dangerously it gives her the leverage she needs to twist into a somersault and throw herself over the top. She clears three shelving units before the soldiers realize what happened, and by then it's too late—she smashes into a shelf, causing it to wobble and ultimately fall on top of a very surprised soldier, who finds himself buried under a number of very heavy crates. Jenny climbs to her feet, sees the top of a second soldier's head on the other side of a shelf that's still standing, and pushes as hard as she can against the crate sitting between them. It flies off the shelf with unexpected force—she's still getting the hang of her own strength—and she hears it impact against the soldier with a loud, wet thud.

Two down, but she's sure she heard three people moving...

She sees the shadow before she sees the person, an indistinct form darting past her right shoulder. She grabs another crate, turns, and throws—a single bullet ricochets off it before it crashes into the side of the shelves on the third row from the door, and she hears a muffled curse as she sees a hand and shoulder disappear behind it. She runs, trying to press her advantage, but when she's only steps away from the shelf she sees a blur of motion, and suddenly a thick pair of boots are flying directly at her face. Her arms go up and she knocks them aside, and the legs attached to them, but even as the man grunts in surprise she reels as something smashes hard against the side of her face. She stumbles, staggers back, and her vision clears just as the man picks himself off the floor.

Blond hair, cold blue eyes: Johann Richter, the man who murdered her great-grandfather in cold blood, faces her for the second time.

* * *

"It's working! I think it's actually working!" Agent Hu shakes with the effort it takes her to generate heat, but she manages to hurl another ball of plasma at the golem, striking its chest. She's not even bothering to fly, at this point—too much effort. Instead, she relies on Jack to keep it occupied while she bombards it from a distance. This tactic isn't working well for Jack, who's starting to feel the effects of the golem's repeated blows, but he throws himself into it with everything he has, trying to focus on a single spot on the thing's leg, attacking it over and over and over until it's forced to spend time fixing it.

But it's whatever Vigilante's doing that hurts it most. Liquid metal erupts from the golem's chest in massive spouts, falling back into itself as it tries and fails to solidify. It can't. Vigilante won't let it.

Occasionally they catch glimpses of the man... or what's left of him. It's usually an arm, though occasionally they see a leg, and once they saw his face, covered in that silvery substance as it streamed down his throat. It's impossible to tell how he's managed to stay inside the golem as long as he has, but it's having an effect: it's down to half of the strange marks on its leg. Everything else is gone.

That's what keeps them fighting. Even though Hu is so exhausted she's about to keel over, even though Jack is starting to feel every crushing blow descending on his head, they fight on. Watching each pip disappear, seeing the marks dwindle as fast as they have… they're close. They're very, very close.

Six marks.

The golem's chest shoots out a jet of silvery liquid. Jack can see Vigilante twisting, desperately clawing his way back into its chest.

Five marks.

The golem's chest collapses in on itself, trying to grind Vigilante to dust. A mangled hand emerges from the silvery liquid, then disappears.

Four marks.

The golem shoots another spout of liquid, this time erupting from its back, arcing over its head, and returning into its chest. That seems to do no good at all—Vigilante isn't seen at all during that display.

Three marks.

The golem stands completely still, save for the liquid patch on its torso that simply won't heal. A low *thummm* radiates from it, and the purple symbol on its torso glows brightly. The *thummm* increases in intensity, and the golem begins to vibrate.

The *thummm* stops. Every piece of the golem transforms into a silver liquid and falls to the ground, forming a silvery pond in front of the wreckage of Warehouse Six.

"What…" Hu stares at the puddle, reaching for words and failing to find them.

The *thummm* begins again, and the liquid flows away from its original spot, farther down the warehouse complex, toward Warehouse Seven. As it moves, it leaves behind a twisted, mangled husk of bone and flesh. Then the liquid twists and flows together, reforming into the shape of the golem, whole and untouched.

Two marks.

"No," Hu whispers. "This can't be happening, come on, we were *so close*!"

The twisted husk of bone and flesh twitches. Something that might be a limb reaches out toward the golem, then falls still.

Jack wipes the sweat from his brow as he prepares for the golem's next attack. He looks down at his hand, and is surprised to see blood.

"I don't think we're gonna make it," he says.

The golem charges.

PART FOURTEEN: DEUS EX MACHINA

Richter's eyes narrow as he recognizes Jenny. He says nothing, but eases into a defensive stance, watching her carefully.

He thinks it's going to be a repeat of last time.

Jenny doesn't jump in swinging—Richter has, for whatever reason, given her a moment. She takes it, allowing herself to catch her breath, then she too eases into a defensive stance.

Focus, Jenny. Don't forget how good he is.

Ready.

Go.

She feints with her right, swings hard with her left. Richter ignores the feint, moves to block the left hook, and just as he bats the blow aside, her right arm closes on his wrist. She twists, pulls, and as he starts to fall forward her left arm locks, and she throws him over her shoulder into a row of shelves.

Thank you, Red Shift.

She moves in to follow up, but Richter grabs the bottom of the shelf above him and kicks, striking her in the knee. Her armor absorbs most of the strike, but it still hits with enough force to knock her knee out from under her. She slips sideways as Richter stands, and his second kick would have struck her in the temple if she hadn't brought up her arm instead. As it is, it grazes the side of her face—the side where she's already bruised. She gasps in pain, but focuses on grabbing the leg and pushing back as she stands. Richter is knocked down, and this time she throws a crate at him.

His eyes widen as he sees the metal box hurtling toward him, but he doesn't panic. He catches the crate and throws it back: Jenny raises her arms in front of her face to keep it from taking her head off, and now *she* is propelled back into shelving.

Richter is on his feet, reaching for his gun. The holster is empty—his gun fell out during the melee. Jenny leaps toward him, forcing him to take a step back, but he counters with a quick jab to her side. She's wearing armor, but Richter is at least as strong as she is, and she gasps as she hears one of the torso plates shatter. Richter follows up with a knuckle strike to the throat, but Jenny grabs the arm and twists, trying to force it behind his back. He grunts in pain, but the elbow of his free arm smashes against the tender side of her face, and she involuntarily loosens her grip enough for him to get free. He turns to face her again, this time drawing a long-bladed knife.

"You've improved," Richter says.

He jabs with the knife; Jenny steps aside to avoid the blow. It's a feint, and her head snaps to the side as his other hand smashes into her jaw. She travels with the force of the blow and turns it into a spinning kick. He turns in time to take the brunt of it on his upper arm and shoulder, then counters with a kick of his own. Her torso plate cracks again, and she feels something sharp biting into her stomach.

Richter jabs with the knife again—not a feint this time. Jenny is ready, lunging back and bringing her arms up to redirect the path of the blade, but she still feels the white heat of pain as it slices across her forehead. It's an unfortunate place to be cut—even shallow cuts bleed heavily, and in a few seconds it'll be getting into her eyes.

He presses his advantage, following up with a quick jab to the stomach, driving the broken piece of armor into her stomach again, then slicing with the knife again. This time Jenny catches the knife hand with both arms and brings it down onto her knee as hard as she can. She can hear bone crunch as the knife drops to the floor, and hears something snap as she pulls and twists his arm as hard as she can. Richter loses his calm, detached demeanor: his face twists into a mask of rage as he strikes her savagely with his good arm. She spins, losing all sense of direction. Richter grabs the back of her armor and throws her across the room with one arm.

She sees the vault doorway as she tumbles, sees a flash of black and yellow armor as someone runs into the room. She hears three shots fire in rapid succession, hears someone grunt in pain, and then the world explodes in a flash of purple light as Jenny slams into the wall, hard. That's it, as far as she's concerned—there's no way she'll be able to clear her head in time to fend off his next attack.

But the attack doesn't come. Instead, when she feels someone grabbing her shoulder, she discovers it's Street Ronin, peering down at her in concern.

"You're hurt," he says.

"Richter." Her voice sounds strange.

"Yeah," he says. "I saw the end of it. You broke his arm."

"Where?" Jenny wipes the blood out of her eyes and tries to focus.

"Gone," Street Ronin says. "He ported out after I shot him."

"You shot him?"

"Don't sound so hopeful," Street Ronin says. "I only winged him. And it was the arm you already broke, so I didn't really do much. He didn't like the odds, though. Keep still. You have a cut on your forehead. Let me get my kit."

He breaks out a first aid kit and Jenny waits patiently while he cleans and tapes over her forehead. When he's done, she uses some of the extra gauze to wipe the rest of the blood out of her eyes, and she finally stands on her own two feet. Her whole head throbs with pain, and she can feel the left side of her face starting to swell.

"Thanks," she says.

"Sure thing." Street Ronin turns his attention to the vault. "Do you know why Richter was in here in the first place?"

"Backups," Jenny says. "I think they were trying to destroy the backups. Which means there might be something useful in here."

Street Ronin looks at the scattered crates and toppled shelving. He sighs. "Well, let's get started. This could take a while."

* * *

Asphalt cracks around him as Jack is pummeled into the ground, the golem pounding his body relentlessly, blow after blow sending him deeper into the street. For a fleeting moment, Jack is tempted to stay down, to give up, to let it win, to stop fighting and *rest*. Somewhere in the distance he hears Agent Hu yelling at the top of her lungs, and the golem stops its attack and turns toward her.

Hu isn't burning any more: she's too tired to keep the flames going. This makes her current tactic—yelling and waving her arms in an attempt to get the golem's attention—both magnificently brave and magnificently stupid. When it works, and the golem turns to face her, she suddenly feels very exposed. When she's not burning, she's as fragile as any other human being.

"Uh..." Hu takes a step back. "Jack?"

Jack groans as he forces himself to climb out of the Jack-sized indentation in the road. His arms and legs feel heavy. It's hard to think straight.

Shouldn't be tired this fast. Shouldn't be this hurt.

Vigilante's body still lies in a heap where the golem left it. It's no longer a twisted mass of bone and flesh—it's actively sorting itself out, regrowing limbs, organs, flesh and hair. Jack tries not to look at it. He wonders, if he manages to hold out long enough, if Vigilante will eventually stand up and rejoin the fight.

I don't think we're going to make it.

Jack gathers his strength and leaps, flying through the air and landing on the golem's back as it advances on Hu. It stops, arms flailing, as he wraps his arms around its head and squeezes with all his strength, as if he's trying to pop its head off its body.

The golem reaches up to grab Jack, trying to pull him off. Jack grits his teeth and tightens his grip.

Earlier in the fight, this very move distracted the golem long enough to give Hu a chance to take a breather, and cost the golem a mark as it tried to throw him off. Now it's distracting, but Jack doesn't have the strength to make it *punishing*. The best he can do is give Hu time to get away.

"Run!" His voice is ragged and raw. "Just... run!"

"Not gonna happen," Hu says. "Only two marks left. We can do this."

"No," Jack says. "I don't think we—"

His strength fails. The golem tears him free of his perch, lifts him high overhead, and drives him back into the ground. It raises its fists, ready to start pummeling him again. Jack steels himself.

This is really gonna hurt.

Somewhere, off in the distance, he hears a car horn, honking wildly. The golem hesitates, half-turning toward the noise.

Hu's eyes go wide. "Grant..."

The car horn gets louder, and with a squeal of tires a slightly beat-up silver Ford Taurus squeals around the corner of Warehouse Two, wheels spinning as the driver points it directly at the golem.

"No!" Hu is shouting at the top of her lungs. "Damn it, Grant, don't you *dare* do this that's my—"

The car horn goes full blast as the tires squeal, and suddenly it shoots forward, bearing down on the golem.

"Oh, *shit*..." Hu watches helplessly as her car races down the road, closing fast. Jack looks up, eyes widening in surprise as he sees the car, and manages to roll off to one side just as the car smashes into the golem's left side.

The hood of the car crumples as it hits the golem's left leg, and the back of the car flips up. The golem doesn't fall, but it's rocked from the blow, and it stares at the car as it flips over, exposing the undercarriage to the sky.

A dark-suited figure blurs into sight next to the upended car, throws something into the undercarriage, then blurs again and vanishes. A heartbeat later the car explodes, engulfing the golem in a fireball.

Hu stands dumbstruck as she watches her car burn.

Grant appears to her right. "Sorry about your car, Hu."

Hu nods wordlessly.

"I couldn't think of anything else to do."

"I get it," Hu says. "I'm still probably going to hit you later. Assuming we survive."

"That's fair," Grant says.

Jack pulls himself off the ground and jogs over to where Hu and Grant stand. They see the golem turn silvery and fall on the remains of the car, dousing the flames, then slowly start to reform.

Hu turns to Grant, eyes wide with alarm. "Travers. Is he—"

"I left him back at the loading platform on Two," Grant says. "Told him to stay clear. What the hell is that thing doing?"

"Healing," Jack says. "The question is, how much will it cost this time?"

Grant frowns, and looks at Hu questioningly.

"It has charges," Hu says.

The silvery form solidifies into the golem once again. They look at its leg. One mark remains.

"Damn," Hu says.

"We can't keep this up," Jack says. "Agent Grant, you need to find the others and tell them not to—"

Something streaks out of the sky and slams into the golem. It explodes, silvery liquid flying in all directions. A sonic boom follows, shaking the walls and rattling what's left of the warehouse windows. A small puddle of liquid attempts to coalesce and reform, but after an initial, halfhearted attempt it goes still.

A man hangs in the air above the golem's liquid remains: six and a half feet tall, dark-skinned, gray sideburns but built like a linebacker. He's dressed in a sleek red-and-black bodysuit that looks none the worse for wear from impact.

"Holy shit," Jack says. "Regiment?"

Roger Whitman focuses his gaze on Jack, and an eyebrow shoots up. "Jack? Jack Barrow?"

"Yeah," Jack says.

"What the hell happened to you?"

Jack nods to the pool of liquid metal lying motionless on the ground.

Regiment notices the pile of flesh quivering and pulsing near the corner of Warehouse Six. "And *what the hell is—*"

"Vigilante," Jack says.

"Really?" Regiment stares at the pile of flesh for a moment longer. "He OK?"

"Probably. Nice timing, Roger. Things were getting pretty bad."

"Speaking of mysterious storms coming out of nowhere with enough force to level a city, where the hell is CB?" Roger turns back to Jack, and his eyes narrow as he notices something for the first time.

"And why the hell are you *naked*?"

PART FIFTEEN: THE FOURTH HORSEMAN

CB forces himself to breathe. It's hard—mucus keeps filling his lungs, and he's constantly coughing and gagging, trying to take a clear breath, but he finds if he focuses on breathing it's easier to handle everything else: the fever, the chills, the pain shooting through his gut. Focusing on a very basic act of survival allows him to move everything else into the background.

It doesn't solve the problem, though: Plague is killing him.

"I didn't even have to try this time." Plague sounds smug. "Last time we met, I really had to work up a sweat to break through your—I don't know. Whatever it is. That thing you have that's protected your sorry ass for as long as we've known each other. But here, in this place? With all this power *swirling around?* I just had to *think* and it happened."

CB coughs, wheezes, and says nothing.

"What, no smartass comment? Well I'm not surprised. Disappointed, I guess. I kinda hoped you might go down swinging. For old times' sake, you know? On the other hand..." Plague chuckles to himself. "I did give you a hell of a disease, didn't I? And you know what the best part is? This is the best part..."

Plague crouches down in front of CB, staring at him hack and cough and try to breathe.

"The best part is, I made it up."

Plague stands and walks over to the Prodigy Harness, staring at the desiccated form of Horace Preston.

"I just came up with a bunch of symptoms, threw 'em together in a big old stew, and put the whole thing in your lap. I don't even know what to call it yet. I don't even know how it *ends*. I mean, I got a few ideas on that front, but..." Plague laughs. "It's amazing what you can do with the right amount of power, CB. You can break down barriers like they were nothing. Before today I'd never be able to invent a disease from scratch. But today? Today, with all this power flying around, just waiting to be *used*... today I did it *twice*."

The sound of the heavy metal door opening at the end of the hall causes both Plague and CB to look up.

"Hey Curveball." It's Agent Grant's voice. CB tries to call out a warning, but all he can do is make tiny choking noises in the back of his throat.

"Hey Curveball, thought you should know that—"

As soon as Agent Grant sees CB on the ground he goes for his gun, but he's not fast enough—his skin turns pallid gray in a matter of seconds, his eyes roll back into his head, and he collapses in a heap.

"And that makes three," Plague says. He walks over to Agent Grant and nudges him with his foot. "Don't worry, your friend ain't gonna die. We'll need someone to interrogate later."

CB tries to get up on his hands and knees, but Plague pushes him over with his boot.

"Stay down, CB. Just lie there and die, OK? Die knowing that you lost. You lost big. You die now, everybody else dies later. God created man, man created gods, and I'm gonna put every single one of 'em in the ground."

Plague laughs again. "Except for the ones we approve of. Except for those chosen few..."

Pause.

"You ain't in that number, CB. I guess you already figured that out. Your services are no longer required..."

A windstorm fills the room, a blur streaks toward Plague and he's slammed into the wall next to the harness. The wall buckles and twists, and as Plague's runes glow brightly, quickly repairing the damage to his body, he looks up to see Roger Whitman standing in front of him. CB immediately feels the pain in his gut subside, his body stops shaking, and after a final racking cough he can breathe again.

Plague's eyes go wide with fear. His fist clenches, and he concentrates, only to gape in surprise as the other man doesn't fall.

"That's what I thought," Roger says, and grabs Plague by the neck, his other fist raised to strike.

Plague's runes glow even brighter. He laughs. "You can't kill me, asshole. Try all you want, but I don't go down. But *you*... I bet with a little time, I could—"

Three gunshots fire in rapid succession. Roger and Plague turn in surprise as CB stands before the Prodigy Harness, gun extended. Horace Preston slumps forward, shot three times: two in the chest, one in the head.

"Sorry, Horace," CB says. "Rest in peace, if you can swing it."

"No..." Plague's voice cracks. "No, that's not fair."

A faint purple glow envelops Plague, and Regiment jerks his hand back as if shocked.

"No!" Plague looks up, eyes wild. "No! You can't do this! Not now! I can still pull this off. *I was so close*, I just need a little more—"

The purple glow flashes, fills the room, and when it's gone, so is Plague.

CB and Roger both stare at the dead body in the Prodigy Harness.

"Was that necessary?" Roger isn't accusing him.

CB sighs heavily. "Yeah. Afraid so. You remember Yuba City."

"I remember," Roger says. "Who was he?"

CB shrugs. "Weather manipulator. Name's Horace Preston. That's all I know."

Agent Grant groans and opens his eyes. "That was really fucking weird."

"Look who's talking." Regiment turns to look down at Agent Grant, adopting a decidedly lighter tone in an attempt to change the mood. "CB, did you know he's a mult?"

CB looks at Grant. "No shit. You make copies?"

"*No.*" Grant almost spits out the word. "...not exactly. Excuse me, I gotta... not be here right now." His outline blurs, then he disappears from the room.

"Teleports, too," Regiment says. "That explains a few things."

He laughs softly, a low rumble in his chest. "Well, here we are again. And it looks like I saved your ass. Again."

"Yeah," CB says. "You know what, Roger? You keep right on doing that. I ain't proud."

Regiment laughs louder this time.

"What are you *doing* here?" CB asks. "Not that I'm complaining. I was trying to figure out how to get in touch with you without tipping off the Feds for *weeks*, but—"

"You're kidding, right?" Roger shakes his head in amusement. "Mysterious, big-ass storm breaks out in the middle of Farraday City—your last known location—and you think we won't think it's you?"

CB raises an eyebrow. "*We?*"

Roger nods, smiling. "Robert wants a word. He sent a ride."

CB blinks. "Robert? Seriously?"

"Seriously," Roger says. "You ready? There's room for everyone. It's a big ride."

CB starts to say yes, then catches himself. "Uh... We gotta take care of some things first. They were doing something down here, Roger. Test. On *people*. There are survivors."

"Agent Grant told me," Roger says. "We're taking them too. It's a big ride."

CB looks at the spot where Plague disappeared, then back at Horace's corpse. He shudders once and turns away.

"OK, Tin Man. Let's go see the Wizard."

WRITER'S NOTES

Curveball Year Two started out with a little problem: the end of Year One.

Don't get me wrong, I was very pleased with the end of Year One. The presence of magic in the "Curveballverse" (I can't think of anything else to call it at the moment, I'm sure I'll come up with something much better after it's too late to do anything about it) was my Big Secret Reveal, and I wanted it to come out of left field and upend everything. I'm pretty pleased with how that turned out, in the end, but it did set up a pretty big challenge for Year Two...

...because now I had to talk about magic.

One of the problems of holding something back and then unloading it on the reader during the climax of a story arc is that the reader, quite reasonably, expects to learn more as the story goes on. So now I had to pull back the covers a little farther, make magic a little more recognizable, and this posed a few challenges.

1. It had to fit. The tone of the world had already been established for eleven issues before magic was introduced. I had to introduce magic in a way that was compatible with what I'd already written.

2. It had to be creepy. Magic was introduced in a way that made it seem like a Very Much Not Good Thing: it was dark, it was evil, it made the protagonist panic a little when he realized what he was dealing with. The great danger of revealing more about something is that when it becomes familiar, it also becomes less threatening. I wanted to preserve that menace.

This caused a few problems, not the least of which is a few issues that were pushed back a month when I tried to write the main story arc that dealt with magic in this run. The sequences on the doomed island of Esperanza tied me into knots and gave me fits as I tried to move the story forward, introduce magic to the reader, keep it creepy, and keep the world feeling right. At the end of 24 issues I wasn't convinced I had hit every mark (I think the tone of the world has changed a bit, for one thing) but I was generally pleased with the outcome. Year Two has some of my favorite writing in it.

I should note that the cover work Pascalle Lepas did for Year Two helped inspire me quite a bit. CB smoking in the foreground, with the Farraday City skyline looming quietly off-kilter in the back, and a large moon hanging quietly overhead really captured the feel, for example... and was a huge inspiration for CB's conversation with the thin man in the bowler hat in Issue 18. I've been very lucky to work with artists who have been able to capture something important about the story that I can use as inspiration, even if they don't necessarily know that's what they're doing at the time.

At the end of it all, after a particularly grueling Issue 24 (which took longer to write than it should have, and wound up being much longer than it should have been) I'm pretty pleased with how Year Two turned out. It did almost everything I wanted it to, and ended almost exactly where I wanted it to end. Almost.

The only problem with Year Two? I set the bar high for Year Three.

Now if you'll excuse me, I gotta go find a ladder. Or some stilts.

C. B. Wright (http://www.curveball.xyz)

ABOUT THE AUTHOR

Writer, former musician, occasional cartoonist, and noted authority on his own opinions, C. B. Wright's weakness for tilting at windmills has influenced every facet of his adult life. He enjoys reading and writing fiction. He also enjoys writing about himself in the third person. He refuses to comment on whether writing about himself in the third person also qualifies as fiction. He currently lives in Alabama with his wife, daughter, dog, and his overpoweringly large ego.

ABOUT CURVEBALL

Curveball is an ongoing story published monthly as web fiction, then through retailers in eBook and paperback formats.

http://www.curveball.xyz

ALSO BY AUTHOR

Curveball Year One: Death of a Hero (eBook, Trade Paperback)

Pay Me, Bug! (eBook, Trade Paperback)

www.ingramcontent.com/pod-product-compliance
Lightning Source LLC
Chambersburg PA
CBHW061319170626
46817CB00001B/231

* 9 7 8 1 9 3 9 6 3 3 2 9 3 *